NIGHT AND DAY

VIRGINIA WOOLF

W9-AXG-233

By Virginia Woolf

THE VOYAGE OUT, 1915

NIGHT AND DAY, 1919

KEW GARDENS, 1919

MONDAY OR TUESDAY, 1921

JACOB'S ROOM, 1922

THE COMMON READER: FIRST SERIES, 1925

MRS. DALLOWAY, 1925

TO THE LIGHTHOUSE, 1927

ORLANDO, 1928

A ROOM OF ONE'S OWN, 1929

THE WAVES, 1931

LETTER TO A YOUNG POET, 1932

THE COMMON READER: SECOND SERIES, 1932

FLUSH: A BIOGRAPHY, 1933

THE YEARS, 1937

THREE GUINEAS, 1938

ROGER FRY: A BIOGRAPHY, 1940

BETWEEN THE ACTS, 1941

THE DEATH OF THE MOTH AND OTHER ESSAYS, 1942

A HAUNTED HOUSE AND OTHER SHORT STORIES, 1944

THE MOMENT AND OTHER ESSAYS, 1947

THE CAPTAIN'S DEATH BED AND OTHER ESSAYS, 1950

A WRITER'S DIARY, 1954

VIRGINIA WOOLF AND LYTTON STRACHEY: LETTERS, 1956

GRANITE AND RAINBOW, 1958

CONTEMPORARY WRITERS, 1965

COLLECTED ESSAYS *(4 vols.)*, 1967

VIRGINIA WOOLF

NIGHT
AND DAY

A HARVEST BOOK

Harcourt Brace Jovanovich, Inc., New York

Library of Congress Cataloging in Publication Data

Woolf, Virginia (Stephen) 1882–1941.
Night and day.

(A Harvest book, HB 263)
I. Title.
PZ3.W884NI10   [PR6045.072]   823'.9'12   73-5730
ISBN 0-15-665600-0 (pbk.)

E   F   G   H   I   J

TO
VANESSA BELL
BUT, LOOKING FOR A PHRASE,
I FOUND NONE TO STAND
BESIDE YOUR NAME

NIGHT AND DAY

NIGHT AND DAY

CHAPTER I

IT was a Sunday evening in October, and in common with many other young ladies of her class, Katharine Hilbery was pouring out tea. Perhaps a fifth part of her mind was thus occupied, and the remaining parts leapt over the little barrier of day which interposed between Monday morning and this rather subdued moment, and played with the things one does voluntarily and normally in the daylight. But although she was silent, she was evidently mistress of a situation which was familiar enough to her, and inclined to let it take its way for the six hundredth time, perhaps, without bringing into play any of her unoccupied faculties. A single glance was enough to show that Mrs. Hilbery was so rich in the gifts which make tea-parties of elderly distinguished people successful, that she scarcely needed any help from her daughter, provided that the tiresome business of teacups and bread and butter was discharged for her.

Considering that the little party had been seated round the tea-table for less than twenty minutes, the animation observable on their faces, and the amount of sound they were producing collectively, were very creditable to the hostess. It suddenly came into Katharine's mind that if some one opened the door at this moment he would think that they were enjoying themselves; he would think, "What an extremely nice house to come into!" and instinctively she laughed, and said something to increase the noise, for the credit of the house presumably, since she herself had not been feeling exhilarated. At the very same moment, rather

9

to her amusement, the door was flung open, and a young man entered the room. Katharine, as she shook hands with him, asked him, in her own mind, "Now, do you think we're enjoying ourselves enormously?" . . . "Mr. Denham, mother," she said aloud, for she saw that her mother had forgotten his name.

That fact was perceptible to Mr. Denham also, and increased the awkwardness which inevitably attends the entrance of a stranger into a room full of people much at their ease, and all launched upon sentences. At the same time, it seemed to Mr. Denham as if a thousand softly padded doors had closed between him and the street outside. A fine mist, the etherealized essence of the fog, hung visibly in the wide and rather empty space of the drawing-room, all silver where the candles were grouped on the tea-table, and ruddy again in the firelight. With the omnibuses and cabs still running in his head, and his body still tingling with his quick walk along the streets and in and out of traffic and foot-passengers, this drawing-room seemed very remote and still; and the faces of the elderly people were mellowed, at some distance from each other, and had a bloom on them owing to the fact that the air in the drawing-room was thickened by blue grains of mist. Mr. Denham had come in as Mr. Fortescue, the eminent novelist, reached the middle of a very long sentence. He kept this suspended while the new-comer sat down, and Mrs. Hilbery deftly joined the severed parts by leaning towards him and remarking:

"Now, what would you do if you were married to in engineer, and had to live in Manchester, Mr. Denham?"

"Surely she could learn Persian," broke in a thin, elderly gentleman. "Is there no retired schoolmaster or man of letters in Manchester with whom she could read Persian?"

"A cousin of ours has married and gone to live in Manchester," Katharine explained. Mr. Denham muttered something, which was indeed all that was required of him, and the novelist went on where he had left off. Privately, Mr. Denham cursed himself very sharply for having exchanged the freedom of the street for this sophisticated drawing-room, where, among other disagreeables, he certainly would not appear at his best. He glanced round him, and saw that, save for Katharine, they were all over forty, the only consolation being that Mr. Fortescue was a considerable celebrity, so that to-morrow one might be glad to have met him.

"Have you ever been to Manchester?" he asked Katharine.

"Never," she replied.

"Why do you object to it, then?"

Katharine stirred her tea, and seemed to speculate, so Denham thought, upon the duty of filling somebody else's cup, but she was really wondering how she was going to keep this strange young man in harmony with the rest. She observed that he was compressing his teacup, so that there was danger lest the thin china might cave inwards. She could see that he was nervous; one would expect a bony young man with his face slightly reddened by the wind, and his hair not altogether smooth, to be nervous in such a party. Further, he probably disliked this kind of thing, and had come out of curiosity, or because her father had invited him —anyhow, he would not be easily combined with the rest.

"I should think there would be no one to talk to in Manchester," she replied at random. Mr. Fortescue had been observing her for a moment or two, as novelists are inclined to observe, and at this remark he smiled, and made it the text for a little further speculation.

"In spite of a slight tendency to exaggeration, Katharine decidedly hits the mark," he said, and lying back in his chair, with his opaque contemplative eyes fixed on the ceiling, and the tips of his fingers pressed together, he depicted, first the horrors of the streets of Manchester, and then the bare, immense moors on the outskirts of the town, and then the scrubby little house in which the girl would live, and then the professors and the miserable young students devoted to the more strenuous works of our younger dramatists, who would visit her, and how her appearance would change by degrees, and how she would fly to London, and how Katharine would have to lead her about, as one leads an eager dog on a chain, past rows of clamorous butchers' shops, poor dear creature.

"Oh, Mr. Fortescue," exclaimed Mrs. Hilbery, as he finished, "I had just written to say how I envied her! I was thinking of the big gardens and the dear old ladies in mittens, who read nothing but the *Spectator,* and snuff the candles. Have they *all* disappeared? I told her she would find the nice things of London without the horrid streets that depress one so."

"There is the University," said the thin gentleman, who had previously insisted upon the existence of people knowing Persian.

"I know there are moors there, because I read about them in a book the other day," said Katharine.

"I am grieved and amazed at the ignorance of my family," Mr. Hilbery remarked. He was an elderly man, with a pair of oval, hazel eyes which were rather bright for his time of life, and relieved the heaviness of his face. He played constantly with a little green stone attached to his watch-chain, thus displaying long and very sensitive fingers, and had a habit of moving his head hither and thither very quickly without altering the position of his large and rather corpulent body, so that he seemed to be providing himself incessantly with food for amusement and reflection with the least possible expenditure of energy. One might suppose that he had passed the time of life when his ambitions were personal, or that he had gratified them as far as he was likely to do, and now employed his considerable acuteness rather to observe and reflect than to attain any result.

Katharine, so Denham decided, while Mr. Fortescue built up another rounded structure of words, had a likeness to each of her parents, but these elements were rather oddly blended. She had the quick, impulsive movements of her mother, the lips parting often to speak, and closing again;

and the dark oval eyes of her father brimming with light upon a basis of sadness, or, since she was too young to have acquired a sorrowful point of view, one might say that the basis was not sadness so much as a spirit given to contemplation and self-control. Judging by her hair, her coloring, and the shape of her features, she was striking, if not actually beautiful. Decision and composure stamped her, a combination of qualities that produced a very marked character, and one that was not calculated to put a young man, who scarcely knew her, at his ease. For the rest, she was tall; her dress was of some quiet color, with old yellow-tinted lace for ornament, to which the spark of an ancient jewel gave its one red gleam. Denham noticed that, although silent, she kept sufficient control of the situation to answer immediately her mother appealed to her for help, and yet it was obvious to him that she attended only with the surface skin of her mind. It struck him that her position at the tea-table, among all these elderly people, was not without its difficulties, and he checked his inclination to find her, or her attitude, generally antipathetic to him. The talk had passed over Manchester, after dealing with it very generously.

"Would it be the Battle of Trafalgar or the Spanish Armada, Katharine?" her mother demanded.

"Trafalgar, mother."

"Trafalgar, of course! How stupid of me! Another cup of tea, with a thin slice of lemon in it, and then, dear Mr. Fortescue, please explain my absurd little puzzle. One can't help believing gentlemen with Roman noses, even if one meets them in omnibuses."

Mr. Hilbery here interposed so far as Denham was concerned, and talked a great deal of sense about the solicitors' profession, and the changes which he had seen in his lifetime. Indeed, Denham properly fell to his lot, owing to the fact that an article by Denham upon some legal matter, published by Mr. Hilbery in his Review, had brought them acquainted. But when a moment later Mrs. Sutton Bailey was announced, he turned to her, and Mr. Denham found himself sitting silent, rejecting possible things to say, beside Katharine, who was silent too. Being much about the same age and both under thirty, they were prohibited from the use of a great many convenient phrases which launch conversation into smooth waters. They were further silenced by Katharine's rather malicious determination not to help this young man, in whose upright and resolute bearing she detected something hostile to her surroundings, by any of the usual feminine amenities. They therefore sat silent, Denham controlling his desire to say something abrupt and explosive, which should shock her into life. But Mrs. Hilbery was immediately sensitive to any silence in the drawing-room, as of a dumb note in a sonorous scale, and leaning across the table she observed, in the curiously tentative detached manner which always gave her phrases the likeness of butterflies flaunting from one sunny spot to another, "D'you know, Mr. Denham, you remind me so much of dear Mr. Ruskin. . . . Is it his tie, Katharine, or his hair, or the way he sits in his chair? Do tell me, Mr. Denham, are you an admirer of Ruskin? Some one, the other day, said to me, 'Oh, no, we don't read Ruskin, Mrs. Hilbery.' What *do* you read, I wonder?—for you can't spend all your time going up in aeroplanes and burrowing into the bowels of the earth."

She looked benevolently at Denham, who said nothing articulate, and then at Katharine, who smiled but said nothing either, upon which Mrs. Hilbery seemed possessed by a brilliant idea, and exclaimed:

"I'm sure Mr. Denham would like to see our things, Katharine. I'm sure he's not like that dreadful young man, Mr. Ponting, who told me that he considered it our duty to live exclusively in the present. After all, what *is* the present? Half of it's the past, and the better half, too, I should say," she added, turning to Mr. Fortescue.

Denham rose, half meaning to go, and thinking that he had seen all that there was to see, but Katharine rose at the same moment, and saying, "Perhaps you would like to see the pictures," led the way across the drawing-room to a smaller room opening out of it.

The smaller room was something like a chapel in a cathedral, or a grotto in a cave, for the booming sound of the traffic in the distance suggested the soft surge of waters, and the oval mirrors, with their silver surface, were like deep pools trembling beneath starlight. But the comparison to a religious temple of some kind was the more apt of the two, for the little room was crowded with relics.

As Katharine touched different spots, lights sprang here and there, and revealed a square mass of red-and-gold books, and then a long skirt in blue-and-white paint lustrous behind glass, and then a mahogany writing-table, with its orderly equipment, and, finally, a picture above the table, to which special illumination was accorded. When Katharine had touched these last lights, she stood back, as much as to say, "There!" Denham found himself looked down upon by the eyes of the great poet, Richard Alardyce, and suffered a little shock which would have led him, had he been wearing a hat, to remove it. The eyes looked at him out of the mellow pinks and yellows of the paint with divine friendliness, which embraced him, and passed on to contemplate the entire world. The paint had so faded that very little but the beautiful large eyes were left, dark in the surrounding dimness.

Katharine waited as though for him to receive a full impression, and then she said:

"This is his writing-table. He used this pen," and she lifted a quill pen and laid it down again. The writing-table was splashed with old ink, and the pen disheveled in service. There lay the gigantic gold-rimmed spectacles, ready to his hand, and beneath the table was a pair of large, worn slippers, one of which Katharine picked up, remarking:

"I think my grandfather must have been at least twice as large as any one is nowadays. This," she went on, as if she knew what she had to say by heart, "is the original manuscript of the 'Ode to Winter.' The early poems are far less corrected than the later.   Would you like to look at it?"

While Mr. Denham examined the manuscript, she glanced up at her grandfather, and, for the thousandth time, fell into a pleasant dreamy state in which she seemed to be the companion of those giant men, of their own lineage, at any rate, and the insignificant present moment was put to shame. That magnificent ghostly head on the canvas, surely, never beheld all the trivialities of a Sunday afternoon, and it did not seem to matter what she and this young man said to each other, for they were only small people.

"This is a copy of the first edition of the poems," she continued, without considering the fact that Mr. Denham was still occupied with the manuscript, "which contains several poems that have not been reprinted, as well as corrections."   She paused for a minute, and then went on, as if these spaces had all been calculated.

"That lady in blue is my great-grandmother, by Millington.   Here is my uncle's walking-stick—he was Sir Richard Warburton, you know, and rode with Havelock to the Relief of Lucknow.   And then, let me see—oh, that's the original Alardyce, 1697, the founder of the family fortunes, with his wife.   Some one gave us this bowl the other day because it has their crest and initials.   We think it must have been given them to celebrate their silver wedding-day."

Here she stopped for a moment, wondering why it was that Mr. Denham said nothing.   Her feeling that he was antagonistic to her, which had lapsed while she thought of her family possessions, returned so keenly that she stopped in the middle of her catalog and looked at him.   Her mother, wishing to connect him reputably with the great dead, had compared him with Mr. Ruskin; and the comparison was in Katharine's mind, and led her to be more critical of the young man than was fair, for a young man paying a call in a tail-coat is in a different element altogether from a head seized at its climax of expressiveness, gazing immutably from behind a sheet of glass, which was all that remained to her of Mr. Ruskin.   He had a singular face—a face built for swiftness and decision rather than for massive contemplation; the forehead broad, the nose long and formidable, the lips clean-shaven and at once dogged and sensitive, the cheeks lean, with a deeply running tide of red blood in them. His eyes, expressive now of the usual masculine impersonality and authority, might reveal more subtle emotions under favorable circumstances, for they were large, and of a clear, brown color; they seemed unexpectedly to hesitate and speculate; but Katharine only looked at him to wonder whether his face would not have come nearer the standard of her dead heroes if it had been adorned with side-whiskers. In his spare build and thin, though healthy, cheeks, she saw tokens of an angular and acrid soul. His voice, she noticed, had a slight vibrating or creaking sound in it, as he laid down the manuscript and said:

"You must be very proud of your family, Miss Hilbery."

"Yes, I am," Katharine answered, and she added, "Do you think there's anything wrong in that?"

"Wrong? How should it be wrong? It must be a bore, though, showing your things to visitors," he added reflectively.

"Not if the visitors like them."

"Isn't it difficult to live up to your ancestors?" he proceeded.

"I dare say I shouldn't try to write poetry," Katharine replied.

"No. And that's what I should hate. I couldn't bear my grandfather to cut me out. And, after all," Denham went on, glancing round him satirically, as Katharine thought, "it's not your grandfather only. You're cut out all the way round. I suppose you come of one of the most disinguished families in England. There are the Warburtons and the Mannings—and you're related to the Otways, aren't you? I read it all in some magazine," he added.

"The Otways are my cousins," Katharine replied.

"Well," said Denham, in a final tone of voice, as if his argument were proved.

"Well," said Katharine, "I don't see that you've proved anything."

Denham smiled, in a peculiarly provoking way. He was amused and gratified to find that he had the power to annoy his oblivious, supercilious hostess, if he could not impress her; though he would have preferred to impress her.

He sat silent, holding the precious little book of poems unopened in his hands, and Katharine watched him, the melancholy or contemplative expression deepening in her eyes as her annoyance faded. She appeared to be considering many things. She had forgotten her duties.

"Well," said Denham again, suddenly opening the little book of poems, as though he had said all that he meant to say or could, with propriety, say. He turned over the pages with great decision, as if he were judging the book in its entirety, the printing and paper and binding, as well as the poetry, and then, having satisfied himself of its good or bad quality, he placed it on the writing-table, and examined the malacca cane with the gold knob which had belonged to the soldier.

"But aren't you proud of your family?" Katharine demanded.

"No," said Denham. "We've never done anything to be proud of—unless you count paying one's bills a matter for pride."

"That sounds rather dull," Katharine remarked.

"You would think us horribly dull," Denham agreed.

"Yes, I might find you dull, but I don't think I should find you ridiculous," Katharine added, as if Denham had actually brought that charge against her family.

"No—because we're not in the least ridiculous. We're a respectable middle-class family, living at Highgate."

"We don't live at Highgate, but we're middle class too, I suppose."

Denham merely smiled, and replacing the malacca cane on the rack, he drew a sword from its ornamental sheath.

"That belonged to Clive, so we say," said Katharine, taking up her duties as hostess again automatically.

"Is it a lie?" Denham inquired.

"It's a family tradition. I don't know that we can prove it."

"You see, we don't have traditions in our family," said Denham.

"You sound very dull," Katharine remarked, for the second time.

"Merely middle class," Denham replied.

"You pay your bills, and you speak the truth. I don't see why you should despise us."

Mr. Denham carefully sheathed the sword which the Hilberys said belonged to Clive.

"I shouldn't like to be you; that's all I said," he replied, as if he were saying what he thought as accurately as he could.

"No, but one never would like to be any one else."

"I should. I should like to be lots of other people."

"Then why not us?" Katharine asked.

Denham looked at her as she sat in her grandfather's arm-chair, drawing her great-uncle's malacca cane smoothly through her fingers, while her background was made up equally of lustrous blue-and-white paint, and crimson books with gilt lines on them. The vitality and composure of her attitude, as of a bright-plumed bird poised easily before further flights, roused him to show her the limitations of her lot. So soon, so easily, would he be forgotten.

"You'll never know anything at first hand," he began, almost savagely. "It's all been done for you. You'll never know the pleasure of buying things after saving up for them, or reading books for the first time, or making discoveries."

"Go on," Katharine observed, as he paused, suddenly doubtful, when he heard his voice proclaiming aloud these facts, whether there was any truth in them.

"Of course, I don't know how you spend your time," he continued, a little stiffly, "but I suppose you have to show people round. You are writing a life of your grandfather, aren't you? And this kind of thing"—he nodded towards the other room, where they could hear bursts of cultivated laughter—"must take up a lot of time."

She looked at him expectantly, as if between them they were decorating a small figure of herself, and she saw him hesitating in the disposition of some bow or sash.

"You've got it very nearly right," she said, "but I only help my mother. I don't write myself."

"Do you do anything yourself?" he demanded.

"What do you mean?" she asked. "I don't leave the house at ten and come back at six."

"I don't mean that."

Mr. Denham had recovered his self-control; he spoke with a quietness which made Katharine rather anxious that he should explain himself, but at the same time she wished to annoy him, to waft him away from her on some light current of ridicule or satire, as she was wont to do with these intermittent young men of her father's.

"Nobody ever does do anything worth doing nowadays," she remarked. "You see"—she tapped the volume of her grandfather's poems—"we don't even print as well as they did, and as for poets or painters or novelists—there are none; so, at any rate, I'm not singular."

"No, we haven't any great men," Denham replied. "I'm very glad that we haven't. I hate great men. The worship of greatness in the nineteenth century seems to me to explain the worthlessness of that generation."

Katharine opened her lips and drew in her breath, as if to reply with equal vigor, when the shutting of a door in the next room withdrew her attention, and they both became conscious that the voices, which had been rising and falling round the tea-table, had fallen silent; the light, even, seemed to have sunk lower. A moment later Mrs. Hilbery appeared in the doorway of the ante-room. She stood looking at them with a smile of expectancy on her face, as if a scene from the drama of the younger generation were being

played for her benefit. She was a remarkable-looking woman, well advanced in the sixties, but owing to the lightness
of her frame and the brightness of her eyes she seemed to
have been wafted over the surface of the years without taking much harm in the passage. Her face was shrunken and
aquiline, but any hint of sharpness was dispelled by the large
blue eyes, at once sagacious and innocent, which seemed to
regard the world with an enormous desire that it should
behave itself nobly, and an entire confidence that it could
do so, if it would only take the pains.

Certain lines on the broad forehead and about the lips
might be taken to suggest that she had known moments of
some difficulty and perplexity in the course of her career,
but these had not destroyed her trustfulness, and she was
clearly still prepared to give every one any number of fresh
chances and the whole system the benefit of the doubt. She
wore a great resemblance to her father, and suggested, as
he did, the fresh airs and open spaces of a younger world.

"Well," she said, "how do you like our things, Mr.
Denham?"

Mr. Denham rose, put his book down, opened his mouth,
but said nothing, as Katharine observed, with some amusement.

Mrs. Hilbery handled the book he had laid down.

"There are some books that *live*," she mused. "They
are young with us, and they grow old with us. Are you
fond of poetry, Mr. Denham? But what an absurd question
to ask! The truth is, dear Mr. Fortescue has almost tired
me out. He is so eloquent and so witty, so searching and
so profound that, after half an hour or so, I feel inclined to
turn out all the lights. But perhaps he'd be more wonderful than ever in the dark. What d'you think, Katharine?
Shall we give a little party in complete darkness? There'd
have to be bright rooms for the bores. . . ."

Here Mr. Denham held out his hand.

"But we've any number of things to show you!" Mrs.
Hilbery exclaimed, taking no notice of it. "Books, pic-

tures, china, manuscripts, and the very chair that Mary Queen of Scots sat in when she heard of Darnley's murder. I must lie down for a little, and Katharine must change her dress (though she's wearing a very pretty one), but if you don't mind being left alone, supper will be at eight. I dare say you'll write a poem of your own while you're waiting. Ah, how I love the firelight! Doesn't our room look charming?"

She stepped back and bade them contemplate the empty drawing-room, with its rich, irregular lights, as the flames leapt and wavered.

"Dear things!" she exclaimed. "Dear chairs and tables! How like old friends they are—faithful, silent friends. Which reminds me, Katharine, little Mr. Anning is coming to-night, and Tite Street, and Cadogan Square. . . . Do remember to get that drawing of your great-uncle glazed. Aunt Millicent remarked it last time she was here, and I know how it would hurt me to see *my* father in a broken glass."

It was like tearing through a maze of diamond-glittering spiders' webs to say good-bye and escape, for at each movement Mrs. Hilbery remembered something further about the villainies of picture-framers or the delights of poetry, and at one time it seemed to the young man that he would be hypnotized into doing what she pretended to want him to do, for he could not suppose that she attached any value whatever to his presence. Katharine, however, made an opportunity for him to leave, and for that he was grateful to her, as one young person is grateful for the understanding of another.

CHAPTER II

THE young man shut the door with a sharper slam than any visitor had used that afternoon, and walked up the street at a great pace, cutting the air with his walking-stick. He was glad to find himself outside that drawing-room, breathing raw fog, and in contact with unpolished people who only wanted their share of the pavement allowed them. He thought that if he had had Mr. or Mrs. or Miss Hilbery out here he would have made them, somehow, feel his superiority, for he was chafed by the memory of halt-ing awkward sentences which had failed to give even the young woman with the sad, but inwardly ironical eyes a hint of his force. He tried to recall the actual words of his little outburst, and unconsciously supplemented them by so many words of greater expressiveness that the irritation of his failure was somewhat assuaged. Sudden stabs of the unmitigated truth assailed him now and then, for he was not inclined by nature to take a rosy view of his conduct, but what with the beat of his foot upon the pavement, and the glimpse which half-drawn curtains offered him of kitchens, dining-rooms, and drawing-rooms, illustrating with mute power different scenes from different lives, his own experience lost its sharpness.

His own experience underwent a curious change. His speed slackened, his head sank a little towards his breast, and the lamplight shone now and again upon a face grown strangely tranquil. His thought was so absorbing that when it became necessary to verify the name of a street, he looked at it for a time before he read it; when he came to a crossing, he seemed to have to reassure himself by two or three taps, such as a blind man gives, upon the curb; and, reaching the Underground station, he blinked in

the bright circle of light, glanced at his watch, decided that
he might still indulge himself in darkness, and walked
straight on.

And yet the thought was the thought with which he had
started. He was still thinking about the people in the house
which he had left; but instead of remembering, with whatever accuracy he could, their looks and sayings, he had consciously taken leave of the literal truth. A turn of the street,
a firelit room, something monumental in the procession of
the lamp-posts, who shall say what accident of light or shape
had suddenly changed the prospect within his mind, and led
him to murmur aloud:

"She'll do. . . . Yes, Katharine Hilbery'll do. . . . I'll
take Katharine Hilbery."

As soon as he had said this, his pace slackened, his head
fell, his eyes became fixed. The desire to justify himself,
which had been so urgent, ceased to torment him, and, as
if released from constraint, so that they worked without
friction or bidding, his faculties leapt forward and fixed, as
a matter of course, upon the form of Katharine Hilbery. It
was marvellous how much they found to feed upon, considering the destructive nature of Denham's criticism in her
presence. The charm, which he had tried to disown, when
under the effect of it, the beauty, the character, the aloofness, which he had been determined not to feel, now possessed him wholly; and when, as happened by the nature of
things, he had exhausted his memory, he went on with his
imagination. He was conscious of what he was about, for
in thus dwelling upon Miss Hilbery's qualities, he showed
a kind of method, as if he required this vision of her for a
particular purpose. He increased her height, he darkened
her hair; but physically there was not much to change in
her. His most daring liberty was taken with her mind,
which, for reasons of his own, he desired to be exalted and
infallible, and of such independence that it was only in
the case of Ralph Denham that it swerved from its high,
swift flight, but where he was concerned, though fastidious

at first, she finally swooped from her eminence to crown him with her approval. These delicious details, however, were to be worked out in all their ramifications at his leisure; the main point was that Katharine Hilbery would do; she would do for weeks, perhaps for months. In taking her he had provided himself with something the lack of which had left a bare place in his mind for a considerable time. He gave a sigh of satisfaction; his consciousness of his actual position somewhere in the neighborhood of Knightsbridge returned to him, and he was soon speeding in the train towards Highgate.

Although thus supported by the knowledge of his new possession of considerable value, he was not proof against the familiar thoughts which the suburban streets and the damp shrubs growing in front gardens and the absurd names painted in white upon the gates of those gardens suggested to him. His walk was uphill, and his mind dwelt gloomily upon the house which he approached, where he would find six or seven brothers and sisters, a widowed mother, and, probably, some aunt or uncle sitting down to an unpleasant meal under a very bright light. Should he put in force the threat which, two weeks ago, some such gathering had wrung from him—the terrible threat that if visitors came on Sunday he should dine alone in his room? A glance in the direction of Miss Hilbery determined him to make his stand this very night, and accordingly, having let himself in, having verified the presence of Uncle Joseph by means of a bowler hat and a very large umbrella, he gave his orders to the maid, and went upstairs to his room.

He went up a great many flights of stairs, and he noticed, as he had very seldom noticed, how the carpet became steadily shabbier, until it ceased altogether, how the walls were discolored, sometimes by cascades of damp, and sometimes by the outlines of picture-frames since removed, how the paper flapped loose at the corners, and a great flake of plaster had fallen from the ceiling. The room itself was a cheer-

less one to return to at this inauspicious hour. A flattened
sofa would, later in the evening, become a bed; one of the
tables concealed a washing apparatus; his clothes and boots
were disagreeably mixed with books which bore the gilt of
college arms; and, for decoration, there hung upon the wall
photographs of bridges and cathedrals and large, unprepos-
sessing groups of insufficiently clothed young men, sitting
in rows one above another upon stone steps. There was a
look of meanness and shabbiness in the furniture and curtains, and nowhere any sign of luxury or even of a cultivated
taste, unless the cheap classics in the book-case were a sign
of an effort in that direction. The only object that threw
any light upon the character of the room's owner was a
large perch, placed in the window to catch the air and sun,
upon which a tame and, apparently, decrepit rook hopped
dryly from side to side. The bird, encouraged by a scratch
behind the ear, settled upon Denham's shoulder. He lit his
gas-fire and settled down in gloomy patience to await his
dinner. After sitting thus for some minutes a small girl
popped her head in to say,

"Mother says, aren't you coming down, Ralph? Uncle
Joseph——"

"They're to bring my dinner up here," said Ralph, peremptorily; whereupon she vanished, leaving the door ajar
in her haste to be gone. After Denham had waited some
minutes, in the course of which neither he nor the rook
took their eyes off the fire, he muttered a curse, ran downstairs, intercepted the parlor-maid, and cut himself a slice
of bread and cold meat. As he did so, the dining-room door
sprang open, a voice exclaimed "Ralph!" but Ralph paid no
attention to the voice, and made off upstairs with his plate.
He set it down in a chair opposite him, and ate with a
ferocity that was due partly to anger and partly to hunger.
His mother, then, was determined not to respect his wishes;
he was a person of no importance in his own family; he was
sent for and treated as a child. He reflected, with a growing
sense of injury, that almost every one of his actions since

opening the door of his room had been won from the grasp of the family system. By rights, he should have been sitting downstairs in the drawing-room describing his afternoon's adventures, or listening to the afternoon's adventures of other people; the room itself, the gas-fire, the arm-chair —all had been fought for; the wretched bird, with half its feathers out and one leg lamed by a cat, had been rescued under protest; but what his family most resented, he reflected, was his wish for privacy. To dine alone, or to sit alone after dinner, was flat rebellion, to be fought with very weapon of underhand stealth or of open appeal. Which did he dislike most—deception or tears? But, at any rate, they could not rob him of his thoughts; they could not make him say where he had been or whom he had seen. That was his own affair; that, indeed, was a step entirely in the right direction, and, lighting his pipe, and cutting up the remains of his meal for the benefit of the rook, Ralph calmed his rather excessive irritation and settled down to think over his prospects.

This particular afternoon was a step in the right direction, because it was part of his plan to get to know people beyond the family circuit, just as it was part of his plan to learn German this autumn, and to review legal books for Mr. Hilbery's *Critical Review*. He had always made plans since he was a small boy; for poverty, and the fact that he was the eldest son of a large family, had given him the habit of thinking of spring and summer, autumn and winter, as so many stages in a prolonged campaign. Although he was still under thirty, this forecasting habit had marked two semicircular lines above his eyebrows, which threatened, at this moment, to crease into their wonted shapes. But instead of settling down to think, he rose, took a small piece of cardboard marked in large letters with the word OUT, and hung it upon the handle of his door. This done, he sharpened a pencil, lit a reading-lamp and opened his book. But still he hesitated to take his seat. He scratched the rook, he walked to the window; he parted the curtains, and looked down upon the city which lay, hazily luminous, beneath him. He looked across the vapors in the direction of Chelsea; looked fixedly for a moment, and then returned to his chair. But the whole thickness of some learned counsel's treatise upon Torts did not screen him satisfactorily. Through the pages he saw a drawing-room, very empty and spacious; he heard low voices, he saw women's figures, he could even smell the scent of the cedar log which flamed in the grate. His mind relaxed its tension, and seemed to be giving out now what it had taken in unconsciously at the time. He could remember Mr. Fortescue's exact words, and the rolling emphasis with which he delivered them, and he began to repeat what Mr. Fortescue had said, in Mr. Fortescue's own manner, about Manchester. His mind then began to wander about the house, and he wondered whether there were other rooms like the drawing-room, and he thought, inconsequently, how beautiful the bathroom must be, and how leisurely it was—the life of these well-kept people, who were, no doubt, still sitting in the same room, only they had changed their clothes, and little Mr. Anning was there, and the aunt who would mind if the glass of her father's picture was broken. Miss Hilbery had changed her dress ("although she's wearing such a pretty one," he heard her mother say), and she was talking to Mr. Anning, who was well over forty, and bald into the bargain, about books. How peaceful and spacious it was; and the peace possessed him so completely that his muscles slackened, his book drooped from his hand, and he forgot that the hour of work was wasting minute by minute.

He was roused by a creak upon the stair. With a guilty start he composed himself, frowned and looked intently at the fifty-sixth page of his volume. A step paused outside his door, and he knew that the person, whoever it might be, was considering the placard, and debating whether to honor its decree or not. Certainly, policy advised him to sit still in autocratic silence, for no custom can take root in a family unless every breach of it is punished severely for the first six months or so. But Ralph was conscious of a distinct wish to be interrupted, and his disappointment was perceptible when he heard the creaking sound rather farther down the stairs, as if his visitor had decided to withdraw. He rose, opened the door with unnecessary abruptness, and waited on the landing. The person stopped simultaneously half a flight downstairs.

"Ralph?" said a voice, inquiringly.

"Joan?"

"I was coming up, but I saw your notice."

"Well, come along in, then." He concealed his desire beneath a tone as grudging as he could make it.

Joan came in, but she was careful to show, by standing upright with one hand upon the mantelpiece, that she was only there for a definite purpose, which discharged, she would go.

She was older than Ralph by some three or four years. Her face was round but worn, and expressed that tolerant but anxious good humor which is the special attribute of elder sisters in large families. Her pleasant brown eyes resembled Ralph's, save in expression, for whereas he seemed to look straightly and keenly at one object, she appeared to be in the habit of considering everything from many different points of view. This made her appear his elder by more years than existed in fact between them. Her gaze rested for a moment or two upon the rook. She then said, without any preface:

"It's about Charles and Uncle John's offer. . . . Mother's been talking to me. She says she can't afford to pay for him after this term. She says she'll have to ask for an overdraft as it is."

"That's simply not true," said Ralph.

"No. I thought not. But she won't believe me when I say it."

Ralph, as if he could foresee the length of this familiar argument, drew up a chair for his sister and sat down himself.

"I'm not interrupting?" she inquired.

Ralph shook his head, and for a time they sat silent. The lines curved themselves in semicircles above their eyes.

"She doesn't understand that one's got to take risks," he observed, finally.

"I believe mother would take risks if she knew that Charles was the sort of boy to profit by it."

"He's got brains, hasn't he?" said Ralph. His tone had taken on that shade of pugnacity which suggested to his sister that some personal grievance drove him to take the line he did. She wondered what it might be, but at once recalled her mind, and assented.

"In some ways he's fearfully backward, though, compared with what you were at his age. And he's difficult at home, too. He makes Molly slave for him."

Ralph made a sound which belittled this particular argument. It was plain to Joan that she had struck one of her brother's perverse moods, and he was going to oppose whatever his mother said. He called her "she," which was a proof of it. She sighed involuntarily, and the sigh annoyed Ralph, and he exclaimed with irritation:

"It's pretty hard lines to stick a boy into an office at seventeen!"

"Nobody *wants* to stick him into an office," she said.

She, too, was becoming annoyed. She had spent the whole of the afternoon discussing wearisome details of education and expense with her mother, and she had come to her brother for help, encouraged, rather irrationally, to expect help by the fact that he had been out somewhere, she didn't know and didn't mean to ask where, all the afternoon.

Ralph was fond of his sister, and her irritation made him think how unfair it was that all these burdens should be laid on her shoulders.

"The truth is," he observed gloomily, "that I ought to have accepted Uncle John's offer. I should have been making six hundred a year by this time."

"I don't think that for a moment," Joan replied quickly, repenting of her annoyance. "The question, to my mind, is, whether we couldn't cut down our expenses in some way."

"A smaller house?"

"Fewer servants, perhaps."

Neither brother nor sister spoke with much conviction, and after reflecting for a moment what these proposed reforms in a strictly economical household meant, Ralph announced very decidedly:

"It's out of the question."

It was out of the question that she should put any more household work upon herself. No, the hardship must fall on him, for he was determined that his family should have as many chances of distinguishing themselves as other families had—as the Hilberys had, for example. He believed secretly and rather defiantly, for it was a fact not capable of proof, that there was something very remarkable about his family.

"If mother won't run risks——"

"You really can't expect her to sell out again."

"She ought to look upon it as an investment; but if she won't, we must find some other way, that's all."

A threat was contained in this sentence, and Joan knew, without asking, what the threat was. In the course of his professional life, which now extended over six or seven years, Ralph had saved, perhaps, three or four hundred pounds. Considering the sacrifices he had made in order to put by this sum it always amazed Joan to find that he used it to gamble with, buying shares and selling them again, increasing it sometimes, sometimes diminishing it, and always running the risk of losing every penny of it in a day's disaster. But although she wondered, she could not help loving him the better for his odd combination of Spartan self-control and what appeared to her romantic and childish folly. Ralph interested her more than any one else in the world, and she often broke off in the middle of one of these economic discussions, in spite of their gravity, to consider some fresh aspect of his character.

"I think you'd be foolish to risk your money on poor old Charles," she observed. "Fond as I am of him, he doesn't seem to me exactly brilliant. . . . Besides, why should you be sacrificed?"

"My dear Joan," Ralph exclaimed, stretching himself out with a gesture of impatience, "don't you see that we've all got to be sacrificed? What's the use of denying it? What's the use of struggling against it? So it always has been, so it always will be. We've got no money and we never shall have any money. We shall just turn round in the mill every day of our lives until we drop and die, worn out, as most people do, when one comes to think of it."

Joan looked at him, opened her lips as if to speak, and closed them again. Then she said, very tentatively:

"Aren't you happy, Ralph?"

"No. Are you? Perhaps I'm as happy as most people, though. God knows whether I'm happy or not. What is happiness?"

He glanced with half a smile, in spite of his gloomy irritation, at his sister. She looked, as usual, as if she were weighing one thing with another, and balancing them together before she made up her mind.

"Happiness," she remarked at length enigmatically, rather as if she were sampling the word, and then she paused. She paused for a considerable space, as if she were considering happiness in all its bearings. "Hilda was here to-day," she suddenly resumed, as if they had never mentioned happiness. "She brought Bobbie—he's a fine boy now." Ralph observed, with an amusement that had a tinge of irony in it, that she was now going to sidle away quickly from this dangerous approach to intimacy on to topics of general and family interest. Nevertheless, he reflected, she was the only one of his family with whom he found it possible to discuss happiness, although he might very well have discussed happiness with Miss Hilbery at their first meeting. He looked critically at Joan, and wished that she did not look so provincial or suburban in her high green dress with the faded trimming, so patient, and almost resigned. He began to wish to tell her about the Hilberys in order to abuse them, for in the miniature battle which so often rages between two quickly following impressions of life, the life of the Hilberys was getting the better of the life of the Denhams in his mind, and he wanted to assure himself that there was some quality in which Joan infinitely surpassed Miss Hilbery. He should have felt that his own sister was more original, and had greater vitality than Miss Hilbery had; but his main impression of Katharine now was of a person of great vitality and composure; and at the moment he could not perceive what poor dear Joan had gained from the fact that she was the granddaughter of a man who kept a shop, and herself earned her own living. The infinite dreariness and sordidness of their life oppressed him in spite of his fundamental belief that, as a family, they were somehow remarkable.

"Shall you talk to mother?" Joan inquired. "Because, you see, the thing's got to be settled, one way or another. Charles must write to Uncle John if he's going there."

Ralph sighed impatiently.

"I suppose it doesn't much matter either way," he exclaimed. "He's doomed to misery in the long run."

A slight flush came into Joan's cheek.

"You know you're talking nonsense," she said. "It doesn't hurt any one to have to earn their own living. I'm very glad I have to earn mine."

Ralph was pleased that she should feel this, and wished her to continue, but he went on, perversely enough.

"Isn't that only because you've forgotten how to enjoy yourself? You never have time for anything decent——"

"As for instance?"

"Well, going for walks, or music, or books, or seeing interesting people. You never do anything that's really worth doing any more than I do."

"I always think you could make this room much nicer, if you liked," she observed.

"What does it matter what sort of room I have when I'm forced to spend all the best years of my life drawing up deeds in an office?"

"You said two days ago that you found the law so interesting."

"So it is if one could afford to know anything about it."

("That's Herbert only just going to bed now," Joan interposed, as a door on the landing slammed vigorously. "And then he won't get up in the morning.")

Ralph looked at the ceiling, and shut his lips closely together. Why, he wondered, could Joan never for one moment detach her mind from the details of domestic life? It seemed to him that she was getting more and more enmeshed in them, and capable of shorter and less frequent flights into the outer world, and yet she was only thirty-three.

"D'you ever pay calls now?" he asked abruptly.

"I don't often have the time. Why do you ask?"

"It might be a good thing, to get to know new people, that's all."

"Poor Ralph!" said Joan suddenly, with a smile. "You think your sister's getting very old and very dull—that's it, isn't it?"

"I don't think anything of the kind," he said stoutly, but he flushed. "But you lead a dog's life, Joan. When you're not working in an office, you're worrying over the rest of us. And I'm not much good to you, I'm afraid."

Joan rose, and stood for a moment warming her hands, and, apparently, meditating as to whether she should say anything more or not. A feeling of great intimacy united the brother and sister, and the semicircular lines above their eyebrows disappeared. No, there was nothing more to be said on either side. Joan brushed her brother's head with her hand as she passed him, murmured good night, and left the room. For some minutes after she had gone Ralph lay quiescent, resting his head on his hand, but gradually his eyes filled with thought, and the line reappeared on his brow, as the pleasant impression of companionship and ancient sympathy waned, and he was left to think on alone.

After a time he opened his book, and read on steadily, glancing once or twice at his watch, as if he had set himself a task to be accomplished in a certain measure of time. Now and then he heard voices in the house, and the closing of bedroom doors, which showed that the building, at the top of which he sat, was inhabited in every one of its cells. When midnight struck, Ralph shut his book, and with a candle in his hand, descended to the ground floor, to ascertain that all lights were extinct and all doors locked. It was a threadbare, well-worn house that he thus examined, as if the inmates had grazed down all luxuriance and plenty to the verge of decency; and in the night, bereft of life, bare places and ancient blemishes were unpleasantly visible. Katharine Hilbery, he thought, would condemn it off-hand.

CHAPTER III

DENHAM had accused Katharine Hilbery of belonging to one of the most distinguished families in England, and if any one will take the trouble to consult Mr. Galton's "Hereditary Genius," he will find that this assertion is not far from the truth. The Alardyces, the Hilberys, the Millingtons, and the Otways seem to prove that intellect is a possession which can be tossed from one member of a certain group to another almost indefinitely, and with apparent certainty that the brilliant gift will be safely caught and held by nine out of ten of the privileged race. They had been conspicuous judges and admirals, lawyers and servants of the State for some years before the richness of the soil culminated in the rarest flower that any family can boast, a great writer, a poet eminent among the poets of England, a Richard Alardyce; and having produced him, they proved once more the amazing virtues of their race by proceeding unconcernedly again with their usual task of breeding distinguished men. They had sailed with Sir John Franklin to the North Pole, and ridden with Havelock to the Relief of Lucknow, and when they were not lighthouses firmly based on rock for the guidance of their generation, they were steady, serviceable candles, illuminating the ordinary chambers of daily life. Whatever profession you looked at, there was a Warburton or an Alardyce, a Millington or a Hilbery somewhere in authority and prominence.

It may be said, indeed, that English society being what it is, no very great merit is required, once you bear a well-known name, to put you into a position where it is easier on the whole to be eminent than obscure. And if this is true of the sons, even the daughters, even in the nine-

teenth century, are apt to become people of importance—
philanthropists and educationalists if they are spinsters, and
the wives of distinguished men if they marry.   It is true
that there were several lamentable exceptions to this rule
in the Alardyce group, which seems to indicate that the
cadets of such houses go more rapidly to the bad than the
children of ordinary fathers and mothers, as if it were somehow a relief to them.   But, on the whole, in these first years
of the twentieth century, the Alardyces and their relations
were keeping their heads well above water.   One finds them
at the tops of professions, with letters after their names;
they sit in luxurious public offices, with private secretaries
attached to them; they write solid books in dark covers, issued by the presses of the two great universities, and when
one of them dies the chances are that another of them writes
his biography.

Now the source of this nobility was, of course, the poet,
and his immediate descendants, therefore, were invested
with greater luster than the collateral branches.   Mrs. Hilbery, in virtue of her position as the only child of the poet,
was spiritually the head of the family, and Katharine, her
daughter, had some superior rank among all the cousins and
connections, the more so because she was an only child.   The
Alardyces had married and intermarried, and their offspring
were generally profuse, and had a way of meeting regularly
in each other's houses for meals and family celebrations
which had acquired a semi-sacred character, and were as
regularly observed as days of feasting and fasting in the
Church.

In times gone by, Mrs. Hilbery had known all the poets,
all the novelists, all the beautiful women and distinguished
men of her time.   These being now either dead or secluded
in their infirm glory, she made her house a meeting-place
for her own relations, to whom she would lament the passing
of the great days of the nineteenth century, when every de-
partment of letters and art was represented in England by
two or three illustrious names.   Where are their successors?

she would ask, and the absence of any poet or painter or novelist of the true caliber at the present day was a text upon which she liked to ruminate, in a sunset mood of benignant reminiscence, which it would have been hard to disturb had there been need. But she was far from visiting their inferiority upon the younger generation. She welcomed them very heartily to her house, told them her stories, gave them sovereigns and ices and good advice, and weaved round them romances which had generally no likeness to the truth.

The quality of her birth oozed into Katharine's consciousness from a dozen different sources as soon as she was able to perceive anything. Above her nursery fireplace hung a photograph of her grandfather's tomb in Poets' Corner, and she was told in one of those moments of grown-up confidence which are so tremendously impressive to the child's mind, that he was buried there because he was a "good and great man." Later, on an anniversary, she was taken by her mother through the fog in a hansom cab, and given a large bunch of bright, sweet-scented flowers to lay upon his tomb. The candles in the church, the singing and the booming of the organ, were all, she thought, in his honor. Again and again she was brought down into the drawing-room to receive the blessing of some awful distinguished old man, who sat, even to her childish eye, somewhat apart, all gathered together and clutching a stick, unlike an ordinary visitor in her father's own arm-chair, and her father himself was there, unlike himself, too, a little excited and very polite. These formidable old creatures used to take her in their arms, look very keenly in her eyes, and then to bless her, and tell her that she must mind and be a good girl, or detect a look in her face something like Richard's as a small boy. That drew down upon her her mother's fervent embrace, and she was sent back to the nursery very proud, and with a mysterious sense of an important and unexplained state of things, which time, by degrees, unveiled to her.

There were always visitors—uncles and aunts and cousins "from India," to be reverenced for their relationship alone, and others of the solitary and formidable class, whom she was enjoined by her parents to "remember all your life." By these means, and from hearing constant talk of great men and their works, her earliest conceptions of the world included an august circle of beings to whom she gave the names of Shakespeare, Milton, Wordsworth, Shelley, and so on, who were, for some reason, much more nearly akin to the Hilberys than to other people. They made a kind of boundary to her vision of life, and played a considerable part in determining her scale of good and bad in her own small affairs. Her descent from one of these gods was no surprise to her, but matter for satisfaction, until, as the years wore on, the privileges of her lot were taken for granted, and certain drawbacks made themselves very manifest. Perhaps it is a little depressing to inherit not lands but an example of intellectual and spiritual virtue; perhaps the conclusiveness of a great ancestor is a little discouraging to those who run the risk of comparison with him. It seems as if, having flowered so splendidly, nothing now remained possible but a steady growth of good, green stalk and leaf. For these reasons, and for others, Katharine had her moments of despondency. The glorious past, in which men and women grew to unexampled size, intruded too much upon the present, and dwarfed it too consistently, to be altogether encouraging to one forced to make her experiment in living when the great age was dead.

She was drawn to dwell upon these matters more than was natural, in the first place owing to her mother's absorption in them, and in the second because a great part of her time was spent in imagination with the dead, since she was helping her mother to produce a life of the great poet. When Katharine was seventeen or eighteen—that is to say, some ten years ago—her mother had enthusiastically announced that now, with a daughter to help her, the biography would soon be published. Notices to this effect found their way into the literary papers, and for some time Katharine worked with a sense of great pride and achievement.

Lately, however, it had seemed to her that they were making no way at all, and this was the more tantalizing because no one with the ghost of a literary temperament could doubt but that they had materials for one of the greatest biographies that has ever been written. Shelves and boxes bulged with the precious stuff. The most private lives of the most interesting people lay furled in yellow bundles of close-written manuscript. In addition to this Mrs. Hilbery had in her own head as bright a vision of that time as now remained to the living, and could give those flashes and thrills to the old words which gave them almost the substance of flesh. She had no difficulty in writing, and covered a page every morning as instinctively as a thrush sings, but nevertheless, with all this to urge and inspire, and the most devout intention to accomplish the work, the book still remained unwritten. Papers accumulated without much furthering their task, and in dull moments Katharine had her doubts whether they would ever produce anything at all fit to lay before the public. Where did the difficulty lie? Not in their materials, alas! nor in their ambitions, but in something more profound, in her own inaptitude, and above all, in her mother's temperament. Katharine would calculate that she had never known her write for more than ten minutes at a time. Ideas came to her chiefly when she was in motion. She liked to perambulate the room with a duster in her hand, with which she stopped to polish the backs of already lustrous books, musing and romancing as she did so. Suddenly the right phrase or the penetrating point of view would suggest itself, and she would drop her duster and write ecstatically for a few breathless moments; and then the mood would pass away, and the duster would be sought for, and the old books polished again. These spells of inspiration never burnt steadily, but flickered over the gigantic mass of the subject as capriciously as a will-o'-the-wisp, lighting now on this

point, now on that.   It was as much as Katharine could do
to keep the pages of her mother's manuscript in order, but
to sort them so that the sixteenth year of Richard Alardyce's life succeeded the fifteenth was beyond her skill.
And yet they were so brilliant, these paragraphs, so nobly
phrased, so lightning-like in their illumination, that the
dead seemed to crowd the very room.   Read continuously,
they produced a sort of vertigo, and set her asking herself
in despair what on earth she was to do with them?   Her
mother refused, also, to face the radical questions of what
to leave in and what to leave out.   She could not decide how
far the public was to be told the truth about the poet's separation from his wife.   She drafted passages to suit either
case, and then liked each so well that she could not decide
upon the rejection of either.

But the book must be written.   It was a duty that they
owed the world, and to Katharine, at least, it meant more
than that, for if they could not between them get this one
book accomplished they had no right to their privileged
position.   Their increment became yearly more and more un-
earned.   Besides, it must be established indisputably that
her grandfather was a very great man.

By the time she was twenty-seven, these thoughts had
become very familiar to her.   They trod their way through
her mind as she sat opposite her mother of a morning at a
table heaped with bundles of old letters and well supplied
with pencils, scissors, bottles of gum, india-rubber bands,
large envelopes, and other appliances for the manufacture
of books.   Shortly before Ralph Denham's visit, Katharine
had resolved to try the effect of strict rules upon her
mother's habits of literary composition.   They were to be
seated at their tables every morning at ten o'clock, with a
clean-swept morning of empty, secluded hours before them.
They were to keep their eyes fast upon the paper, and nothing was to tempt them to speech, save at the stroke of the
hour when ten minutes for relaxation were to be allowed
them.   If these rules were observed for a year, she made

out on a sheet of paper that the completion of the book was certain, and she laid her scheme before her mother with a feeling that much of the task was already accomplished. Mrs. Hilbery examined the sheet of paper very carefully. Then she clapped her hands and exclaimed enthusiastically:

"Well done, Katharine! What a wonderful head for business you've got! Now I shall keep this before me, and every day I shall make a little mark in my pocketbook, and on the last day of all—let me think, what shall we do to celebrate the last day of all? If it weren't the winter we could take a jaunt to Italy. They say Switzerland's very lovely in the snow, except for the cold. But, as you say, the great thing is to finish the book. Now let me see——"

When they inspected her manuscripts, which Katharine had put in order, they found a state of things well calculated to dash their spirits, if they had not just resolved on reform. They found, to begin with, a great variety of very imposing paragraphs with which the biography was to open; many of these, it is true, were unfinished, and resembled triumphal arches standing upon one leg, but, as Mrs. Hilbery observed, they could be patched up in ten minutes, if she gave her mind to it. Next, there was an account of the ancient home of the Alardyces, or rather, of spring in Suffolk, which was very beautifully written, although not essential to the story. However, Katharine had put together a string of names and dates, so that the poet was capably brought into the world, and his ninth year was reached without further mishap. After that, Mrs. Hilbery wished, for sentimental reasons, to introduce the recollections of a very fluent old lady, who had been brought up in the same village, but these Katharine decided must go. It might be advisable to introduce here a sketch of contemporary poetry contributed by Mr. Hilbery, and thus terse and learned and altogether out of keeping with the rest, but Mrs. Hilbery was of opinion that it was too bare, and made one feel altogether like a good little girl in a lecture-room, which was not at all in keeping with her father. It was put on one side.

Now came the period of his early manhood, when various affairs of the heart must either be concealed or revealed; here again Mrs. Hilbery was of two minds, and a thick packet of manuscript was shelved for further consideration.

Several years were now altogether omitted, because Mrs. Hilbery had found something distasteful to her in that period, and had preferred to dwell upon her own recollections as a child. After this, it seemed to Katharine that the book became a wild dance of will-o'-the-wisps, without form or continuity, without coherence even, or any attempt to make a narrative. Here were twenty pages upon her grandfather's taste in hats, an essay upon contemporary china, a long account of a summer day's expedition into the country, when they had missed their train, together with fragmentary visions of all sorts of famous men and women, which seemed to be partly imaginary and partly authentic. There were, moreover, thousands of letters, and a mass of faithful recollections contributed by old friends, which had grown yellow now in their envelopes, but must be placed somewhere, or their feelings would be hurt. So many volumes had been written about the poet since his death that she had also to dispose of a great number of misstatements, which involved minute researches and much correspondence. Sometimes Katharine brooded, half crushed, among her papers; sometimes she felt that it was necessary for her very existence that she should free herself from the past; at others, that the past had completely displaced the present, which, when one resumed life after a morning among the dead, proved to be of an utterly thin and inferior composition.

The worst of it was that she had no aptitude for literature. She did not like phrases. She had even some natural antipathy to that process of self-examination, that perpetual effort to understand one's own feeling, and express it beautifully, fitly, or energetically in language, which constituted so great a part of her mother's existence. She was, on the contrary, inclined to be silent; she shrank from expressing herself even in talk, let alone in writing. As this disposition

was highly convenient in a family much given to the manufacture of phrases, and seemed to argue a corresponding
capacity for action, she was, from her childhood even, put
in charge of household affairs.   She had the reputation,
which nothing in her manner contradicted, of being the
most practical of people.   Ordering meals, directing servants, paying bills, and so contriving that every clock ticked
more or less accurately in time, and a number of vases were
always full of fresh flowers was supposed to be a natural
endowment of hers, and, indeed, Mrs. Hilbery often observed that it was poetry the wrong side out.   From a very
early age, too, she had to exert herself in another capacity;
she had to counsel and help and generally sustain her
mother.   Mrs. Hilbery would have been perfectly well able
to sustain herself if the world had been what the world is
not.   She was beautifully adapted for life in another planet.
But the natural genius she had for conducting affairs there
was of no real use to her here.   Her watch, for example,
was a constant source of surprise to her, and at the age of
sixty-five she was still amazed at the ascendancy which rules
and reasons exerted over the lives of other people.   She had
never learnt her lesson, and had constantly to be punished
for her ignorance.   But as that ignorance was combined
with a fine natural insight which saw deep whenever it saw
at all, it was not possible to write Mrs. Hilbery off among
the dunces; on the contrary, she had a way of seeming the
wisest person in the room.   But, on the whole, she found
it very necessary to seek support in her daughter.

Katharine, thus, was a member of a very great profession which has, as yet, no title and very little recognition,
although the labor of mill and factory is, perhaps, no more
severe and the results of less benefit to the world.   She
lived at home.   She did it very well, too.   Any one coming
to the house in Cheyne Walk felt that here was an orderly
place, shapely, controlled—a place where life had been
trained to show to the best advantage, and, though composed
of different elements, made to appear harmonious and with

a character of its own. Perhaps it was the chief triumph of Katharine's art that Mrs. Hilbery's character predominated. She and Mr. Hilbery appeared to be a rich background for her mother's more striking qualities.

Silence being, thus, both natural to her and imposed upon her, the only other remark that her mother's friends were in the habit of making about it was that it was neither a stupid silence nor an indifferent silence. But to what quality it owed its character, since character of some sort it had, no one troubled themselves to inquire. It was understood that she was helping her mother to produce a great book. She was known to manage the household. She was certainly beautiful. That accounted for her satisfactorily. But it would have been a surprise, not only to other people but to Katharine herself, if some magic watch could have taken count of the moments spent in an entirely different occupation from her ostensible one. Sitting with faded papers before her, she took part in a series of scenes such as the taming of wild ponies upon the American prairies, or the conduct of a vast ship in a hurricane round a black promontory of rock, or in others more peaceful, but marked by her complete emancipation from her present surroundings and, needless to say, by her surpassing ability in her new vocation. When she was rid of the pretense of paper and pen, phrase-making and biography, she turned her attention in a more legitimate direction, though, strangely enough, she would rather have confessed her wildest dreams of hurricane and prairie than the fact that, upstairs, alone in her room, she rose early in the morning or sat up late at night to . . . work at mathematics. No force on earth would have made her confess that. Her actions when thus engaged were furtive and secretive, like those of some nocturnal animal. Steps had only to sound on the staircase, and she slipped her paper between the leaves of a great Greek dictionary which she had purloined from her father's room for this purpose. It was only at night, indeed, that she felt secure enough from surprise to concentrate her mind to the utmost.

Perhaps the unwomanly nature of the science made her instinctively wish to conceal her love of it. But the more profound reason was that in her mind mathematics were directly opposed to literature. She would not have cared to confess how infinitely she preferred the exactitude, the star-like impersonality, of figures to the confusion, agitation, and vagueness of the finest prose. There was something a little unseemly in thus opposing the tradition of her family; something that made her feel wrong-headed, and thus more than ever disposed to shut her desires away from view and cherish them with extraordinary fondness. Again and again she was thinking of some problem when she should have been thinking of her grandfather. Waking from these trances, she would see that her mother, too, had lapsed into some dream almost as visionary as her own, for the people who played their parts in it had long been numbered among the dead. But, seeing her own state mirrored in her mother's face, Katharine would shake herself awake with a sense of irritation. Her mother was the last person she wished to resemble, much though she admired her. Her common sense would assert itself almost brutally, and Mrs. Hilbery, looking at her with her odd sidelong glance, that was half malicious and half tender, would liken her to "your wicked old Uncle Judge Peter, who used to be heard delivering sentence of death in the bathroom. Thank Heaven, Katharine, I've not a drop of *him* in me!"

CHAPTER IV

AT about nine o'clock at night, on every alternate Wednesday, Miss Mary Datchet made the same resolve, that she would never again lend her rooms for any purposes whatsoever. Being, as they were, rather large and conveniently situated in a street mostly dedicated to offices off the Strand, people who wished to meet, either for purposes of enjoyment, or to discuss art, or to reform the State, had a way of suggesting that Mary had better be asked to lend them her rooms. She always met the request with the same frown of well-simulated annoyance, which presently dissolved in a kind of half-humorous, half-surly shrug, as of a large dog tormented by children who shakes his ears. She would lend her room, but only on condition that all the arrangements were made by her. This fortnightly meeting of a society for the free discussion of everything entailed a great deal of moving, and pulling, and ranging of furniture against the wall, and placing of breakable and precious things in safe places. Miss Datchet was quite capable of lifting a kitchen table on her back, if need were, for although well-proportioned and dressed becomingly, she had the appearance of unusual strength and determination.

She was some twenty-five years of age, but looked older because she earned, or intended to earn, her own living, and had already lost the look of the irresponsible spectator, and taken on that of the private in the army of workers. Her gestures seemed to have a certain purpose, the muscles round eyes and lips were set rather firmly, as though the senses had undergone some discipline, and were held ready for a call on them. She had contracted two faint lines between her eyebrows, not from anxiety but from thought,

47

and it was quite evident that all the feminine instincts of pleasing, soothing, and charming were crossed by others in no way peculiar to her sex. For the rest she was brown-eyed, a little clumsy in movement, and suggested country birth and a descent from respectable hard-working ancestors, who had been men of faith and integrity rather than doubters or fanatics.

At the end of a fairly hard day's work it was certainly something of an effort to clear one's room, to pull the mattress off one's bed, and lay it on the floor, to fill a pitcher with cold coffee, and to sweep a long table clear for plates and cups and saucers, with pyramids of little pink biscuits between them; but when these alterations were effected, Mary felt a lightness of spirit come to her, as if she had put off the stout stuff of her working hours and slipped over her entire being some vesture of thin, bright silk. She knelt before the fire and looked out into the room. The light fell softly, but with clear radiance, through shades of yellow and blue paper, and the room, which was set with one or two sofas resembling grassy mounds in their lack of shape, looked unusually large and quiet. Mary was led to think of the heights of a Sussex down, and the swelling green circle of some camp of ancient warriors. The moonlight would be falling there so peacefully now, and she could fancy the rough pathway of silver upon the wrinkled skin of the sea.

"And here we are," she said, half aloud, half satirically, yet with evident pride, "talking about art."

She pulled a basket containing balls of differently colored wools and a pair of stockings which needed darning towards her, and began to set her fingers to work; while her mind, reflecting the lassitude of her body, went on perversely, conjuring up visions of solitude and quiet, and she pictured herself laying aside her knitting and walking out on to the down, and hearing nothing but the sheep cropping the grass close to the roots, while the shadows of the little trees moved very slightly this way and that in the moonlight, as

the breeze went through them. But she was perfectly conscious of her present situation, and derived some pleasure
from the reflection that she could rejoice equally in solitude,
and in the presence of the many very different people who
were now making their way, by divers paths, across London
to the spot where she was sitting.

As she ran her needle in and out of the wool, she thought
of the various stages in her own life which made her present
position seem the culmination of successive miracles. She
thought of her clerical father in his country parsonage, and
of her mother's death, and of her own determination to ob-
tain education, and of her college life, which had merged,
not so very long ago, in the wonderful maze of London,
which still seemed to her, in spite of her constitutional
level-headedness, like a vast electric light, casting radiance
upon the myriads of men and women who crowded round
it. And here she was at the very center of it all, that center
which was constantly in the minds of people in remote Cana-
dian forests and on the plains of India, when their thoughts
turned to England. The nine mellow strokes, by which she
was now apprised of the hour, were a message from the
great clock at Westminster itself. As the last of them died
away, there was a firm knocking on her own door, and she
rose and opened it. She returned to the room, with a look
of steady pleasure in her eyes, and she was talking to Ralph
Denham, who followed her.

"Alone?" he said, as if he were pleasantly surprised by
that fact.

"I am sometimes alone," she replied.

"But you expect a great many people," he added, looking
round him. "It's like a room on the stage. Who is it
to-night?"

"William Rodney, upon the Elizabethan use of metaphor.
I expect a good solid paper, with plenty of quotations from
the classics."

Ralph warmed his hands at the fire, which was flapping
bravely in the grate, while Mary took up her stocking again.

"I suppose you are the only woman in London who darns her own stockings," he observed.

"I'm only one of a great many thousands really," she replied, "though I must admit that I was thinking myself very remarkable when you came in. And now that you're here I don't think myself remarkable at all. How horrid of you! But I'm afraid you're much more remarkable than I am. You've done much more than I've done."

"If that's your standard, you've nothing to be proud of," said Ralph grimly.

"Well, I must reflect with Emerson that it's being and not doing that matters," she continued.

"Emerson?" Ralph exclaimed, with derision. "You don't mean to say you read Emerson?"

"Perhaps it wasn't Emerson; but why shouldn't I read Emerson?" she asked, with a tinge of anxiety.

"There's no reason that I know of. It's the combination that's odd—books and stockings. The combination is very odd." But it seemed to recommend itself to him. Mary gave a little laugh, expressive of happiness, and the particular stitches that she was now putting into her work appeared to her to be done with singular grace and felicity. She held out the stocking and looked at it approvingly.

"You always say that," she said. "I assure you it's a common 'combination,' as you call it, in the houses of the clergy. The only thing that's odd about me is that I enjoy them both—Emerson and the stocking."

A knock was heard, and Ralph exclaimed:

"Damn those people! I wish they weren't coming!"

"It's only Mr. Turner, on the floor below," said Mary, and she felt grateful to Mr. Turner for having alarmed Ralph, and for having given a false alarm.

"Will there be a crowd?" Ralph asked, after a pause.

"There'll be the Morrises and the Crashaws, and Dick Osborne, and Septimus, and all that set. Katharine Hilbery is coming, by the way, so William Rodney told me."

"Katharine Hilbery!" Ralph exclaimed.

"You know her?" Mary asked, with some surprise.

"I went to a tea-party at her house."

Mary pressed him to tell her all about it, and Ralph was not at all unwilling to exhibit proofs of the extent of his knowledge. He described the scene with certain additions and exaggerations which interested Mary very much.

"But, in spite of what you say, I do admire her," she said. "I've only seen her once or twice, but she seems to me to be what one calls a 'personality.'"

"I didn't mean to abuse her. I only felt that she wasn't very sympathetic to me."

"They say she's going to marry that queer creature Rodney."

"Marry Rodney? Then she must be more deluded than I thought her."

"Now that's my door, all right," Mary exclaimed, carefully putting her wools away, as a succession of knocks reverberated unnecessarily, accompanied by a sound of people stamping their feet and laughing. A moment later the room was full of young men and women, who came in with a peculiar look of expectation, exclaimed "Oh!" when they saw Denham, and then stood still, gaping rather foolishly.

The room very soon contained between twenty and thirty people, who found seats for the most part upon the floor, occupying the mattresses, and hunching themselves together into triangular shapes. They were all young and some of them seemed to make a protest by their hair and dress, and something somber and truculent in the expression of their faces, against the more normal type, who would have passed unnoticed in an omnibus or an underground railway. It was notable that the talk was confined to groups, and was, at first, entirely spasmodic in character, and muttered in undertones as if the speakers were suspicious of their fellow-guests.

Katharine Hilbery came in rather late, and took up a position on the floor, with her back against the wall. She looked round quickly, recognized about half a dozen people, to whom she nodded, but failed to see Ralph, or, if so, had already forgotten to attach any name to him. But in a second these heterogeneous elements were all united by the voice of Mr. Rodney, who suddenly strode up to the table, and began very rapidly in high-strained tones:

"In undertaking to speak of the Elizabethan use of metaphor in poetry——"

All the different heads swung slightly or steadied themselves into a position in which they could gaze straight at the speaker's face, and the same rather solemn expression was visible on all of them. But, at the same time, even the faces that were most exposed to view, and therefore most tautly under control, disclosed a sudden impulsive tremor which, unless directly checked, would have developed into an outburst of laughter. The first sight of Mr. Rodney was irresistibly ludicrous. He was very red in the face, whether from the cool November night or nervousness, and every movement, from the way he wrung his hands to the way he jerked his head to right and left, as though a vision drew him now to the door, now to the window, bespoke his horrible discomfort under the stare of so many eyes. He was scrupulously well dressed, and a pearl in the center of his tie seemed to give him a touch of aristocratic opulence. But the rather prominent eyes and the impulsive stammering manner, which seemed to indicate a torrent of ideas intermittently pressing for utterance and always checked in their course by a clutch of nervousness, drew no pity, as in the case of a more imposing personage, but a desire to laugh, which was, however, entirely lacking in malice. Mr. Rodney was evidently so painfully conscious of the oddity of his appearance, and his very redness and the starts to which his body was liable gave such proof of his own discomfort, that there was something endearing in this ridiculous susceptibility, although most people would probably have echoed Denham's private exclamation, "Fancy marrying a creature like that!"

His paper was carefully written out, but in spite of this precaution Mr. Rodney managed to turn over two sheets instead of one, to choose the wrong sentence where two were written together, and to discover his own handwriting suddenly illegible. When he found himself possessed of a coherent passage, he shook it at his audience almost aggressively, and then fumbled for another. After a distressing search a fresh discovery would be made, and produced in the same way, until, by means of repeated attacks, he had stirred his audience to a degree of animation quite remarkable in these gatherings. Whether they were stirred by his enthusiasm for poetry or by the contortions which a human being was going through for their benefit, it would be hard to say. At length Mr. Rodney sat down impulsively in the middle of a sentence, and, after a pause of bewilderment, the audience expressed its relief at being able to laugh aloud in a decided outburst of applause.

Mr. Rodney acknowledged this with a wild glance round him, and, instead of waiting to answer questions, he jumped up, thrust himself through the seated bodies into the corner where Katharine was sitting, and exclaimed, very audibly:

"Well, Katharine, I hope I've made a big enough fool of myself even for you! It was terrible! terrible! terrible!"

"Hush! You must answer their questions," Katharine whispered, desiring, at all costs, to keep him quiet. Oddly enough, when the speaker was no longer in front of them, there seemed to be much that was suggestive in what he had said. At any rate, a pale-faced young man with sad eyes was already on his feet, delivering an accurately worded speech with perfect composure. William Rodney listened with a curious lifting of his upper lip, although his face was still quivering slightly with emotion.

"Idiot!" he whispered. "He's misunderstood every word I said!"

"Well then, answer him," Katharine whispered back.

"No, I shan't! They'd only laugh at me. Why did I

let you persuade me that these sort of people care for literature?" he continued.

There was much to be said both for and against Mr.
Rodney's paper. It had been crammed with assertions that
such-and-such passages, taken liberally from English,
French, and Italian, are the supreme pearls of literature.
Further, he was fond of using metaphors which, com-
pounded in the study, were apt to sound either cramped or
out of place as he delivered them in fragments. Literature
was a fresh garland of spring flowers, he said, in which
yew-berries and the purple nightshade mingled with the
various tints of the anemone; and somehow or other this
garland encircled marble brows. He had read very badly
some very beautiful quotations. But through his manner
and his confusion of language there had emerged some passion of feeling which, as he spoke, formed in the majority of
the audience a little picture or an idea which each now was
eager to give expression to. Most of the people there proposed to spend their lives in the practice either of writing
or painting, and merely by looking at them it could be seen
that, as they listened to Mr. Purvis first, and then to Mr.
Greenhalgh, they were seeing something done by these gentlemen to a possession which they thought to be their own.
One person after another rose, and, as with an ill-balanced
axe, attempted to hew out his conception of art a little more
clearly, and sat down with the feeling that, for some reason
which he could not grasp, his strokes had gone awry. As
they sat down they turned almost invariably to the person
sitting next them, and rectified and continued what they had
just said in public. Before long, therefore, the groups on
the mattresses and the groups on the chairs were all in
communication with each other, and Mary Datchet, who
had begun to darn stockings again, stooped down and remarked to Ralph:

"That was what I call a first-rate paper."

Both of them instinctively turned their eyes in the direction of the reader of the paper. He was lying back

against the wall, with his eyes apparently shut, and his chin sunk upon his collar. Katharine was turning over the pages of his manuscript as if she were looking for some passage that had particularly struck her, and had a difficulty in finding it.

"Let's go and tell him how much we liked it," said Mary, thus suggesting an action which Ralph was anxious to take, though without her he would have been too proud to do it, for he suspected that he had more interest in Katharine than she had in him.

"That was a very interesting paper," Mary began, without any shyness, seating herself on the floor opposite to Rodney and Katharine. "Will you lend me the manuscript to read in peace?"

Rodney, who had opened his eyes on their approach, regarded her for a moment in suspicious silence.

"Do you say that merely to disguise the fact of my ridiculous failure?" he asked.

Katharine looked up from her reading with a smile.

"He says he doesn't mind what we think of him," she remarked. "He says we don't care a rap for art of any kind."

"I asked her to pity me, and she teases me!" Rodney exclaimed.

"I don't intend to pity you, Mr. Rodney," Mary remarked, kindly, but firmly. "When a paper's a failure, nobody says anything; whereas now, just listen to them!"

The sound, which filled the room, with its hurry of short syllables, its sudden pauses, and its sudden attacks, might be compared to some animal hubbub, frantic and inarticulate.

"D'you think that's all about my paper?" Rodney inquired, after a moment's attention, with a distinct brightening of expression.

"Of course it is," said Mary. "It was a very suggestive paper."

She turned to Denham for confirmation, and he corroborated her.

"It's the ten minutes after a paper is read that proves whether it's been a success or not," he said. "If I were you, Rodney, I should be very pleased with myself."

This commendation seemed to comfort Mr. Rodney completely, and he began to bethink him of all the passages in his paper which deserved to be called "suggestive."

"Did you agree at all, Denham, with what I said about Shakespeare's later use of imagery? I'm afraid I didn't altogether make my meaning plain."

Here he gathered himself together, and by means of a series of frog-like jerks, succeeded in bringing himself close to Denham.

Denham answered him with the brevity which is the result of having another sentence in the mind to be addressed to another person. He wished to say to Katharine: "Did you remember to get that picture glazed before your aunt came to dinner?" but, besides having to answer Rodney, he was not sure that the remark, with its assertion of intimacy, would not strike Katharine as impertinent. She was listening to what some one in another group was saying. Rodney, meanwhile, was talking about the Elizabethan dramatists.

He was a curious-looking man since, upon first sight, especially if he chanced to be talking with animation, he appeared, in some way, ridiculous; but, next moment, in repose, his face, with its large nose, thin cheeks and lips expressing the utmost sensibility, somehow recalled a Roman head bound with laurel, cut upon a circle of semi-transparent reddish stone. It had dignity and character. By profession a clerk in a Government office, he was one of those martyred spirits to whom literature is at once a source of divine joy and of almost intolerable irritation. Not content to rest in their love of it, they must attempt to practise it themselves, and they are generally endowed with very little facility in composition. They condemn whatever they produce. Moreover, the violence of their feelings is such that they seldom meet with adequate sympathy, and being rendered very sensitive by their cultivated perceptions, suffer constant slights both to their own persons and to the thing they worship. But Rodney could never resist making trial of the sympathies of any one who seemed favorably disposed, and Denham's praise had stimulated his very susceptible vanity.

"You remember the passage just before the death of the Duchess?" he continued, edging still closer to Denham, and adjusting his elbow and knee in an incredibly angular combination. Here, Katharine, who had been cut off by these maneuvers from all communication with the outer world, rose, and seated herself upon the window-sill, where she was joined by Mary Datchet. The two young women could thus survey the whole party. Denham looked after them, and made as if he were tearing handfuls of grass up by the roots from the carpet. But as it fell in accurately with his conception of life that all one's desires were bound to be frustrated, he concentrated his mind upon literature, and determined, philosophically, to get what he could out of that.

Katharine was pleasantly excited. A variety of courses was open to her. She knew several people slightly, and at any moment one of them might rise from the floor and come and speak to her; on the other hand, she might select somebody for herself, or she might strike into Rodney's discourse, to which she was intermittently attentive. She was conscious of Mary's body beside her, but, at the same time, the consciousness of being both of them women made it unnecessary to speak to her. But Mary, feeling, as she had said, that Katharine was a "personality," wished so much to speak to her that in a few moments she did.

"They're exactly like a flock of sheep, aren't they?" she said, referring to the noise that rose from the scattered bodies beneath her.

Katharine turned and smiled.

"I wonder what they're making such a noise about?" she said.

"The Elizabethans, I suppose."

"No, I don't think it's got anything to do with the Elizabethans. There! Didn't you hear them say, 'Insurance Bill'?"

"I wonder why men always talk about politics?" Mary speculated. "I suppose, if we had votes, we should, too."

"I dare say we should. And you spend your life in getting us votes, don't you?"

"I do," said Mary, stoutly. "From ten to six every day I'm at it."

Katharine looked at Ralph Denham, who was now pounding his way through the metaphysics of metaphor with Rodney, and was reminded of his talk that Sunday afternoon. She connected him vaguely with Mary.

"I suppose you're one of the people who think we should all have professions," she said, rather distantly, as if feeling her way among the phantoms of an unknown world.

"Oh dear no," said Mary at once.

"Well, I think I do," Katharine continued, with half a sigh. "You will always be able to say that you've done something, whereas, in a crowd like this, I feel rather melancholy."

"In a crowd? Why in a crowd?" Mary asked, deepening the two lines between her eyes, and hoisting herself nearer to Katharine upon the window-sill.

"Don't you see how many different things these people care about? And I want to beat them down—I only mean," she corrected herself, "that I want to assert myself, and it's difficult, if one hasn't a profession."

Mary smiled, thinking that to beat people down was a process that should present no difficulty to Miss Katharine Hilbery. They knew each other so slightly that the beginning of intimacy, which Katharine seemed to initiate by talking about herself, had something solemn in it, and they were silent, as if to decide whether to proceed or not. They tested the ground.

"Ah, but I want to trample upon their prostrate bodies!" Katharine announced, a moment later, with a laugh, as if at the train of thought which had led her to this conclusion.

"One doesn't necessarily trample upon people's bodies because one runs an office," Mary remarked.

"No. Perhaps not," Katharine replied. The conversation lapsed, and Mary saw Katharine looking out into the room rather moodily with closed lips, the desire to talk about herself or to initiate a friendship having, apparently, left her. Mary was struck by her capacity for being thus easily silent, and occupied with her own thoughts. It was a habit that spoke of loneliness and a mind thinking for itself. When Katharine remained silent Mary was slightly embarrassed.

"Yes, they're very like sheep," she repeated, foolishly.

"And yet they are very clever—at least," Katharine added, "I suppose they have all read Webster."

"Surely you don't think that a proof of cleverness? I've read Webster, I've read Ben Jonson, but I don't think myself clever—not exactly, at least."

"I think you must be very clever," Katharine observed.

"Why? Because I run an office?"

"I wasn't thinking of that. I was thinking how you live alone in this room, and have parties."

Mary reflected for a second.

"It means, chiefly, a power of being disagreeable to one's own family, I think. I have that, perhaps. I didn't want to live at home, and I told my father. He didn't like it. . . . But then I have a sister, and you haven't, have you?"

"No, I haven't any sisters."

"You are writing a life of your grandfather?" Mary pursued.

Katharine seemed instantly to be confronted by some familiar thought from which she wished to escape. She replied, "Yes, I am helping my mother," in such a way that

Mary felt herself baffled, and put back again into the position in which she had been at the beginning of their talk. It seemed to her that Katharine possessed a curious power of drawing near and receding, which sent alternate emotions through her far more quickly than was usual, and kept her in a condition of curious alertness. Desiring to classify her, Mary bethought her of the convenient term "egoist."

"She's an egoist," she said to herself, and stored that word up to give to Ralph one day when, as it would certainly fall out, they were discussing Miss Hilbery.

"Heavens, what a mess there'll be to-morrow morning!" Katharine exclaimed. "I hope you don't sleep in this room, Miss Datchet?"

Mary laughed.

"What are you laughing at?" Katharine demanded.

"I won't tell you."

"Let me guess. You were laughing because you thought I'd changed the conversation?"

"No."

"Because you think——" She paused.

"If you want to know, I was laughing at the way you said Miss Datchet."

"Mary, then. Mary, Mary, Mary."

So saying, Katharine drew back the curtain in order, perhaps, to conceal the momentary flush of pleasure which is caused by coming perceptibly nearer to another person.

"Mary Datchet," said Mary. "It's not such an imposing name as Katharine Hilbery, I'm afraid."

They both looked out of the window, first up at the hard silver moon, stationary among a hurry of little grey-blue clouds, and then down upon the roofs of London, with all their upright chimneys, and then below them at the empty moonlit pavement of the street, upon which the joint of each paving-stone was clearly marked out. Mary then saw Katharine raise her eyes again to the moon, with a contemplative look in them, as though she were setting that moon against the moon of other nights, held in memory. Some one in the room behind them made a joke about star-gazing, which destroyed their pleasure in it, and they looked back into the room again.

Ralph had been watching for this moment, and he instantly produced his sentence.

"I wonder, Miss Hilbery, whether you remembered to get that picture glazed?" His voice showed that the question was one that had been prepared.

"Oh, you idiot!" Mary exclaimed, very nearly aloud, with a sense that Ralph had said something very stupid. So, after three lessons in Latin grammar, one might correct a fellow student, whose knowledge did not embrace the ablative of *mensa*.

"Picture—what picture?" Katharine asked. "Oh, at home, you mean—that Sunday afternoon. Was it the day Mr. Fortescue came? Yes, I think I remembered it."

The three of them stood for a moment awkwardly silent, and then Mary left them in order to see that the great pitcher of coffee was properly handled, for beneath all her education she preserved the anxieties of one who owns china.

Ralph could think of nothing further to say; but could one have stripped off his mask of flesh, one would have seen that his will-power was rigidly set upon a single object— that Miss Hilbery should obey him. He wished her to stay there until, by some measures not yet apparent to him, he had conquered her interest. These states of mind transmit themselves very often without the use of language, and it was evident to Katharine that this young man had fixed his mind upon her. She instantly recalled her first impressions of him, and saw herself again proffering family relics. She reverted to the state of mind in which he had left her that Sunday afternoon. She supposed that he judged her very severely. She argued naturally that, if this were the case, the burden of the conversation should rest with him. But she submitted so far as to stand perfectly still, her eyes upon the opposite wall, and her lips very nearly closed, though the desire to laugh stirred them slightly.

"You know the names of the stars, I suppose?" Denham remarked, and from the tone of his voice one might have thought that he grudged Katharine the knowledge he attributed to her.

She kept her voice steady with some difficulty.

"I know how to find the Pole star if I'm lost."

"I don't suppose that often happens to you."

"No. Nothing interesting ever happens to me," she said.

"I think you make a system of saying disagreeable things, Miss Hilbery," he broke out, again going further than he meant to. "I suppose it's one of the characteristics of your class. They never talk seriously to their inferiors."

Whether it was that they were meeting on neutral ground to-night, or whether the carelessness of an old grey coat that Denham wore gave an ease to his bearing that he lacked in conventional dress, Katharine certainly felt no impulse to consider him outside the particular set in which she lived.

"In what sense are you my inferior?" she asked, looking at him gravely, as though honestly searching for his meaning. The look gave him great pleasure. For the first time he felt himself on perfectly equal terms with a woman whom he wished to think well of him, although he could not have explained why her opinion of him mattered one way or another. Perhaps, after all, he only wanted to have something of her to take home to think about. But he was not destined to profit by his advantage.

"I don't think I understand what you mean," Katharine repeated, and then she was obliged to stop and answer some one who wished to know whether she would buy a ticket for an opera from them, at a reduction. Indeed, the temper of the meeting was now unfavorable to separate conversation; it had become rather debauched and hilarious, and people who scarcely knew each other were making use of Christian names with apparent cordiality, and had reached that kind of gay tolerance and general friendliness which human beings in England only attain after sitting together for three hours or so, and the first cold blast in the air of the street freezes them into isolation once more. Cloaks were being flung round the shoulders, hats swiftly pinned to the head; and Denham had the mortification of seeing Katharine helped to prepare herself by the ridiculous Rodney. It was not the convention of the meeting to say good-bye, or necessarily even to nod to the person with whom one was talking; but, nevertheless, Denham was disappointed by the completeness with which Katharine parted from him, without any attempt to finish her sentence. She left with Rodney.

CHAPTER V

DENHAM had no conscious intention of following
Katharine, but, seeing her depart, he took his hat and
ran rather more quickly down the stairs than he would have
done if Katharine had not been in front of him. He over-
took a friend of his, by name Harry Sandys, who was going
the same way, and they walked together a few paces behind
Katharine and Rodney.

The night was very still, and on such nights, when the
traffic thins away, the walker becomes conscious of the moon
in the street, as if the curtains of the sky had been drawn
apart, and the heaven lay bare, as it does in the country.
The air was softly cool, so that people who had been sitting
talking in a crowd found it pleasant to walk a little before
deciding to stop an omnibus or encounter light again in an
underground railway. Sandys, who was a barrister with a
philosophic tendency, took out his pipe, lit it, murmured
"hum" and "ha," and was silent. The couple in front of
them kept their distance accurately, and appeared, so far as
Denham could judge by the way they turned towards each
other, to be talking very constantly. He observed that when
a pedestrian going the opposite way forced them to part
they came together again directly afterwards. Without
intending to watch them he never quite lost sight of the
yellow scarf twisted round Katharine's head, or the light
overcoat which made Rodney look fashionable among the
crowd. At the Strand he supposed that they would separate,
but instead they crossed the road, and took their way down
one of the narrow passages which lead through ancient
courts to the river. Among the crowd of people in the big
thoroughfares Rodney seemed merely to be lending Kath-

arine his escort, but now, when passengers were rare and the footsteps of the couple were distinctly heard in the silence, Denham could not help picturing to himself some change in their conversation. The effect of the light and shadow, which seemed to increase their height, was to make them mysterious and significant, so that Denham had no feeling of irritation with Katharine, but rather a half-dreamy acquiescence in the course of the world. Yes, she did very well to dream about—but Sandys had suddenly begun to talk. He was a solitary man who had made his friends at college and always addressed them as if they were still undergraduates arguing in his room, though many months or even years had passed in some cases between the last sentence and the present one. The method was a little singular, but very restful, for it seemed to ignore completely all accidents of human life, and to span very deep abysses with a few simple words.

On this occasion he began, while they waited for a minute on the edge of the Strand:

"I hear that Bennett has given up his theory of truth."

Denham returned a suitable answer, and he proceeded to explain how this decision had been arrived at, and what changes it involved in the philosophy which they both accepted. Meanwhile Katharine and Rodney drew further ahead, and Denham kept, if that is the right expression for an involuntary action, one filament of his mind upon them, while with the rest of his intelligence he sought to understand what Sandys was saying.

As they passed through the courts thus talking, Sandys laid the tip of his stick upon one of the stones forming a time-worn arch, and struck it meditatively two or three times in order to illustrate something very obscure about the complex nature of one's apprehension of facts. During the pause which this necessitated, Katharine and Rodney turned the corner and disappeared. For a moment Denham stopped involuntarily in his sentence, and continued it with a sense of having lost something.

Unconscious that they were observed, Katharine and Rodney had come out on the Embankment. When they had crossed the road, Rodney slapped his hand upon the stone parapet above the river and exclaimed:

"I promise I won't say another word about it, Katharine! But do stop a minute and look at the moon upon the water."

Katharine paused, looked up and down the river, and snuffed the air.

"I'm sure one can smell the sea, with the wind blowing this way," she said.

They stood silent for a few moments while the river shifted in its bed, and the silver and red lights which were laid upon it were torn by the current and joined together again. Very far off up the river a steamer hooted with its hollow voice of unspeakable melancholy, as if from the heart of lonely mist-shrouded voyagings.

"Ah!" Rodney cried, striking his hand once more upon the balustrade, "why can't one say how beautiful it all is? Why am I condemned for ever, Katharine, to feel what I can't express? And the things I can give there's no use in my giving. Trust me, Katharine," he added hastily, "I won't speak of it again. But in the presence of beauty— look at the iridescence round the moon!—one feels—one feels—— Perhaps if you married me—I'm half a poet, you see, and I can't pretend not to feel what I do feel. If I could write—ah, that would be another matter. I shouldn't bother you to marry me then, Katharine."

He spoke these disconnected sentences rather abruptly, with his eyes alternately upon the moon and upon the stream.

"But for me I suppose you would recommend marriage?" said Katharine, with her eyes fixed on the moon.

"Certainly I should. Not for you only, but for all women. Why, you're nothing at all without it; you're only half alive; using only half your faculties; you must feel that for yourself. That is why——" Here he stopped himself, and they began to walk slowly along the Embankment, the moon fronting them.

"With how sad steps she climbs the sky,
How silently and with how wan a face,"

Rodney quoted.

"I've been told a great many unpleasant things about myself to-night," Katharine stated, without attending to him. "Mr. Denham seems to think it his mission to lecture me, though I hardly know him. By the way, William, you know him; tell me, what is he like?"

William drew a deep sigh.

"We may lecture you till we're blue in the face——   "

"Yes—but what's he like?"

"And we write sonnets to your eyebrows, you cruel practical creature. Denham?" he added, as Katharine remained silent. "A good fellow, I should think. He cares, naturally, for the right sort of things, I expect. But you mustn't marry him, though. He scolded you, did he—what did he say?"

"What happens with Mr. Denham is this: He comes to tea. I do all I can to put him at his ease. He merely sits and scowls at me. Then I show him our manuscripts. At this he becomes really angry, and tells me I've no business to call myself a middle-class woman. So we part in a huff; and next time we meet, which was to-night, he walks straight up to me, and says, 'Go to the Devil!' That's the sort of behavior my mother complains of. I want to know, what does it mean?"

She paused and, slackening her steps, looked at the lighted train drawing itself smoothly over Hungerford Bridge.

"It means, I should say, that he finds you chilly and unsympathetic."

Katharine laughed with round, separate notes of genuine amusement.

"It's time I jumped into a cab and hid myself in my own house," she exclaimed.

"Would your mother object to my being seen with you? No one could possibly recognize us, could they?" Rodney inquired, with some solicitude.

Katharine looked at him, and perceiving that his solicitude was genuine, she laughed again, but with an ironical note in her laughter.

"You may laugh, Katharine, but I can tell you that if any of your friends saw us together at this time of night they would talk about it, and I should find that very disagreeable. But why do you laugh?"

"I don't know. Because you're such a queer mixture, I think. You're half poet and half old maid."

"I know I always seem to you highly ridiculous. But I can't help having inherited certain traditions and trying to put them into practice."

"Nonsense, William. You may come of the oldest family in Devonshire, but that's no reason why you should mind being seen alone with me on the Embankment."

"I'm ten years older than you are, Katharine, and I know more of the world than you do."

"Very well. Leave me and go home."

Rodney looked back over his shoulder and perceived that they were being followed at a short distance by a taxicab, which evidently awaited his summons. Katharine saw it, too, and exclaimed:

"Don't call that cab for me, William. I shall walk."

"Nonsense, Katharine; you'll do nothing of the kind. It's nearly twelve o'clock, and we've walked too far as it is."

Katharine laughed and walked on so quickly that both Rodney and the taxicab had to increase their pace to keep up with her.

"Now, William," she said, "if people see me racing along the Embankment like this they *will* talk. You had far better say good-night, if you don't want people to talk."

At this William beckoned, with a despotic gesture, to the cab with one hand, and with the other he brought Katharine to a standstill.

"Don't let the man see us struggling, for God's sake!" he murmured. Katharine stood for a moment quite still.

"There's more of the old maid in you than the poet," she observed briefly.

William shut the door sharply, gave the address to the driver, and turned away, lifting his hat punctiliously high in farewell to the invisible lady.

He looked back after the cab twice, suspiciously, half expecting that she would stop it and dismount; but it bore her swiftly on, and was soon out of sight. William felt in the mood for a short soliloquy of indignation, for Katharine had contrived to exasperate him in more ways than one.

"Of all the unreasonable, inconsiderate creatures I've ever known, she's the worst!" he exclaimed to himself, striding back along the Embankment. "Heaven forbid that I should ever make a fool of myself with her again. Why, I'd sooner marry the daughter of my landlady than Katharine Hilbery! She'd leave me not a moment's peace—and she'd never understand me—never, never, never!"

Uttered aloud and with vehemence so that the stars of Heaven might hear, for there was no human being at hand, these sentiments sounded satisfactorily irrefutable. Rodney quieted down, and walked on in silence, until he perceived some one approaching him, who had something, either in his walk or his dress, which proclaimed that he was one of William's acquaintances before it was possible to tell which of them he was. It was Denham who, having parted from Sandys at the bottom of his staircase, was now walking to the Tube at Charing Cross, deep in the thoughts which his talk with Sandys had suggested. He had forgotten the meeting at Mary Datchet's rooms, he had forgotten Rodney, and metaphors and Elizabethan drama, and could have sworn that he had forgotten Katharine Hilbery, too, although that was more disputable. His mind was scaling the highest pinnacles of its alps, where there was only starlight and the untrodden snow. He cast strange eyes upon Rodney, as they encountered each other beneath a lamp-post.

"Ha!" Rodney exclaimed.

If he had been in full possession of his mind, Denham

would probably have passed on with a salutation. But the shock of the interruption made him stand still, and before he knew what he was doing, he had turned and was walking with Rodney in obedience to Rodney's invitation to come to his rooms and have something to drink. Denham had no wish to drink with Rodney, but he followed him passively enough. Rodney was gratified by this obedience. He felt inclined to be communicative with this silent man, who possessed so obviously all the good masculine qualities in which Katharine now seemed lamentably deficient.

"You do well, Denham," he began impulsively, "to have nothing to do with young women. I offer you my experience—if one trusts them one invariably has cause to repent. Not that I have any reason at this moment," he added hastily, "to complain of them. It's a subject that crops up now and again for no particular reason. Miss Datchet, I dare say, is one of the exceptions. Do you like Miss Datchet?"

These remarks indicated clearly enough that Rodney's nerves were in a state of irritation, and Denham speedily woke to the situation of the world as it had been one hour ago. He had last seen Rodney walking with Katharine. He could not help regretting the eagerness with which his mind returned to these interests, and fretted him with the old trivial anxieties. He sank in his own esteem. Reason bade him break from Rodney, who clearly tended to become confidential, before he had utterly lost touch with the problems of high philosophy. He looked along the road, and marked a lamp-post at a distance of some hundred yards, and decided that he would part from Rodney when they reached this point.

"Yes, I like Mary; I don't see how one could help liking her," he remarked cautiously, with his eye on the lamp-post.

"Ah, Denham, you're so different from me. You never give yourself away. I watched you this evening with Katharine Hilbery. My instinct is to trust the person I'm talking to. That's why I'm always being taken in, I suppose."

Denham seemed to be pondering this statement of Rodney's, but, as a matter of fact, he was hardly conscious of
Rodney and his revelations, and was only concerned to make
him mention Katharine again before they reached the lamp-
post.

"Who's taken you in now?" he asked. "Katharine Hilbery?"

Rodney stopped and once more began beating a kind of
rhythm, as if he were marking a phrase in a symphony,
upon the smooth stone balustrade of the Embankment.

"Katharine Hilbery," he repeated, with a curious little
chuckle. "No, Denham, I have no illusions about that
young woman. I think I made that plain to her to-night.
But don't run away with a false impression," he continued
eagerly, turning and linking his arm through Denham's, as
though to prevent him from escaping; and, thus compelled,
Denham passed the monitory lamp-post, to which, in passing, he breathed an excuse, for how could he break away
when Rodney's arm was actually linked in his? "You must
not think that I have any bitterness against her—far from it.
It's not altogether her fault, poor girl. She lives, you know,
one of those odious, self-centered lives—at least, I think
them odious for a woman—feeding her wits upon everything, having control of everything, getting far too much
her own way at home—spoilt, in a sense, feeling that every
one is at her feet, and so not realizing how she hurts—that
is, how rudely she behaves to people who haven't all her
advantages. Still, to do her justice, she's no fool," he
added, as if to warn Denham not to take any liberties. "She
has taste. She has sense. She can understand you when
you talk to her. But she's a woman, and there's an end of
it," he added, with another little chuckle, and dropped
Denham's arm.

"And did you tell her all this to-night?" Denham asked.

"Oh dear me, no. I should never think of telling Katharine the truth about herself. That wouldn't do at all. One

has to be in an attitude of adoration in order to get on with Katharine.

"Now I've learnt that she's refused to marry him why don't I go home?" Denham thought to himself. But he went on walking beside Rodney, and for a time they did not speak, though Rodney hummed snatches of a tune out of an opera by Mozart. A feeling of contempt and liking combine very naturally in the mind of one to whom another has just spoken unpremeditatedly, revealing rather more of his private feelings than he intended to reveal. Denham began to wonder what sort of person Rodney was, and at the same time Rodney began to think about Denham.

"You're a slave like me, I suppose?" he asked.

"A solicitor, yes."

"I sometimes wonder why we don't chuck it. Why don't you emigrate, Denham? I should have thought that would suit you."

"I've a family."

"I'm often on the point of going myself. And then I know I couldn't live without this"—and he waved his hand towards the City of London, which wore, at this moment, the appearance of a town cut out of gray-blue cardboard, and pasted flat against the sky, which was of a deeper blue.

"There are one or two people I'm fond of, and there's a little good music, and a few pictures, now and then—just enough to keep one dangling about here. Ah, but I couldn't live with savages! Are you fond of books? Music? Pictures? D'you care at all for first editions? I've got a few nice things up here, things I pick up cheap, for I can't afford to give what they ask."

They had reached a small court of high eighteenth-century houses, in one of which Rodney had his rooms. They climbed a very steep staircase, through whose uncurtained windows the moonlight fell, illuminating the banisters with their twisted pillars, and the piles of plates set on the window-sills, and jars half-full of milk. Rodney's rooms were small, but the sitting-room window looked out into a court-

yard, with its flagged pavement, and its single tree, and
across to the flat red-brick fronts of the opposite houses,
which would not have surprised Dr. Johnson, if he had
come out of his grave for a turn in the moonlight. Rodney
lit his lamp, pulled his curtains, offered Denham a chair,
and, flinging the manuscript of his paper on the Elizabethan
use of Metaphor on to the table, exclaimed:

"Oh dear me, what a waste of time! But it's over now,
and so we may think no more about it."

He then busied himself very dexterously in lighting a fire,
producing glasses, whisky, a cake, and cups and saucers.
He put on a faded crimson dressing-gown, and a pair of red
slippers, and advanced to Denham with a tumbler in one
hand and a well-burnished book in the other.

"The Baskerville Congreve," said Rodney, offering it to
his guest. "I couldn't read him in a cheap edition."

When he was seen thus among his books and his valuables,
amiably anxious to make his visitor comfortable, and moving about with something of the dexterity and grace of a
Persian cat, Denham relaxed his critical attitude, and felt
more at home with Rodney than he would have done with
many men better known to him. Rodney's room was the
room of a person who cherishes a great many personal
tastes, guarding them from the rough blasts of the public
with scrupulous attention. His papers and his books rose in
jagged mounds on table and floor, round which he skirted
with nervous care lest his dressing-gown might disarrange
them ever so slightly. On a chair stood a stack of photographs of statues and pictures, which it was his habit to exhibit, one by one, for the space of a day or two. The books
on his shelves were as orderly as regiments of soldiers, and
the backs of them shone like so many bronze beetle-wings;
though, if you took one from its place you saw a shabbier
volume behind it, since space was limited. An oval Venetian
mirror stood above the fireplace, and reflected duskily in its
spotted depths the faint yellow and crimson of a jarful of
tulips which stood among the letters and pipes and cigarettes

upon the mantelpiece. A small piano occupied a corner of
the room, with the score of "Don Giovanni" open upon the
bracket.

"Well, Rodney," said Denham, as he filled his pipe and
looked about him, "this is all very nice and comfortable."

Rodney turned his head half round and smiled, with the
pride of a proprietor, and then prevented himself from
smiling.

"Tolerable," he muttered.

"But I dare say it's just as well that you have to earn
your own living."

"If you mean that I shouldn't do anything good with
leisure if I had it, I dare say you're right. But I should be
ten times as happy with my whole day to spend as I liked."

"I doubt that," Denham replied.

They sat silent, and the smoke from their pipes joined
amicably in a blue vapor above their heads.

"I could spend three hours every day reading Shakespeare," Rodney remarked. "And there's music and pictures, let alone the society of the people one likes."

"You'd be bored to death in a year's time."

"Oh, I grant you I should be bored if I did nothing. But
I should write plays."

"H'm!"

"I should write plays," he repeated. "I've written three-
quarters of one already, and I'm only waiting for a holiday
to finish it. And it's not bad—no, some of it's really rather
nice."

The question arose in Denham's mind whether he should
ask to see this play, as, no doubt, he was expected to do.
He looked rather stealthily at Rodney, who was tapping the
coal nervously with a poker, and quivering almost physically,
so Denham thought, with desire to talk about this play of
his, and vanity unrequited and urgent. He seemed very
much at Denham's mercy, and Denham could not help liking
him, partly on that account.

"Well, . . . will you let me see the play?" Denham asked,

and Rodney looked immediately appeased, but, nevertheless, he sat silent for a moment, holding the poker perfectly upright in the air, regarding it with his rather prominent eyes, and opening his lips and shutting them again.

"Do you really care for this kind of thing?" he asked at length, in a different tone of voice from that in which he had been speaking. And, without waiting for an answer, he went on, rather querulously: "Very few people care for poetry. I dare say it bores you."

"Perhaps," Denham remarked.

"Well, I'll lend it you," Rodney announced, putting down the poker.

As he moved to fetch the play, Denham stretched a hand to the bookcase beside him, and took down the first volume which his fingers touched. It happened to be a small and very lovely edition of Sir Thomas Browne, containing the "Urn Burial," the "Hydriotaphia," and the "Garden of Cyrus," and, opening it at a passage which he knew very nearly by heart, Denham began to read and, for some time, continued to read.

Rodney resumed his seat, with his manuscript on his knee, and from time to time he glanced at Denham, and then joined his finger-tips and crossed his thin legs over the fender, as if he experienced a good deal of pleasure. At length Denham shut the book, and stood, with his back to the fireplace, occasionally making an inarticulate humming sound which seemed to refer to Sir Thomas Browne. He put his hat on his head, and stood over Rodney, who still lay stretched back in his chair, with his toes within the fender.

"I shall look in again some time," Denham remarked, upon which Rodney held up his hand, containing his manuscript, without saying anything except—"If you like."

Denham took the manuscript and went. Two days later he was much surprised to find a thin parcel on his breakfast-plate, which, on being opened, revealed the very copy of Sir Thomas Browne which he had studied so intently in Rodney's rooms. From sheer laziness he returned no thanks, but he thought of Rodney from time to time with interest, disconnecting him from Katharine, and meant to go round one evening and smoke a pipe with him. It pleased Rodney thus to give away whatever his friends genuinely admired. His library was constantly being diminished.

CHAPTER VI

OF all the hours of an ordinary working week-day, which are the pleasantest to look forward to and to look back upon? If a single instance is of use in framing a theory, it may be said that the minutes between nine-twenty-five and nine-thirty in the morning had a singular charm for Mary Datchet. She spent them in a very enviable frame of mind; her contentment was almost unalloyed. High in the air as her flat was, some beams from the morning sun reached her even in November, striking straight at curtain, chair, and carpet, and painting there three bright, true spaces of green, blue, and purple, upon which the eye rested with a pleasure which gave physical warmth to the body.

There were few mornings when Mary did not look up, as she bent to lace her boots, and as she followed the yellow rod from curtain to breakfast-table she usually breathed some sigh of thankfulness that her life provided her with such moments of pure enjoyment. She was robbing no one of anything, and yet, to get so much pleasure from simple things, such as eating one's breakfast alone in a room which had nice colors in it, clean from the skirting of the boards to the corners of the ceiling, seemed to suit her so thoroughly that she used at first to hunt about for some one to apologize to, or for some flaw in the situation. She had now been six months in London, and she could find no flaw, but that, as she invariably concluded by the time her boots were laced, was solely and entirely due to the fact that she had her work. Every day, as she stood with her dispatch-box in her hand at the door of her flat, and gave one look back into the room to see that everything was straight before she left, she said to herself that she was very glad that she was going to leave it all, that to have sat there all day long, in the enjoyment of leisure, would have been intolerable.

Out in the street she liked to think herself one of the workers who, at this hour, take their way in rapid single file along all the broad pavements of the city, with their heads slightly lowered, as if all their effort were to follow each other as closely as might be; so that Mary used to figure to herself a straight rabbit-run worn by their unswerving feet upon the pavement. But she liked to pretend that she was indistinguishable from the rest, and that when a wet day drove her to the Underground or omnibus, she gave and took her share of crowd and wet with clerks and typists and commercial men, and shared with them the serious business of winding-up the world to tick for another four-and-twenty hours.

Thus thinking, on the particular morning in question, she made her away across Lincoln's Inn Fields and up Kingsway, and so through Southampton Row until she reached her office in Russell Square. Now and then she would pause and look into the window of some bookseller or flower shop, where, at this early hour, the goods were being arranged, and empty gaps behind the plate glass revealed a state of undress. Mary felt kindly disposed towards the shopkeepers, and hoped that they would trick the midday public into purchasing, for at this hour of the morning she ranged herself entirely on the side of the shopkeepers and bank clerks, and regarded all who slept late and had money to spend as her enemy and natural prey. And directly she had crossed the road at Holborn, her thoughts all came naturally and regularly to roost upon her work, and she forgot that she was, properly speaking, an amateur worker, whose services were unpaid, and could hardly be said to wind the world up for its daily task, since the world, so far, had shown very little desire to take the boons which Mary's society for woman's suffrage had offered it.

She was thinking all the way up Southampton Row of notepaper and foolscap, and how an economy in the use of paper might be effected (without, of course, hurting Mrs. Seal's feelings), for she was certain that the great organizers always pounce, to begin with, upon trifles like these, and build up their triumphant reforms upon a basis of absolute solidity; and, without acknowledging it for a moment, Mary Datchet was determined to be a great organizer, and had already doomed her society to reconstruction of the most radical kind. Once or twice lately, it is true, she had started, broad awake, before turning into Russell Square, and denounced herself rather sharply for being already in a groove, capable, that is, of thinking the same thoughts every morning at the same hour, so that the chestnut-colored brick of the Russell Square houses had some curious connection with her thoughts about office economy, and served also as a sign that she should get into trim for meeting Mr. Clacton, or Mrs. Seal, or whoever might be beforehand with her at the office. Having no religious belief, she was the more conscientious about her life, examining her position from time to time very seriously, and nothing annoyed her more than to find one of these bad habits nibbling away unheeded at the precious substance. What was the good, after all, of being a woman if one didn't keep fresh, and cram one's life with all sorts of views and experiments? Thus she always gave herself a little shake, as she turned the corner, and, as often as not, reached her own door whistling a snatch of a Somersetshire ballad.

The suffrage office was at the top of one of the large Russell Square houses, which had once been lived in by a great city merchant and his family, and was now let out in slices to a number of societies which displayed assorted initials upon doors of ground glass, and kept, each of them, a typewriter which clicked busily all day long. The old house, with its great stone staircase, echoed hollowly to the sound of typewriters and of errand-boys from ten to six. The noise of different typewriters already at work, disseminating their views upon the protection of native races, or the value of cereals as foodstuffs, quickened Mary's steps, and she always ran up the last flight of steps which led to her own landing, at whatever hour she came, so as to get her type-writer to take its place in competition with the rest.

She sat herself down to her letters, and very soon all these speculations were forgotten, and the two lines drew themselves between her eyebrows, as the contents of the letters, the office furniture, and the sounds of activity in the next room gradually asserted their sway upon her. By eleven o'clock the atmosphere of concentration was running so strongly in one direction that any thought of a different order could hardly have survived its birth more than a moment or so. The task which lay before her was to organize a series of entertainments, the profits of which were to benefit the society, which drooped for want of funds. It was her first attempt at organization on a large scale, and she meant to achieve something remarkable. She meant to use the cumbrous machine to pick out this, that, and the other interesting person from the muddle of the world, and to set them for a week in a pattern which must catch the eyes of Cabinet Ministers, and the eyes once caught, the old arguments were to be delivered with unexampled originality. Such was the scheme as a whole; and in contemplation of it she would become quite flushed and excited, and have to remind herself of all the details that intervened between her and success.

The door would open, and Mr. Clacton would come in to search for a certain leaflet buried beneath a pyramid of leaflets. He was a thin, sandy-haired man of about thirty-five, spoke with a Cockney accent, and had about him a frugal look, as if nature had not dealt generously with him in any way, which, naturally, prevented him from dealing generously with other people. When he had found his leaflet, and offered a few jocular hints upon keeping papers in order, the typewriting would stop abruptly, and Mrs. Seal would burst into the room with a letter which needed explanation in her hand. This was a more serious interruption than the other, because she never knew exactly what she wanted, and half a dozen requests would bolt from her, no one of which was clearly stated. Dressed in plum-colored velveteen, with short, gray hair, and a face that seemed permanently flushed with philanthropic enthusiasm, she was always in a hurry, and always in some disorder. She wore two crucifixes, which got themselves entangled in a heavy gold chain upon her breast, and seemed to Mary expressive of her mental ambiguity. Only her vast enthusiasm and her worship of Miss Markham, one of the pioneers of the society, kept her in her place, for which she had no sound qualification.

So the morning wore on, and the pile of letters grew, and Mary felt, at last, that she was the center ganglion of a very fine network of nerves which fell over England, and one of these days, when she touched the heart of the system, would begin feeling and rushing together and emitting their splendid blaze of revolutionary fireworks—for some such metaphor represents what she felt about her work, when her brain had been heated by three hours of application.

Shortly before one o'clock Mr. Clacton and Mrs. Seal desisted from their labors, and the old joke about luncheon, which came out regularly at this hour, was repeated with scarcely any variation of words. Mr. Clacton patronized a vegetarian restaurant; Mrs. Seal brought sandwiches, which she ate beneath the plane-trees in Russell Square; while Mary generally went to a gaudy establishment, upholstered in red plush, near by, where, much to the vegetarian's disapproval, you could buy steak, two inches thick, or a roast section of fowl, swimming in a pewter dish.

"The bare branches against the sky do one so much *good*," Mrs. Seal asserted, looking out into the Square.

"But one can't lunch off trees, Sally," said Mary.

"I confess I don't know how you manage it, Miss Datchet," Mr. Clacton remarked. "I should sleep all the afternoon, I know, if I took a heavy meal in the middle of the day."

"What's the very latest thing in literature?" Mary asked, good-humoredly pointing to the yellow-covered volume beneath Mr. Clacton's arm, for he invariably read some new French author at lunch-time, or squeezed in a visit to a picture gallery, balancing his social work with an ardent culture of which he was secretly proud, as Mary had very soon divined.

So they parted and Mary walked away, wondering if they guessed that she really wanted to get away from them, and supposing that they had not quite reached that degree of subtlety. She bought herself an evening paper, which she read as she ate, looking over the top of it again and again at the queer people who were buying cakes or imparting their secrets, until some young woman whom she knew came in, and she called out, "Eleanor, come and sit by me," and they finished their lunch together, parting on the strip of pavement among the different lines of traffic with a pleasant feeling that they were stepping once more into their separate places in the great and eternally moving pattern of human life.

But, instead of going straight back to the office to-day, Mary turned into the British Museum, and strolled down the gallery with the shapes of stone until she found an empty seat directly beneath the gaze of the Elgin marbles. She looked at them, and seemed, as usual, borne up on some wave of exaltation and emotion, by which her life at once became solemn and beautiful—an impression which was due as much, perhaps, to the solitude and chill and silence of the gallery as to the actual beauty of the statues. One must suppose, at least, that her emotions were not purely esthetic, because, after she had gazed at the Ulysses for a minute or two, she began to think about Ralph Denham. So secure did she feel with these silent shapes that she almost yielded to an impulse to say "I am in love with you" aloud. The presence of this immense and enduring beauty made her almost alarmingly conscious of her desire, and at the same time proud of a feeling which did not display anything like the same proportions when she was going about her daily work.

She repressed her impulse to speak aloud, and rose and wandered about rather aimlessly among the statues until she found herself in another gallery devoted to engraved obelisks and winged Assyrian bulls, and her emotion took another turn. She began to picture herself traveling with Ralph in a land where these monsters were couchant in the sand. "For," she thought to herself, as she gazed fixedly at some information printed behind a piece of glass, "the wonderful thing about you is that you're ready for anything; you're not in the least conventional, like most clever men."

And she conjured up a scene of herself on a camel's back, in the desert, while Ralph commanded a whole tribe of natives.

"That is what you can do," she went on, moving on to the next statue. "You always make people do what you want."

A glow spread over her spirit, and filled her eyes with brightness. Nevertheless, before she left the Museum she was very far from saying, even in the privacy of her own mind, "I am in love with you," and that sentence might very well never have framed itself. She was, indeed, rather annoyed with herself for having allowed such an ill-considered breach of her reserve, weakening her powers of resistance, she felt, should this impulse return again. For, as she walked along the street to her office, the force of all her customary objections to being in love with any one overcame her. She did not want to marry at all. It seemed to her that there was something amateurish in bringing love into touch with a perfectly straightforward friendship, such as hers was with Ralph, which, for two years now, had based itself upon common interests in impersonal topics, such as the housing of the poor, or the taxation of land values.

But the afternoon spirit differed intrinsically from the morning spirit. Mary found herself watching the flight of a bird, or making drawings of the branches of the plane-trees upon her blotting-paper. People came in to see Mr. Clacton on business, and a seductive smell of cigarette smoke issued from his room. Mrs. Seal wandered about with newspaper cuttings, which seemed to her either "quite splendid" or "really too bad for words." She used to paste these into books, or send them to her friends, having first drawn a broad bar in blue pencil down the margin, a proceeding which signified equally and indistinguishably the depths of her reprobation or the heights of her approval.

About four o'clock on that same afternoon Katharine Hilbery was walking up Kingsway. The question of tea presented itself. The street lamps were being lit already, and as she stood still for a moment beneath one of them, she tried to think of some neighboring drawing-room where there would be firelight and talk congenial to her mood. That mood, owing to the spinning traffic and the evening veil of unreality, was ill-adapted to her home surroundings. Perhaps, on the whole, a shop was the best place in which to preserve this queer sense of heightened existence. At the same time she wished to talk. Remembering Mary Datchet and her repeated invitations, she crossed the road, turned into Russell Square, and peered about, seeking for numbers with a sense of adventure that was out of all proportion to the deed itself. She found herself in a dimly lighted hall, unguarded by a porter, and pushed open the first swing door. But the office-boy had never heard of Miss Datchet. Did she belong to the S.R.F.R.? Katharine shook her head with a smile of dismay. A voice from within shouted, "No. The S.G.S.—top floor."

Katharine mounted past innumerable glass doors, with initials on them, and became steadily more and more doubtful of the wisdom of her venture. At the top she paused for a moment to breathe and collect herself. She heard the typewriter and formal professional voices inside, not belonging, she thought, to any one she had ever spoken to. She touched the bell, and the door was opened almost immediately by Mary herself. Her face had to change its expression entirely when she saw Katharine.

"You!" she exclaimed. "We thought you were the printer." Still holding the door open, she called back, "No, Mr. Clacton, it's not Penningtons. I should ring them up again—double three double eight, Central. Well, this is a surprise. Come in," she added. "You're just in time for tea."

The light of relief shone in Mary's eyes. The boredom of the afternoon was dissipated at once, and she was glad that Katharine had found them in a momentary press of activity, owing to the failure of the printer to send back certain proofs.

The unshaded electric light shining upon the table covered with papers dazed Katharine for a moment. After the confusion of her twilight walk, and her random thoughts, life in this small room appeared extremely concentrated and bright. She turned instinctively to look out of the window, which was uncurtained, but Mary immediately recalled her.

"It was very clever of you to find your way," she said, and Katharine wondered, as she stood there, feeling, for the moment, entirely detached and unabsorbed, why she had come. She looked, indeed, to Mary's eyes strangely out of place in the office. Her figure in the long cloak, which took deep folds, and her face, which was composed into a mask of sensitive apprehension, disturbed Mary for a moment with a sense of the presence of some one who was of another world, and, therefore, subversive of her world. She became immediately anxious that Katharine should be impressed by the importance of her world, and hoped that neither Mrs. Seal nor Mr. Clacton would appear until the impression of importance had been received. But in this she was disappointed. Mrs. Seal burst into the room holding a kettle in her hand, which she set upon the stove, and then, with inefficient haste, she set light to the gas, which flared up, exploded, and went out.

"Always the way, always the way," she muttered. "Kit

Markham is the only person who knows how to deal with the thing."

Mary had to go to her help, and together they spread the table, and apologized for the disparity between the cups and the plainness of the food.

"If we had known Miss Hilbery was coming, we should have bought a cake," said Mary, upon which Mrs. Seal looked at Katharine for the first time, suspiciously, because she was a person who needed cake.

Here Mr. Clacton opened the door, and came in, holding a typewritten letter in his hand, which he was reading aloud.

"Salford's affiliated," he said.

"Well done, Salford!" Mrs. Seal exclaimed enthusiastically, thumping the teapot which she held upon the table, in token of applause.

"Yes, these provincial centers seem to be coming into line at last," said Mr. Clacton, and then Mary introduced him to Miss Hilbery, and he asked her, in a very formal manner, if she were interested "in our work."

"And the proofs still not come?" said Mrs. Seal, putting both her elbows on the table, and propping her chin on her hands, as Mary began to pour out tea. "It's too bad—too bad. At this rate we shall miss the country post. Which reminds me, Mr. Clacton, don't you think we should circularize the provinces with Partridge's last speech? What? You've not read it? Oh, it's the best thing they've had in the House this Session. Even the Prime Minister——"

But Mary cut her short.

"We don't allow shop at tea, Sally," she said firmly. "We fine her a penny each time she forgets, and the fines go to buying a plum cake," she explained, seeking to draw Katharine into the community. She had given up all hope of impressing her.

"I'm sorry, I'm sorry," Mrs. Seal apologized. "It's my misfortune to be an enthusiast," she said, turning to Katharine. "My father's daughter could hardly be anything else. I think I've been on as many committees as most people.

Waifs and Strays, Rescue Work, Church Work, C. O. S.—
local branch—besides the usual civic duties which fall to one
as a householder. But I've given them all up for our work
here, and I don't regret it for a second," she added. "This
is the root question, I feel; until women have votes——"

"It'll be sixpence, at least, Sally," said Mary, bringing
her fist down on the table. "And we're all sick to death of
women and their votes."

Mrs. Seal looked for a moment as though she could hardly
believe her ears, and made a deprecating "tut-tut-tut" in
her throat, looking alternately at Katharine and Mary, and
shaking her head as she did so. Then she remarked, rather
confidentially to Katharine, with a little nod in Mary's direction:

"She's doing more for the cause than any of us. She's
giving her youth—for, alas! when I was young there were
domestic circumstances——" she sighed, and stopped short.

Mr. Clacton hastily reverted to the joke about luncheon,
and explained how Mrs. Seal fed on a bag of biscuits under
the trees, whatever the weather might be, rather, Katharine
thought, as though Mrs. Seal were a pet dog who had convenient tricks.

"Yes, I took my little bag into the square," said Mrs.
Seal, with the self-conscious guilt of a child owning some
fault to its elders. "It was really very sustaining, and the
bare boughs against the sky do one so much *good*. But I
shall have to give up going into the square," she proceeded,
wrinkling her forehead. "The injustice of it! Why should
I have a beautiful square all to myself, when poor women
who need rest have nowhere at all to sit?" She looked
fiercely at Katharine, giving her short locks a little shake.
"It's dreadful what a tyrant one still is, in spite of all one's
efforts. One tries to lead a decent life, but one can't. Of
course, directly one thinks of it, one sees that *all* squares
should be open to *every* one. Is there any society with that
object, Mr. Clacton? If not, there should be, surely."

"A most excellent object," said Mr. Clacton in his professional manner. "At the same time, one must deplore the ramification of organizations, Mrs. Seal. So much excellent effort thrown away, not to speak of pounds, shillings, and pence. Now how many organizations of a philanthropic nature do you suppose there are in the City of London itself, Miss Hilbery?" he added, screwing his mouth into a queer little smile, as if to show that the question had its frivolous side.

Katharine smiled, too. Her unlikeness to the rest of them had, by this time, penetrated to Mr. Clacton, who was not naturally observant, and he was wondering who she was; this same unlikeness had subtly stimulated Mrs. Seal to try and make a convert of her. Mary, too, looked at her almost as if she begged her to make things easy. For Katharine had shown no disposition to make things easy. She had scarcely spoken, and her silence, though grave and even thoughtful, seemed to Mary the silence of one who criticizes.

"Well, there are more in this house than I'd any notion of," she said. "On the ground floor you protect natives, on the next you emigrate women and tell people to eat nuts——"

"Why do you say that 'we' do these things?" Mary interposed, rather sharply. "We're not responsible for all the cranks who choose to lodge in the same house with us."

Mr. Clacton cleared his throat and looked at each of the young ladies in turn. He was a good deal struck by the appearance and manner of Miss Hilbery, which seemed to him to place her among those cultivated and luxurious people of whom he used to dream. Mary, on the other hand, was more of his own sort, and a little too much inclined to order him about. He picked up crumbs of dry biscuit and put them into his mouth with incredible rapidity.

"You don't belong to our society, then?" said Mrs. Seal.

"No, I'm afraid I don't," said Katharine, with such ready candor that Mrs. Seal was nonplussed, and stared at her with a puzzled expression, as if she could not classify her among the varieties of human beings known to her.

"But surely——" she began.

"Mrs. Seal is an enthusiast in these matters," said Mr. Clacton, almost apologetically. "We have to remind her sometimes that others have a right to their views even if they differ from our own. . . . *Punch* has a very funny picture this week, about a Suffragist and an agricultural laborer. Have you seen this week's *Punch*, Miss Datchet?"

Mary laughed, and said "No."

Mr. Clacton then told them the substance of the joke, which, however, depended a good deal for its success upon the expression which the artist had put into the people's faces. Mrs. Seal sat all the time perfectly grave. Directly he had done speaking she burst out:

"But surely, if you care about the welfare of your sex at all, you must wish them to have the vote?"

"I never said I didn't wish them to have the vote," Katharine protested.

"Then why aren't you a member of our society?" Mrs. Seal demanded.

Katharine stirred her spoon round and round, stared into the swirl of the tea, and remained silent. Mr. Clacton, meanwhile, framed a question which, after a moment's hesitation, he put to Katharine.

"Are you in any way related, I wonder, to the poet Alardyce? His daughter, I believe, married a Mr. Hilbery."

"Yes; I'm the poet's granddaughter," said Katharine, with a little sigh, after a pause; and for a moment they were all silent.

"The poet's granddaughter!" Mrs. Seal repeated, half to herself, with a shake of her head, as if that explained what was otherwise inexplicable.

The light kindled in Mr. Clacton's eye.

"Ah, indeed. That interests me very much," he said. "I owe a great debt to your grandfather, Miss Hilbery. At one time I could have repeated the greater part of him by heart.

But one gets out of the way of reading poetry, unfortunately. You don't remember him, I suppose?"

A sharp rap at the door made Katharine's answer inaudible. Mrs. Seal looked up with renewed hope in her eyes, and exclaiming:

"The proofs at last!" ran to open the door. "Oh, it's only Mr. Denham!" she cried, without any attempt to conceal her disappointment. Ralph, Katharine supposed, was a frequent visitor, for the only person he thought it necessary to greet was herself, and Mary at once explained the strange fact of her being there by saying:

"Katharine has come to see how one runs an office."

Ralph felt himself stiffen uncomfortably, as he said:

"I hope Mary hasn't persuaded you that she knows how to run an office?"

"What, doesn't she?" said Katharine, looking from one to the other.

At these remarks Mrs. Seal began to exhibit signs of discomposure, which displayed themselves by a tossing movement of her head, and, as Ralph took a letter from his pocket, and placed his finger upon a certain sentence, she forestalled him by exclaiming in confusion:

"Now, I know what you're going to say, Mr. Denham! But it was the day Kit Markham was here, and she upsets one so—with her wonderful vitality, always thinking of something new that we ought to be doing and aren't—and I was conscious at the time that my dates were mixed. It had nothing to do with Mary at all, I assure you."

"My dear Sally, don't apologize," said Mary, laughing. "Men are such pedants—they don't know what things matter, and what things don't."

"Now, Denham, speak up for our sex," said Mr. Clacton in a jocular manner, indeed, but like most insignificant men he was very quick to resent being found fault with by a woman, in argument with whom he was fond of calling himself "a mere man." He wished, however, to enter into a literary conservation with Miss Hilbery, and thus let the matter drop.

"Doesn't it seem strange to you, Miss Hilbery," he said, "that the French, with all their wealth of illustrious names, have no poet who can compare with your grandfather? Let me see. There's Chénier and Hugo and Alfred de Musset—wonderful men, but, at the same time, there's a richness, a freshness about Alardyce——"

Here the telephone bell rang, and he had to absent himself with a smile and a bow which signified that, although literature is delightful, it is not work. Mrs. Seal rose at the same time, but remained hovering over the table, delivering herself of a tirade against party government. "For if I were to tell you what I know of back-stairs intrigue, and what can be done by the power of the purse, you wouldn't credit me, Mr. Denham, you wouldn't, indeed. Which is why I feel that the only work for my father's daughter—for he was one of the pioneers, Mr. Denham, and on his tombstone I had that verse from the Psalms put, about the sowers and the seed. . . . And what wouldn't I give that he should be alive now, seeing what we're going to see——" but reflecting that the glories of the future depended in part upon the activity of her typewriter, she bobbed her head, and hurried back to the seclusion of her little room, from which immediately issued sounds of enthusiastic, but obviously erratic, composition.

Mary made it clear at once, by starting a fresh topic of general interest, that though she saw the humor of her colleague, she did not intend to have her laughed at.

"The standard of morality seems to me frightfully low," she observed reflectively, pouring out a second cup of tea, "especially among women who aren't well educated. They don't see that small things matter, and that's where the leakage begins, and then we find ourselves in difficulties—I very nearly lost my temper yesterday," she went on, looking at Ralph with a little smile, as though he knew what happened when she lost her temper. "It makes me very angry when people tell me lies—doesn't it make you angry?" she asked Katharine.

"But considering that every one tells lies," Katharine remarked, looking about the room to see where she had put down her umbrella and her parcel, for there was an intimacy in the way in which Mary and Ralph addressed each other which made her wish to leave them. Mary, on the other hand, was anxious, superficially at least, that Katharine should stay and so fortify her in her determination not to be in love with Ralph.

Ralph, while lifting his cup from his lips to the table, had made up his mind that if Miss Hilbery left, he would go with her.

"I don't think that I tell lies, and I don't think that Ralph tells lies, do you, Ralph?" Mary continued.

Katharine laughed, with more gayety, as it seemed to Mary, than she could properly account for. What was she laughing at? At them, presumably. Katharine had risen, and was glancing hither and thither, at the presses and the cupboards, and all the machinery of the office, as if she included them all in her rather malicious amusement, which caused Mary to keep her eyes on her straightly and rather fiercely, as if she were a gay-plumed, mischievous bird, who might light on the topmost bough and pick off the ruddiest cherry, without any warning. Two women less like each other could scarcely be imagined, Ralph thought, looking from one to the other. Next moment, he too, rose, and nodding to Mary, as Katharine said good-bye, opened the door for her, and followed her out.

Mary sat still and made no attempt to prevent them from going. For a second or two after the door had shut on them her eyes rested on the door with a straightforward fierceness in which, for a moment, a certain degree of bewilderment seemed to enter; but, after a brief hesitation, she put down her cup and proceeded to clear away the tea-things.

The impulse which had driven Ralph to take this action was the result of a very swift little piece of reasoning, and thus, perhaps, was not quite so much of an impulse as it seemed. It passed through his mind that if he missed this chance of talking to Katharine, he would have to face an enraged ghost, when he was alone in his room again, demanding an explanation of his cowardly indecision. It was better, on the whole, to risk present discomfiture than to waste an evening bandying excuses and constructing impossible scenes with this uncompromising section of himself. For ever since he had visited the Hilberys he had been much at the mercy of a phantom Katharine, who came to him when he sat alone, and answered him as he would have her answer, and was always beside him to crown those varying triumphs which were transacted almost every night, in imaginary scenes, as he walked through the lamplit streets home from the office. To walk with Katharine in the flesh would either feed that phantom with fresh food, which, as all who nourish dreams are aware, is a process that becomes necessary from time to time, or refine it to such a degree of thinness that it was scarcely serviceable any longer; and that, too, is sometimes a welcome change to a dreamer. And all the time Ralph was well aware that the bulk of Katharine was not represented in his dreams at all, so that when he met her he was bewildered by the fact that she had nothing to do with his dream of her.

When, on reaching the street, Katharine found that Mr. Denham proceeded to keep pace by her side, she was surprised and, perhaps, a little annoyed. She, too, had her margin of imagination, and to-night her activity in this obscure region of the mind required solitude. If she had had her way, she would have walked very fast down the Tottenham Court Road, and then sprung into a cab and raced swiftly home. The view she had had of the inside of an office was of the nature of a dream to her. Shut off up there, she compared Mrs. Seal, and Mary Datchet, and Mr. Clacton to enchanted people in a bewitched tower, with the spiders' webs looping across the corners of the room, and all the tools of the necromancer's craft at hand; for so aloof and unreal and apart from the normal world did they seem to her, in the house of innumerable typewriters, murmuring their incantations and concocting their drugs, and flinging their frail spiders' webs over the torrent of life which rushed down the streets outside.

She may have been conscious that there was some exaggeration in this fancy of hers, for she certainly did not wish to share it with Ralph. To him, she supposed, Mary Datchet, composing leaflets for Cabinet Ministers among her typewriters, represented all that was interesting and genuine; and, accordingly, she shut them both out from all share in the crowded street, with its pendant necklace of lamps, its lighted windows, and its throng of men and women, which exhilarated her to such an extent that she very nearly forgot her companion. She walked very fast, and the effect of people passing in the opposite direction was to produce a queer dizziness both in her head and in Ralph's, which set their bodies far apart. But she did her duty by her companion almost unconsciously.

"Mary Datchet does that sort of work very well. . . . She's responsible for it, I suppose?"

"Yes. The others don't help at all. . . . Has she made a convert of you?"

"Oh no. That is, I'm a convert already."

"But she hasn't persuaded you to work for them?"

"Oh dear no—that wouldn't do at all."

So they walked on down the Tottenham Court Road, parting and coming together again, and Ralph felt much as though he were addressing the summit of a poplar in a high gale of wind.

"Suppose we get on to that omnibus?" he suggested.

Katharine acquiesced, and they climbed up, and found themselves alone on top of it.

"But which way are you going?" Katharine asked, waking a little from the trance into which movement among moving things had thrown her.

"I'm going to the Temple," Ralph replied, inventing a

destination on the spur of the moment. He felt the change come over her as they sat down and the omnibus began to move forward. He imagined her contemplating the avenue in front of them with those honest sad eyes which seemed to set him at such a distance from them. But the breeze was blowing in their faces; it lifted her hat for a second, and she drew out a pin and stuck it in again,—a little action which seemed, for some reason, to make her rather more fallible. Ah, if only her hat would blow off, and leave her altogether disheveled, accepting it from his hands!

"This is like Venice," she observed, raising her hand. "The motor-cars, I mean, shooting about so quickly, with their lights."

"I've never seen Venice," he replied. "I keep that and some other things for my old age."

"What are the other things?" she asked.

"There's Venice and India and, I think, Dante, too."

She laughed.

"Think of providing for one's old age! And would you refuse to see Venice if you had the chance?"

Instead of answering her, he wondered whether he should tell her something that was quite true about himself, and as he wondered, he told her.

"I've planned out my life in sections ever since I was a child, to make it last longer. You see, I'm always afraid that I'm missing something——"

"And so am I!" Katharine exclaimed. "But, after all," she added, "why should you miss anything?"

"Why? Because I'm poor, for one thing," Ralph rejoined. "You, I suppose, can have Venice and India and Dante every day of your life."

She said nothing for a moment, but rested one hand, which was bare of glove, upon the rail in front of her, meditating upon a variety of things, of which one was that this strange young man pronounced Dante as she was used to hearing it pronounced, and another, that he had, most unexpectedly, a feeling about life that was familiar to her.

Perhaps, then, he was the sort of person she might take an interest in, if she came to know him better, and as she had placed him among those whom she would never want to know better, this was enough to make her silent. She hastily recalled her first view of him, in the little room where the relics were kept, and ran a bar through half her impressions, as one cancels a badly written sentence, having found the right one.

"But to know that one might have things doesn't alter the fact that one hasn't got them," she said, in some confusion. "How could I go to India, for example? Besides," she began impulsively, and stopped herself. Here the conductor came round, and interrupted them. Ralph waited for her to resume her sentence, but she said no more.

"I have a message to give your father," he remarked. "Perhaps you would give it him, or I could come——"

"Yes, do come," Katharine replied.

"Still, I don't see why you shouldn't go to India," Ralph began, in order to keep her from rising, as she threatened to do.

But she got up in spite of him, and said good-bye with her usual air of decision, and left him with a quickness which Ralph connected now with all her movements. He looked down and saw her standing on the pavement edge, an alert, commanding figure, which waited its season to cross, and then walked boldly and swiftly to the other side. That gesture and action would be added to the picture he had of her, but at present the real woman completely routed the phantom one.

CHAPTER VII

A ND little Augustus Pelham said to me, 'It's the younger generation knocking at the door,' and I said to him, 'Oh, but the younger generation comes in without knocking, Mr. Pelham.' Such a feeble little joke, wasn't it, but down it went into his notebook all the same."

"Let us congratulate ourselves that we shall be in the grave before that work is published," said Mr. Hilbery.

The elderly couple were waiting for the dinner-bell to ring and, for their daughter to come into the room. Their arm-chairs were drawn up on either side of the fire, and each sat in the same slightly crouched position, looking into the coals, with the expressions of people who have had their share of experiences and wait, rather passively, for something to happen. Mr. Hilbery now gave all his attention to a piece of coal which had fallen out of the grate, and to selecting a favorable position for it among the lumps that were burning already. Mrs. Hilbery watched him in silence, and the smile changed on her lips as if her mind still played with the events of the afternoon.

When Mr. Hilbery had accomplished his task, he resumed his crouching position again, and began to toy with the little green stone attached to his watch-chain. His deep, oval-shaped eyes were fixed upon the flames, but behind the superficial glaze seemed to brood an observant and whimsical spirit, which kept the brown of the eye still unusually vivid. But a look of indolence, the result of skepticism or of a taste too fastidious to be satisfied by the prizes and conclusions so easily within his grasp, lent him an expression almost of melancholy. After sitting thus for a time, he seemed to reach some point in his thinking which demonstrated its futility, upon which he sighed and stretched his hand for a book lying on the table by his side.

Directly the door opened he closed the book, and the eyes of father and mother both rested on Katharine as she came towards them. The sight seemed at once to give them a motive which they had not had before. To them she appeared, as she walked towards them in her light evening dress, extremely young, and the sight of her refreshed them, were it only because her youth and ignorance made their knowledge of the world of some value.

"The only excuse for you, Katharine, is that dinner is still later than you are," said Mr. Hilbery, putting down his spectacles.

"I don't mind her being late when the result is so charming," said Mrs. Hilbery, looking with pride at her daughter. "Still, I don't know that I *like* your being out so late, Katharine," she continued. "You took a cab, I hope?"

Here dinner was announced, and Mr. Hilbery formally led his wife downstairs on his arm. They were all dressed for dinner, and, indeed, the prettiness of the dinner-table merited that compliment. There was no cloth upon the table, and the china made regular circles of deep blue upon the shining brown wood. In the middle there was a bowl of tawny red and yellow chrysanthemums, and one of pure white, so fresh that the narrow petals were curved backwards into a firm white ball. From the surrounding walls the heads of three famous Victorian writers surveyed this entertainment, and slips of paper pasted beneath them testified in the great man's own handwriting that he was yours sincerely or affectionately or for ever. The father and daughter would have been quite content, apparently, to eat their dinner in silence, or with a few cryptic remarks expressed in a shorthand which could not be understood by the servants. But silence depressed Mrs. Hilbery, and far from minding the presence of maids, she would often address herself to them, and was never altogether unconscious of their approval or disapproval of her remarks. In the first place she called them to witness that the room was darker than usual, and had all the lights turned on.

"That's more cheerful," she exclaimed. "D'you know, Katharine, that ridiculous goose came to tea with me? Oh, how I wanted you! He tried to make epigrams all the time, and I got so nervous, expecting them, you know, that I spilt the tea—and he made an epigram about that!"

"Which ridiculous goose?" Katharine asked her father.

"Only one of my geese, happily, makes epigrams—Augustus Pelham, of course," said Mrs. Hilbery.

"I'm not sorry that I was out," said Katharine.

"Poor Augustus!" Mrs. Hilbery exclaimed. "But we're all too hard on him. Remember how devoted he is to his tiresome old mother."

"That's only because she is his mother. Any one connected with himself——"

"No, no, Katharine—that's too bad. That's—what's the word I mean, Trevor, something long and Latin—the sort of word you and Katharine know——"

Mr. Hilbery suggested "cynical."

"Well, that'll do. I don't believe in sending girls to college, but I should teach them that sort of thing. It makes one feel so dignified, bringing out these little allusions, and passing on gracefully to the next topic. But I don't know what's come over me—I actually had to ask Augustus the name of the lady Hamlet was in love with, as you were out, Katharine, and Heaven knows what he mayn't put down about me in his diary."

"I wish," Katharine started, with great impetuosity, and checked herself. Her mother always stirred her to feel and think quickly, and then she remembered that her father was there, listening with attention.

"What is it you wish?" he asked, as she paused.

He often surprised her, thus, into telling him what she had not meant to tell him; and then they argued, while Mrs. Hilbery went on with her own thoughts.

"I wish mother wasn't famous. I was out at tea, and they would talk to me about poetry."

"Thinking you must be poetical, I see—and aren't you?"

"Who's been talking to you about poetry, Katharine?" Mrs. Hilbery demanded, and Katharine was committed to giving her parents an account of her visit to the Suffrage office.

"They have an office at the top of one of the old houses in Russell Square. I never saw such queer-looking people. And the man discovered I was related to the poet, and talked to me about poetry. Even Mary Datchet seems different in that atmosphere."

"Yes, the office atmosphere is very bad for the soul," said Mr. Hilbery.

"I don't remember any offices in Russell Square in the old days, when Mamma lived there," Mrs. Hilbery mused, "and I can't fancy turning one of those noble great rooms into a stuffy little Suffrage office. Still, if the clerks read poetry there must be something nice about them."

"No, because they don't read it as we read it," Katharine insisted.

"But it's nice to think of them reading your grandfather, and not filling up those dreadful little forms all day long," Mrs. Hilbery persisted, her notion of office life being derived from some chance view of a scene behind the counter at her bank, as she slipped the sovereigns into her purse.

"At any rate, they haven't made a convert of Katharine, which was what I was afraid of," Mr. Hilbery remarked.

"Oh no," said Katharine very decidedly, "I wouldn't work with them for anything."

"It's curious," Mr. Hilbery continued, agreeing with his daughter, "how the sight of one's fellow-enthusiasts always chokes one off. They show up the faults of one's cause so much more plainly than one's antagonists. One can be enthusiastic in one's study, but directly one comes into touch with the people who agree with one, all the glamor goes. So I've always found," and he proceeded to tell them, as he peeled his apple, how he committed himself once, in his youthful days, to make a speech at a political meeting, and went there ablaze with enthusiasm for the ideals of his own side; but while his leaders spoke, he became gradually converted to the other way of thinking, if thinking it could be called, and had to feign illness in order to avoid making a fool of himself—an experience which had sickened him of public meetings.

Katharine listened and felt as she generally did when her father, and to some extent her mother, described their feelings, that she quite understood and agreed with them, but, at the same time, saw something which they did not see, and always felt some disappointment when they fell short of her vision, as they always did. The plates succeeded each other swiftly and noiselessly in front of her, and the table was decked for dessert, and as the talk murmured on in familiar grooves, she sat there, rather like a judge, listening to her parents, who did, indeed, feel it very pleasant when they made her laugh.

Daily life in a house where there are young and old is full of curious little ceremonies and pieties, which are discharged quite punctually, though the meaning of them is obscure, and a mystery has come to brood over them which lends even a superstitious charm to their performance. Such was the nightly ceremony of the cigar and the glass of port, which were placed on the right hand and on the left hand of Mr. Hilbery, and simultaneously Mrs. Hilbery and Katharine left the room. All the years they had lived together they had never seen Mr. Hilbery smoke his cigar or drink his port, and they would have felt it unseemly if, by chance, they had surprised him as he sat there. These short, but clearly marked, periods of separation between the sexes were always used for an intimate postscript to what had been said at dinner, the sense of being women together coming out most strongly when the male sex was, as if by some religious rite, secluded from the female. Katharine knew by heart the sort of mood that possessed her as she walked upstairs to the drawing-room, her mother's arm in hers; and she could anticipate the pleasure with which, when she had turned on the lights, they both regarded the drawing-room, fresh swept and set in order for the last section of the day, with the red parrots swinging on the chintz curtains, and the arm-chairs warming in the blaze. Mrs. Hilbery stood over the fire, with one foot on the fender, and her skirts slightly raised.

"Oh, Katharine," she exclaimed, "how you've made me think of Mamma and the old days in Russell Square! I can see the chandeliers, and the green silk of the piano, and Mamma sitting in her cashmere shawl by the window, singing till the little ragamuffin boys outside stopped to listen. Papa sent me in with a bunch of violets while he waited round the corner. It must have been a summer evening. That was before things were hopeless. . . ."

As she spoke an expression of regret, which must have come frequently to cause the lines which now grew deep round the lips and eyes, settled on her face. The poet's marriage had not been a happy one. He had left his wife, and after some years of a rather reckless existence, she had died, before her time. This disaster had led to great irregularities of education, and, indeed, Mrs. Hilbery might be said to have escaped education altogether. But she had been her father's companion at the season when he wrote the finest of his poems. She had sat on his knee in taverns and other haunts of drunken poets, and it was for her sake, so people said, that he had cured himself of his dissipation, and become the irreproachable literary character that the world knows, whose inspiration had deserted him. As Mrs. Hilbery grew old she thought more and more of the past, and this ancient disaster seemed at times almost to prey upon her mind, as if she could not pass out of life herself without laying the ghost of her parent's sorrow to rest.

Katharine wished to comfort her mother, but it was difficult to do this satisfactorily when the facts themselves were so much of a legend. The house in Russell Square, for example, with its noble rooms, and the magnolia-tree in the garden, and the sweet-voiced piano, and the sound of feet coming down the corridors, and other properties of size and romance—had they any existence? Yet why should Mrs. Alardyce live all alone in this gigantic mansion, and, if she did not live alone, with whom did she live? For its own sake, Katharine rather liked this tragic story, and would have been glad to hear the details of it, and to have been able to discuss them frankly. But this it became less and less possible to do, for though Mrs. Hilbery was constantly reverting to the story, it was always in this tentative and restless fashion, as though by a touch here and there she could set things straight which had been crooked these sixty years. Perhaps, indeed, she no longer knew what the truth was.

"If they'd lived now," she concluded, "I feel it wouldn't have happened. People aren't so set upon tragedy as they were then. If my father had been able to go round the world, or if she'd had a rest cure, everything would have come right. But what could I do? And then they had bad friends, both of them, who made mischief. Ah, Katharine, when you marry, be quite, quite sure that you love your husband!"

The tears stood in Mrs. Hilbery's eyes.

While comforting her, Katharine thought to herself, "Now this is what Mary Datchet and Mr. Denham don't understand. This is the sort of position I'm always getting into. How simple it must be to live as they do!" for all the evening she had been comparing her home and her father and mother with the Suffrage office and the people there.

"But, Katharine," Mrs. Hilbery continued, with one of her sudden changes of mood, "though, Heaven knows, I don't want to see you married, surely if ever a man loved a woman, William loves you. And it's a nice, rich-sounding name too—Katharine Rodney, which, unfortunately, doesn't mean that he's got any money, because he hasn't."

The alteration of her name annoyed Katharine, and she observed, rather sharply, that she didn't want to marry any one.

"It's very dull that you can only marry one husband, certainly," Mrs. Hilbery reflected. "I always wish that you could marry everybody who wants to marry you. Perhaps they'll come to that in time, but meanwhile I confess that dear William——" But here Mr. Hilbery came in, and the more solid part of the evening began. This consisted in the reading aloud by Katharine from some prose work or other, while her mother knitted scarves intermittently on a little circular frame, and her father read the newspaper, not so attentively but that he could comment humorously now and again upon the fortunes of the hero and the heroine. The Hilberys subscribed to a library, which delivered books on Tuesdays and Fridays, and Katharine did her best to interest her parents in the works of living and highly respectable authors; but Mrs. Hilbery was perturbed by the very look of the light, gold-wreathed volumes, and would make little faces as if she tasted something bitter as the reading went on; while Mr. Hilbery would treat the moderns with a curious elaborate banter such as one might apply to the antics of a promising child. So this evening, after five pages or so of one of these masters, Mrs. Hilbery protested that it was all too clever and cheap and nasty for words.

"Please, Katharine, read us something *real*."

Katharine had to go to the bookcase and choose a portly volume in sleek, yellow calf, which had directly a sedative effect upon both her parents. But the delivery of the evening post broke in upon the periods of Henry Fielding, and Katharine found that her letters needed all her attention.

CHAPTER VIII

SHE took her letters up to her room with her, having persuaded her mother to go to bed directly Mr. Hilbery
left them, for so long as she sat in the same room as her
mother, Mrs. Hilbery might, at any moment, ask for a sight
of the poet. A very hasty glance through many sheets had
shown Katharine that, by some coincidence, her attention
had to be directed to many different anxieties simultaneously.
In the first place, Rodney had written a very full account of
his state of mind, which was illustrated by a sonnet, and he
demanded a reconsideration of their position, which agitated
Katharine more than she liked. Then there were two letters
which had to be laid side by side and compared before she
could make out the truth of their story, and even when she
knew the facts she could not decide what to make of them;
and finally she had to reflect upon a great many pages from
a cousin who found himself in financial difficulties, which
forced him to the uncongenial occupation of teaching the
young ladies of Bungay to play upon the violin.

But the two letters which each told the same story differently were the chief source of her perplexity. She was
really rather shocked to find it definitely established that her
own second cousin, Cyril Alardyce, had lived for the last
four years with a woman who was not his wife, who had
borne him two children, and was now about to bear him another. This state of things had been discovered by Mrs.
Milvain, her aunt Celia, a zealous inquirer into such matters, whose letter was also under consideration. Cyril, she
said, must be made to marry the woman at once; and Cyril,
rightly or wrongly, was indignant with such interference
with his affairs, and would not own that he had any cause
to be ashamed of himself. Had he any cause to be ashamed

of himself, Katharine wondered; and she turned to her aunt again.

"Remember," she wrote, in her profuse, emphatic statement, "that he bears your grandfather's name, and so will the child that is to be born. The poor boy is not so much to blame as the woman who deluded him, thinking him a gentleman, which he *is,* and having money, which he has *not.*"

"What would Ralph Denham say to this?" thought Katharine, beginning to pace up and down her bedroom. She twitched aside the curtains, so that, on turning, she was faced by darkness, and looking out, could just distinguish the branches of a plane-tree and the yellow lights of some one else's windows.

"What would Mary Datchet and Ralph Denham say?" she reflected, pausing by the window, which, as the night was warm, she raised, in order to feel the air upon her face, and to lose herself in the nothingness of night. But with the air the distant humming sound of far-off crowded thoroughfares was admitted to the room. The incessant and tumultuous hum of the distant traffic seemed, as she stood there, to represent the thick texture of her life, for her life was so hemmed in with the progress of other lives that the sound of its own advance was inaudible. People like Ralph and Mary, she thought, had it all their own way, and an empty space before them, and, as she envied them, she cast her mind out to imagine an empty land where all this petty intercourse of men and women, this life made up of the dense crossings and entanglements of men and women, had no existence whatever. Even now, alone, at night, looking out into the shapeless mass of London, she was forced to remember that there was one point and here another with which she had some connection. William Rodney, at this very moment, was seated in a minute speck of light somewhere to the east of her, and his mind was occupied, not with his book, but with her. She wished that no one in the whole world would think of her. However, there was no way of escaping from one's fellow-beings, she concluded, and shut the window with a sigh, and returned once more to her letters.

She could not doubt but that William's letter was the most genuine she had yet received from him. He had come to the conclusion that he could not live without her, he wrote. He believed that he knew her, and could give her happiness, and that their marriage would be unlike other marriages. Nor was the sonnet, in spite of its accomplishment, lacking in passion, and Katharine, as she read the pages through again, could see in what direction her feelings ought to flow, supposing they revealed themselves. She would come to feel a humorous sort of tenderness for him, a zealous care for his susceptibilities, and, after all, she considered, thinking of her father and mother, what is love?

Naturally, with her face, position, and background, she had experience of young men who wished to marry her, and made protestations of love, but, perhaps because she did not return the feeling, it remained something of a pageant to her. Not having experience of it herself, her mind had unconsciously occupied itself for some years in dressing up an image of love, and the marriage that was the outcome of love, and the man who inspired love, which naturally dwarfed any examples that came her way. Easily, and without correction by reason, her imagination made pictures, superb backgrounds casting a rich though phantom light upon the facts in the foreground. Splendid as the waters that drop with resounding thunder from high ledges of rock, and plunge downwards into the blue depths of night, was the presence of love she dreamt, drawing into it every drop of the force of life, and dashing them all asunder in the superb catastrophe in which everything was surrendered, and nothing might be reclaimed. The man, too, was some magnanimous hero, riding a great horse by the shore of the sea. They rode through forests together, they galloped by the rim of the sea. But waking, she was able to contemplate a perfectly loveless marriage, as the thing one did actually in real life, for possibly the people who dream thus are those who do the most prosaic things.

At this moment she was much inclined to sit on into the night, spinning her light fabric of thoughts until she tired of their futility, and went to her mathematics; but, as she knew very well, it was necessary that she should see her father before he went to bed. The case of Cyril Alardyce must be discussed, her mother's illusions and the rights of the family attended to. Being vague herself as to what all this amounted to, she had to take counsel with her father. She took her letters in her hand and went downstairs. It was past eleven, and the clocks had come into their reign, the grandfather's clock in the hall ticking in competition with the small clock on the landing. Mr. Hilbery's study ran out behind the rest of the house, on the ground floor, and was a very silent, subterranean place, the sun in daytime casting a mere abstract of light through a skylight upon his books and the large table, with its spread of white papers, now illumined by a green reading-lamp. Here Mr. Hilbery sat editing his review, or placing together documents by means of which it could be proved that Shelley had written "of" instead of "and," or that the inn in which Byron had slept was called the "Nag's Head" and not the "Turkish Knight," or that the Christian name of Keats's uncle had been John rather than Richard, for he knew more minute details about these poets than any man in England, probably, and was preparing an edition of Shelley which scrupulously observed the poet's system of punctuation. He saw the humor of these researches, but that did not prevent him from carrying them out with the utmost scrupulosity.

He was lying back comfortably in a deep arm-chair smoking a cigar, and ruminating the fruitful question as to whether Coleridge had wished to marry Dorothy Wordsworth, and what, if he had done so, would have been the consequences to him in particular, and to literature in general. When Katharine came in he reflected that he knew what she had come for, and he made a pencil note before he

spoke to her. Having done this, he saw that she was reading, and he watched her for a moment without saying anything. She was reading "Isabella and the Pot of Basil," and
her mind was full of the Italian hills and the blue daylight,
and the hedges set with little rosettes of red and white roses.
Feeling that her father waited for her, she sighed and said,
shutting her book:

"I've had a letter from Aunt Celia about Cyril, father.
. . . It seems to be true—about his marriage. What are
we to do?"

"Cyril seems to have been behaving in a very foolish
manner," said Mr. Hilbery, in his pleasant and deliberate
tones.

Katharine found some difficulty in carrying on the conversation, while her father balanced his finger-tips so judi-
ciously, and seemed to reserve so many of his thoughts for
himself.

"He's about done for himself, I should say," he continued.
Without saying anything, he took Katharine's letters out
of her hand, adjusted his eyeglasses, and read them through.

At length he said "Humph!" and gave the letters back to
her.

"Mother knows nothing about it," Katharine remarked.
"Will you tell her?"

"I shall tell your mother. But I shall tell her that there
is nothing whatever for us to do."

"But the marriage?" Katharine asked, with some diffidence.

Mr. Hilbery said nothing, and stared into the fire.

"What in the name of conscience did he do it for?" he
speculated at last, rather to himself than to her.

Katharine had begun to read her aunt's letter over again,
and she now quoted a sentence. "Ibsen and Butler. . . .
He has sent me a letter full of quotations—nonsense, though
clever nonsense."

"Well, if the younger generation want to carry on its life
on those lines, it's none of our affair," he remarked.

"But isn't it our affair, perhaps, to make them get married?" Katharine asked rather wearily.

"Why the dickens should they apply to me?" her father demanded with sudden irritation.

"Only as the head of the family——"

"But I'm not the head of the family. Alfred's the head of the family. Let them apply to Alfred," said Mr. Hilbery, relapsing again into his arm-chair. Katharine was aware that she had touched a sensitive spot, however, in mentioning the family.

"I think, perhaps, the best thing would be for me to go and see them," she observed.

"I won't have you going anywhere near them," Mr. Hilbery replied with unwonted decision and authority. "Indeed, I don't understand why they've dragged you into the business at all—I don't see that it's got anything to do with you."

"I've always been friends with Cyril," Katharine observed.

"But did he ever tell you anything about this?" Mr. Hilbery asked rather sharply.

Katharine shook her head. She was, indeed, a good deal hurt that Cyril had not confided in her—did he think, as Ralph Denham or Mary Datchet might think, that she was, for some reason, unsympathetic—hostile even?

"As to your mother," said Mr. Hilbery, after a pause, in which he seemed to be considering the color of the flames, "you had better tell her the facts. She'd better know the facts before every one begins to talk about it, though why Aunt Celia thinks it necessary to come, I'm sure I don't know. And the less talk there is the better."

Granting the assumption that gentlemen of sixty who are highly cultivated, and have had much experience of life, probably think of many things which they do not say, Katharine could not help feeling rather puzzled by her father's attitude, as she went back to her room. What a distance he was from it all! How superficially he smoothed these events into a semblance of decency which harmonized with his own view of life! He never wondered what Cyril had felt, nor did the hidden aspects of the case tempt him to examine into them. He merely seemed to realize, rather languidly, that Cyril had behaved in a way which was foolish, because other people did not behave in that way. He seemed to be looking through a telescope at little figures hundreds of miles in the distance.

Her selfish anxiety not to have to tell Mrs. Hilbery what had happened made her follow her father into the hall after breakfast the next morning in order to question him.

"Have you told mother?" she asked. Her manner to her father was almost stern, and she seemed to hold endless depths of reflection in the dark of her eyes.

Mr. Hilbery sighed.

"My dear child, it went out of my head." He smoothed his silk hat energetically, and at once affected an air of hurry. "I'll send a note round from the office. . . . I'm late this morning, and I've any amount of proofs to get through."

"That wouldn't do at all," Katharine said decidedly. "She must be told—you or I must tell her. We ought to have told her at first."

Mr. Hilbery had now placed his hat on his head, and his hand was on the door-knob. An expression which Katharine knew well from her childhood, when he asked her to shield him in some neglect of duty, came into his eyes; malice, humor, and irresponsibility were blended in it. He nodded his head to and fro significantly, opened the door with an adroit movement, and stepped out with a lightness unexpected at his age. He waved his hand once to his daughter, and was gone. Left alone, Katharine could not help laughing to find herself cheated as usual in domestic bargainings with her father, and left to do the disagreeable work which belonged, by rights, to him.

CHAPTER IX

KATHARINE disliked telling her mother about Cyril's misbehavior quite as much as her father did, and for much the same reasons. They both shrank, nervously, as people fear the report of a gun on the stage, from all that would have to be said on this occasion. Katharine, moreover, was unable to decide what she thought of Cyril's misbehavior. As usual, she saw something which her father and mother did not see, and the effect of that something was to suspend Cyril's behavior in her mind without any qualification at all. They would think whether it was good or bad; to her it was merely a thing that had happened.

When Katharine reached the study, Mrs. Hilbery had already dipped her pen in the ink.

"Katharine," she said, lifting it in the air, "I've just made out such a queer, strange thing about your grandfather. I'm three years and six months older than he was when he died. I couldn't very well have been his mother, but I might have been his elder sister, and that seems to me such a pleasant fancy. I'm going to start quite fresh this morning, and get a lot done."

She began her sentence, at any rate, and Katharine sat down at her own table, untied the bundle of old letters upon which she was working, smoothed them out absent-mindedly, and began to decipher the faded script. In a minute she looked across at her mother, to judge her mood. Peace and happiness had relaxed every muscle in her face; her lips were parted very slightly, and her breath came in smooth, controlled inspirations like those of a child who is surrounding itself with a building of bricks, and increasing in ecstasy as each brick is placed in position. So Mrs. Hilbery was raising round her the skies and trees of the past with every stroke of her pen, and recalling the voices of the dead. Quiet as the room was, and undisturbed by the sounds of the present moment, Katharine could fancy that here was a deep pool of past time, and that she and her mother were bathed in the light of sixty years ago. What could the present give, she wondered, to compare with the rich crowd of gifts bestowed by the past? Here was a Thursday morning in process of manufacture; each second was minted fresh by the clock upon the mantelpiece. She strained her ears and could just hear, far off, the hoot of a motor-car and the rush of wheels coming nearer and dying away again, and the voices of men crying old iron and vegetables in one of the poorer streets at the back of the house. Rooms, of course, accumulate their suggestions, and any room in which one has been used to carry on any particular occupation gives off memories of moods, of ideas, of postures that have been seen in it; so that to attempt any different kind of work there is almost impossible.

Katharine was unconsciously affected, each time she entered her mother's room, by all these influences, which had had their birth years ago, when she was a child, and had something sweet and solemn about them, and connected themselves with early memories of the cavernous glooms and sonorous echoes of the Abbey where her grandfather lay buried. All the books and pictures, even the chairs and tables, had belonged to him, or had reference to him; even the china dogs on the mantelpiece and the little shepherdesses with their sheep had been bought by him for a penny a piece from a man who used to stand with a tray of toys in Kensington High Street, as Katharine had often heard her mother tell. Often she had sat in this room, with her mind fixed so firmly on those vanished figures that she could almost see the muscles round their eyes and lips, and had given to each his own voice, with its tricks of accent, and his coat and his cravat. Often she had seemed to herself to be moving among them, an invisible ghost among the living, better acquainted with them than with her own friends, because she knew their secrets and possessed a divine foreknowledge of their destiny. They had been so unhappy, such muddlers, so wrong-headed, it seemed to her. She could have told them what to do, and what not to do. It was a melancholy fact that they would pay no heed to her, and were bound to come to grief in their own antiquated way. Their behavior was often grotesquely irrational; their conventions monstrously absurd; and yet, as she brooded upon them, she felt so closely attached to them that it was useless to try to pass judgment upon them. She very nearly lost consciousness that she was a separate being, with a future of her own. On a morning of slight depression, such as this, she would try to find some sort of clue to the muddle which their old letters presented; some reason which seemed to make it worth while to them; some aim which they kept steadily in view—but she was interrupted.

Mrs. Hilbery had risen from her table, and was standing looking out of the window at a string of barges swimming up the river.

Katharine watched her. Suddenly Mrs. Hilbery turned abruptly, and exclaimed:

"I really believe I'm bewitched! I only want three sentences, you see, something quite straightforward and commonplace, and I can't find 'em."

She began to pace up and down the room, snatching up her duster; but she was too much annoyed to find any relief, as yet, in polishing the backs of books.

"Besides," she said, giving the sheet she had written to Katharine, "I don't believe this'll do. Did your grandfather ever visit the Hebrides, Katharine?" She looked in a strangely beseeching way at her daughter. "My mind got running on the Hebrides, and I couldn't help writing a little description of them. Perhaps it would do at the beginning of a chapter. Chapters often begin quite differently from the way they go on, you know." Katharine read what her mother had written. She might have been a schoolmaster criticizing a child's essay. Her face gave Mrs. Hilbery, who watched it anxiously, no ground for hope.

"It's very beautiful," she stated, "but, you see, mother, we ought to go from point to point——"

"Oh, I know," Mrs. Hilbery exclaimed. "And that's just what I can't do. Things keep coming into my head. It isn't that I don't know everything and feel everything (who did know him, if I didn't?), but I can't put it down, you see. There's a kind of blind spot," she said, touching her forehead, "there. And when I can't sleep o' nights, I fancy I shall die without having done it."

From exultation she had passed to the depths of depression which the imagination of her death aroused. The depression communicated itself to Katharine. How impotent they were, fiddling about all day long with papers! And the clock was striking eleven and nothing done! She watched her mother, now rummaging in a great brass-bound box which stood by her table, but she did not go to her help. Of course, Katharine reflected, her mother had now lost some paper, and they would waste the rest of the morning looking for it. She cast her eyes down in irritation, and read again her mother's musical sentences about the silver gulls, and the roots of little pink flowers washed by pellucid streams, and the blue mists of hyacinths, until she was struck by her mother's silence. She raised her eyes. Mrs. Hilbery had emptied a portfolio containing old photographs over her table, and was looking from one to another.

"Surely, Katharine," she said, "the men were far handsomer in those days than they are now, in spite of their odious whiskers? Look at old John Graham, in his white waistcoat—look at Uncle Harley. That's Peter the man-servant, I suppose. Uncle John brought him back from India."

Katharine looked at her mother, but did not stir or answer. She had suddenly become very angry, with a rage which their relationship made silent, and therefore doubly powerful and critical. She felt all the unfairness of the

claim which her mother tacitly made to her time and sympathy, and what Mrs. Hilbery took, Katharine thought bitterly, she wasted. Then, in a flash, she remembered that
she had still to tell her about Cyril's misbehavior. Her
anger immediately dissipated itself; it broke like some wave
that has gathered itself high above the rest; the waters
were resumed into the sea again, and Katharine felt
once more full of peace and solicitude, and anxious only that
her mother should be protected from pain. She crossed the
room instinctively, and sat on the arm of her mother's chair.
Mrs. Hilbery leant her head against her daughter's body.

"What is nobler," she mused, turning over the photographs, "than to be a woman to whom every one turns, in
sorrow or difficulty? How have the young women of your
generation improved upon that, Katharine? I can see them
now, sweeping over the lawns at Melbury House, in their
flounces and furbelows, so calm and stately and imperial
(and the monkey and the little black dwarf following behind), as if nothing mattered in the world but to be beautiful
and kind. But they did more than we do, I sometimes think.
They *were,* and that's better than doing. They seem to me
like ships, like majestic ships, holding on their way, not
shoving or pushing, not fretted by little things, as we are,
but taking their way, like ships with white sails."

Katharine tried to interrupt this discourse, but the opportunity did not come, and she could not forbear to turn over
the pages of the album in which the old photographs were
stored. The faces of these men and women shone forth
wonderfully after the hubbub of living faces, and seemed,
as her mother had said, to wear a marvelous dignity and
calm, as if they had ruled their kingdoms justly and deserved great love. Some were of almost incredible beauty,
others were ugly enough in a forcible way, but none were
dull or bored or insignificant. The superb stiff folds of the
crinolines suited the women; the cloaks and hats of the gentlemen seemed full of character. Once more Katharine felt
the serene air all round her, and seemed far off to hear the

solemn beating of the sea upon the shore. But she knew that she must join the present on to this past.

Mrs. Hilbery was rambling on, from story to story.

"That's Janie Mannering," she said, pointing to a superb, white-haired dame, whose satin robes seemed strung with pearls. "I must have told you how she found her cook drunk under the kitchen table when the Empress was coming to dinner, and tucked up her velvet sleeves (she always dressed like an Empress herself), cooked the whole meal, and appeared in the drawing-room as if she'd been sleeping on a bank of roses all day. She could do anything with her hands—they all could—make a cottage or embroider a petticoat.

"And that's Queenie Colquhoun," she went on, turning the pages, "who took her coffin out with her to Jamaica, packed with lovely shawls and bonnets, because you couldn't get coffins in Jamaica, and she had a horror of dying there (as she did), and being devoured by the white ants. And there's Sabine, the loveliest of them all; ah! it was like a star rising when she came into the room. And that's Miriam, in her coachman's cloak, with all the little capes on, and she wore great top-boots underneath. You young people may say you're unconventional, but you're nothing compared with her."

Turning the page, she came upon the picture of a very masculine, handsome lady, whose head the photographer had adorned with an imperial crown.

"Ah, you wretch!" Mrs. Hilbery exclaimed, "what a wicked old despot you were, in your day! How we all bowed down before you! 'Maggie,' she used to say, 'if it hadn't been for me, where would you be now?' And it was true; she brought them together, you know. She said to my father, 'Marry her,' and he did; and she said to poor little Clara, 'Fall down and worship him,' and she did; but she got up again, of course. What else could one expect? She was a mere child—eighteen—and half dead with fright, too. But that old tyrant never repented. She used to say that she had given them three perfect months, and no one had a right to more; and I sometimes think, Katharine, that's true, you know. It's more than most of us have, only we have to pretend, which was a thing neither of them could ever do. I fancy," Mrs. Hilbery mused, "that there was a kind of sincerity in those days between men and women which, with all your outspokenness, you haven't got."

Katharine again tried to interrupt. But Mrs. Hilbery had been gathering impetus from her recollections, and was now in high spirits.

"They must have been good friends at heart," she resumed, "because she used to sing his songs. Ah, how did it go?" and Mrs. Hilbery, who had a very sweet voice, trolled out a famous lyric of her father's which had been set to an absurdly and charmingly sentimental air by some early Victorian composer.

"It's the vitality of them!" she concluded, striking her fist against the table. "That's what we haven't got! We're virtuous, we're earnest, we go to meetings, we pay the poor their wages, but we don't live as they lived. As often as not, my father wasn't in bed three nights out of the seven, but always fresh as paint in the morning. I hear him now, come singing up the stairs to the nursery, and tossing the loaf for breakfast on his sword-stick, and then off we went for a day's pleasuring—Richmond, Hampton Court, the Surrey Hills. Why shouldn't we go, Katharine? It's going to be a fine day."

At this moment, just as Mrs. Hilbery was examining the weather from the window, there was a knock at the door. A slight, elderly lady came in, and was saluted by Katharine, with very evident dismay, as "Aunt Celia!" She was dismayed because she guessed why Aunt Celia had come. It was certainly in order to discuss the case of Cyril and the woman who was not his wife, and owing to her procrastination Mrs. Hilbery was quite unprepared. Who could be more unprepared? Here she was, suggesting that all three of them should go on a jaunt to Blackfriars to inspect the site of Shakespeare's theater, for the weather was hardly settled enough for the country.

To this proposal Mrs. Milvain listened with a patient smile, which indicated that for many years she had accepted such eccentricities in her sister-in-law with bland philosophy. Katharine took up her position at some distance, standing with her foot on the fender, as though by so doing she could get a better view of the matter. But, in spite of her aunt's presence, how unreal the whole question of Cyril and his morality appeared! The difficulty, it now seemed, was not to break the news gently to Mrs. Hilbery, but to make her understand it. How was one to lasso her mind, and tether it to this minute, unimportant spot? A matter-of-fact statement seemed best.

"I think Aunt Celia has come to talk about Cyril, mother," she said rather brutally. "Aunt Celia has discovered that Cyril is married. He has a wife and children."

"No, he is *not* married," Mrs. Milvain interposed, in low tones, addressing herself to Mrs. Hilbery. "He has two children, and another on the way."

Mrs. Hilbery looked from one to the other in bewilderment.

"We thought it better to wait until it was proved before we told you," Katharine added.

"But I met Cyril only a fortnight ago at the National Gallery!" Mrs. Hilbery exclaimed. "I don't believe a word of it," and she tossed her head with a smile on her lips at Mrs. Milvain, as though she could quite understand her mistake, which was a very natural mistake, in the case of a childless woman, whose husband was something very dull in the Board of Trade.

"I didn't *wish* to believe it, Maggie," said Mrs. Milvain. "For a long time I *couldn't* believe it. But now I've seen, and I *have* to believe it."

"Katharine," Mrs. Hilbery demanded, "does your father know of this?"

Katharine nodded.

"Cyril married!" Mrs. Hilbery repeated. "And never telling us a word, though we've had him in our house since he was a child—noble William's son! I can't believe my ears!"

Feeling that the burden of proof was laid upon her, Mrs. Milvain now proceeded with her story. She was elderly and fragile, but her childlessness seemed always to impose these painful duties on her, and to revere the family, and to keep it in repair, had now become the chief object of her life. She told her story in a low, spasmodic, and somewhat broken voice.

"I have suspected for some time that he was not happy. There were new lines on his face. So I went to his rooms, when I knew he was engaged at the poor men's college. He lectures there—Roman law, you know, or it may be Greek. The landlady said Mr. Alardyce only slept there about once a fortnight now. He looked so ill, she said. She had seen him with a young person. I suspected something directly. I went to his room, and there was an envelope on the mantel-piece, and a letter with an address in Seton Street, off the Kennington Road."

Mrs. Hilbery fidgeted rather restlessly, and hummed fragments of her tune, as if to interrupt.

"I went to Seton Street," Aunt Celia continued firmly. "A very low place—lodging-houses, you know, with canaries in the window. Number seven just like all the others. I rang, I knocked; no one came. I went down the area. I am certain I saw some one inside—children—a cradle. But no reply—no reply." She sighed, and looked straight in front of her with a glazed expression in her half-veiled blue eyes.

"I stood in the street," she resumed, "in case I could catch a sight of one of them. It seemed a very long time. There were rough men singing in the public-house round the corner. At last the door opened, and some one—it must have been the woman herself—came right past me. There was only the pillar-box between us."

"And what did she look like?" Mrs. Hilbery demanded.

"One could see how the poor boy had been deluded," was all that Mrs. Milvain vouchsafed by way of description.

"Poor thing!" Mrs. Hilbery exclaimed.

"Poor *Cyril!*" Mrs. Milvain said, laying a slight emphasis upon Cyril.

"But they've got nothing to live upon," Mrs. Hilbery continued. "If he'd come to us like a man," she went on, "and said, 'I've been a fool,' one would have pitied him; one would have tried to help him. There's nothing so disgraceful after all—But he's been going about all these years, pretending, letting one take it for granted, that he was single. And the poor deserted little wife——"

"She is *not* his wife," Aunt Celia interrupted.

"I've never heard anything so detestable!" Mrs. Hilbery wound up, striking her fist on the arm of her chair. As she realized the facts she became thoroughly disgusted, although, perhaps, she was more hurt by the concealment of the sin than by the sin itself. She looked splendidly roused and indignant; and Katharine felt an immense relief and pride in her mother. It was plain that her indignation was very genuine, and that her mind was as perfectly focused upon the facts as any one could wish—more so, by a long way, than Aunt Celia's mind, which seemed to be timidly circling, with a morbid pleasure, in these unpleasant shades. She and her mother together would take the situation in hand, visit Cyril, and see the whole thing through.

"We must realize Cyril's point of view first," she said, speaking directly to her mother, as if to a contemporary, but before the words were out of her mouth, there was more confusion outside, and Cousin Caroline, Mrs. Hilbery's maiden cousin, entered the room. Although she was by birth an Alardyce, and Aunt Celia a Hilbery, the complexities of the family relationship were such that each was at once first and second cousin to the other, and thus aunt and cousin to the culprit Cyril, so that his misbehavior was almost as much Cousin Caroline's affair as Aunt Celia's.

Cousin Caroline was a lady of very imposing height and circumference, but in spite of her size and her handsome trappings, there was something exposed and unsheltered in her expression, as if for many summers her thin red skin and hooked nose and reduplication of chins, so much resembling the profile of a cockatoo, had been bared to the weather; she was, indeed, a single lady; but she had, it was the habit to say, "made a life for herself," and was thus entitled to be heard with respect.

"This unhappy business," she began, out of breath as she was. "If the train had not gone out of the station just as I arrived, I should have been with you before. Celia has doubtless told you. You will agree with me, Maggie. He must be made to marry her at once—for the sake of the children——"

"But does he refuse to marry her?" Mrs. Hilbery inquired, with a return of her bewilderment.

"He has written an absurd perverted letter, all quotations," Cousin Caroline puffed. "He thinks he's doing a very fine thing, where we only see the folly of it. . . . The girl's every bit as infatuated as he is—for which I blame him."

"*She* entangled *him*," Aunt Celia intervened, with a very curious smoothness of intonation, which seemed to convey a vision of threads weaving and interweaving a close, white mesh round their victim.

"It's no use going into the rights and wrongs of the affair now, Celia," said Cousin Caroline with some acerbity, for she believed herself the only practical one of the family, and regretted that, owing to the slowness of the kitchen clock, Mrs. Milvain had already confused poor dear Maggie with her own incomplete version of the facts. "The mischief's done, and very ugly mischief too. Are we to allow the third child to be born out of wedlock? (I am sorry to have to say these things before you, Katharine.) He will bear your name, Maggie—your father's name, remember."

"But let us hope it will be a girl," said Mrs. Hilbery.

Katharine, who had been looking at her mother constantly, while the chatter of tongues held sway, perceived that the look of straightforward indignation had already vanished; her mother was evidently casting about in her mind for some method of escape, or bright spot, or sudden illumination which should show to the satisfaction of everybody that all had happened, miraculously but incontestably, for the best.

"It's detestable—quite detestable!" she repeated, but in tones of no great assurance; and then her face lit up with a smile which, tentative at first, soon became almost assured. "Nowadays, people don't think so badly of these things as they used to do," she began. "It will be horribly uncomfortable for them sometimes, but if they are brave, clever children, as they will be, I dare say it'll make remarkable people of them in the end. Robert Browning used to say that every great man has Jewish blood in him, and we must try to look at it in that light. And, after all, Cyril has acted on principle. One may disagree with his principle, but, at least, one can respect it—like the French Revolution, or Cromwell cutting the King's head off. Some of the most terrible things in history have been done on principle," she concluded.

"I'm afraid I take a very different view of principle," Cousin Caroline remarked tartly.

"Principle!" Aunt Celia repeated, with an air of deprecating such a word in such a connection. "I will go to-morrow and see him," she added.

"But why should you take these disagreeable things upon yourself, Celia?" Mrs. Hilbery interposed, and Cousin Caroline thereupon protested with some further plan involving sacrifice of herself.

Growing weary of it all, Katharine turned to the window, and stood among the folds of the curtain, pressing close to the window-pane, and gazing disconsolately at the river much in the attitude of a child depressed by the meaningless talk of its elders. She was much disappointed in her mother

—and in herself too. The little tug which she gave to the blind, letting it fly up to the top with a snap, signified her annoyance. She was very angry, and yet impotent to give expression to her anger, or know with whom she was angry. How they talked and moralized and made up stories to suit their own version of the becoming, and secretly praised their own devotion and tact! No; they had their dwelling in a mist, she decided; hundreds of miles away—away from what? "Perhaps it would be better if I married William," she thought suddenly, and the thought appeared to loom through the mist like solid ground. She stood there, thinking of her own destiny, and the elder ladies talked on, until they had talked themselves into a decision to ask the young woman to luncheon, and tell her, very friendlily, how such behavior appeared to women like themselves, who knew the world. And then Mrs. Hilbery was struck by a better idea.

CHAPTER X

MESSRS. GRATELEY AND HOOPER, the solicitors in whose firm Ralph Denham was clerk, had their office in Lincoln's Inn Fields, and there Ralph Denham appeared every morning very punctually at ten o'clock. His punctuality, together with other qualities, marked him out among the clerks for success, and indeed it would have been safe to wager that in ten years' time or so one would find him at the head of his profession, had it not been for a peculiarity which sometimes seemed to make everything about him uncertain and perilous. His sister Joan had already been disturbed by his love of gambling with his savings. Scrutinizing him constantly with the eye of affection, she had become aware of a curious perversity in his temperament which caused her much anxiety, and would have caused her still more if she had not recognized the germs of it in her own nature. She could fancy Ralph suddenly sacrificing his entire career for some fantastic imagination; some cause or idea or even (so her fancy ran) for some woman seen from a railway train, hanging up clothes in a back yard. When he had found this beauty or this cause, no force, she knew, would avail to restrain him from pursuit of it. She suspected the East also, and always fidgeted herself when she saw him with a book of Indian travels in his hand, as though he were sucking contagion from the page. On the other hand, no common love affair, had there been such a thing, would have caused her a moment's uneasiness where Ralph was concerned. He was destined in her fancy for something splendid in the way of success or failure, she knew not which.

And yet nobody could have worked harder or done better

in all the recognized stages of a young man's life than Ralph had done, and Joan had to gather materials for her fears from trifles in her brother's behavior which would have escaped any other eye. It was natural that she should be anxious. Life had been so arduous for all of them from the start that she could not help dreading any sudden relaxation of his grasp upon what he held, though, as she knew from inspection of her own life, such sudden impulse to let go and make away from the discipline and the drudgery was sometimes almost irresistible. But with Ralph, if he broke away, she knew that it would be only to put himself under harsher constraint; she figured him toiling through sandy deserts under a tropical sun to find the source of some river or the haunt of some fly; she figured him living by the labor of his hands in some city slum, the victim of one of those terrible theories of right and wrong which were current at the time; she figured him prisoner for life in the house of a woman who had seduced him by her misfortunes. Half proudly, and wholly anxiously, she framed such thoughts, as they sat, late at night, talking together over the gas-stove in Ralph's bedroom.

It is likely that Ralph would not have recognized his own dream of a future in the forecasts which disturbed his sister's peace of mind. Certainly, if any one of them had been put before him he would have rejected it with a laugh, as the sort of life that held no attractions for him. He could not have said how it was that he had put these absurd notions into his sister's head. Indeed, he prided himself upon being well broken into a life of hard work, about which he had no sort of illusions. His vision of his own future, unlike many such forecasts, could have been made public at any moment without a blush; he attributed to himself a strong brain, and conferred on himself a seat in the House of Commons at the age of fifty, a moderate fortune, and, with luck, an unimportant office in a Liberal Government. There was nothing extravagant in a forecast of that kind, and certainly nothing dishonorable. Nevertheless, as his sister guessed, it needed all Ralph's strength of will, together with the pressure of circumstances, to keep his feet moving in the path which led that way. It needed, in particular, a constant repetition of a phrase to the effect that he shared the common fate, found it best of all, and wished for no other; and by repeating such phrases he acquired punctuality and habits of work, and could very plausibly demonstrate that to be a clerk in a solicitor's office was the best of all possible lives, and that other ambitions were vain.

But, like all beliefs not genuinely held, this one depended very much upon the amount of acceptance it received from other people, and in private, when the pressure of public opinion was removed, Ralph let himself swing very rapidly away from his actual circumstances upon strange voyages which, indeed, he would have been ashamed to describe. In these dreams, of course, he figured in noble and romantic parts, but self-glorification was not the only motive of them. They gave outlet to some spirit which found no work to do in real life, for, with the pessimism which his lot forced upon him, Ralph had made up his mind that there was no use for what, contemptuously enough, he called dreams, in the world which we inhabit. It sometimes seemed to him that this spirit was the most valuable possession he had; he thought that by means of it he could set flowering waste tracts of the earth, cure many ills, or raise up beauty where none now existed; it was, too, a fierce and potent spirit which would devour the dusty books and parchments on the office wall with one lick of its tongue, and leave him in a min-ute standing in nakedness, if he gave way to it. His endeav-or, for many years, had been to control the spirit, and at the age of twenty-nine he thought he could pride himself upon a life rigidly divided into the hours of work and those of dreams; the two lived side by side without harming each other. As a matter of fact, this effort at discipline had been helped by the interests of a difficult profession, but the old conclusion to which Ralph had come when he left college still held sway in his mind, and tinged his views with the melancholy belief that life for most people compels the exercise of the lower gifts and wastes the precious ones, until it forces us to agree that there is little virtue, as well as little profit, in what once seemed to us the noblest part of our inheritance.

Denham was not altogether popular either in his office or among his family. He was too positive, at this stage of his career, as to what was right and what wrong, too proud of his self-control, and, as is natural in the case of persons not altogether happy or well suited in their conditions, too apt to prove the folly of contentment, if he found any one who confessed to that weakness. In the office his rather ostentatious efficiency annoyed those who took their own work more lightly, and, if they foretold his advancement, it was not altogether sympathetically. Indeed, he appeared to be rather a hard and self-sufficient young man, with a queer temper, and manners that were uncompromisingly abrupt, who was consumed with a desire to get on in the world, which was natural, these critics thought, in a man of no means, but not engaging.

The young men in the office had a perfect right to these opinions, because Denham showed no particular desire for their friendship. He liked them well enough, but shut them up in that compartment of life which was devoted to work. Hitherto, indeed, he had found little difficulty in arranging his life as methodically as he arranged his expenditure, but about this time he began to encounter experiences which were not so easy to classify. Mary Datchet had begun this confusion two years ago by bursting into laughter at some remark of his, almost the first time they met. She could not explain why it was. She thought him quite astonishingly odd. When he knew her well enough to tell her how he spent Monday and Wednesday and Saturday, she was still more amused; she laughed till he laughed, too, without knowing why. It seemed to her very odd that he should know as much about breeding bulldogs as any man in England; that he had a collection of wild flowers found near London; and his weekly visit to old Miss Trotter at Ealing, who was an authority upon the science of Heraldry, never failed to excite her laughter. She wanted to know everything, even the kind of cake which the old lady supplied on these occasions; and their summer excursions to churches in the neighborhood of London for the purpose of taking rubbings of the brasses became most important festivals, from the interest she took in them. In six months she knew more about his odd friends and hobbies than his own brothers and sisters knew, after living with him all his life; and Ralph found this very pleasant, though disordering, for his own view of himself had always been profoundly serious.

Certainly it was very pleasant to be with Mary Datchet and to become, directly the door was shut, quite a different sort of person, eccentric and lovable, with scarcely any likeness to the self most people knew. He became less serious, and rather less dictatorial at home, for he was apt to hear Mary laughing at him, and telling him, as she was fond of doing, that he knew nothing at all about anything. She made him, also, take an interest in public questions, for which she had a natural liking; and was in process of turning him from Tory to Radical, after a course of public meetings, which began by boring him acutely, and ended by exciting him even more than they excited her.

But he was reserved; when ideas started up in his mind, he divided them automatically into those he could discuss with Mary, and those he must keep for himself. She knew this and it interested her, for she was accustomed to find young men very ready to talk about themselves, and had come to listen to them as one listens to children, without any thought of herself. But with Ralph, she had very little of this maternal feeling, and, in consequence, a much keener sense of her own individuality.

Late one afternoon Ralph stepped along the Strand to an interview with a lawyer upon business. The afternoon light was almost over, and already streams of greenish and yellowish artificial light were being poured into an atmosphere which, in country lanes, would now have been soft with the smoke of wood fires; and on both sides of the road the shop windows were full of sparkling chains and highly polished leather cases, which stood upon shelves made of thick plate-glass. None of these different objects was seen separately by Denham, but from all of them he drew an impression of stir and cheerfulness. Thus it came about that he saw Katharine Hilbery coming towards him, and looked straight at her, as if she were only an illustration of the argument that was going forward in his mind. In this spirit he noticed the rather set expression in her eyes, and the slight, half-conscious movement of her lips, which, together with her height and the distinction of her dress, made her look as if the scurrying crowd impeded her, and her direction were different from theirs. He noticed this calmly; but suddenly, as he passed her, his hands and knees began to tremble, and his heart beat painfully. She did not see him, and went on repeating to herself some lines which had stuck to her memory: "It's life that matters, nothing but life—the process of discovering—the everlasting and perpetual process, not the discovery itself at all." Thus occupied, she did not see Denham, and he had not the courage to stop her. But immediately the whole scene in the Strand wore that curious look of order and purpose which is imparted to the most heterogeneous things when music sounds; and so pleasant was this impression that he was very glad that he had not stopped her, after all. It grew slowly fainter, but lasted until he stood outside the barrister's chambers.

When his interview with the barrister was over, it was too late to go back to the office. His sight of Katharine had put him queerly out of tune for a domestic evening. Where should he go? To walk through the streets of London until he came to Katharine's house, to look up at the windows and fancy her within, seemed to him possible for a moment; and then he rejected the plan almost with a blush as, with a curious division of consciousness, one plucks a flower sentimentally and throws it away, with a blush, when

it is actually picked. No, he would go and see Mary Datchet. By this time she would be back from her work.

To see Ralph appear unexpectedly in her room threw
Mary for a second off her balance. She had been cleaning
knives in her little scullery, and when she had let him in she
went back again, and turned on the cold-water tap to its
fullest volume, and then turned it off again. "Now," she
thought to herself, as she screwed it tight, "I'm not going to
let these silly ideas come into my head. . . . Don't you
think Mr. Asquith deserves to be hanged?" she called back
into the sitting-room, and when she joined him, drying her
hands, she began to tell him about the latest evasion on the
part of the Government with respect to the Women's Suffrage Bill. Ralph did not want to talk about politics, but
he could not help respecting Mary for taking such an interest
in public questions. He looked at her as she leant forward,
poking the fire, and expressing herself very clearly in phrases
which bore distantly the taint of the platform, and he
thought, "How absurd Mary would think me if she knew
that I almost made up my mind to walk all the way to
Chelsea in order to look at Katharine's windows. She
wouldn't understand it, but I like her very much as she is."

For some time they discussed what the women had better
do; and as Ralph became genuinely interested in the question, Mary unconsciously let her attention wander, and a
great desire came over her to talk to Ralph about her own
feelings; or, at any rate, about something personal, so that
she might see what he felt for her; but she resisted this wish.
But she could not prevent him from feeling her lack of
interest in what he was saying, and gradually they both became silent. One thought after another came up in Ralph's
mind, but they were all, in some way, connected with Katharine, or with vague feelings of romance and adventure such
as she inspired. But he could not talk to Mary about such
thoughts; and he pitied her for knowing nothing of what he
was feeling. "Here," he thought, "is where we differ from
women; they have no sense of romance."

"Well, Mary," he said at length, "why don't you say something amusing?"

His tone was certainly provoking, but, as a general rule, Mary was not easily provoked. This evening, however, she replied rather sharply:

"Because I've got nothing amusing to say, I suppose."

Ralph thought for a moment, and then remarked:

"You work too hard. I don't mean your health," he added, as she laughed scornfully, "I mean that you seem to me to be getting wrapped up in your work."

"And is that a bad thing?" she asked, shading her eyes with her hand.

"I think it is," he returned abruptly.

"But only a week ago you were saying the opposite." Her tone was defiant, but she became curiously depressed. Ralph did not perceive it, and took this opportunity of lecturing her, and expressing his latest views upon the proper conduct of life. She listened, but her main impression was that he had been meeting some one who had influenced him. He was telling her that she ought to read more, and to see that there were other points of view as deserving of attention as her own. Naturally, having last seen him as he left the office in company with Katharine, she attributed the change to her; it was likely that Katharine, on leaving the scene which she had so clearly despised, had pronounced some such criticism, or suggested it by her own attitude. But she knew that Ralph would never admit that he had been influenced by anybody.

"You don't read enough, Mary," he was saying. "You ought to read more poetry."

It was true that Mary's reading had been rather limited to such works as she needed to know for the sake of examinations; and her time for reading in London was very little. For some reason, no one likes to be told that they do not read enough poetry, but her resentment was only visible in the way she changed the position of her hands, and in the fixed look in her eyes. And then she thought to herself.

"I'm behaving exactly as I said I wouldn't behave," whereupon she relaxed all her muscles and said, in her reasonable way:

"Tell me what I ought to read, then."

Ralph had unconsciously been irritated by Mary, and he now delivered himself of a few names of great poets which were the text for a discourse upon the imperfection of Mary's character and way of life.

"You live with your inferiors," he said, warming unreasonably, as he knew, to his text. "And you get into a groove because, on the whole, it's rather a pleasant groove. And you tend to forget what you're there for. You've the feminine habit of making much of details. You don't see when things matter and when they don't. And that's what's the ruin of all these organizations. That's why the Suffragists have never done anything all these years. What's the point of drawing-room meetings and bazaars? You want to have ideas, Mary; get hold of something big; never mind making mistakes, but don't niggle. Why don't you throw it all up for a year, and travel?—see something of the world. Don't be content to live with half a dozen people in a backwater all your life. But you won't," he concluded.

"I've rather come to that way of thinking myself—about myself, I mean," said Mary, surprising him by her acquiescence. "I should like to go somewhere far away."

For a moment they were both silent. Ralph then said:

"But look here, Mary, you haven't been taking this seriously, have you?" His irritation was spent, and the depression, which she could not keep out of her voice, made him feel suddenly with remorse that he had been hurting her.

"You won't go away, will you?" he asked. And as she said nothing, he added, "Oh no, don't go away."

"I don't know exactly what I mean to do," she replied. She hovered on the verge of some discussion of her plans, but she received no encouragement. He fell into one of his queer silences, which seemed to Mary, in spite of all her precautions, to have reference to what she also could not prevent herself from thinking about—their feeling for each other and their relationship. She felt that the two lines of thought bored their way in long, parallel tunnels which came very close indeed, but never ran into each other.

When he had gone, and he left her without breaking his silence more than was needed to wish her good night, she sat on for a time, reviewing what he had said. If love is a devastating fire which melts the whole being into one mountain torrent, Mary was no more in love with Denham than she was in love with her poker or her tongs. But probably these extreme passions are very rare, and the state of mind thus depicted belongs to the very last stages of love, when the power to resist has been eaten away, week by week or day by day. Like most intelligent people, Mary was something of an egoist, to the extent, that is, of attaching great importance to what she felt, and she was by nature enough of a moralist to like to make certain, from time to time, that her feelings were creditable to her. When Ralph left her she thought over her state of mind, and came to the conclusion that it would be a good thing to learn a language—say Italian or German. She then went to a drawer, which she had to unlock, and took from it certain deeply scored manuscript pages. She read them through, looking up from her reading every now and then and thinking very intently for a few seconds about Ralph. She did her best to verify all the qualities in him which gave rise to emotions in her; and persuaded herself that she accounted reasonably for them all. Then she looked back again at her manuscript, and decided that to write grammatical English prose is the hardest thing in the world. But she thought about herself a great deal more than she thought about grammatical English prose or about Ralph Denham, and it may therefore be disputed whether she was in love, or, if so, to which branch of the family her passion belonged.

CHAPTER XI

"IT'S life that matters, nothing but life—the process of discovering, the everlasting and perpetual process," said Katharine, as she passed under the archway, and so into the wide space of King's Bench Walk, "not the discovery itself at all." She spoke the last words looking up at Rodney's windows, which were a semilucent red color, in her honor, as she knew. He had asked her to tea with him. But she was in a mood when it is almost physically disagreeable to interrupt the stride of one's thought, and she walked up and down two or three times under the trees before approaching his staircase. She liked getting hold of some book which neither her father or mother had read, and keeping it to herself, and gnawing its contents in privacy, and pondering the meaning without sharing her thoughts with any one, or having to decide whether the book was a good one or a bad one. This evening she had twisted the words of Dostoevsky to suit her mood—a fatalistic mood—to proclaim that the process of discovery was life, and that, presumably, the nature of one's goal mattered not at all. She sat down for a moment upon one of the seats; felt herself carried along in the swirl of many things; decided, in her sudden way, that it was time to heave all this thinking overboard, and rose, leaving a fishmonger's basket on the seat behind her. Two minutes later her rap sounded with authority upon Rodney's door.

"Well, William," she said, "I'm afraid I'm late."

It was true, but he was so glad to see her that he forgot his annoyance. He had been occupied for over an hour in making things ready for her, and he now had his reward in seeing her look right and left, as she slipped her cloak from her shoulders, with evident satisfaction, although she said nothing. He had seen that the fire burnt well; jam-pots were on the table, tin covers shone in the fender, and the shabby comfort of the room was extreme. He was dressed in his old crimson dressing-gown, which was faded irregularly, and had bright new patches on it, like the paler grass which one finds on lifting a stone. He made the tea, and Katharine drew off her gloves, and crossed her legs with a gesture that was rather masculine in its ease. Nor did they talk much until they were smoking cigarettes over the fire, having placed their teacups upon the floor between them.

They had not met since they had exchanged letters about their relationship. Katharine's answer to his protestation had been short and sensible. Half a sheet of notepaper contained the whole of it, for she merely had to say that she was not in love with him, and so could not marry him, but their friendship would continue, she hoped, unchanged. She had added a postscript in which she stated, "I like your sonnet very much."

So far as William was concerned, this appearance of ease was assumed. Three times that afternoon he had dressed himself in a tail-coat, and three times he had discarded it for an old dressing-gown; three times he had placed his pearl tie-pin in position, and three times he had removed it again, the little looking-glass in his room being the witness of these changes of mind. The question was, which would Katharine prefer on this particular afternoon in December? He read her note once more, and the postscript about the sonnet settled the matter. Evidently she admired most the poet in him; and as this, on the whole, agreed with his own opinion, he decided to err, if anything, on the side of shabbiness. His demeanor was also regulated with premeditation; he spoke little, and only on impersonal matters; he wished her to realize that in visiting him for the first time alone she was doing nothing remarkable, although, in fact, that was a point about which he was not at all sure.

Certainly Katharine seemed quite unmoved by any disturbing thoughts; and if he had been completely master of himself, he might, indeed, have complained that she was a trifle absent-minded. The ease, the familiarity of the situation alone with Rodney, among teacups and candles, had more effect upon her than was apparent. She asked to look at his books, and then at his pictures. It was while she held a photograph from the Greek in her hands that she exclaimed, impulsively, if incongruously:

"My oysters! I had a basket," she explained, "and I've left it somewhere. Uncle Dudley dines with us to-night. What in the world have I done with them?"

She rose and began to wander about the room. William rose also, and stood in front of the fire, muttering, "Oysters, oysters—your basket of oysters!" but though he looked vaguely here and there, as if the oysters might be on the top of the bookshelf, his eyes returned always to Katharine. She drew the curtain and looked out among the scanty leaves of the plane-trees.

"I had them," she calculated, "in the Strand; I sat on a seat. Well, never mind," she concluded, turning back into the room abruptly, "I dare say some old creature is enjoying them by this time."

"I should have thought that you never forgot anything," William remarked, as they settled down again.

"That's part of the myth about me, I know," Katharine replied.

"And I wonder," William proceeded, with some caution, "what the truth about you is? But I know this sort of thing doesn't interest you," he added hastily, with a touch of peevishness.

"No; it doesn't interest me very much," she replied candidly.

"What shall we talk about then?" he asked.

She looked rather whimsically round the walls of the room.

"However we start, we end by talking about the same thing—about poetry, I mean. I wonder if you realize,

William, that I've never read even Shakespeare? It's rather wonderful how I've kept it up all these years."

"You've kept it up for ten years very beautifully, as far as I'm concerned," he said.

"Ten years? So long as that?"

"And I don't think it's always bored you," he added.

She looked into the fire silently. She could not deny that the surface of her feeling was absolutely unruffled by anything in William's character; on the contrary, she felt certain that she could deal with whatever turned up. He gave her peace, in which she could think of things that were far removed from what they talked about. Even now, when he sat within a yard of her, how easily her mind ranged hither and thither! Suddenly a picture presented itself before her, without any effort on her part as pictures will, of herself in these very rooms; she had come in from a lecture, and she held a pile of books in her hand, scientific books, and books about mathematics and astronomy which she had mastered. She put them down on the table over there. It was a picture plucked from her life two or three years hence, when she was married to William; but here she checked herself abruptly.

She could not entirely forget William's presence, because, in spite of his efforts to control himself, his nervousness was apparent. On such occasions his eyes protruded more than ever, and his face had more than ever the appearance of being covered with a thin crackling skin, through which every flush of his volatile blood showed itself instantly. By this time he had shaped so many sentences and rejected them, felt so many impulses and subdued them, that he was a uniform scarlet.

"You may say you don't read books," he remarked, "but, all the same, you know about them. Besides, who wants you to be learned? Leave that to the poor devils who've got nothing better to do. You—you—ahem!——"

"Well, then, why don't you read me something before I go?" said Katharine, looking at her watch.

"Katharine, you've only just come! Let me see now, what have I got to show you?" He rose, and stirred about the papers on his table, as if in doubt; he then picked up a manuscript, and after spreading it smoothly upon his knee, he looked up at Katharine suspiciously. He caught her smiling.

"I believe you only ask me to read out of kindness," he burst out. "Let's find something else to talk about. Who have you been seeing?"

"I don't generally ask things out of kindness," Katharine observed; "however, if you don't want to read, you needn't."

William gave a queer snort of exasperation, and opened his manuscript once more, though he kept his eyes upon her face as he did so. No face could have been graver or more judicial.

"One can trust you, certainly, to say unpleasant things," he said, smoothing out the page, clearing his throat, and reading half a stanza to himself. "Ahem! The Princess is lost in the wood, and she hears the sound of a horn. (This would all be very pretty on the stage, but I can't get the effect here.) Anyhow, Sylvano enters, accompanied by the rest of the gentlemen of Gratian's court. I begin where he soliloquizes." He jerked his head and began to read.

Although Katharine had just disclaimed any knowledge of literature, she listened attentively. At least, she listened to the first twenty-five lines attentively, and then she frowned. Her attention was only aroused again when Rodney raised his finger—a sign, she knew, that the meter was about to change.

His theory was that every mood has its meter. His mastery of meters was very great; and, if the beauty of a drama depended upon the variety of measures in which the personages speak, Rodney's plays must have challenged the works of Shakespeare. Katharine's ignorance of Shakespeare did not prevent her from feeling fairly certain that plays should not produce a sense of chill stupor in the audience, such as overcame her as the lines flowed on, sometimes long and sometimes short, but always delivered with the same lilt of voice, which seemed to nail each line firmly on to the same spot in the hearer's brain. Still, she reflected, these sorts of skill are almost exclusively masculine; women neither practice them nor know how to value them; and one's husband's proficiency in this direction might legitimately increase one's respect for him, since mystification is no bad basis for respect. No one could doubt that William was a scholar. The reading ended with the finish of the Act; Katharine had prepared a little speech.

"That seems to me extremely well written, William; although, of course, I don't know enough to criticize in detail."

"But it's the skill that strikes you—not the emotion?"

"In a fragment like that, of course, the skill strikes one most."

"But perhaps—have you time to listen to one more short piece? the scene between the lovers? There's some real feeling in that, I think. Denham agrees that it's the best thing I've done."

"You've read it to Ralph Denham?" Katharine inquired, with surprise. "He's a better judge than I am. What did he say?"

"My dear Katharine," Rodney exclaimed, "I don't ask you for criticism, as I should ask a scholar. I dare say there are only five men in England whose opinion of my work matters a straw to me. But I trust you where feeling is concerned. I had you in my mind often when I was writing those scenes. I kept asking myself, 'Now is this the sort of thing Katharine would like?' I always think of you when I'm writing, Katharine, even when it's the sort of thing you wouldn't know about. And I'd rather—yes, I really believe I'd rather—you thought well of my writing than any one in the world."

This was so genuine a tribute to his trust in her that Katharine was touched.

"You think too much of me altogether, William," she said, forgetting that she had not meant to speak in this way.

"No, Katharine, I don't," he replied, replacing his manuscript in the drawer. "It does me good to think of you."

So quiet an answer, followed as it was by no expression of love, but merely by the statement that if she must go he would take her to the Strand, and would, if she could wait a moment, change his dressing-gown for a coat, moved her to the warmest feeling of affection for him that she had yet experienced. While he changed in the next room, she stood by the bookcase, taking down books and opening them, but reading nothing on their pages.

She felt certain that she would marry Rodney. How could one avoid it? How could one find fault with it? Here she sighed, and, putting the thought of marriage away, fell into a dream state, in which she became another person, and the whole world seemed changed. Being a frequent visitor to that world, she could find her way there unhesitatingly. If she had tried to analyze her impressions, she would have said that there dwelt the realities of the appearances which figure in our world; so direct, powerful, and unimpeded were her sensations there, compared with those called forth in actual life. There dwelt the things one might have felt, had there been cause; the perfect happiness of which here we taste the fragment; the beauty seen here in flying glimpses only. No doubt much of the furniture of this world was drawn directly from the past, and even from the England of the Elizabethan age. However the embellishment of this imaginary world might change, two qualities were constant in it. It was a place where feelings were liberated from the constraint which the real world puts upon them; and the process of awakenment was always marked by resignation and a kind of stoical acceptance of facts. She met no acquaintance there, as Denham did, miraculously transfigured; she played no heroic part. But there certainly she loved some magnanimous hero, and as they swept together among the leaf-hung trees of an unknown world, they shared the feelings which came fresh and fast as the waves on the shore. But the sands of her liberation were running fast; even through the forest branches came sounds of Rodney moving things on his dressing-table; and Katharine woke herself from this excursion by shutting the cover of the book she was holding, and replacing it in the bookshelf.

"William," she said, speaking rather faintly at first, like one sending a voice from sleep to reach the living. "William," she repeated firmly, "if you still want me to marry you, I will."

Perhaps it was that no man could expect to have the most momentous question of his life settled in a voice so level, so toneless, so devoid of joy or energy. At any rate William made no answer. She waited stoically. A moment later he stepped briskly from his dressing-room, and observed that if she wanted to buy more oysters he thought he knew where they could find a fishmonger's shop still open. She breathed deeply a sigh of relief.

Extract from a letter sent a few days later by Mrs. Hilbery to her sister-in-law, Mrs. Milvain:

" . . . How stupid of me to forget the name in my telegram. Such a nice, rich, English name, too, and, in addition, he has all the graces of intellect; he has read literally *everything*. I tell Katharine, I shall always put him on my right side at dinner, so as to have him by me when people begin talking about characters in Shakespeare. They won't be rich, but they'll be very, very happy. I was sitting in my room late one night, feeling that nothing nice would ever happen to me again, when I heard Katharine outside in the passage, and I thought to myself, 'Shall I call her in?' and then I thought (in that hopeless, dreary way one does think, with the fire going out and one's birthday just over), 'Why should I lay my troubles on *her?*' But my little self-control had its reward, for next moment she tapped at the door and came in, and sat on the rug, and though we neither of us said anything, I felt so happy all of a second that I couldn't help crying, 'Oh, Katharine, when you come to my age, how I hope you'll have a daughter, too!' You know how silent Katharine is. She was so silent, for such a long time, that in my foolish, nervous state I dreaded something, I don't quite know what. And then she told me how, after all, she had made up her mind. She had written. She expected him to-morrow. At first I wasn't glad at all. I didn't want her to marry any one; but when she said, 'It will make no difference. I shall always care for you and father most,' then I saw how selfish I was, and I told her she must give him everything, everything, everything! I told her I should be thankful to come second. But why, when everything's turned out just as one always hoped it would turn out, why then can one do nothing but cry, nothing but feel a desolate old woman whose life's been a failure, and now is nearly over, and age is so cruel? But Katharine said to me, 'I am happy. I'm very happy.' And then I thought, though it all seemed so desperately dismal at the time, Katharine had said she was happy, and I should have a son, and it would all turn out so much more wonderfully than I could possibly imagine, for though the sermons don't say so, I do believe the world is meant for us to be happy in. She told me that they would live quite near us, and see us every day; and she would go on with the Life, and we should finish it as we had meant to. And, after all, it would be far more horrid if she didn't marry—or suppose she married some one we couldn't endure? Suppose she had fallen in love with some one who was married already?

"And though one never thinks any one good enough for the people one's fond of, he has the kindest, truest instincts, I'm sure, and though he seems nervous and his manner is not commanding, I only think these things because it's Katharine. And now I've written this, it comes over me that, of course, all the time, Katharine has what he hasn't. She does command, she isn't nervous; it comes naturally to her to rule and control. It's time that she should give all this to some one who will need her when we aren't there, save in our spirits, for whatever people say, I'm sure I shall come back to this wonderful world where one's been so happy and so miserable, where, even now, I seem to see myself stretching out my hands for another present from the great Fairy Tree whose boughs are still hung with enchanting toys, though they are rarer now, perhaps, and between the branches one sees no longer the blue sky, but the stars and the tops of the mountains.

"One doesn't know any more, does one? One hasn't any advice to give one's children. One can only hope that they will have the same vision and the same power to believe, without which life would be so meaningless. That is what I ask for Katharine and her husband."

CHAPTER XII

I S Mr. Hilbery at home, or Mrs. Hilbery?" Denham asked, of the parlor maid in Chelsea, a week later.

"No, sir. But Miss Hilbery is at home," the girl answered.

Ralph had anticipated many answers, but not this one, and now it was unexpectedly made plain to him that it was the chance of seeing Katharine that had brought him all the way to Chelsea on pretence of seeing her father.

He made some show of considering the matter, and was taken upstairs to the drawing-room. As upon that first occasion, some weeks ago, the door closed as if it were a thousand doors softly excluding the world; and once more Ralph received an impression of a room full of deep shadows, firelight, unwavering silver candle flames, and empty spaces to be crossed before reaching the round table in the middle of the room, with its frail burden of silver trays and china teacups. But this time Katharine was there by herself; the volume in her hand showed that she expected no visitors.

Ralph said something about hoping to find her father.

"My father is out," she replied. "But if you can wait, I expect him soon."

It might have been due merely to politeness, but Ralph felt that she received him almost with cordiality. Perhaps she was bored by drinking tea and reading a book all alone; at any rate, she tossed the book on to a sofa with a gesture of relief.

"Is that one of the moderns whom you despise?" he asked, smiling at the carelessness of her gesture.

"Yes," she replied. "I think even you would despise him."

"Even I?" he repeated. "Why even I?"

"You said you liked modern things; I said I hated them."

This was not a very accurate report of their conversation among the relics, perhaps, but Ralph was flattered to think that she remembered anything about it.

"Or did I confess that I hated all books?" she went on, seeing him look up with an air of inquiry. "I forget——"

"Do you hate all books?" he asked.

"It would be absurd to say that I hate all books when I've only read ten, perhaps; but——" Here she pulled herself up short.

"Well?"

"Yes, I do hate books," she continued. "Why do you want to be for ever talking about your feelings? That's what I can't make out. And poetry's all about feelings—novels are all about feelings."

She cut a cake vigorously into slices, and providing a tray with bread and butter for Mrs. Hilbery, who was in her room with a cold, she rose to go upstairs.

Ralph held the door open for her, and then stood with clasped hands in the middle of the room. His eyes were bright, and, indeed, he scarcely knew whether they beheld dreams or realities. All down the street and on the doorstep, and while he mounted the stairs, his dream of Katharine possessed him; on the threshold of the room he had dismissed it, in order to prevent too painful a collision between what he dreamt of her and what she was. And in five minutes she had filled the shell of the old dream with the flesh of life; looked with fire out of phantom eyes. He glanced about him with bewilderment at finding himself among her chairs and tables; they were solid, for he grasped the back of the chair in which Katharine had sat; and yet they were unreal; the atmosphere was that of a dream. He summoned all the faculties of his spirit to seize what the minutes had to give him; and from the depths of his mind there rose unchecked a joyful recognition of the truth that human nature surpasses, in its beauty, all that our wildest dreams bring us hints of.

Katharine came into the room a moment later. He stood watching her come towards him, and thought her more beautiful and strange than his dream of her; for the real Katharine could speak the words which seemed to crowd behind the forehead and in the depths of the eyes, and the commonest sentence would be flashed on by this immortal light. And she overflowed the edges of the dream; he remarked that her softness was like that of some vast snowy owl; she wore a ruby on her finger.

"My mother wants me to tell you," she said, "that she hopes you have begun your poem. She says every one ought to write poetry. . . . All my relations write poetry," she went on. "I can't bear to think of it sometimes—because, of course, it's none of it any good. But then one needn't read it——"

"You don't encourage me to write a poem," said Ralph.

"But you're not a poet, too, are you?" she inquired, turning upon him with a laugh.

"Should I tell you if I were?"

"Yes. Because I think you speak the truth," she said, searching him for proof of this apparently, with eyes now almost impersonally direct. It would be easy, Ralph thought, to worship one so far removed, and yet of so straight a nature; easy to submit recklessly to her, without thought of future pain.

"Are you a poet?" she demanded. He felt that her question had an unexplained weight of meaning behind it, as if she sought an answer to a question that she did not ask.

"No. I haven't written any poetry for years," he replied. "But all the same, I don't agree with you. I think it's the only thing worth doing."

"Why do you say that?" she asked, almost with impatience, tapping her spoon two or three times against the side of her cup.

"Why?" Ralph laid hands on the first words that came

to mind. "Because, I suppose, it keeps an ideal alive which might die otherwise."

A curious change came over her face, as if the flame of her mind were subdued; and she looked at him ironically and with the expression which he had called sad before, for want of a better name for it.

"I don't know that there's much sense in having ideals," she said.

"But you have them," he replied energetically. "Why do we call them ideals? It's a stupid word. Dreams, I mean——"

She followed his words with parted lips, as though to answer eagerly when he had done; but as he said, "Dreams, I mean," the door of the drawing-room swung open, and so remained for a perceptible instant. They both held themselves silent, her lips still parted.

Far off, they heard the rustle of skirts. Then the owner of the skirts appeared in the doorway, which she almost filled, nearly concealing the figure of a very much smaller lady who accompanied her.

"My aunts!" Katharine murmured, under her breath. Her tone had a hint of tragedy in it, but no less, Ralph thought, than the situation required. She addressed the larger lady as Aunt Millicent; the smaller was Aunt Celia, Mrs. Milvain, who had lately undertaken the task of marrying Cyril to his wife. Both ladies, but Mrs. Cosham (Aunt Millicent) in particular, had that look of heightened, smoothed, incarnadined existence which is proper to elderly ladies paying calls in London about five o'clock in the afternoon. Portraits by Romney, seen through glass, have something of their pink, mellow look, their blooming softness, as of apricots hanging upon a red wall in the afternoon sun. Mrs. Cosham was so appareled with hanging muffs, chains, and swinging draperies that it was impossible to detect the shape of a human being in the mass of brown and black which filled the arm-chair. Mrs. Milvain was a much slighter figure; but the same doubt as to the precise lines of her contour filled Ralph, as he regarded them, with dismal foreboding. What remark of his would ever reach these fabulous and fantastic characters?—for there was something fantastically unreal in the curious swayings and noddings of Mrs. Cosham, as if her equipment included a large wire spring. Her voice had a high-pitched, cooing note, which prolonged words and cut them short until the English language seemed no longer fit for common purposes. In a moment of nervousness, so Ralph thought, Katharine had turned on innumerable electric lights. But Mrs. Cosham had gained impetus (perhaps her swaying movements had that end in view) for sustained speech; and she now addressed Ralph deliberately and elaborately.

"I come from Woking, Mr. Popham. You may well ask me, why Woking? and to that I answer, for perhaps the hundredth time, because of the sunsets. We went there for the sunsets, but that was five-and-twenty years ago. Where are the sunsets now? Alas! There is no sunset now nearer than the South Coast." Her rich and romantic notes were accompanied by a wave of a long white hand, which, when waved, gave off a flash of diamonds, rubies, and emeralds. Ralph wondered whether she more resembled an elephant, with a jeweled head-dress, or a superb cockatoo, balanced insecurely upon its perch, and pecking capriciously at a lump of sugar.

"Where are the sunsets now?" she repeated. "Do you find sunsets now, Mr. Popham?"

"I live at Highgate," he replied.

"At Highgate? Yes, Highgate has its charms; your Uncle John lived at Highgate," she jerked in the direction of Katharine. She sank her head upon her breast, as if for a moment's meditation, which past, she looked up and observed: "I dare say there are very pretty lanes in Highgate. I can recollect walking with your mother, Katharine, through lanes blossoming with wild hawthorn. But where is the hawthorn now? You remember that exquisite description in De Quincey, Mr. Popham?—but I forget, you, in your generation, with all your activity and enlightenment, at which I can only marvel"—here she displayed both her beautiful white hands—"do not read De Quincey. You have your Belloc, your Chesterton, your Bernard Shaw—why should you read De Quincey?"

"But I do read De Quincey," Ralph protested, "more than Belloc and Chesterton, anyhow."

"Indeed!" exclaimed Mrs. Cosham, with a gesture of surprise and relief mingled. "You are, then, a *rara avis* in your generation. I am delighted to meet any one who reads De Quincey."

Here she hollowed her hand into a screen, and, leaning towards Katharine, inquired, in a very audible whisper, "Does your friend *write*?"

"Mr. Denham," said Katharine, with more than her usual clearness and firmness, "writes for the Review. He is a lawyer."

"The clean-shaven lips, showing the expression of the mouth! I recognize them at once. I always feel at home with lawyers, Mr. Denham——"

"They used to come about us so much in the old days," Mrs. Milvain interposed, the frail, silvery notes of her voice falling with the sweet tone of an old bell.

"You say you live at Highgate," she continued. "I wonder whether you happen to know if there is an old house called Tempest Lodge still in existence—an old white house in a garden?"

Ralph shook his head, and she sighed.

"Ah, no; it must have been pulled down by this time, with all the other old houses. There were such pretty lanes in those days. That was how your uncle met your Aunt Emily, you know," she addressed Katharine. "They walked home through the lanes."

"A sprig of May in her bonnet," Mrs. Cosham ejaculated, reminiscently.

"And next Sunday he had violets in his buttonhole. And that was how we guessed."

Katharine laughed. She looked at Ralph. His eyes were meditative, and she wondered what he found in this old gossip to make him ponder so contentedly. She felt, she hardly knew why, a curious pity for him.

"Uncle John—yes, 'poor John,' you always called him. Why was that?" she asked, to make them go on talking, which, indeed, they needed little invitation to do.

"That was what his father, old Sir Richard, always called him. Poor John, or the fool of the family," Mrs. Milvain hastened to inform them. "The other boys were so brilliant, and he could never pass his examinations, so they sent him to India—a long voyage in those days, poor fellow. You had your own room, you know, and you did it up. But he will get his knighthood and a pension, I believe," she said, turning to Ralph, "only it is not England."

"No," Mrs. Cosham confirmed her, "it is not England. In those days we thought an Indian Judgeship about equal to a county-court judgeship at home. His Honor—a pretty title, but still, not at the top of the tree. However," she sighed, "if you have a wife and seven children, and people nowadays very quickly forget your father's name—well, you have to take what you can get," she concluded.

"And I fancy," Mrs. Milvain resumed, lowering her voice rather confidentially, "that John would have done more if it hadn't been for his wife, your Aunt Emily. She was a very good woman, devoted to him, of course, but she was not ambitious for him, and if a wife isn't ambitious for her husband, especially in a profession like the law, clients soon get to know of it. In our young days, Mr. Denham, we used to say that we knew which of our friends would become judges, by looking at the girls they married. And so it was, and so, I fancy, it always will be. I don't think," she added, summing up these scattered remarks, "that any man is really happy unless he succeeds in his profession."

Mrs. Cosham approved of this sentiment with more ponderous sagacity from her side of the tea-table, in the first place by swaying her head, and in the second by remarking:

"No, men are not the same as women. I fancy Alfred Tennyson spoke the truth about that as about many other things. How I wish he'd lived to write 'The Prince'—a sequel to 'The Princess'! I confess I'm almost tired of Princesses. We want some one to show us what a good man can be. We have Laura and Beatrice, Antigone and Cordelia, but we have no heroic man. How do you, as a poet, account for that, Mr. Denham?"

"I'm not a poet," said Ralph good-humoredly. "I'm only a solicitor."

"But you write, too?" Mrs. Cosham demanded, afraid lest she should be balked of her priceless discovery, a young man truly devoted to literature.

"In my spare time," Denham reassured her.

"In your spare time!" Mrs. Cosham echoed. "That is a proof of devotion, indeed." She half closed her eyes, and indulged herself in a fascinating picture of a briefless barrister lodged in a garret, writing immortal novels by the light of a farthing dip. But the romance which fell upon the figures of great writers and illumined their pages was no false radiance in her case. She carried her pocket Shakespeare about with her, and met life fortified by the words of the poets. How far she saw Denham, and how far she confused him with some hero of fiction, it would be hard to say. Literature had taken possession even of her memories. She was matching him, presumably, with certain characters in the old novels, for she came out, after a pause, with:

"Um—um—Pendennis—Warrington—I could never forgive Laura," she pronounced energetically, "for not marrying George, in spite of everything. George Eliot did the very same thing; and Lewes was a little frog-faced man, with the manner of a dancing master. But Warrington, now, had everything in his favor; intellect, passion, romance, distinction, and the connection was a mere piece of undergraduate folly. Arthur, I confess, has always seemed to me a bit of a fop; I can't imagine how Laura married him. But you say you're a solicitor, Mr. Denham. Now there are one

or two things I should like to ask you—about Shakespeare——" She drew out her small, worn volume with
some difficulty, opened it, and shook it in the air. "They
say, nowadays, that Shakespeare was a lawyer. They say,
that accounts for his knowledge of human nature. There's
a fine example for you, Mr. Denham. Study your clients,
young man, and the world will be the richer one of these
days, I have no doubt. Tell me, how do we come out of it,
now; better or worse than you expected?"

Thus called upon to sum up the worth of human nature
in a few words, Ralph answered unhesitatingly:

"Worse, Mrs. Cosham, a good deal worse. I'm afraid
the ordinary man is a bit of a rascal——"

"And the ordinary woman?"

"No, I don't like the ordinary woman either——"

Ah, dear me, I've no doubt that's very true, very true."
Mrs. Cosham sighed. "Swift would have agreed with you,
anyhow——" She looked at him, and thought that there
were signs of distinct power in his brow. He would do
well, she thought, to devote himself to satire.

"Charles Lavington, you remember, was a solicitor," Mrs.
Milvain interposed, rather resenting the waste of time involved in talking about fictitious people when you might be
talking about real people. "But you wouldn't remembe
him, Katharine."

"Mr. Lavington? Oh, yes, I do," said Katharine, waking
from other thoughts with her little start. "The summer we
had a house near Tenby. I remember the field and the pond
with the tadpoles, and making haystacks with Mr. Lavington."

"She is right. There *was* a pond with tadpoles," Mrs.
Cosham corroborated. "Millais made studies of it for
'Ophelia.' Some say that is the best picture he ever
painted——"

"And I remember the dog chained up in the yard, and the
dead snakes hanging in the toolhouse."

"It was at Tenby that you were chased by the bull," Mrs

Milvain continued. "But that you couldn't remember, though it's true you were a wonderful child. Such eyes she had, Mr. Denham! I used to say to her father, 'She's watching us, and summing us all up in her little mind.' And they had a nurse in those days," she went on, telling her story with charming solemnity to Ralph, "who was a good woman, but engaged to a sailor. When she ought to have been attending to the baby, her eyes were on the sea. And Mrs. Hilbery allowed this girl—Susan her name was—to have him to stay in the village. They abused her goodness, I'm sorry to say, and while they walked in the lanes, they stood the perambulator alone in a field where there was a bull. The animal became enraged by the red blanket in the perambulator, and Heaven knows what might have happened if a gentleman had not been walking by in the nick of time, and rescued Katharine in his arms!"

"I think the bull was only a cow, Aunt Celia," said Katharine.

"My darling, it was a great red Devonshire bull, and not long after it gored a man to death and had to be destroyed. And your mother forgave Susan—a thing I could never have done."

"Maggie's sympathies were entirely with Susan and the sailor, I am sure," said Mrs. Cosham, rather tartly. "My sister-in-law," she continued, "has laid her burdens upon Providence at every crisis in her life, and Providence, I must confess, has responded nobly, so far——"

"Yes," said Katharine, with a laugh, for she liked the rashness which irritated the rest of the family. "My mother's bulls always turn into cows at the critical moment."

"Well," said Mrs. Milvain, "I'm glad you have some one to protect you from bulls now."

"I can't imagine William protecting any one from bulls," said Katharine.

It happened that Mrs. Cosham had once more produced her pocket volume of Shakespeare, and was consulting Ralph upon an obscure passage in "Measure for Measure."

He did not at once seize the meaning of what Katharine and her aunt were saying; William, he supposed, referred to some small cousin, for he now saw Katharine as a child in a pinafore; but, nevertheless, he was so much distracted that his eye could hardly follow the words on the paper. A moment later he heard them speak distinctly of an engagement ring.

"I like rubies," he heard Katharine say.

> *"To be imprison'd in the viewless winds,*
> *And blown with restless violence round about*
> *The pendant world. . . ."*

Mrs. Cosham intoned; at the same instant "Rodney" fitted itself to "William" in Ralph's mind. He felt convinced that Katharine was engaged to Rodney. His first sensation was one of violent rage with her for having deceived him throughout the visit, fed him with pleasant old wives' tales, let him see her as a child playing in a meadow, shared her youth with him, while all the time she was a stranger entirely, and engaged to marry Rodney.

But was it possible? Surely it was not possible. For in his eyes she was still a child. He paused so long over the book that Mrs. Cosham had time to look over his shoulder and ask her niece:

"And have you settled upon a house yet, Katharine?"

This convinced him of the truth of the monstrous idea. He looked up at once and said:

"Yes, it's a difficult passage."

His voice had changed so much, he spoke with such curtness and even with such contempt, that Mrs. Cosham looked at him fairly puzzled. Happily she belonged to a generation which expected uncouthness in its men, and she merely felt convinced that this Mr. Denham was very, very clever. She took back her Shakespeare, as Denham seemed to have no more to say, and secreted it once more about her person with the infinitely pathetic resignation of the old.

"Katharine's engaged to William Rodney," she said, by

way of filling in the pause; "a very old friend of ours. He has a wonderful knowledge of literature, too—wonderful." She nodded her head rather vaguely. "You should meet each other."

Denham's one wish was to leave the house as soon as he could; but the elderly ladies had risen, and were proposing to visit Mrs. Hilbery in her bedroom, so that any move on his part was impossible. At the same time, he wished to say something, but he knew not what, to Katharine alone. She took her aunts upstairs, and returned, coming towards him once more with an air of innocence and friendliness that amazed him.

"My father will be back," she said. "Won't you sit down?" and she laughed, as if now they might share a perfectly friendly laugh at the tea-party.

But Ralph made no attempt to seat himself.

"I must congratulate you," he said. "It was news to me." He saw her face change, but only to become graver than before.

"My engagement?" she asked. "Yes, I am going to marry William Rodney."

Ralph remained standing with his hand on the back of a chair in absolute silence. Abysses seemed to plunge into darkness between them. He looked at her, but her face showed that she was not thinking of him. No regret or consciousness of wrong disturbed her.

"Well, I must go," he said at length.

She seemed about to say something, then changed her mind and said merely:

"You will come again, I hope. We always seem"—she hesitated—"to be interrupted."

He bowed and left the room.

Ralph strode with extreme swiftness along the Embankment. Every muscle was taut and braced as if to resist some sudden attack from outside. For the moment it seemed as if the attack were about to be directed against his body, and his brain thus was on the alert, but without understanding.

Finding himself, after a few minutes, no longer under observation, and no attack delivered, he slackened his pace, the
pain spread all through him, took possession of every gov-
erning seat, and met with scarcely any resistance from
powers exhausted by their first effort at defence. He took
his way languidly along the river embankment, away from
home rather than towards it. The world had him at its
mercy. He made no pattern out of the sights he saw. He
felt himself now, as he had often fancied other people,
adrift on the stream, and far removed from control of it, a
man with no grasp upon circumstances any longer. Old
battered men loafing at the doors of public-houses now
seemed to be his fellows, and he felt, as he supposed them
to feel, a mingling of envy and hatred towards those who
passed quickly and certainly to a goal of their own. They,
too, saw things very thin and shadowy, and were wafted
about by the lightest breath of wind. For the substantial
world, with its prospect of avenues leading on and on to the
invisible distance, had slipped from him, since Katharine
was engaged. Now all his life was visible, and the straight,
meager path had its ending soon enough. Katharine was
engaged, and she had deceived him, too. He felt for corners
of his being untouched by his disaster; but there was no
limit to the flood of damage; not one of his possessions was
safe now. Katharine had deceived him; she had mixed herself with every thought of his, and reft of her they seemed
false thoughts which he would blush to think again. His
life seemed immeasurably impoverished.

He sat himself down, in spite of the chilly fog which
obscured the farther bank and left its lights suspended upon
a blank surface, upon one of the riverside seats, and let the
tide of disillusionment sweep through him. For the time
being all bright points in his life were blotted out; all prom-
inences leveled. At first he made himself believe that Katharine had treated him badly, and drew comfort from the
thought that, left alone, she would recollect this, and think
of him and tender him, in silence, at any rate, an apology.

But this grain of comfort failed him after a second or two, for, upon reflection, he had to admit that Katharine owed him nothing. Katharine had promised nothing, taken nothing; to her his dreams had meant nothing. This, indeed, was the lowest pitch of his despair. If the best of one's feelings means nothing to the person most concerned in those feelings, what reality is left us? The old romance which had warmed his days for him, the thoughts of Katharine which had painted every hour, were now made to appear foolish and enfeebled. He rose, and looked into the river, whose swift race of dun-colored waters seemed the very spirit of futility and oblivion.

"In what can one trust, then?" he thought, as he leant there. So feeble and insubstantial did he feel himself that he repeated the word aloud.

"In what can one trust? Not in men and women. Not in one's dreams about them. There's nothing—nothing, nothing left at all."

Now Denham had reason to know that he could bring to birth and keep alive a fine anger when he chose. Rodney provided a good target for that emotion. And yet at the moment, Rodney and Katharine herself seemed disembodied ghosts. He could scarcely remember the look of them. His mind plunged lower and lower. Their marriage seemed of no importance to him. All things had turned to ghosts; the whole mass of the world was insubstantial vapor, surrounding the solitary spark in his mind, whose burning point he could remember, for it burnt no more. He had once cherished a belief, and Katharine had embodied this belief, and she did so no longer. He did not blame her; he blamed nothing, nobody; he saw the truth. He saw the dun-colored race of waters and the blank shore. But life is vigorous; the body lives, and the body, no doubt, dictated the reflection, which now urged him to movement, that one may cast away the forms of human beings, and yet retain the passion which seemed inseparable from their existence in the flesh. Now this passion burnt on his horizon, as the winter sun makes a greenish pane in the west through thinning clouds. His eyes were set on something infinitely far and remote; by that light he felt he could walk, and would, in future, have to find his way. But that was all there was left to him of a populous and teeming world.

CHAPTER XIII

THE lunch hour in the office was only partly spent by Denham in the consumption of food. Whether fine or wet, he passed most of it pacing the gravel paths in Lincoln's Inn Fields. The children got to know his figure, and the sparrows expected their daily scattering of breadcrumbs. No doubt, since he often gave a copper and almost always a handful of bread, he was not as blind to his surroundings as he thought himself.

He thought that these winter days were spent in long hours before white papers radiant in electric light; and in short passages through fog-dimmed streets. When he came back to his work after lunch he carried in his head a picture of the Strand, scattered with omnibuses, and of the purple shapes of leaves pressed flat upon the gravel, as if his eyes had always been bent upon the ground. His brain worked incessantly, but his thought was attended with so little joy that he did not willingly recall it; but drove ahead, now in this direction, now in that; and came home laden with dark books borrowed from a library.

Mary Datchet, coming from the Strand at lunch-time, saw him one day taking his turn, closely buttoned in an overcoat, and so lost in thought that he might have been sitting in his own room.

She was overcome by something very like awe by the sight of him; then she felt much inclined to laugh, although her pulse beat faster. She passed him, and he never saw her. She came back and touched him on the shoulder.

"Gracious, Mary!" he exclaimed. "How you startled me!"

"Yes. You looked as if you were walking in your sleep," she said. "Are you arranging some terrible love affair? Have you got to reconcile a desperate couple?"

"I wasn't thinking about my work," Ralph replied, rather hastily. "And, besides, that sort of thing's not in my line," he added, rather grimly.

The morning was fine, and they had still some minutes of leisure to spend. They had not met for two or three weeks, and Mary had much to say to Ralph; but she was not certain how far he wished for her company. However, after a turn or two, in which a few facts were communicated, he suggested sitting down, and she took the seat beside him. The sparrows came fluttering about them, and Ralph produced from his pocket the half of a roll saved from his luncheon. He threw a few crumbs among them.

"I've never seen sparrows so tame," Mary observed, by way of saying something.

"No," said Ralph. "The sparrows in Hyde Park aren't as tame as this. If we keep perfectly still, I'll get one to settle on my arm."

Mary felt that she could have forgone this display of animal good temper, but seeing that Ralph, for some curious reason, took a pride in the sparrows, she bet him sixpence that he would not succeed

"Done!" he said; and his eye, which had been gloomy, showed a spark of light. His conversation was now addressed entirely to a bald cock-sparrow, who seemed bolder than the rest; and Mary took the opportunity of looking at him. She was not satisfied; his face was worn, and his expression stern. A child came bowling its hoop through the concourse of birds, and Ralph threw his last crumbs of bread into the bushes with a snort of impatience.

"That's what always happens—just as I've almost got him," he said. "Here's your sixpence, Mary. But you've only got it thanks to that brute of a boy. They oughtn't to be allowed to bowl hoops here——"

"Oughtn't to be allowed to bowl hoops My dear Ralph, what nonsense!"

"You always say that," he complained; "and it isn't nonsense. What's the point of having a garden if one can't watch birds in it? The street does all right for hoops. And if children can't be trusted in the streets, their mothers should keep them at home."

Mary made no answer to this remark, but frowned.

She leant back on the seat and looked about her at the great houses breaking the soft gray-blue sky with their chimneys.

"Ah, well," she said, "London's a fine place to live in. I believe I could sit and watch people all day long. I like my fellow-creatures. . . ."

Ralph sighed impatiently.

"Yes, I think so, when you come to know them," she added, as if his disagreement had been spoken.

"That's just when I don't like them," he replied. "Still, I don't see why you shouldn't cherish that illusion, if it pleases you." He spoke without much vehemence of agreement or disagreement. He seemed chilled.

"Wake up, Ralph! You're half asleep!" Mary cried, turning and pinching his sleeve. "What have you been doing with yourself? Moping? Working? Despising the world, as usual?"

As he merely shook his head, and filled his pipe, she went on:

"It's a bit of a pose, isn't it?"

"Not more than most things," he said.

"Well," Mary remarked, "I've a great deal to say to you, but I must go on—we have a committee." She rose, but hesitated, looking down upon him rather gravely. "You don't look happy, Ralph," she said. "Is it anything, or is it nothing?"

He did not immediately answer her, but rose, too, and walked with her towards the gate. As usual, he did not speak to her without considering whether what he was about to say was the sort of thing that he could say to her.

"I've been bothered," he said at length. "Partly by work, and partly by family troubles. Charles has been behaving like a fool. He wants to go out to Canada as a farmer——"

"Well, there's something to be said for that," said Mary; and they passed the gate, and walked slowly round the Fields again, discussing difficulties which, as a matter of fact, were more or less chronic in the Denham family, and only now brought forward to appease Mary's sympathy, which, however, soothed Ralph more than he was aware of. She made him at least dwell upon problems which were real in the sense that they were capable of solution; and the true cause of his melancholy, which was not susceptible to such treatment, sank rather more deeply into the shades of his mind.

Mary was attentive; she was helpful. Ralph could not help feeling grateful to her, the more so, perhaps, because he had not told her the truth about his state; and when they reached the gate again he wished to make some affectionate objection to her leaving him. But his affection took the rather uncouth form of expostulating with her about her work.

"What d'you want to sit on a committee for?" he asked. "It's waste of your time, Mary."

"I agree with you that a country walk would benefit the world more," she said. "Look here," she added suddenly, "why don't you come to us at Christmas? It's almost the best time of year."

"Come to you at Disham?" Ralph repeated.

"Yes. We won't interfere with you. But you can tell me later," she said, rather hastily, and then started off in the direction of Russell Square. She had invited him on the impulse of the moment, as a vision of the country came before her; and now she was annoyed with herself for having done so, and then she was annoyed at being annoyed.

"If I can't face a walk in a field alone with Ralph," she reasoned, "I'd better buy a cat and live in a lodging at Ealing, like Sally Seal—and he won't come. Or did he mean that he *would* come?"

She shook her head. She really did not know what he

had meant. She never felt quite certain; but now she was more than usually baffled. Was he concealing something from her? His manner had been odd; his deep absorption had impressed her; there was something in him that she had not fathomed, and the mystery of his nature laid more of a spell upon her than she liked. Moreover, she could not prevent herself from doing now what she had often blamed others of her sex for doing—from endowing her friend with a kind of heavenly fire, and passing her life before it for his sanction.

Under this process, the committee rather dwindled in importance; the Suffrage shrank; she vowed she would work harder at the Italian language; she thought she would take up the study of birds. But this program for a perfect life threatened to become so absurd that she very soon caught herself out in the evil habit, and was rehearsing her speech to the committee by the time the chestnut-colored bricks of Russell Square came in sight. Indeed, she never noticed them. She ran upstairs as usual, and was completely awakened to reality by the sight of Mrs. Seal, on the landing outside the office, inducing a very large dog to drink water out of a tumbler.

"Miss Markham has already arrived," Mrs. Seal remarked, with due solemnity, "and this is her dog."

"A very fine dog, too," said Mary, patting him on the head.

"Yes. A magnificent fellow," Mrs. Seal agreed. "A kind of St. Bernard, she tells me—so like Kit to have a St. Bernard. And you guard your mistress well, don't you, Sailor? You see that wicked men don't break into her larder when she's out at *her* work—helping poor souls who have lost their way. . . . But we're late—we must begin!" and scattering the rest of the water indiscriminately over the floor, she hurried Mary into the committee-room.

CHAPTER XIV

MR. CLACTON was in his glory. The machinery which he had perfected and controlled was now about to turn out its bi-monthly product, a committee meeting; and his pride in the perfect structure of these assemblies was great. He loved the jargon of committee-rooms; he loved the way in which the door kept opening as the clock struck the hour, in obedience to a few strokes of his pen on a piece of paper; and when it had opened sufficiently often, he loved to issue from his inner chamber with documents in his hands, visibly important, with a preoccupied expression on his face that might have suited a Prime Minister advancing to meet his Cabinet. By his orders the table had been decorated beforehand with six sheets of blotting-paper, with six pens, six ink-pots, a tumbler and a jug of water, a bell, and, in deference to the taste of the lady members, a vase of hardy chrysanthemums. He had already surreptitiously straightened the sheets of blotting-paper in relation to the ink-pots, and now stood in front of the fire engaged in conversation with Miss Markham. But his eye was on the door, and when Mary and Mrs. Seal entered, he gave a little laugh and observed to the assembly which was scattered about the room:

"I fancy, ladies and gentlemen, that we are ready to commence."

So speaking, he took his seat at the head of the table, and arranging one bundle of papers upon his right and another upon his left, called upon Miss Datchet to read the minutes of the previous meeting. Mary obeyed. A keen observer might have wondered why it was necessary for the secretary to knit her brows so closely over the tolerably matter-of-fact statement before her. Could there be any doubt in her mind that it had been resolved to circularize the provinces with Leaflet No. 3, or to issue a statistical diagram showing the proportion of married women to spinsters in New Zealand; or that the net profits of Mrs. Hipsley's Bazaar had reached a total of five pounds eight shillings and twopence halfpenny?

Could any doubt as to the perfect sense and propriety of these statements be disturbing her? No one could have guessed, from the look of her, that she was disturbed at all. A pleasanter and saner woman than Mary Datchet was never seen within a committee-room. She seemed a compound of the autumn leaves and the winter sunshine; less poetically speaking, she showed both gentleness and strength, an indefinable promise of soft maternity blending with her evident fitness for honest labor. Nevertheless, she had great difficulty in reducing her mind to obedience; and her reading lacked conviction, as if, as was indeed the case, she had lost the power of visualizing what she read. And directly the list was completed, her mind floated to Lincoln's Inn Fields and the fluttering wings of innumerable sparrows. Was Ralph still enticing the bald-headed cock-sparrow to sit upon his hand? Had he succeeded? Would he ever succeed? She had meant to ask him why it is that the sparrows in Lincoln's Inn Fields are tamer than the sparrows in Hyde Park—perhaps it is that the passers-by are rarer, and they come to recognize their benefactors. For the first half-hour of the committee meeting, Mary had thus to do battle with the skeptical presence of Ralph Denham, who threatened to have it all his own way. Mary tried half a dozen methods of ousting him. She raised her voice, she articulated distinctly, she looked firmly at Mr. Clacton's bald head, she began to write a note. To her annoyance, her pencil drew a little round figure on the blotting-paper, which, she could not deny, was really a bald-headed cock-sparrow. She looked again at Mr. Clacton; yes, he was bald, and so are cock-sparrows. Never was a secretary tormented by so many unsuitable suggestions, and they all came, alas! with something ludicrously grotesque about them, which might, at any moment, provoke her to such flippancy as would shock her colleagues for ever. The thought of what she might say made her bite her lips, as if her lips would protect her.

But all these suggestions were but flotsam and jetsam cast to the surface by a more profound disturbance, which, as she could not consider it at present, manifested its existence by these grotesque nods and beckonings. Consider it, she must, when the committee was over. Meanwhile, she was behaving scandalously; she was looking out of the window, and thinking of the color of the sky, and of the decorations on the Imperial Hotel, when she ought to have been shepherding her colleagues, and pinning them down to the matter in hand. She could not bring herself to attach more weight to one project than to another. Ralph had said— she could not stop to consider what he had said, but he had somehow divested the proceedings of all reality. And then, without conscious effort, by some trick of the brain, she found herself becoming interested in some scheme for organizing a newspaper campaign. Certain articles were to be written; certain editors approached. What line was it advisable to take? She found herself strongly disapproving of what Mr. Clacton was saying. She committed herself to the opinion that now was the time to strike hard. Directly she had said this, she felt that she had turned upon Ralph's ghost; and she became more and more in earnest, and anxious to bring the others round to her point of view. Once more, she knew exactly and indisputably what is right and what is wrong. As if emerging from a mist, the old foes of the public good loomed ahead of her—capitalists, newspaper proprietors, anti-suffragists, and, in some ways most pernicious of all, the masses who take no interest one way or another—among whom, for the time being, she certainly discerned the features of Ralph Denham. Indeed, when Miss Markham asked her to suggest the names of a few friends of hers, she expressed herself with unusual bitterness:

"My friends think all this kind of thing useless." She felt that she was really saying that to Ralph himself.

"Oh, they're that sort, are they?" said Miss Markham, with a little laugh; and with renewed vigor their legions charged the foe.

Mary's spirits had been low when she entered the committee-room; but now they were considerably improved. She knew the ways of this world; it was a shapely, orderly place; she felt convinced of its right and its wrong; and the feeling that she was fit to deal a heavy blow against her enemies warmed her heart and kindled her eye. In one of those flights of fancy, not characteristic of her but tiresomely frequent this afternoon, she envisaged herself battered with rotten eggs upon a platform, from which Ralph vainly begged her to descend. But——

"What do I matter compared with the cause?" she said, and so on. Much to her credit, however teased by foolish fancies, she kept the surface of her brain moderate and vigilant, and subdued Mrs. Seal very tactfully more than once when she demanded, "Action!—everywhere!—at once!" as became her father's daughter.

The other members of the committee, who were all rather elderly people, were a good deal impressed by Mary, and inclined to side with her and against each other, partly, perhaps, because of her youth. The feeling that she controlled them all filled Mary with a sense of power; and she felt that no work can equal in importance, or be so exciting as, the work of making other people do what you want them to do. Indeed, when she had won her point she felt a slight degree of contempt for the people who had yielded to her.

The committee now rose, gathered together their papers, shook them straight, placed them in their attaché-cases, snapped the locks firmly together, and hurried away, having, for the most part, to catch trains, in order to keep other appointments with other committees, for they were all busy people. Mary, Mrs. Seal, and Mr. Clacton were left alone; the room was hot and untidy, the pieces of pink blotting-paper were lying at different angles upon the table, and the tumbler was half full of water, which some one had poured out and forgotten to drink.

Mrs. Seal began preparing the tea, while Mr. Clacton retired to his room to file the fresh accumulation of documents. Mary was too much excited even to help Mrs. Seal with the cups and saucers. She flung up the window and stood by it, looking out. The street lamps were already lit; and through the mist in the square one could see little figures hurrying across the road and along the pavement, on the farther side. In her absurd mood of lustful arrogance, Mary looked at the little figures and thought, "If I liked I could make you go in there or stop short; I could make you walk in single file or in double file; I could do what I liked with you." Then Mrs. Seal came and stood by her.

"Oughtn't you to put something round your shoulders, Sally?" Mary asked, in rather a condescending tone of voice, feeling a sort of pity for the enthusiastic ineffective little woman. But Mrs. Seal paid no attention to the suggestion.

"Well, did you enjoy yourself?" Mary asked, with a little laugh.

Mrs. Seal drew a deep breath, restrained herself, and then burst out, looking out, too, upon Russell Square and Southampton Row, and at the passers-by, "Ah, if only one could get every one of those people into this room, and make them understand for five minutes! But they *must* see the truth some day. . . . If only one could *make* them see it. . . ."

Mary knew herself to be very much wiser than Mrs. Seal, and when Mrs. Seal said anything, even if it was what Mary herself was feeling, she automatically thought of all that there was to be said against it. On this occasion her arrogant feeling that she could direct everybody dwindled away.

"Let's have our tea," she said, turning back from the window and pulling down the blind. "It was a good meeting—didn't you think so, Sally?" she let fall, casually, as she sat down at the table. Surely Mrs. Seal must realize that Mary had been extraordinarily efficient?

"But we go at such a snail's pace," said Sally, shaking her head impatiently.

At this Mary burst out laughing, and all her arrogance was dissipated.

"You can afford to laugh," said Sally, with another shake of her head, "but I can't. I'm fifty-five, and I dare say I shall be in my grave by the time we get it—if we ever do."

"Oh, no, you won't be in your grave," said Mary, kindly.

"It'll be such a great day," said Mrs. Seal, with a toss of her locks. "A great day, not only for us, but for civilization. That's what I feel, you know, about these meetings. Each one of them is a step onwards in the great march— humanity, you know. We do want the people after us to have a better time of it—and so many don't see it. I wonder how it is that they don't see it?"

She was carrying plates and cups from the cupboard as she spoke, ˙so that her sentences were more than usually broken apart. Mary could not help looking at the odd little priestess of humanity with something like admiration. While she had been thinking about herself, Mrs. Seal had thought of nothing but her vision.

"You mustn't wear yourself out, Sally, if you want to see the great day," she said, rising and trying to take a plate of biscuits from Mrs. Seal's hands.

"My dear child, what else is my old body good for?" she exclaimed, clinging more tightly than before to her plate of biscuits. "Shouldn't I be proud to give everything I have to the cause?—for I'm not an intelligence like you. There were domestic circumstances—I'd like to tell you one of these days—so I say foolish things. I lose my head, you know. You don't. Mr. Clacton doesn't. It's a great mistake, to lose one's head. But my heart's in the right place. And I'm so glad Kit has a big dog, for I didn't think her looking well."

They had their tea, and went over many of the points that

had been raised in the committee rather more intimately than
had been possible then; and they all felt an agreeable sense
of being in some way behind the scenes; of having their
hands upon strings which, when pulled, would completely
change the pageant exhibited daily to those who read the
newspapers. Although their views were very different, this
sense united them and made them almost cordial in their
manners to each other.

Mary, however, left the tea-party rather early, desiring
both to be alone, and then to hear some music at the Queen's
Hall. She fully intended to use her loneliness to think out
her position with regard to Ralph; but although she walked
back to the Strand with this end in view, she found her mind
uncomfortably full of different trains of thought. She
started one and then another. They seemed even to take
their color from the street she happened to be in. Thus the
vision of humanity appeared to be in some way connected
with Bloomsbury, and faded distinctly by the time she
crossed the main road; then a belated organ-grinder in Holborn set her thoughts dancing incongruously; and by the
time she was crossing the great misty square of Lincoln's
Inn Fields, she was cold and depressed again, and horribly
clear-sighted. The dark removed the stimulus of human
companionship, and a tear actually slid down her cheek, ac-
companying a sudden conviction within her that she loved
Ralph, and that he didn't love her. All dark and empty now
was the path where they had walked that morning, and the
sparrows silent in the bare trees. But the lights in her own
building soon cheered her; all these different states of mind
were submerged in the deep flood of desires, thoughts, perceptions, antagonisms, which washed perpetually at the base
of her being, to rise into prominence in turn when the conditions of the upper world were favorable. She put off the
hour of clear thought until Christmas, saying to herself, as
she lit her fire, that it is impossible to think anything out in
London; and, no doubt, Ralph wouldn't come at Christmas,
and she would take long walks into the heart of the country,

and decide this question and all the others that puzzled her. Meanwhile, she thought, drawing her feet up on to the fender, life was full of complexity; life was a thing one must love to the last fiber of it.

She had sat there for five minutes or so, and her thoughts had had time to grow dim, when there came a ring at her bell. Her eye brightened; she felt immediately convinced that Ralph had come to visit her. Accordingly, she waited a moment before opening the door; she wanted to feel her hands secure upon the reins of all the troublesome emotions which the sight of Ralph would certainly arouse. She composed herself unnecessarily, however, for she had to admit, not Ralph, but Katharine and William Rodney. Her first impression was that they were both extremely well dressed. She felt herself shabby and slovenly beside them, and did not know how she should entertain them, not could she guess why they had come. She had heard nothing of their engagement. But after the first disappointment, she was pleased, for she felt instantly that Katharine was a personality, and, moreover, she need not now exercise her self-control.

"We were passing and saw a light in your window, so we came up," Katharine explained, standing and looking very tall and distinguished and rather absent-minded.

"We have been to see some pictures," said William. "Oh, dear," he exclaimed, looking about him, "this room reminds me of one of the worst hours in my existence—when I read a paper, and you all sat round and jeered at me. Katharine was the worst. I could feel her gloating over every mistake I made. Miss Datchet was kind. Miss Datchet just made it possible for me to get through, I remember."

Sitting down, he drew off his light yellow gloves, and began slapping his knees with them. His vitality was pleasant, Mary thought, although he made her laugh. The very look of him was inclined to make her laugh. His rather prominent eyes passed from one young woman to the other,

and his lips perpetually formed words which remained unspoken.

"We have been seeing old masters at the Grafton Gallery," said Katharine, apparently paying no attention to
William, and accepting a cigarette which Mary offered her.
She leant back in her chair, and the smoke which hung about
her face seemed to withdraw her still further from the
others.

"Would you believe it, Miss Datchet," William continued,
"Katharine doesn't like Titian. She doesn't like apricots,
she doesn't like peaches, she doesn't like green peas. She
likes the Elgin marbles, and gray days without any sun.
She's a typical example of the cold northern nature. I come
from Devonshire——"

Had they been quarreling, Mary wondered, and had they,
for that reason, sought refuge in her room, or were they
engaged, or had Katharine just refused him? She was
completely baffled.

Katharine now reappeared from her veil of smoke,
knocked the ash from her cigarette into the fireplace, and
looked, with an odd expression of solicitude, at the irritable
man.

"Perhaps, Mary," she said tentatively, "you wouldn't
mind giving us some tea? We did try to get some, but the
shop was so crowded, and in the next one there was a band
playing; and most of the pictures, at any rate, were very
dull, whatever you may say, William." She spoke with a
kind of guarded gentleness.

Mary, accordingly, retired to make preparations in the
pantry.

"What in the world are they after?" she asked of her own
reflection in the little looking-glass which hung there. She
was not left to doubt much longer, for, on coming back into
the sitting-room with the tea-things, Katharine informed
her, apparently having been instructed so to do by William,
of their engagement.

"William," she said, "thinks that perhaps you don't know. We are going to be married."

Mary found herself shaking William's hand, and addressing her congratulations to him, as if Katharine were inaccessible; she had, indeed, taken hold of the tea-kettle.

"Let me see," Katharine said, "one puts hot water into the cups first, doesn't one? You have some dodge of your own, haven't you, William, about making tea?"

Mary was half inclined to suspect that this was said in order to conceal nervousness, but if so, the concealment was unusually perfect. Talk of marriage was dismissed. Katharine might have been seated in her own drawing-room, controlling a situation which presented no sort of difficulty to her trained mind. Rather to her surprise, Mary found herself making conversation with William about old Italian pictures, while Katharine poured out tea, cut cake, kept William's plate supplied, without joining more than was necessary in the conversation. She seemed to have taken possession of Mary's room, and to handle the cups as if they belonged to her. But it was done so naturally that it bred no resentment in Mary; on the contrary, she found herself putting her hand on Katharine's knee, affectionately, for an instant. Was there something maternal in this assumption of control? And thinking of Katharine as one who would soon be married, these maternal airs filled Mary's mind with a new tenderness, and even with awe. Katharine seemed very much older and more experienced than she was.

Meanwhile Rodney talked. If his appearance was superficially against him, it had the advantage of making his solid merits something of a surprise. He had kept notebooks; he knew a great deal about pictures. He could compare different examples in different galleries, and his authoritative answers to intelligent questions gained not a little, Mary felt, from the smart taps which he dealt, as he delivered them, upon the lumps of coal. She was impressed.

"Your tea, William," said Katharine gently.

He paused, gulped it down, obediently, and continued.

And then it struck Mary that Katharine, in the shade of her broad-brimmed hat, and in the midst of the smoke, and in the obscurity of her character, was, perhaps, smiling to herself, not altogether in the maternal spirit. What she said was very simple, but her words, even "Your tea, William," were set down as gently and cautiously and exactly as the feet of a Persian cat stepping among China ornaments. For the second time that day Mary felt herself baffled by something inscrutable in the character of a person to whom she felt herself much attracted. She thought that if she were engaged to Katharine, she, too, would find herself very soon using those fretful questions with which William evidently teased his bride. And yet Katharine's voice was humble.

"I wonder how you find the time to know all about pictures as well as books?" she asked.

"How do I find the time?" William answered, delighted, Mary guessed, at this little compliment. "Why, I always travel with a notebook. And I ask my way to the picture gallery the very first thing in the morning. And then I meet men, and talk to them. There's a man in my office who knows all about the Flemish school. I was telling Miss Datchet about the Flemish school. I picked up a lot of it from him—it's a way men have—Gibbons, his name is. You must meet him. We'll ask him to lunch. And this not caring about art," he explained, turning to Mary, "it's one of Katharine's poses, Miss Datchet. Did you know she posed? She pretends that she's never read Shakespeare. And why should she read Shakespeare, since she *is* Shakespeare—Rosalind, you know," and he gave his queer little chuckle. Somehow this compliment appeared very old-fashioned and almost in bad taste. Mary actually felt herself blush, as if he had said "the sex" or "the ladies." Constrained, perhaps, by nervousness, Rodney continued in the same vein.

"She knows enough—enough for all decent purposes. What do you women want with learning, when you have so much else—everything, I should say—everything. Leave us something, eh, Katharine?"

"Leave you something?" said Katharine, apparently waking from a brown study. "I was thinking we must be going——"

"Is it to-night that Lady Ferrilby dines with us? No, we mustn't be late," said Rodney, rising. "D'you know the Ferrilbys, Miss Datchet? They own Trantem Abbey," he added, for her information, as she looked doubtful. "And if Katharine makes herself very charming to-night, perhaps 'll lend it to us for the honeymoon."

"I agree that may be a reason. Otherwise she's a dull woman," said Katharine. "At least," she added, as if to qualify her abruptness, "I find it difficult to talk to her."

"Because you expect every one else to take all the trouble. I've seen her sit silent a whole evening," he said, turning to Mary, as he had frequently done already. "Don't you find that, too? Sometimes when we're alone, I've counted the time on my watch"—here he took out a large gold watch, and tapped the glass—"the time between one remark and the next. And once I counted ten minutes and twenty seconds, and then, if you'll believe me, she only said 'Um!' "

"I'm sure I'm sorry," Katharine apologized. "I know it's a bad habit, but then, you see, at home——"

The rest of her excuse was cut short, so far as Mary was concerned, by the closing of the door. She fancied she could hear William finding fresh fault on the stairs. A moment later, the door-bell rang again, and Katharine reappeared, having left her purse on a chair. She soon found it, and said, pausing for a moment at the door, and speaking differently as they were alone:

"I think being engaged is very bad for the character." She shook her purse in her hand until the coins jingled, as if she alluded merely to this example of her forgetfulness. But the remark puzzled Mary; it seemed to refer to something else; and her manner had changed so strangely, now that William was out of hearing, that she could not help looking at her for an explanation. She looked almost stern, so that Mary, trying to smile at her, only succeeded in producing a silent stare of interrogation.

As the door shut for the second time, she sank on to the floor in front of the fire, trying, now that their bodies were not there to distract her, to piece together her impressions of them as a whole. And, though priding herself, with all other men and women, upon an infallible eye for character, she could not feel at all certain that she knew what motives inspired Katharine Hilbery in life. There was something that carried her on smoothly, out of reach—something, yes, but what?—something that reminded Mary of Ralph. Oddly enough, he gave her the same feeling, too, and with him, too, she felt baffled. Oddly enough, for no two people, she hastily concluded, were more unlike. And yet both had this hidden impulse, this incalculable force—this thing they cared for and didn't talk about—oh, what was it?

CHAPTER XV

THE village of Disham lies somewhere on the rolling piece of cultivated ground in the neighborhood of Lincoln, no so far inland but that a sound, bringing rumors of the sea, can be heard on summer nights or when the winter storms fling the waves upon the long beach. So large is the church, and in particular the church tower, in comparison with the little street of cottages which compose the village, that the traveler is apt to cast his mind back to the Middle Ages, as the only time when so much piety could have been kept alive. So great a trust in the Church can surely not belong to our day, and he goes on to conjecture that every one of the villagers has reached the extreme limit of human life. Such are the reflections of the superficial stranger, and his sight of the population, as it is represented by two or three men hoeing in a turnip-field, a small child carrying a jug, and a young woman shaking a piece of carpet outside her cottage door, will not lead him to see anything very much out of keeping with the Middle Ages in the village of Disham as it is to-day. These people, though they seem young enough, look so angular and so crude that they remind him of the little pictures painted by monks in the capital letters of their manuscripts. He only half understands what they say, and speaks very loud and clearly, as though, indeed, his voice had to carry through a hundred years or more before it reached them. He would have a far better chance of understanding some dweller in Paris or Rome, Berlin or Madrid, than these countrymen of his who have lived for the last two thousand years not two hundred miles from the City of London.

The Rectory stands about half a mile beyond the village.

It is a large house, and has been growing steadily for some centuries round the great kitchen, with its narrow red tiles, as the Rector would point out to his guests on the first night of their arrival, taking his brass candlestick, and bidding them mind the steps up and the steps down, and notice the immense thickness of the walls, the old beams across the ceiling, the staircases as steep as ladders, and the attics, with their deep, tent-like roofs, in which swallows bred, and once a white owl. But nothing very interesting or very beautiful had resulted from the different additions made by the different rectors.

The house, however, was surrounded by a garden, in which the Rector took considerable pride. The lawn, which fronted the drawing-room windows, was a rich and uniform green, unspotted by a single daisy, and on the other side of it two straight paths led past beds of tall, standing flowers to a charming grassy walk, where the Rev. Wyndham Datchet would pace up and down at the same hour every morning, with a sundial to measure the time for him. As often as not, he carried a book in his hand, into which he would glance, then shut it up, and repeat the rest of the ode from memory. He had most of Horace by heart, and had got into the habit of connecting this particular walk with certain odes which he repeated duly, at the same time noting the condition of his flowers, and stooping now and again to pick any that were withered or overblown. On wet days, such was the power of habit over him, he rose from his chair at the same hour, and paced his study for the same length of time, pausing now and then to straighten some book in the bookcase, or alter the position of the two brass crucifixes standing upon cairns of serpentine stone upon the mantelpiece. His children had a great respect for him, credited him with far more learning than he actually possessed, and saw that his habits were not interfered with, if possible. Like most people who do things methodically, the Rector himself had more strength of purpose and power of self-sacrifice than of intellect or of originality. On cold and windy nights he rode off to visit sick people, who might need him, without a murmur; and by virtue of doing dull duties punctually, he was much employed upon committees and local Boards and Councils; and at this period of his life (he was sixty-eight) he was beginning to be commiserated by tender old ladies for the extreme leanness of his person, which, they said, was worn out upon the roads when it should have been resting before a comfortable fire. His elder daughter, Elizabeth, lived with him and managed the house, and already much resembled him in dry sincerity and methodical habit of mind; of the two sons one, Richard, was an estate agent, the other, Christopher, was reading for the Bar. At Christmas, naturally, they met together; and for a month past the arrangement of the Christmas week had been much in the mind of mistress and maid, who prided themselves every year more confidently upon the excellence of their equipment. The late Mrs. Datchet had left an excellent cupboard of linen, to which Elizabeth had succeeded at the age of nineteen, when her mother died, and the charge of the family rested upon the shoulders of the eldest daughter. She kept a fine flock of yellow chickens, sketched a little, certain rose-trees in the garden were committed specially to her care; and what with the care of the house, the care of the chickens, and the care of the poor, she scarcely knew what it was to have an idle minute. An extreme rectitude of mind, rather than any gift, gave her weight in the family. When Mary wrote to say that she had asked Ralph Denham to stay with them, she added, out of deference to Elizabeth's character, that he was very nice, though rather queer, and had been overworking himself in London. No doubt Elizabeth would conclude that Ralph was in love with her, but there could be no doubt either that not a word of this would be spoken by either of them, unless, indeed, some catastrophe made mention of it unavoidable.

Mary went down to Disham without knowing whether Ralph intended to come; but two or three days before Christmas she received a telegram from Ralph, asking her to take a room for him in the village. This was followed by a letter explaining that he hoped he might have his meals with them; but quiet, essential for his work, made it necessary to sleep out.

Mary was walking in the garden with Elizabeth, and inspecting the roses, when the letter arrived.

"But that's absurd," said Elizabeth decidedly, when the plan was explained to her. "There are five spare rooms, even when the boys are here. Besides, he wouldn't get a room in the village. And he oughtn't to work if he's overworked."

"But perhaps he doesn't want to see so much of us," Mary thought to herself, although outwardly she assented, and felt grateful to Elizabeth for supporting her in what was, of course, her desire. They were cutting roses at the time, and laying them, head by head, in a shallow basket.

"If Ralph were here, he'd find this very dull," Mary thought, with a little shiver of irritation, which led her to place her rose the wrong way in the basket. Meanwhile, they had come to the end of the path, and while Elizabeth straightened some flowers, and made them stand upright within their fence of string, Mary looked at her father, who was pacing up and down, with his hand behind his back and his head bowed in meditation. Obeying an impulse which sprang from some desire to interrupt this methodical marching, Mary stepped on to the grass walk and put her hand on his arm.

"A flower for your buttonhole, father," she said, presenting a rose.

"Eh, dear?" said Mr. Datchet, taking the flower, and holding it at an angle which suited his bad eyesight, without pausing in his walk.

"Where does this fellow come from? One of Elizabeth's roses—I hope you asked her leave. Elizabeth doesn't like having her roses picked without her leave, and quite right, too."

He had a habit, Mary remarked, and she had never noticed it so clearly before, of letting his sentences tail away in a continuous murmur, whereupon he passed into a state of abstraction, presumed by his children to indicate some train of thought too profound for utterance.

"What?" said Mary, interrupting, for the first time in her life, perhaps, when the murmur ceased. He made no reply. She knew very well that he wished to be left alone, but she stuck to his side much as she might have stuck to some sleep-walker, whom she thought it right gradually to awaken. She could think of nothing to rouse him with except:

"The garden's looking very nice, father."

"Yes, yes, yes," said Mr. Datchet, running his words together in the same abstracted manner, and sinking his head yet lower upon his breast. And suddenly, as they turned their steps to retrace their way, he jerked out:

"The traffic's very much increased, you know. More rolling-stock needed already. Forty trucks went down yesterday by the 12.15—counted them myself. They've taken off the 9.3, and given us an 8.30 instead—suits the business men, you know. You came by the old 3.10 yesterday, I suppose?"

She said "Yes," as he seemed to wish for a reply, and then he looked at his watch, and made off down the path towards the house, holding the rose at the same angle in front of him. Elizabeth had gone round to the side of the house, where the chickens lived, so that Mary found herself alone, holding Ralph's letter in her hand. She was uneasy. She had put off the season for thinking things out very successfully, and now that Ralph was actually coming, the next day, she could only wonder how her family would impress him. She thought it likely that her father would discuss the train service with him; Elizabeth would be bright and sensible, and always leaving the room to give messages to the servants. Her brothers had already said that they would give him a day's shooting. She was content to leave the problem of Ralph's relations to the young men obscure, trusting that they would find some common ground of masculine agreement. But what would he think of *her?* Would he see that she was different from the rest of the family? She devised a plan for taking him to her sitting-room, and artfully leading the talk towards the English poets, who now occupied prominent places in her little bookcase. Moreover, she might give him to understand, privately, that she, too, thought her family a queer one—queer, yes, but not dull. That was the rock past which she was bent on steering him. And she thought how she would draw his attention to Edward's passion for Jorrocks, and the enthusiasm which led Christopher to collect moths and butterflies though he was now twenty-two. Perhaps Elizabeth's sketching, if the fruits were invisible, might lend color to the general effect which she wished to produce of a family, eccentric and limited, perhaps, but not dull. Edward, she perceived, was rolling the lawn, for the sake of exercise; and the sight of him, with pink cheeks, bright little brown eyes, and a general resemblance to a clumsy young cart-horse in its winter coat of dusty brown hair, made Mary violently ashamed of her ambitious scheming. She loved him precisely as he was; she loved them all; and as she walked by his side, up and down, and down and up, her strong moral sense administered a sound drubbing to the vain and romantic element aroused in her by the mere thought of Ralph. She felt quite certain that, for good or for bad, she was very like the rest of her family.

Sitting in the corner of a third-class railway carriage, on the afternoon of the following day, Ralph made several inquiries of a commercial traveler in the opposite corner. They centered round a village called Lampsher, not three miles, he understood, from Lincoln; was there a big house in Lampsher, he asked, inhabited by a gentleman of the name of Otway?

The traveler knew nothing, but rolled the name of Otway on his tongue, reflectively, and the sound of it gratified

Ralph amazingly. It gave him an excuse to take a letter from his pocket in order to verify the address.

"Stogdon House, Lampsher, Lincoln," he read out.

"You'll find somebody to direct you at Lincoln," said the man; and Ralph had to confess that he was not bound there this very evening.

"I've got to walk over from Disham," he said, and in the heart of him could not help marveling at the pleasure which he derived from making a bagman in a train believe what he himself did not believe. For the letter, though signed by Katharine's father, contained no invitation or warrant for thinking that Katharine herself was there; the only fact it disclosed was that for a fortnight this address would be Mr. Hilbery's address. But when he looked out of the window, it was of her he thought; she, too, had seen these gray fields, and, perhaps, she was there where the trees ran up a slope, and one yellow light shone now, and then went out again, at the foot of the hill. The light shone in the windows of an old gray house, he thought. He lay back in his corner and forgot the commercial traveler altogether. The process of visualizing Katharine stopped short at the old gray manor-house; instinct warned him that if he went much further with this process reality would soon force itself in; he could not altogether neglect the figure of William Rodney. Since the day when he had heard from Katharine's lips of her engagement, he had refrained from investing his dream of her with the details of real life. But the light of the late afternoon glowed green behind the straight trees, and became a symbol of her. The light seemed to expand his heart. She brooded over the gray fields, and was with him now in the railway carriage, thoughtful, silent, and infinitely tender; but the vision pressed too close, and must be dismissed, for the train was slackening. Its abrupt jerks shook him wide awake, and he saw Mary Datchet, a sturdy russet figure, with a dash of scarlet about it, as the carriage slid down the platform. A tall youth who accompanied her shook him by the hand, took his bag, and led the way without uttering one articulate word.

Never are voices so beautiful as on a winter's evening, when dusk almost hides the body, and they seem to issue from nothingness with a note of intimacy seldom heard by day. Such an edge was there in Mary's voice when she greeted him. About her seemed to hang the mist of the winter hedges, and the clear red of the bramble leaves. He felt himself at once stepping on to the firm ground of an entirely different world, but he did not allow himself to yield to the pleasure of it directly. They gave him his choice of driving with Edward or of walking home across the fields with Mary—not a shorter way, they explained, but Mary thought it a nicer way. He decided to walk with her, being conscious, indeed, that he got comfort from her presence. What could be the cause of her cheerfulness, he wondered, half ironically, and half enviously, as the pony-cart started briskly away, and the dusk swam between their eyes and the tall form of Edward, standing up to drive, with the reins in one hand and the whip in the other. People from the village, who had been to the market town, were climbing into their gigs, or setting off home down the road together in little parties. Many salutations were addressed to Mary, who shouted back, with the addition of the speaker's name. But soon she led the way over a stile, and along a path worn slightly darker than the dim green surrounding it. In front of them the sky now showed itself of a reddish-yellow, like a slice of some semilucent stone behind which a lamp burnt, while a fringe of black trees with distinct branches stood against the light, which was obscured in one direction by a hump of earth, in all other directions the land lying flat to the very verge of the sky. One of the swift and noiseless birds of the winter's night seemed to follow them across the field, circling a few feet in front of them, disappearing and returning again and again.

Mary had gone this walk many hundred times in the course of her life, generally alone, and at different stages the ghosts of past moods would flood her mind with a whole scene or train of thought merely at the sight of three trees from a particular angle, or at the sound of the pheasant clucking in the ditch. But to-night the circumstances were strong enough to oust all other scenes; and she looked at the field and the trees with an involuntary intensity as if they had no such associations for her.

"Well, Ralph," she said, "this is better than Lincoln's Inn Fields, isn't it? Look, there's a bird for you! Oh, you've brought glasses, have you? Edward and Christopher mean to make you shoot. Can you shoot? I shouldn't think so——"

"Look here, you must explain," said Ralph. "Who are these young men? Where am I staying?"

"You are staying with us, of course," she said boldly. "Of course, you're staying with us—you don't mind coming, do you?"

"If I had, I shouldn't have come," he said sturdily. They walked on in silence; Mary took care not to break it for a time. She wished Ralph to feel, as she thought he would, all the fresh delights of the earth and air. She was right. In a moment he expressed his pleasure, much to her comfort.

"This is the sort of country I thought you'd live in, Mary," he said, pushing his hat back on his head, and looking about him. "Real country. No gentlemen's seats."

He snuffed the air, and felt more keenly than he had done for many weeks the pleasure of owning a body.

"Now we have to find our way through a hedge," said Mary. In the gap of the hedge Ralph tore up a poacher's wire, set across a hole to trap a rabbit.

"It's quite right that they should poach," said Mary, watching him tugging at the wire. "I wonder whether it was Alfred Duggins or Sid Rankin? How can one expect them not to, when they only make fifteen shillings a week? Fifteen shillings a week," she repeated, coming out on the other side of the hedge, and running her fingers through her hair to rid herself of a bramble which had attached itself to her. "I could live on fifteen shillings a week—easily."

"Could you?" said Ralph. "I don't believe you could," he added.

"Oh yes. They have a cottage thrown in, and a garden where one can grow vegetables. It wouldn't be half bad," said Mary, with a soberness which impressed Ralph very much.

"But you'd get tired of it," he urged.

"I sometimes think it's the only thing one would never get tired of," she replied.

The idea of a cottage where one grew one's own vegetables and lived on fifteen shillings a week, filled Ralph with an extraordinary sense of rest and satisfaction.

"But wouldn't it be on the main road, or next door to a woman with six squalling children, who'd always be hanging her washing out to dry across your garden?"

"The cottage I'm thinking of stands by itself in a little orchard."

"And what about the Suffrage?" he asked, attempting sarcasm.

"Oh, there are other things in the world besides the Suffrage," she replied, in an off-hand manner which was slightly mysterious.

Ralph fell silent. It annoyed him that she should have plans of which he knew nothing; but he felt that he had no right to press her further. His mind settled upon the idea of life in a country cottage. Conceivably, for he could not examine into it now, here lay a tremendous possibility; a solution of many problems. He struck his stick upon the earth, and stared through the dusk at the shape of the country.

"D'you know the points of the compass?" he asked.

"Well, of course," said Mary. "What d'you take me for? —a Cockney like you?" She then told him exactly where the north lay, and where the south.

"It's my native land, this," she said. "I could smell my way about it blindfold."

As if to prove this boast, she walked a little quicker, so that Ralph found it difficult to keep pace with her. At the same time, he felt drawn to her as he had never been before; partly, no doubt, because she was more independent of him than in London, and seemed to be attached firmly to a world where he had no place at all. Now the dusk had fallen to such an extent that he had to follow her implicitly, and even lean his hand on her shoulder when they jumped a bank into a very narrow lane. And he felt curiously shy of her when she began to shout through her hands at a spot of light which swung upon the mist in a neighboring field. He shouted, too, and the light stood still.

"That's Christopher, come in already, and gone to feed his chickens," she said.

She introduced him to Ralph, who could see only a tall figure in gaiters, rising from a fluttering circle of soft feathery bodies, upon whom the light fell in wavering discs, calling out now a bright spot of yellow, now one of greenish-black and scarlet. Mary dipped her hand in the bucket he carried, and was at once the center of a circle also; and as she cast her grain she talked alternately to the birds and to her brother, in the same clucking, half-inarticulate voice, as it sounded to Ralph, standing on the outskirts of the fluttering feathers in his black overcoat.

He had removed his overcoat by the time they sat round the dinner-table, but nevertheless he looked very strange among the others. A country life and breeding had preserved in them all a look which Mary hesitated to call either innocent or youthful, as she compared them, now sitting round in an oval, softly illuminated by candlelight; and yet it was something of the kind, yes, even in the case of the Rector himself. Though superficially marked with lines, his face was a clear pink, and his blue eyes had the long-sighted, peaceful expression of eyes seeking the turn of the road, or a distant light through rain, or the darkness of winter. She looked at Ralph. He had never appeared to her more concentrated and full of purpose; as if behind his forehead were massed so much experience that he could choose for himself which part of it he would display and which part he would keep to himself. Compared with that dark and stern countenance, her brothers' faces, bending low over their soup-plates, were mere circles of pink, unmolded flesh.

"You came by the 3.10, Mr. Denham?" said the Reverend Wyndham Datchet, tucking his napkin into his collar, so that almost the whole of his body was concealed by a large white diamond. "They treat us very well, on the whole. Considering the increase of traffic, they treat us very well indeed. I have the curiosity sometimes to count the trucks on the goods' trains, and they're well over fifty—well over fifty, at this season of the year."

The old gentleman had been roused agreeably by the presence of this attentive and well-informed young man, as was evident by the care with which he finished the last words in his sentences, and his slight exaggeration in the number of trucks on the trains. Indeed, the chief burden of the talk fell upon him, and he sustained it to-night in a manner which caused his sons to look at him admiringly now and then; for they felt shy of Denham, and were glad not to have to talk themselves. The store of information about the present and past of this particular corner of Lincolnshire which old Mr. Datchet produced really surprised his children, for though they knew of its existence, they had forgotten its extent, as they might have forgotten the amount of family plate stored in the plate-chest, until some rare celebration brought it forth.

After dinner, parish business took the Rector to his study, and Mary proposed that they should sit in the kitchen.

"It's not the kitchen really," Elizabeth hastened to explain to her guest, "but we call it so——"

"It's the nicest room in the house," said Edward.

"It's got the old rests by the side of the fireplace, where the men hung their guns," said Elizabeth, leading the way, with a tall brass candlestick in her hand, down a passage. "Show Mr. Denham the steps, Christopher. . . . When the Ecclesiastical Commissioners were here two years ago they said this was the most interesting part of the house. These narrow bricks prove that it is five hundred years old—five hundred years, I think—they may have said six." She, too, felt an impulse to exaggerate the age of the bricks, as her father had exaggerated the number of trucks. A big lamp hung down from the center of the ceiling and, together with a fine log fire, illuminated a large and lofty room, with rafters running from wall to wall, a floor of red tiles, and a substantial fireplace built up of those narrow red bricks which were said to be five hundred years old. A few rugs and a sprinkling of arm-chairs had made this ancient kitchen into a sitting-room. Elizabeth, after pointing out the gun-racks, and the hooks for smoking hams, and other evidence of incontestable age, and explaining that Mary had had the idea of turning the room into a sitting-room—otherwise it was used for hanging out the wash and for the men to change in after shooting—considered that she had done her duty as hostess, and sat down in an upright chair directly beneath the lamp, beside a very long and narrow oak table. She placed a pair of horn spectacles upon her nose, and drew towards her a basketful of threads and wools. In a few minutes a smile came to her face, and remained there for the rest of the evening.

"Will you come out shooting with us to-morrow?" said Christopher, who had, on the whole, formed a favorable impression of his sister's friend.

"I won't shoot, but I'll come with you," said Ralph.

"Don't you care about shooting?" asked Edward, whose suspicions were not yet laid to rest.

"I've never shot in my life," said Ralph, turning and looking him in the face, because he was not sure how this confession would be received.

"You wouldn't have much chance in London, I suppose,"

said Christopher. "But won't you find it rather dull—just watching us?"

"I shall watch birds," Ralph replied, with a smile.

"I can show you the place for watching birds," said Edward, "if that's what you like doing. I know a fellow who comes down from London about this time every year to watch them. It's a great place for the wild geese and the ducks. I've heard this man say that it's one of the best places for birds in the country."

"It's about the best place in England," Ralph replied. They were all gratified by this praise of their native county; and Mary now had the pleasure of hearing these short questions and answers lose their undertone of suspicious inspection, so far as her brothers were concerned, and develop into a genuine conversation about the habits of birds which afterwards turned to a discussion as to the habits of solicitors, in which it was scarcely necessary for her to take part. She was pleased to see that her brothers liked Ralph, to the extent, that is, of wishing to secure his good opinion. Whether or not he liked them it was impossible to tell from his kind but experienced manner. Now and then she fed the fire with a fresh log, and as the room filled with the fine, dry heat of burning wood, they all, with the exception of Elizabeth, who was outside the range of the fire, felt less and less anxious about the effect they were making, and more and more inclined for sleep. At this moment a vehement scratching was heard on the door.

"Piper!—oh, damn!—I shall have to get up," murmured Christopher.

"It's not Piper, it's Pitch," Edward grunted.

"All the same, I shall have to get up," Christopher grumbled. He let in the dog, and stood for a moment by the door, which opened into the garden, to revive himself with a draught of the black, starlit air.

"Do come in and shut the door!" Mary cried, half turning in her chair.

"We shall have a fine day to-morrow," said Christopher

with complacency, and he sat himself on the floor at her
feet, and leant his back against her knees, and stretched out
his long stockinged legs to the fire—all signs that he felt no
longer any restraint at the presence of the stranger. He
was the youngest of the family, and Mary's favorite, partly
because his character resembled hers, as Edward's character
resembled Elizabeth's. She made her knees a comfortable
rest for his head, and ran her fingers through his hair.

"I should like Mary to stroke my head like that," Ralph
thought to himself suddenly, and he looked at Christopher,
almost affectionately, for calling forth his sister's caresses.
Instantly he thought of Katharine, the thought of her being
surrounded by the spaces of night and the open air; and
Mary, watching him, saw the lines upon his forehead suddenly deepen. He stretched out an arm and placed a log
upon the fire, constraining himself to fit it carefully into
the frail red scaffolding, and also to limit his thoughts to
this one room.

Mary had ceased to stroke her brother's head; he moved
it impatiently between her knees, and, much as though he
were a child, she began once more to part the thick, reddish-
colored locks this way and that. But a far stronger passion
had taken possession of her soul than any her brother could
inspire in her, and, seeing Ralph's change of expression, her
hand almost automatically continued its movements, while
her mind plunged desperately for some hold upon slippery
banks.

CHAPTER XVI

INTO that same black night, almost, indeed, into the very same layer of starlit air, Katharine Hilbery was now gazing, although not with a view to the prospects of a fine day for duck shooting on the morrow. She was walking up and down a gravel path in the garden of Stogdon House, her sight of the heavens being partially intercepted by the light leafless hoops of a pergola. Thus a spray of clematis would completely obscure Cassiopeia, or blot out with its black pattern myriads of miles of the Milky Way. At the end of the pergola, however, there was a stone seat, from which the sky could be seen completely swept clear of any earthly interruption, save to the right, indeed, where a line of elm-trees was beautifully sprinkled with stars, and a low stable building had a full drop of quivering silver just issuing from the mouth of the chimney. It was a moonless night, but the light of the stars was sufficient to show the outline of the young woman's form, and the shape of her face gazing gravely, indeed almost sternly, into the sky. She had come out into the winter's night, which was mild enough, not so much to look with scientific eyes upon the stars, as to shake herself free from certain purely terrestrial discontents. Much as a literary person in like circumstances would begin, absent-mindedly, pulling out volume after volume, so she stepped into the garden in order to have the stars at hand, even though she did not look at them. Not to be happy, when she was supposed to be happier than she would ever be again—that, as far as she could see, was the origin of a discontent which had begun almost as soon as she arrived, two days before, and seemed now so intolerable that she had left the family party, and come out here to consider it by herself. It was not she who thought herself unhappy, but her cousins, who thought it for her. The house was full of cousins, much of her age, or even younger, and among them they had some terribly bright eyes. They seemed always on the search for something between her and Rodney, which they expected to find, and yet did not find; and when they searched, Katharine became aware of wanting what she had not been conscious of wanting in London, alone with William and her parents. Or, if she did not want it, she missed it. And this state of mind depressed her, because she had been accustomed always to give complete satisfaction, and her self-love was now a little ruffled. She would have liked to break through the reserve habitual to her in order to justify her engagement to some one whose opinion she valued. No one had spoken a word of criticism, but they left her alone with William; not that that would have mattered, if they had not left her alone so politely; and, perhaps, that would not have mattered if they had not seemed so queerly silent, almost respectful, in her presence, which gave way to criticism, she felt, out of it.

Looking now and then at the sky, she went through the list of her cousins' names: Eleanor, Humphrey, Marmaduke, Silvia, Henry, Cassandra, Gilbert, and Mostyn— Henry, the cousin who taught the young ladies of Bungay to play upon the violin, was the only one in whom she could confide, and as she walked up and down beneath the hoops of the pergola, she did begin a little speech to him, which ran something like this:

"To begin with, I'm very fond of William. You can't deny that. I know him bettter than any one, almost. But why I'm marrying him is, partly, I admit—I'm being quite honest with you, and you mustn't tell any one—partly because I want to get married. I want to have a house of my own. It isn't possible at home. It's all very well for you, Henry; you can go your own way. I have to be there always. Besides, you know what our house is. You wouldn't be happy either, if you didn't do something. It isn't that I haven't the time at home—it's the atmosphere."

Here, presumably, she imagined that her cousin, who had listened with his usual intelligent sympathy, raised his eyebrows a little, and interposed:

"Well, but what do you want to do?"

Even in this purely imaginary dialogue, Katharine found it difficult to confide her ambition to an imaginary companion.

"I should like," she began, and hesitated quite a long time before she forced herself to add, with a change of voice, "to study mathematics—to know about the stars."

Henry was clearly amazed, but too kind to express all his doubts; he only said something about the difficulties of mathematics, and remarked that very little was known about the stars.

Katharine thereupon went on with the statement of her case.

"I don't care much whether I ever get to know anything—but I want to work out something in figures—something that hasn't got to do with human beings. I don't want people particularly. In some ways, Henry, I'm a humbug—I mean, I'm not what you all take me for. I'm not domestic, or very practical or sensible, really. And if I could calculate things, and use a telescope, and have to work out figures, and know to a fraction where I was wrong, I should be perfectly happy, and I believe I should give William all he wants."

Having reached this point, instinct told her that she had passed beyond the region in which Henry's advice could be of any good; and, having rid her mind of its superficial annoyance, she sat herself upon the stone seat, raised her eyes unconsciously and thought about the deeper questions which she had to decide, she knew, for herself. Would she, indeed, give William all he wanted? In order to decide the question, she ran her mind rapidly over her little collection of significant sayings, looks, compliments, gestures, which had marked their intercourse during the last day or two. He had been annoyed because a box, containing some clothes specially chosen by him for her to wear, had been taken to the wrong station, owing to her neglect in the matter of labels. The box had arrived in the nick of time, and he had remarked, as she came downstairs on the first night, that he had never seen her look more beautiful. She outshone all her cousins. He had discovered that she never made an ugly movement; he also said that the shape of her head made it possible for her, unlike most women, to wear her hair low. He had twice reproved her for being silent at dinner; and once for never attending to what he said. He had been surprised at the excellence of her French accent, but he thought it was selfish of her not to go with her mother to call upon the Middletons, because they were old family friends and very nice people. One the whole, the balance was nearly even; and, writing down a kind of conclusion in her mind which finished the sum for the present, at least, she changed the focus of her eyes, and saw nothing but the stars.

To-night they seemed fixed with unusual firmness in the blue, and flashed back such a ripple of light into her eyes that she found herself thinking that to-night the stars were happy. Without knowing or caring more for Church practices than most people of her age, Katharine could not look into the sky at Christmas time without feeling that, at this one season, the Heavens bend over the earth with sympathy, and signal with immortal radiance that they, too, take part in her festival. Somehow, it seemed to her that they were even now beholding the procession of kings and wise men upon some road on a distant part of the earth. And yet, after gazing for another second, the stars did their usual work upon the mind, froze to cinders the whole of our short human history, and reduced the human body to an ape-like, furry form, crouching amid the brushwood of a barbarous clod of mud. This stage was soon succeeded by another, in which there was nothing in the universe save stars and the light of stars; as she looked up the pupils of her eyes so dilated with starlight that the whole of her seemed dissolved in silver and spilt over the ledges of the stars for ever and ever indefinitely through space. Somehow simultaneously, though incongruously, she was riding with the magnanimous hero upon the shore or under forest trees, and so might have continued were it not for the rebuke forcibly administered by the body, which, content with the normal conditions of life, in no way furthers any attempt on the part of the mind to alter them. She grew cold, shook herself, rose, and walked towards the house.

By the light of the stars, Stogdon House looked pale and romantic, and about twice its natural size. Built by a retired admiral in the early years of the nineteenth century, the curving bow windows of the front, now filled with reddish-yellow light, suggested a portly three-decker, sailing seas where those dolphins and narwhals who disport themselves upon the edges of old maps were scattered with an impartial hand. A semicircular flight of shallow steps led to a very large door, which Katharine had left ajar. She hesitated, cast her eyes over the front of the house, marked that a light burnt in one small window upon an upper floor, and pushed the door open. For a moment she stood in the square hall, among many horned skulls, sallow globes, cracked oil-paintings, and stuffed owls, hesitating, it seemed, whether she should open the door on her right, through which the stir of life reached her ears. Listening for a moment, she heard a sound which decided her, apparently, not to enter; her uncle, Sir Francis, was playing his nightly game of whist; it appeared probable that he was losing.

She went up the curving stairway, which represented the one attempt at ceremony in the otherwise rather dilapidated mansion, and down a narrow passage until she came to the room whose light she had seen from the garden. Knocking, she was told to come in. A young man, Henry Otway, was reading, with his feet on the fender. He had a fine head, the brow arched in the Elizabethan manner, but the gentle, honest eyes were rather skeptical than glowing with the

Elizabethan vigor. He gave the impression that he had not
yet found the cause which suited his temperament.

He turned, put down his book, and looked at her. He
noticed her rather pale, dew-drenched look, as of one whose
mind is not altogether settled in the body. He had often
laid his difficulties before her, and guessed, in some ways
hoped, that perhaps she now had need of him. At the same
time, she carried on her life with such independence that
he scarcely expected any confidence to be expressed in
words.

"You have fled, too, then?" he said, looking at her cloak.
Katharine had forgotten to remove this token of her star-
gazing.

"Fled?" she asked. "From whom d'you mean? Oh, the
family party. Yes, it was hot down there, so I went into
the garden."

"And aren't you very cold?" Henry inquired, placing coal
on the fire, drawing a chair up to the grate, and laying aside
her cloak. Her indifference to such details often forced
Henry to act the part generally taken by women in such deal-
ings. It was one of the ties between them.

"Thank you, Henry," she said. "I'm not disturbing you?"

"I'm not here. I'm at Bungay," he replied. "I'm giving
a music lesson to Harold and Julia. That was why I had to
leave the table with the ladies—I'm spending the night there,
and I shan't be back till late on Christmas Eve."

"How I wish——" Katharine began, and stopped short.
"I think these parties are a great mistake," she added briefly,
and sighed.

"Oh, horrible!" he agreed; and they both fell silent.

Her sigh made him look at her. Should he venture to
ask her why she sighed? Was her reticence about her own
affairs as inviolable as it had often been convenient for
rather an egoistical young man to think it? But since her
engagement to Rodney, Henry's feeling towards her had
become rather complex; equally divided between an impulse
to hurt her and an impulse to be tender to her; and all the

time he suffered a curious irritation from the sense that she was drifting away from him for ever upon unknown seas. On her side, directly Katharine got into his presence, and the sense of the stars dropped from her, she knew that any intercourse between people is extremely partial; from the whole mass of her feelings, only one or two could be selected for Henry's inspection, and therefore she sighed. Then she looked at him, and their eyes meeting, much more seemed to be in common between them than had appeared possible. At any rate they had a grandfather in common; at any rate there was a kind of loyalty between them sometimes found between relations who have no other cause to like each other, as these two had.

"Well, what's the date of the wedding?" said Henry, the malicious mood now predominating.

"I think some time in March," she replied.

"And afterwards?" he asked.

"We take a house, I suppose, somewhere in Chelsea."

"It's very interesting," he observed, stealing another look at her.

She lay back in her arm-chair, her feet high upon the side of the grate, and in front of her, presumably to screen her eyes, she held a newspaper from which she picked up a sentence or two now and again. Observing this, Henry remarked:

"Perhaps marriage will make you more human."

At this she lowered the newspaper an inch or two, but said nothing. Indeed, she sat quite silent for over a minute.

"When you consider things like the stars, our affairs don't seem to matter very much, do they?" she said suddenly.

"I don't think I ever do consider things like the stars," Henry replied. "I'm not sure that that's not the explanation, though," he added, now observing her steadily.

"I doubt whether there is an explanation," she replied rather hurriedly, not clearly understanding what he meant.

"What? No explanation of anything?" he inquired, with a smile.

"Oh, things happen. That's about all," she let drop in her casual, decided way.

"That certainly seems to explain some of your actions," Henry thought to himself.

"One thing's about as good as another, and one's got to do something," he said aloud, expressing what he supposed to be her attitude, much in her accent. Perhaps she detected the imitation, for looking gently at him, she said, with ironical composure:

"Well, if you believe that your life must be simple, Henry."

"But I don't believe it," he said shortly.

"No more do I," she replied.

"What about the stars?" he asked a moment later. "I understand that you rule your life by the stars?"

She let this pass, either because she did not attend to it, or because the tone was not to her liking.

Once more she paused, and then she inquired:

"But do *you* always understand why you do everything? Ought one to understand? People like my mother understand," she reflected. "Now I must go down to them, I suppose, and see what's happening."

"What could be happening?" Henry protested.

"Oh, they may want to settle something," she replied vaguely, putting her feet on the ground, resting her chin on her hands, and looking out of her large dark eyes contemplatively at the fire.

"And then there's William," she added, as if by an afterthought.

Henry very nearly laughed, but restrained himself.

"Do they know what coals are made of, Henry?" she asked, a moment later.

"Mares' tails, I believe," he hazarded.

"Have you ever been down a coal-mine?" she went on.

"Don't let's talk about coal-mines, Katharine," he protested. "We shall probably never see each other again. When you're married——"

Tremendously to his surprise, he saw the tears stand in her eyes.

"Why do you all tease me?" she said. "It isn't kind."

Henry could not pretend that he was altogether ignorant of her meaning, though, certainly, he had never guessed that she minded the teasing. But before he knew what to say, her eyes were clear again, and the sudden crack in the surface was almost filled up.

"Things aren't easy, anyhow," she stated.

Obeying an impulse of genuine affection, Henry spoke.

"Promise me, Katharine, that if I can ever help you, you will let me."

She seemed to consider, looking once more into the red of the fire, and decided to refrain from any explanation.

"Yes, I promise that," she said at length, and Henry felt himself gratified by her complete sincerity, and began to tell her now about the coal-mine, in obedience to her love of facts.

They were, indeed, descending the shaft in a small cage, and could hear the picks of the miners, something like the gnawing of rats, in the earth beneath them, when the door was burst open, without any knocking.

"Well, here you are!" Rodney exclaimed. Both Katharine and Henry turned round very quickly and rather guiltily. Rodney was in evening dress. It was clear that his temper was ruffled.

"That's where you've been all the time," he repeated, looking at Katharine.

"I've only been here about ten minutes," she replied.

"My dear Katharine, you left the drawing-room over an hour ago."

She said nothing.

"Does it very much matter?" Henry asked.

Rodney found it hard to be unreasonable in the presence of another man, and did not answer him.

"They don't like it," he said. "It isn't kind to old people

to leave them alone—although I've no doubt it's much more amusing to sit up here and talk to Henry."

"We were discussing coal-mines," said Henry urbanely.

"Yes. But we were talking about much more interesting things before that," said Katharine.

From the apparent determination to hurt him with which she spoke, Henry thought that some sort of explosion on Rodney's part was about to take place.

"I can quite understand that," said Rodney, with his little chuckle, leaning over the back of his chair and tapping the woodwork lightly with his fingers. They were all silent, and the silence was acutely uncomfortable to Henry, at least.

"Was it very dull, William?" Katharine suddenly asked, with a complete change of tone and a little gesture of her hand.

"Of course it was dull," William said sulkily.

"Well, you stay and talk to Henry, and I'll go down," she replied.

She rose as she spoke, and as she turned to leave the room, she laid her hand, with a curiously caressing gesture, upon Rodney's shoulder. Instantly Rodney clasped her hand in his, with such an impulse of emotion that Henry was annoyed, and rather ostentatiously opened a book.

"I shall come down with you," said William, as she drew back her hand, and made as if to pass him.

"Oh no," she said hastily. "You stay here and talk to Henry."

"Yes, do," said Henry, shutting up his book again. His invitation was polite, without being precisely cordial. Rodney evidently hesitated as to the course he should pursue, but seeing Katharine at the door, he exclaimed:

"No. I want to come with you."

She looked back, and said in a very commanding tone, and with an expression of authority upon her face:

"It's useless for you to come. I shall go to bed in ten minutes. Good night."

She nodded to them both, but Henry could not help noticing that her last nod was in his direction. Rodney sat down rather heavily.

His mortification was so obvious that Henry scarcely liked to open the conversation with some remark of a literary character. On the other hand, unless he checked him, Rodney might begin to talk about his feelings, and irreticence is apt to be extremely painful, at any rate in prospect. He therefore adopted a middle course; that is to say, he wrote a note upon the fly-leaf of his book, which ran, "The situation is becoming most uncomfortable." This he decorated with those flourishes and decorative borders which grow of themselves upon these occasions; and as he did so, he thought to himself that whatever Katharine's difficulties might be, they did not justify her behavior. She had spoken with a kind of brutality which suggested that, whether it is natural or assumed, women have a peculiar blindness to the feelings of men.

The penciling of this note gave Rodney time to recover himself. Perhaps, for he was a very vain man, he was more hurt that Henry had seen him rebuffed than by the rebuff itself. He was in love with Katharine, and vanity is not decreased but increased by love, especially, one may hazard, in the presence of one's own sex. But Rodney enjoyed the courage which springs from that laughable and lovable defect, and when he had mastered his first impulse, in some way to make a fool of himself, he drew inspiration from the perfect fit of his evening dress. He chose a cigarette, tapped it on the back of his hand, displayed his exquisite pumps on the edge of the fender, and summoned his self-respect.

"You've several big estates round here, Otway," he began. "Any good hunting? Let me see, what pack would it be? Who's your great man?"

"Sir William Budge, the sugar king, has the biggest estate. He bought out poor Stanham, who went bankrupt."

"Which Stanham would that be? Verney or Alfred?"

"Alfred. . . . I don't hunt myself. You're a great hunts-

man, aren't you? You have a great reputation as a horseman, anyhow," he added, desiring to help Rodney in his
effort to recover his complacency.

"Oh, I love riding," Rodney replied. "Could I get a horse
down here? Stupid of me! I forgot to bring any clothes.
I can't imagine, though, who told you I was anything of
a rider?"

To tell the truth, Henry labored under the same difficulty;
he did not wish to introduce Katharine's name, and, therefore, he replied vaguely that he had always heard that Rodney was a great rider. In truth, he had heard very little
about him, one way or another, accepting him as a figure
often to be found in the background at his aunt's house, and
inevitably, though inexplicably, engaged to his cousin.

"I don't care much for shooting," Rodney continued; "but
one has to do it, unless one wants to be altogether out of
things. I dare say there's some very pretty country round
here. I stayed once at Bolham Hall. Young Cranthorpe
was up with you, wasn't he? He married old Lord Bolham's daughter. Very nice people—in their way."

"I don't mix in that society," Henry remarked, rather
shortly. But Rodney, now started on an agreeable current
of reflection, could not resist the temptation of pursuing it a
little further. He appeared to himself as a man who moved
easily in very good society, and knew enough about the true
values of life to be himself above it.

"Oh, but you should," he went on. "It's well worth staying there, anyhow, once a year. They make one very comfortable, and the women are ravishing."

"The women?" Henry thought to himself, with disgust.
"What could any woman see in you?" His tolerance was
rapidly becoming exhausted, but he could not help liking
Rodney nevertheless, and this appeared to him strange, for
he was fastidious, and such words in another mouth would
have condemned the speaker irreparably. He began, in
short, to wonder what kind of creature this man who was
to marry his cousin might be. Could any one, except a

rather singular character, afford to be so ridiculously vain?

"I don't think I should get on in that society," he replied. "I don't think I should know what to say to Lady Rose if I met her."

"I don't find any difficulty," Rodney chuckled. "You talk to them about their children, if they have any, or their accomplishments—painting, gardening, poetry—they're so delightfully sympathetic. Seriously, you know I think a woman's opinion of one's poetry is always worth having. Don't ask them for their reasons. Just ask them for their feelings. Katharine, for example——"

"Katharine," said Henry, with an emphasis upon the name, almost as if he resented Rodney's use of it, "Katharine is very unlike most women."

"Quite," Rodney agreed. "She is——" He seemed about to describe her, and he hesitated for a long time. "She's looking very well," he stated, or rather almost inquired, in a different tone from that in which he had been speaking. Henry bent his head.

"But, as a family, you're given to moods, eh?"

"Not Katharine," said Henry, with decision.

"Not Katharine," Rodney repeated, as if he weighed the meaning of the words. "No, perhaps you're right. But her engagement has changed her. Naturally," he added, "one would expect that to be so." He waited for Henry to confirm this statement, but Henry remained silent.

"Katharine has had a difficult life, in some ways," he continued. "I expect that marriage will be good for her. She has great powers."

"Great," said Henry, with decision.

"Yes—but now what direction d'you think they take?"

Rodney had completely dropped his pose as a man of the world, and seemed to be asking Henry to help him in a difficulty.

"I don't know," Henry hesitated cautiously.

"D'you think children—a household—that sort of thing —d'you think that'll satisfy her? Mind, I'm out all day."

"She would certainly be very competent," Henry stated.

"Oh, she's wonderfully competent," said Rodney. "But —I get absorbed in my poetry. Well, Katharine hasn't got that. She admires my poetry, you know, but that wouldn't be enough for her?"

"No," said Henry. He paused. "I think you're right," he added, as if he were summing up his thoughts. "Katharine hasn't found herself yet. Life isn't altogether real to her yet—I sometimes think——"

"Yes?" Rodney inquired, as if he were eager for Henry to continue. "That is what I——" he was going on, as Henry remained silent, but the sentence was not finished, for the door opened, and they were interrupted by Henry's younger brother Gilbert, much to Henry's relief, for he had already said more than he liked.

CHAPTER XVII

WHEN the sun shone, as it did with unusual brightness that Christmas week, it revealed much that was faded and not altogether well-kept-up in Stogdon House and its grounds. In truth, Sir Francis had retired from service under the Government of India with a pension that was not adequate, in his opinion, to his services, as it certainly was not adequate to his ambitions. His career had not come up to his expectations, and although he was a very fine, white-whiskered, mahogany-colored old man to look at, and had laid down a very choice cellar of good reading and good stories, you could not long remain ignorant of the fact that some thunder-storm had soured them; he had a grievance. This grievance dated back to the middle years of the last century, when, owing to some official intrigue, his merits had been passed over in a disgraceful manner in favor of another, his junior.

The rights and wrongs of the story, presuming that they had some existence in fact, were no longer clearly known to his wife and children; but this disappointment had played a very large part in their lives, and had poisoned the life of Sir Francis much as a disappointment in love is said to poison the whole life of a woman. Long brooding on his failure, continual arrangement and rearrangement of his deserts and rebuffs, had made Sir Francis much of an egoist, and in his retirement his temper became increasingly difficult and exacting.

His wife now offered so little resistance to his moods that she was practically useless to him. He made his daughter Eleanor into his chief confidante, and the prime of her life was being rapidly consumed by her father. To her he dictated the memoirs which were to avenge his memory, and she had to assure him constantly that his treatment had been a disgrace. Already, at the age of thirty-five, her cheeks were whitening as her mother's had whitened, but for her there would be no memories of Indian suns and Indian rivers, and clamor of children in a nursery; she would have very little of substance to think about when she sat, as Lady Otway now sat, knitting white wool, with her eyes fixed almost perpetually upon the same embroidered bird upon the same fire-screen. But then Lady Otway was one of the people for whom the great make-believe game of English social life has been invented; she spent most of her time in pretending to herself and her neighbors that she was a dignified, important, much-occupied person, of considerable social standing and sufficient wealth. In view of the actual state of things this game needed a great deal of skill; and, perhaps, at the age she had reached—she was over sixty—she played far more to deceive herself than to deceive any one else. Moreover, the armor was wearing thin; she forgot to keep up appearances more and more.

The worn patches in the carpets, and the pallor of the drawing-room, where no chair or cover had been renewed for some years, were due not only to the miserable pension, but to the wear and tear of twelve children, eight of whom were sons. As often happens in these large families, a distinct dividing-line could be traced, about half-way in the succession, where the money for educational purposes had run short, and the six younger children had grown up far more economically than the elder. If the boys were clever, they won scholarships, and went to school; if they were not clever, they took what the family connection had to offer them. The girls accepted situations occasionally, but there were always one or two at home, nursing sick animals, tending silkworms, or playing the flute in their bedrooms. The distinction between the elder children and the younger corresponded almost to the distinction between a higher class and a lower one, for with only a haphazard education and insufficient allowances, the younger children had picked up accomplishments, friends, and points of view which were not to be found within the walls of a public school or of a Government office. Between the two divisions there was considerable hostility, the elder trying to patronize the younger, the younger refusing to respect the elder; but one feeling united them and instantly closed any risk of a breach —their common belief in the superiority of their own family to all others. Henry was the eldest of the younger group, and their leader; he bought strange books and joined odd societies; he went without a tie for a whole year, and had six shirts made of black flannel. He had long refused to take a seat either in a shipping office or in a tea-merchant's warehouse; and persisted, in spite of the disapproval of uncles and aunts, in practising both violin and piano, with the result that he could not perform professionally upon either. Indeed, for thirty-two years of life he had nothing more substantial to show than a manuscript book containing the score of half an opera. In this protest of his, Katharine had always given him her support, and as she was generally held to be an extremely sensible person, who dressed too well to be eccentric, he had found her support of some use. Indeed, when she came down at Christmas she usually spent a great part of her time in private conferences with Henry and with Cassandra, the youngest girl, to whom the silkworms belonged. With the younger section she had a great reputation for common sense, and for something that they despised but inwardly respected and called knowledge of the world—that is to say, of the way in which respectable elderly people, going to their clubs and dining out with ministers, think and behave. She had more than once played the part of ambassador between Lady Otway and her children. That poor lady, for instance, consulted her for advice when, one day, she opened Cassandra's bedroom door on a mission of discovery, and found the ceiling hung with mulberry-leaves, the windows blocked with cages, and the tables

stacked with home-made machines for the manufacture of
silk dresses.

"I wish you could help her to take an interest in something that other people are interested in, Katharine," she
observed, rather plaintively, detailing her grievances. "It's
all Henry's doing, you know, giving up her parties and taking to these nasty insects. It doesn't follow that if a man
can do a thing a woman may too."

The morning was sufficiently bright to make the chairs
and sofas in Lady Otway's private sitting-room appear
more than usually shabby, and the gallant gentlemen, her
brothers and cousins, who had defended the Empire and left
their bones on many frontiers, looked at the world through
a film of yellow which the morning light seemed to have
drawn across their photographs. Lady Otway sighed, it
may be at the faded relics, and turned, with resignation, to
her balls of wool, which, curiously and characteristically,
were not an ivory-white, but rather a tarnished yellow-
white. She had called her niece in for a little chat. She had
always trusted her, and now more than ever, since her engagement to Rodney, which seemed to Lady Otway extremely suitable, and just what one would wish for one's
own daughter. Katharine unwittingly increased her reputation for wisdom by asking to be given knitting-needles too.

"It's so very pleasant," said Lady Otway, "to knit while
one's talking. And now, my dear Katharine, tell me about
your plans."

The emotions of the night before, which she had sup-
pressed in such a way as to keep her awake till dawn, had
left Katharine a little jaded, and thus more matter-of-fact
than usual. She was quite ready to discuss her plans—
houses and rents, servants and economy—without feeling
that they concerned her very much. As she spoke, knitting
methodically meanwhile, Lady Otway noted, with approval,
the upright, responsible bearing of her niece, to whom the
prospect of marriage had brought some gravity most be-

coming in a bride, and yet, in these days, most rare. Yes, Katharine's engagement had changed her a little.

"What a perfect daughter, or daughter-in-law!" she thought to herself, and could not help contrasting her with Cassandra, surrounded by innumerable silkworms in her bedroom

"Yes," she continued, glancing at Katharine, with the round, greenish eyes which were as inexpressive as moist marbles, "Katharine is like the girls of my youth. We took the serious things of life seriously." But just as she was deriving satisfaction from his thought, and was producing some of the hoarded wisdom which none of her own daughters, alas! seemed now to need, the door opened, and Mrs. Hilbery came in, or rather, did not come in, but stood in the doorway and smiled, having evidently mistaken the room.

"I never *shall* know my way about this house!" she exclaimed. "I'm on my way to the library, and I don't want to interrupt. You and Katharine were having a little chat?"

The presence of her sister-in-law made Lady Otway slightly uneasy. How could she go on with what she was saying in Maggie's presence? for she was saying something that she had never said, all these years, to Maggie herself.

"I was telling Katharine a few little commonplaces about marriage," she said, with a little laugh. "Are none of my children looking after you, Maggie?"

"Marriage," said Mrs. Hilbery, coming into the room, and nodding her head once or twice, "I always say marriage is a school. And you don't get the prizes unless you go to school. Charlotte has won all the prizes," she added, giving her sister-in-law a little pat, which made Lady Otway more uncomfortable still. She half laughed, muttered something, and ended on a sigh.

"Aunt Charlotte was saying that it's no good being married unless you submit to your husband," said Katharine, framing her aunt's words into a far more definite shape than they had really worn; and when she spoke thus she did not appear at all old-fashioned. Lady Otway looked at her and paused for a moment.

"Well, I really don't advise a woman who wants to have things her own way to get married," she said, beginning a fresh row rather elaborately.

Mrs. Hilbery knew something of the circumstances which, as she thought, had inspired this remark. In a moment her face was clouded with sympathy which she did not quite know how to express.

"What a shame it was!" she exclaimed, forgetting that her train of thought might not be obvious to her listeners. "But, Charlotte, it would have been much worse if Frank had disgraced himself in any way. And it isn't what our husbands *get,* but what they *are.* I used to dream of white horses and palanquins, too; but still, I like the ink-pots best. And who knows?" she concluded, looking at Katharine, "your father may be made a baronet to-morrow."

Lady Otway, who was Mr. Hilbery's sister, knew quite well that, in private, the Hilberys called Sir Francis "that old Turk," and though she did not follow the drift of Mrs. Hilbery's remarks, she knew what prompted them.

"But if you can give way to your husband," she said, speaking to Katharine, as if there were a separate understanding between them, "a happy marriage is the happiest thing in the world."

"Yes," said Katharine, "but——" She did not mean to finish her sentence, she merely wished to induce her mother and her aunt to go on talking about marriage, for she was in the mood to feel that other people could help her if they would. She went on knitting, but her fingers worked with a decision that was oddly unlike the smooth and contemplative sweep of Lady Otway's plump hand. Now and then she looked swiftly at her mother, then at her aunt. Mrs. Hilbery held a book in her hand, and was on her way, as Katharine guessed, to the library, where another paragraph was to be added to that varied assortment of paragraphs, the Life of Richard Alardyce. Normally, Katharine would have hurried her mother downstairs, and seen that no excuse for distraction came her way. Her attitude towards the poet's life, however, had changed with other changes; and she was content to forget all about her scheme of hours. Mrs. Hilbery was secretly delighted. Her relief at finding herself excused manifested itself in a series of sidelong glances of sly humor in her daughter's direction, and the indulgence put her in the best of spirits. Was she to be allowed merely to sit and talk? It was so much pleasanter to sit in a nice room filled with all sorts of interesting odds and ends which she hadn't looked at for a year, at least, than to seek out one date which contradicted another in a dictionary.

"We've all had perfect husbands," she concluded, generously forgiving Sir Francis all his faults in a lump. "Not that I think a bad temper is really a fault in a man. I don't mean a bad temper," she corrected herself, with a glance obviously in the direction of Sir Francis. "I should say a quick, impatient temper. Most, in fact *all* great men have had bad tempers—except your grandfather, Katharine," and here she sighed, and suggested that, perhaps, she ought to go down to the library.

"But in the ordinary marriage, is it necessary to give way to one's husband?" said Katharine, taking no notice of her mother's suggestion, blind even to the depression which had now taken possession of her at the thought of her own inevitable death.

"I should say yes, certainly," said Lady Otway, with a decision most unusual for her.

"Then one ought to make up one's mind to that before one is married," Katharine mused, seeming to address herself.

Mrs. Hilbery was not much interested in these remarks, which seemed to have a melancholy tendency, and to revive her spirits she had recourse to an infallible remedy—she looked out of the window.

"Do look at that lovely little blue bird!" she exclaimed, and her eye looked with extreme pleasure at the soft sky, at the trees, at the green fields visible behind those trees, and at the leafless branches which surrounded the body of the small blue tit. Her sympathy with nature was exquisite.

"Most women know by instinct whether they can give it or not," Lady Otway slipped in quickly, in rather a low voice, as if she wanted to get this said while her sister-in-law's attention was diverted. "And if not—well then, my advice would be—don't marry."

"Oh, but marriage is the happiest life for a woman," said Mrs. Hilbery, catching the word marriage, as she brought her eyes back to the room again. Then she turned her mind to what she had said.

"It's the most *interesting* life," she corrected herself. She looked at her daughter with a look of vague alarm. It was the kind of maternal scrutiny which suggests that, in looking at her daughter a mother is really looking at herself. She was not altogether satisfied; but she purposely made no attempt to break down the reserve which, as a matter of fact, was a quality she particularly admired and depended upon in her daughter. But when her mother said that marriage was the most interesting life, Katharine felt, as she was apt to do suddenly, for no definite reason, that they understood each other, in spite of differing in every possible way. Yet the wisdom of the old seems to apply more to feelings which we have in common with the rest of the human race than to our feelings as individuals, and Katharine knew that only some one of her own age could follow her meaning. Both these elderly women seemed to her to have been content with so little happiness, and at the moment she had not sufficient force to feel certain that their version of marriage was the wrong one. In London, certainly, this temperate attitude toward her own marriage had seemed to her just. Why had she now changed? Why did it now depress her? It never occurred to her that her own conduct could be anything of a puzzle to her mother, or that elder people are as much affected by the young as the young are by them. And yet it was true that love—passion—whatever

one chose to call it, had played far less part in Mrs. Hilbery's
life than might have seemed likely, judging from her enthusiastic and imaginative temperament. She had always
been more interested by other things. Lady Otway, strange
though it seemed, guessed more accurately at Katharine's
state of mind than her mother did.

"Why don't we all live in the country?" exclaimed Mrs.
Hilbery, once more looking out of the window. "I'm sure
one would think such beautiful things if one lived in the
country. No horrid slum houses to depress one, no trams
or motor-cars; and the people all looking so plump and
cheerful. Isn't there some little cottage near you, Charlotte,
which would do for us, with a spare room, perhaps, in case
we asked a friend down? And we should save so much
money that we should be able to travel——"

"Yes. You would find it very nice for a week or two, no
doubt," said Lady Otway. "But what hour would you like
the carriage this morning?" she continued, touching the bell.

"Katharine shall decide," said Mrs. Hilbery, feeling herself unable to prefer one hour to another. "And I was just
going to tell you, Katharine, how, when I woke this morning, everything seemed so clear in my head that if I'd had a
pencil I believe I could have written quite a long chapter.
When we're out on our drive I shall find us a house. A few
trees round it, and a little garden, a pond with a Chinese
duck, a study for your father, a study for me, and a sitting
room for Katharine, because then she'll be a married lady."

At this Katharine shivered a little, drew up to the fire,
and warmed her hands by spreading them over the topmost
peak of the coal. She wished to bring the talk back to marriage again, in order to hear Aunt Charlotte's views, but she
did not know how to do this.

"Let me look at your engagement-ring, Aunt Charlotte,"
she said, noticing her own.

She took the cluster of green stones and turned it round
and round, but she did not know what to say next.

"That poor old ring was a sad disappointment to me

when I first had it," Lady Otway mused. "I'd set my heart
on a diamond ring, but I never liked to tell Frank, naturally.
He bought it at Simla."

Katharine turned the ring round once more, and gave it
back to her aunt without speaking. And while she turned
it round her lips set themselves firmly together, and it
seemed to her that she could satisfy William as these women
had satisfied their husbands; she could pretend to like emeralds when she preferred diamonds. Having replaced her
ring, Lady Otway remarked that it was chilly, though not
more so than one must expect at this time of year. Indeed,
one ought to be thankful to see the sun at all, and she advised
them both to dress warmly for their drive. Her aunt's stock
of commonplaces, Katharine sometimes suspected, had been
laid in on purpose to fill silences with, and had little to do
with her private thoughts. But at this moment they seemed
terribly in keeping with her own conclusions, so that she
took up her knitting again and listened, chiefly with a view
to confirming herself in the belief that to be engaged to
marry some one with whom you are not in love is an inevitable step in a world where the existence of passion is only a
traveller's story brought from the heart of deep forests and
told so rarely that wise people doubt whether the story can
be true. She did her best to listen to her mother asking for
news of John, and to her aunt replying with the authentic
history of Hilda's engagement to an officer in the Indian
Army, but she cast her mind alternately towards forest
paths and starry blossoms, and towards pages of neatly written mathematical signs. When her mind took this turn her
marriage seemed no more than an archway through which
it was necessary to pass in order to have her desire. At such
times the current of her nature ran in its deep narrow channel with great force and with an alarming lack of consideration for the feelings of others. Just as the two elder ladies
had finished their survey of the family prospects, and Lady
Otway was nervously anticipating some general statement
as to life and death from her sister-in-law, Cassandra burst

into the room with the news that the carriage was at the door.

"Why didn't Andrews tell me himself?" said Lady Otway, peevishly, blaming her servants for not living up to her ideals.

When Mrs. Hilbery and Katharine arrived in the hall, ready dressed for their drive, they found that the usual discussion was going forward as to the plans of the rest of the family. In token of this, a great many doors were opening and shutting, two or three people stood irresolutely on the stairs, now going a few steps up, and now a few steps down, and Sir Francis himself had come out from his study, with the *Times* under his arm, and a complaint about noise and draughts from the open door which, at least, had the effect of bundling the people who did not want to go into the carriage, and sending those who did not want to stay back to their rooms. It was decided that Mrs. Hilbery, Katharine, Rodney, and Henry should drive to Lincoln, and any one else who wished to go should follow on bicycles or in the pony-cart. Every one who stayed at Stogdon House had to make this expedition to Lincoln in obedience to Lady Otway's conception of the right way to entertain her guests, which she had imbibed from reading in fashionable papers of the behavior of Christmas parties in ducal houses. The carriage horses were both fat and aged, still they matched; the carriage was shaky and uncomfortable, but the Otway arms were visible on the panels. Lady Otway stood on the topmost step, wrapped in a white shawl, and waved her hand almost mechanically until they had turned the corner under the laurel-bushes, when she retired indoors with a sense that she had played her part, and a sigh at the thought that none of her children felt it necessary to play theirs.

The carriage bowled along smoothly over the gently curving road. Mrs. Hilbery dropped into a pleasant, inattentive state of mind, in which she was conscious of the running green lines of the hedges, of the swelling ploughland, and of the mild blue sky, which served her, after the first five minutes, for a pastoral background to the drama of human life; and then she thought of a cottage garden, with the flash of yellow daffodils against blue water; and what with the arrangement of these different prospects, and the shaping of two or three lovely phrases, she did not notice that the young people in the carriage were almost silent. Henry, indeed, had been included against his wish, and revenged himself by observing Katharine and Rodney with disillusioned eyes; while Katharine was in a state of gloomy self-suppression which resulted in complete apathy. When Rodney spoke to her she either said "Hum!" or assented so listlessly that he addressed his next remark to her mother. His deference was agreeable to her, his manners were exemplary; and when the church towers and factory chimneys of the town came into sight, she roused herself, and recalled memories of the fair summer of 1853, which fitted in harmoniously with what she was dreaming of the future.

CHAPTER XVIII

B UT other passengers were approaching Lincoln mean-while by other roads on foot. A county town draws the inhabitants of all vicarages, farms, country houses, and wayside cottages, within a radius of ten miles at least, once or twice a week to its streets; and among them, on this occasion, were Ralph Denham and Mary Datchet. They despised the roads, and took their way across the fields; and yet, from their appearance, it did not seem as if they cared much where they walked so long as the way did not actually trip them up. When they left the Vicarage, they had begun an argument which swung their feet along so rhythmically in time with it that they covered the ground at over four miles an hour, and saw nothing of the hedge-rows, the swelling plowland, or the mild blue sky. What they saw were the Houses of Parliament and the Government Offices in Whitehall. They both belonged to the class which is conscious of having lost its birthright in these great structures and is seeking to build another kind of lodging for its own notion of law and government. Purposely, per-haps, Mary did not agree with Ralph; she loved to feel her mind in conflict with his, and to be certain that he spared her female judgment no ounce of his male muscularity. He seemed to argue as fiercely with her as if she were his brother. They were alike, however, in believing that it behooved them to take in hand the repair and reconstruction of the fabric of England. They agreed in thinking that nature has not been generous in the endowment of our coun-cilors. They agreed, unconsciously, in a mute love for the muddy field through which they tramped, with eyes nar-rowed close by the concentration of their minds. At length

they drew breath, let the argument fly away into the limbo
of other good arguments, and, leaning over a gate, opened
their eyes for the first time and looked about them. Their
feet tingled with warm blood and their breath rose in steam
around them. The bodily exercise made them both feel
more direct and less self-conscious than usual, and Mary,
indeed, was overcome by a sort of light-headedness which
made it seem to her that it mattered very little what happened next. It mattered so little, indeed, that she felt herself on the point of saying to Ralph:

"I love you; I shall never love anybody else. Marry me
or leave me; think what you like of me—I don't care a
straw." At the moment, however, speech or silence seemed
immaterial, and she merely clapped her hands together, and
looked at the distant woods with the rust-like bloom on their
brown, and the green and blue landscape through the steam
of her own breath. It seemed a mere toss-up whether she
said, "I love you," or whether she said, "I love the beech-
trees," or only "I love—I love."

"Do you know, Mary," Ralph suddenly interrupted her,
"I've made up my mind."

Her indifference must have been superficial, for it disappeared at once. Indeed, she lost sight of the trees, and
saw her own hand upon the topmost bar of the gate with
extreme distinctness, while he went on:

"I've made up my mind to chuck my work and live down
here. I want you to tell me about that cottage you spoke of.
However, I suppose there'll be no difficulty about getting a
cottage, will there?" He spoke with an assumption of carelessness as if expecting her to dissuade him.

She still waited, as if for him to continue; she was convinced that in some roundabout way he approached the
subject of their marriage.

"I can't stand the office any longer," he proceeded. "I
don't know what my family will say; but I'm sure I'm right.
Don't you think so?"

"Live down here by yourself?" she asked.

"Some old woman would do for me, I suppose," he replied. "I'm sick of the whole thing," he went on, and opened the gate with a jerk.   They began to cross the next field walking side by side.

"I tell you, Mary, it's utter destruction, working away, day after day, at stuff that doesn't matter a damn to any one.   I've stood eight years of it, and I'm not going to stand it any longer.   I suppose this all seems to you mad, though?"

By this time Mary had recovered her self-control.

"No.   I thought you weren't happy," she said.

"Why did you think that?" he asked, with some surprise.

"Don't you remember that morning in Lincoln's Inn Fields?" she asked.

"Yes," said Ralph, slackening his pace and remembering Katharine and her engagement, the purple leaves stamped into the path, the white paper radiant under the electric light, and the hopelessness which seemed to surround all these things.

"You're right, Mary," he said, with something of an effort, "though I don't know how you guessed it."

She was silent, hoping that he might tell her the reason of his unhappiness, for his excuses had not deceived her.

"I was unhappy—very unhappy," he repeated.   Some six weeks separated him from that afternoon when he had sat upon the Embankment watching his visions dissolve in mist as the waters swam past and the sense of his desolation still made him shiver.   He had not recovered in the least from that depression.   Here was an opportunity for making himself face it, as he felt that he ought to; for, by this time, no doubt, it was only a sentimental ghost, better exorcised by ruthless exposure to such an eye as Mary's, than allowed to underlie all his actions and thoughts as had been the case ever since he first saw Katharine Hilbery pouring out tea. He must begin, however, by mentioning her name, and this he found it impossible to do.   He persuaded himself that he he persuaded himself that his feeling had very little to do could make an honest statement without speaking her name; with her.

"Unhappiness is a state of mind," he said, "by which I mean that it is not necessarily the result of any particular cause."

This rather stilted beginning did not please him, and it became more and more obvious to him that, whatever he might say, his unhappiness had been directly caused by Katharine.

"I began to find my life unsatisfactory," he started afresh. "It seemed to me meaningless." He paused again, but felt that this, at any rate, was true, and that on these lines he could go on.

"All this money-making and working ten hours a day in an office, what's it *for*? When one's a boy, you see, one's head is so full of dreams that it doesn't seem to matter what one does. And if you're ambitious, you're all right; you've got a reason for going on. Now my reasons ceased to satisfy me. Perhaps I never had any. That's very likely now I come to think of it. (What reason is there for anything, though?) Still, it's impossible, after a certain age, to take oneself in satisfactorily. And I know what carried me on"—for a good reason now occurred to him—"I wanted to be the savior of my family and all that kind of thing. I wanted them to get on in the world. That was a lie, of course—a kind of self-glorification, too. Like most people, I suppose, I've lived almost entirely among delusions, and now I'm at the awkward stage of finding it out. I want another delusion to go on with. That's what my unhappiness amounts to, Mary."

There were two reasons that kept Mary very silent during this speech, and drew curiously straight lines upon her face. In the first place, Ralph made no mention of marriage; in the second, he was not speaking the truth.

"I don't think it will be difficult to find a cottage," she said, with cheerful hardness, ignoring the whole of this statement. "You've got a little money, haven't you? Yes," she concluded, "I don't see why it shouldn't be a very good plan."

They crossed the field in complete silence. Ralph was

surprised by her remark and a little hurt, and yet, on the whole, rather pleased. He had convinced himself that it was impossible to lay his case truthfully before Mary, and, secretly, he was relieved to find that he had not parted with his dream to her. She was, as he had always found her, the sensible, loyal friend, the woman he trusted; whose sympathy he could count upon, provided he kept within certain limits. He was not displeased to find that those limits were very clearly marked. When they had crossed the next hedge she said to him:

"Yes, Ralph, it's time you made a break. I've come to the same conclusion myself. Only it won't be a country cottage in my case; it'll be America. America!" she cried. "That's the place for me! They'll teach me something about organizing a movement there, and I'll come back and show you how to do it."

If she meant consciously or unconsciously to belittle the seclusion and security of a country cottage, she did not succeed; for Ralph's determination was genuine. But she made him visualize her in her own character, so that he looked quickly at her, as she walked a little in front of him across the plowed field; for the first time that morning he saw her independently of him or of his preoccupation with Katharine. He seemed to see her marching ahead, a rather clumsy but powerful and independent figure, for whose courage he felt the greatest respect.

"Don't go away, Mary!" he exclaimed, and stopped.

"That's what you said before, Ralph," she returned, without looking at him. "You want to go away yourself and you don't want me to go away. That's not very sensible, is it?"

"Mary," he cried, stung by the remembrance of his exacting and dictatorial ways with her, "what a brute I've been to you!"

It took all her strength to keep the tears from springing, and to thrust back her assurance that she would forgive him till Doomsday if he chose. She was preserved from doing so only by a stubborn kind of respect for herself which lay at the root of her nature and forbade surrender, even in moments of almost overwhelming passion. Now, when all was tempest and high-running waves, she knew of a land where the sun shone clear upon Italian grammars and files of docketed papers. Nevertheless, from the skeleton pallor of that land and the rocks that broke its surface, she knew that her life there would be harsh and lonely almost beyond endurance. She walked steadily a little in front of him across the plowed field. Their way took them round the verge of a wood of thin trees standing at the edge of a steep fold in the land. Looking between the tree-trunks, Ralph saw laid out on the perfectly flat and richly green meadow at the bottom of the hill a small gray manor-house, with ponds, terraces, and clipped hedges in front of it, a farm building or so at the side, and a screen of fir-trees rising behind, all perfectly sheltered and self-sufficient. Behind the house the hill rose again, and the trees on the farther summit stood upright against the sky, which appeared of a more intense blue between their trunks. His mind at once was filled with a sense of the actual presence of Katharine; the gray house and the intense blue sky gave him the feeling of her presence close by. He leant against a tree, forming her name beneath his breath:

"Katharine, Katharine," he said aloud, and then, looking round, saw Mary walking slowly away from him, tearing a long spray of ivy from the trees as she passed them. She seemed so definitely opposed to the vision he held in his mind that he returned to it with a gesture of impatience.

"Katharine, Katharine," he repeated, and seemed to himself to be with her. He lost his sense of all that surrounded him; all substantial things—the hour of the day, what we have done and are about to do, the presence of other people and the support we derive from seeing their belief in a common reality—all this slipped from him. So he might have felt if the earth had dropped from his feet, and the empty blue had hung all round him, and the air had been steeped

in the presence of one woman. The chirp of a robin on the
bough above his head awakened him, and his awakenment
was accompanied by a sigh. Here was the world in which
he had live; here the plowed field, the high road yonder,
and Mary, stripping ivy from the trees. When he came up
with her he linked his arm through hers and said:

"Now, Mary, what's all this about America?"

There was a brotherly kindness in his voice which seemed
to her magnanimous, when she reflected that she had cut
short his explanations and shown little interest in his change
of plan. She gave him her reasons for thinking that she
might profit by such a journey, omitting the one reason
which had set all the rest in motion. He listened attentively,
and made no attempt to dissuade her. In truth, he found
himself curiously eager to make certain of her good sense,
and accepted each fresh proof of it with satisfaction, as
though it helped him to make up his mind about something.
She forgot the pain he had caused her, and in place of it
she became conscious of a steady tide of well-being which
harmonized very aptly with the tramp of their feet upon
the dry road and the support of his arm. The comfort was
the more glowing in that it seemed to be the reward of her
determination to behave to him simply and without attempting to be other than she was. Instead of making out an
interest in the poets, she avoided them instinctively, and
dwelt rather insistently upon the practical nature of her
gifts.

In a practical way she asked for particulars of his cottage,
which hardly existed in his mind, and corrected his vagueness.

"You must see that there's water," she insisted, with an
exaggeration of interest. She avoided asking him what he
meant to do in this cottage, and, at last, when all the practical details had been thrashed out as much as possible, he
rewarded her by a more intimate statement.

"One of the rooms," he said, "must be my study, for, you
see, Mary, I'm going to write a book." Here he withdrew

his arm from hers, lit his pipe, and they tramped on in a sagacious kind of comradeship, the most complete they had attained in all their friendship.

"And what's your book to be about?" she said, as boldly as if she had never come to grief with Ralph in talking about books. He told her unhesitatingly that he meant to write the history of the English village from Saxon days to the present time. Some such plan had lain as a seed in his mind for many years; and now that he had decided, in a flash, to give up his profession, the seed grew in the space of twenty minutes both tall and lusty. He was surprised himself at the positive way in which he spoke. It was the same with the question of his cottage. That had come into existence, too, in an unromantic shape—a square white house standing just off the high road, no doubt, with a neighbor who kept a pig and a dozen squalling children; for these plans were shorn of all romance in his mind, and the pleasure he derived from thinking of them was checked directly it passed a very sober limit. So a sensible man who has lost his chance of some beautiful inheritance might tread out the narrow bounds of his actual dwelling-place, and assure himself that life is supportable within its demesne, only one must grow turnips and cabbages, not melons and pomegranates. Certainly Ralph took some pride in the resources of his mind, and was insensibly helped to right himself by Mary's trust in him. She wound her ivy spray round her ash-plant, and for the first time for many days, when alone with Ralph, set no spies upon her motives, sayings, and feelings, but surrendered herself to complete happiness.

Thus talking, with easy silences and some pauses to look at the view over the hedge and to decide upon the species of a little gray-brown bird slipping among the twigs, they walked into Lincoln, and after strolling up and down the main street, decided upon an inn where the rounded window suggested substantial fare, nor were they mistaken. For over a hundred and fifty years hot joints, potatoes, greens, and apple puddings had been served to generations of coun-

try gentlemen, and now, sitting at a table in the hollow of
the bow window, Ralph and Mary took their share of this
perennial feast.   Looking across the joint, half-way through
the meal, Mary wondered whether Ralph would ever come
to look quite like the other people in the room.   Would he
be absorbed among the round pink faces, pricked with little
white bristles, the calves fitted in shiny brown leather, the
black-and-white check suits, which were sprinkled about in
the same room with them?   She half hoped so; she thought
that it was only in his mind that he was different.   She did
not wish him to be too different from other people.   The
walk had given him a ruddy color, too, and his eyes were lit
up by a steady, honest light, which could not make the
simplest farmer feel ill at ease, or suggest to the most devout
of clergymen a disposition to sneer at his faith.   She loved
the steep cliff of his forehead, and compared it to the brow
of a young Greek horseman, who reins his horse back so
sharply that it half falls on its haunches.   He always seemed
to her like a rider on a spirited horse.   And there was an
exaltation to her in being with him, because there was a risk
that he would not be able to keep to the right pace among
other people.   Sitting opposite him at the little table in the
window, she came back to that state of careless exaltation
which had overcome her when they halted by the gate, but
now it was accompanied by a sense of sanity and security,
for she felt that they had a feeling in common which scarcely
needed embodiment in words.   How silent he was! leaning
his forehead on his hand, now and then, and again looking
steadily and gravely at the backs of the two men at the next
table, with so little self-consciousness that she could almost
watch his mind placing one thought solidly upon the top of
another; she thought that she could feel him thinking,
through the shade of her fingers, and she could anticipate the
exact moment when he would put an end to his thought and
turn a little in his chair and say:

"Well, Mary——?" inviting her to take up the thread of
thought where he had dropped it.

And at that very moment he turned just so, and said:

"Well, Mary?" with the curious touch of diffidence which she loved in him.

She laughed, and she explained her laugh on the spur of the moment by the look of the people in the street below. There was a motor-car with an old lady swathed in blue veils, and a lady's maid on the seat opposite, holding a King Charles's spaniel; there was a country-woman wheeling a perambulator full of sticks down the middle of the road; there was a bailiff in gaiters discussing the state of the cattle market with a dissenting minister—so she defined them.

She ran over this list without any fear that her companion would think her trivial. Indeed, whether it was due to the warmth of the room or to the good roast beef, or whether Ralph had achieved the process which is called making up one's mind, certainly he had given up testing the good sense, the independent character, the intelligence shown in her remarks. He had been building one of those piles of thought, as ramshackle and fantastic as a Chinese pagoda, half from words let fall by gentlemen in gaiters, half from the litter in his own mind, about duck shooting and legal history, about the Roman occupation of Lincoln and the relations of country gentlemen with their wives, when, from all this disconnected rambling, there suddenly formed itself in his mind the idea that he would ask Mary to marry him. The idea was so spontaneous that it seemed to shape itself of its own accord before his eyes. It was then that he turned round and made use of his old, instinctive phrase:

"Well, Mary——?"

As it presented itself to him at first, the idea was so new and interesting that he was half inclined to address it, without more ado, to Mary herself. His natural instinct to divide his thoughts carefully into two different classes before he expressed them to her prevailed. But as he watched her looking out of the window and describing the old lady, the woman with the perambulator, the bailiff and the dissenting minister, his eyes filled involuntarily with tears. He would have liked to lay his head on her shoulder and sob, while she parted his hair with her fingers and soothed him and said:

"There, there. Don't cry! Tell me why you're crying——"; and they would clasp each other tight, and her arms would hold him like his mother's. He felt that he was very lonely, and that he was afraid of the other people in the room.

"How damnable this all is!" he exclaimed abruptly.

"What are you talking about?" she replied, rather vaguely, still looking out of the window.

He resented this divided attention more than, perhaps, he knew, and he thought how Mary would soon be on her way to America.

"Mary," he said, "I want to talk to you. Haven't we nearly done? Why don't they take away these plates?"

Mary felt his agitation without looking at him; she felt convinced that she knew what it was that he wished to say to her.

"They'll come all in good time," she said; and felt it necessary to display her extreme calmness by lifting a salt-cellar and sweeping up a little heap of bread-crumbs.

"I want to apologize," Ralph continued, not quite knowing what he was about to say, but feeling some curious instinct which urged him to commit himself irrevocably, and to prevent the moment of intimacy from passing.

"I think I've treated you very badly. That is, I've told you lies. Did you guess that I was lying to you? Once in Lincoln's Inn Fields and again to-day on our walk. I am a liar, Mary. Did you know that? Do you think you do know me?"

"I think I do," she said.

At this point the waiter changed their plates.

"It's true I don't want you to go to America," he said, looking fixedly at the table-cloth. "In fact, my feelings towards you seem to be utterly and damnably bad," he said energetically, although forced to keep his voice low.

"If I weren't a selfish beast I should tell you to have

nothing more to do with me. And yet, Mary, in spite of the fact that I believe what I'm saying, I also believe that it's good we should know each other—the world being what it is, you see——" and by a nod of his head he indicated the other occupants of the room, "for, of course, in an ideal state of things, in a decent community even, there's no doubt you shouldn't have anything to do with me—seriously, that is."

"You forget that I'm not an ideal character, either," said Mary, in the same low and very earnest tones, which, in spite of being almost inaudible, surrounded their table with an atmosphere of concentration which was quite perceptible to the other diners, who glanced at them now and then with a queer mixture of kindness, amusement, and curiosity.

"I'm much more selfish than I let on, and I'm worldly a little—more than you think, anyhow. I like bossing things —perhaps that's my greatest fault. I've none of your passion for——" here she hesitated, and glanced at him, as if to ascertain what his passion was for—"for the truth," she added, as if she had found what she sought indisputably.

"I've told you I'm a liar," Ralph repeated obstinately.

"Oh, in little things, I dare say," she said impatiently. "But not in real ones, and that's what matters. I dare say I'm more truthful than you are in small ways. But I could never care"—she was surprised to find herself speaking the word, and had to force herself to speak it out—"for any one who was a liar in that way. I love the truth a certain amount—a considerable amount—but not in the way you love it." Her voice sank, became inaudible, and wavered as if she could scarcely keep herself from tears.

"Good heavens!" Ralph exclaimed to himself. "She loves me! Why did I never see it before? She's going to cry; no, but she can't speak."

The certainty overwhelmed him so that he scarcely knew what he was doing; the blood rushed to his cheeks, and although he had quite made up his mind to ask her to marry him, the certainty that she loved him seemed to change the situation so completely that he could not do it. He did not dare to look at her. If she cried, he did not know what he should do. It seemed to him that something of a terrible and devastating nature had happened. The waiter changed their plates once more.

In his agitation Ralph rose, turned his back upon Mary, and looked out of the window. The people in the street seemed to him only a dissolving and combining pattern of black particles; which, for the moment, represented very well the involuntary procession of feelings and thoughts which formed and dissolved in rapid succession in his own mind. At one moment he exulted in the thought that Mary loved him; at the next, it seemed that he was without feeling for her; her love was repulsive to him. Now he felt urged to marry her at once; now to disappear and never see her again. In order to control this disorderly race of thought he forced himself to read the name on the chemist's shop directly opposite him; then to examine the objects in the shop windows, and then to focus his eyes exactly upon a little group of women looking in at the great windows of a large draper's shop. This discipline having given him at least a superficial control of himself, he was about to turn and ask the waiter to bring the bill, when his eye was caught by a tall figure walking quickly along the opposite pavement —a tall figure, upright, dark, and commanding, much detached from her surroundings. She held her gloves in her left hand, and the left hand was bare. All this Ralph noticed and enumerated and recognized before he put a name to the whole—Katharine Hilbery. She seemed to be looking for somebody. Her eyes, in fact, scanned both sides of the street, and for one second were raised directly to the bow window in which Ralph stood; but she looked away again instantly without giving any sign that she had seen him. This sudden apparition had an extraordinary effect upon him. It was as if he had thought of her so intensely that his mind had formed the shape of her, rather than that he had seen her in the flesh outside in the street. And yet he had not been thinking of her at all. The impression was so intense that he could not dismiss it, nor even think whether he had seen her or merely imagined her. He sat down at once, and said, briefly and strangely, rather to himself than to Mary:

"That was Katharine Hilbery."

"Katharine Hilbery? What do you mean?" she asked, hardly understanding from his manner whether he had seen her or not.

"Katharine Hilbery," he repeated. "But she's gone now."

"Katharine Hilbery!" Mary thought, in an instant of blinding revelation; "I've always known it was Katharine Hilbery!" She knew it all now.

After a moment of downcast stupor, she raised her eyes, looked steadily at Ralph, and caught his fixed and dreamy gaze leveled at a point far beyond their surroundings, a point that she had never reached in all the time that she had known him. She noticed the lips just parted, the fingers loosely clenched, the whole attitude of rapt contemplation, which fell like a veil between them. She noticed everything about him; if there had been other signs of his utter alienation she would have sought them out, too, for she felt that it was only by heaping one truth upon another that she could keep herself sitting there, upright. The truth seemed to support her; it struck her, even as she looked at his face, that the light of truth was shining far away beyond him; the light of truth, she seemed to frame the words as she rose to go, shines on a world not to be shaken by our personal calamities.

Ralph handed her her coat and her stick. She took them, fastened the coat securely, grasped the stick firmly. The ivy spray was still twisted about the handle; this one sacrifice, she thought, she might make to sentimentality and personality, and she picked two leaves from the ivy and put them in her pocket before she disencumbered her stick of the rest of it. She grasped the stick in the middle, and settled her fur cap closely upon her head, as if she must be

in trim for a long and stormy walk. Next, standing in the
middle of the road, she took a slip of paper from her purse,
and read out loud a list of commissions entrusted to her—
fruit, butter, string, and so on; and all the time she never
spoke directly to Ralph or looked at him.

Ralph heard her giving orders to attentive, rosy-cheeked
men in white aprons, and in spite of his own preoccupation,
he commented upon the determination with which she made
her wishes known. Once more he began, automatically, to
take stock of her characteristics. Standing thus, superficially observant and stirring the sawdust on the floor meditatively with the toe of his boot, he was roused by a musical
and familiar voice behind him, accompanied by a light touch
upon his shoulder.

"I'm not mistaken? Surely Mr. Denham? I caught a
glimpse of your coat through the window, and I felt sure
that I knew your coat. Have you seen Katharine or William? I'm wandering about Lincoln looking for the ruins."

It was Mrs. Hilbery; her entrance created some stir in
the shop; many people looked at her.

"First of all, tell me where I am," she demanded, but,
catching sight of the attentive shopman, she appealed to
him. "The ruins—my party is waiting for me at the ruins.
The Roman ruins—or Greek, Mr. Denham? Your town
has a great many beautiful things in it, but I wish it hadn't
so many ruins. I never saw such delightful little pots of
honey in my life—are they made by your own bees? Please
give me one of those little pots, and tell me how I shall find
my way to the ruins."

"And now," she continued, having received the information and the pot of honey, having been introduced to Mary,
and having insisted that they should accompany her back
to the ruins, since in a town with so many turnings, such
prospects, such delightful little half-naked boys dabbling in
pools, such Venetian canals, such old blue china in the curiosity shops, it was impossible for one person all alone to
find her way to the ruins. "Now," she exclaimed, "please

tell me what you're doing here, Mr. Denham—for you *are* Mr. Denham, aren't you?" she inquired, gazing at him with a sudden suspicion of her own accuracy. "The brilliant young man who writes for the Review, I mean? Only yesterday my husband was telling me he thought you one of the cleverest young men he knew. Certainly, you've been the messenger of Providence to me, for unless I'd seen you I'm sure I should never have found the ruins at all."

They had reached the Roman arch when Mrs. Hilbery caught sight of her own party, standing like sentinels facing up and down the road so as to intercept her if, as they expected, she had got lodged in some shop.

"I've found something much better than ruins!" she exclaimed. "I've found two friends who told me how to find you, which I could never have done without them. They must come and have tea with us. What a pity that we've just had luncheon." Could they not somehow revoke that meal?

Katharine, who had gone a few steps by herself down the road, and was investigating the window of an ironmonger, as if her mother might have got herself concealed among mowing-machines and garden-shears, turned sharply on hearing her voice, and came towards them. She was a great deal surprised to see Denham and Mary Datchet. Whether the cordiality with which she greeted them was merely that which is natural to a surprise meeting in the country, or whether she was really glad to see them both, at any rate she exclaimed with unusual pleasure as she shook hands:

"I never knew you lived here. Why didn't you say so, and we could have met? And are you staying with Mary?" she continued, turning to Ralph. "What a pity we didn't meet before."

Thus confronted at a distance of only a few feet by the real body of the woman about whom he had dreamt so many million dreams, Ralph stammered; he made a clutch at his self-control; the color either came to his cheeks or left them, he knew not which; but he was determined to face her and track down in the cold light of day whatever vestige of

truth there might be in his persistent imaginations. He did
not succeed in saying anything. It was Mary who spoke
for both of them. He was struck dumb by finding that
Katharine was quite different, in some strange way, from
his memory, so that he had to dismiss his old view in order
to accept the new one. The wind was blowing her crimson
scarf across her face; the wind had already loosened her
hair, which looped across the corner of one of the large,
dark eyes which, so he used to think, looked sad; now they
looked bright with the brightness of the sea struck by an
unclouded ray; everything about her seemed rapid, fragmentary, and full of a kind of racing speed. He realized
suddenly that he had never seen her in the daylight before.

Meanwhile, it was decided that it was too late to go in
search of ruins as they had intended; and the whole party
began to walk towards the stables where the carriage had
been put up.

"Do you know," said Katharine, keeping slightly in advance of the rest with Ralph, "I thought I saw you this
morning, standing at a window. But I decided that it
couldn't be you. And it must have been you all the same."

"Yes, I thought I saw you—but it wasn't you," he replied.

This remark, and the rough strain in his voice, recalled
to her memory so many difficult speeches and abortive meetings that she was jerked directly back to the London drawing-room, the family relics, and the tea-table; and at the
same time recalled some half-finished or interrupted remark
which she had wanted to make herself or to hear from him
—she could not remember what it was.

"I expect it was me," she said. "I was looking for my
mother. It happens every time we come to Lincoln. In
fact, there never was a family so unable to take care of itself
as ours is. Not that it very much matters, because some
one always turns up in the nick of time to help us out of our
scrapes. Once I was left in a field with a bull when I was
a baby—but where did we leave the carriage? Down that
street or the next? The next, I think." She glanced back

and saw that the others were following obediently, listening to certain memories of Lincoln upon which Mrs. Hilbery had started. "But what are you doing here?" she asked.

"I'm buying a cottage. I'm going to live here—as soon as I can find a cottage, and Mary tells me there'll be no difficulty about that."

"But," she exclaimed, almost standing still in her surprise, "you will give up the Bar, then?" It flashed across her mind that he must already be engaged to Mary.

"The solicitor's office? Yes. I'm giving that up."

"But why?" she asked. She answered herself at once, with a curious change from rapid speech to an almost melancholy tone. "I think you're very wise to give it up. You will be much happier."

At this very moment, when her words seemed to be striking a path into the future for him, they stepped into the yard of an inn, and there beheld the family coach of the Otways, to which one sleek horse was already attached, while the second was being led out of the stable door by the hostler.

"I don't know what one means by happiness," he said briefly, having to step aside in order to avoid a groom with a bucket. "Why do you think I shall be happy? I don't expect to be anything of the kind. I expect to be rather less unhappy. I shall write a book and curse my charwoman— if happiness consists in that. What do you think?"

She could not answer because they were immediately surrounded by other members of the party—by Mrs. Hilbery, and Mary, Henry Otway, and William.

Rodney went up to Katharine immediately and said to her:

"Henry is going to drive home with your mother, and I suggest that they should put us down half-way and let us walk back."

Katharine nodded her head. She glanced at him with an oddly furtive expression.

"Unfortunately we go in opposite directions, or we might

have given you a lift," he continued to Denham. His manner was unusually peremptory; he seemed anxious to hasten the departure, and Katharine looked at him from time to time, as Denham noticed, with an expression half of inquiry, half of annoyance. She at once helped her mother into her cloak, and said to Mary:

"I want to see you. Are you going back to London at once? I will write." She half smiled at Ralph, but her look was a little overcast by something she was thinking, and in a very few minutes the Otway carriage rolled out of the stable yard and turned down the high road leading to the village of Lampsher.

The return drive was almost as silent as the drive from home had been in the morning; indeed, Mrs. Hilbery leant back with closed eyes in her corner, and either slept or feigned sleep, as her habit was in the intervals between the seasons of active exertion, or continued the story which she had begun to tell herself that morning.

About two miles from Lampsher the road ran over the rounded summit of the heath, a lonely spot marked by an obelisk of granite, setting forth the gratitude of some great lady of the eighteenth century who had been set upon by highwaymen at this spot and delivered from death just as hope seemed lost. In summer it was a pleasant place, for the deep woods on either side murmured, and the heather, which grew thick round the granite pedestal, made the light breeze taste sweetly; in winter the sighing of the trees was deepened to a hollow sound, and the heath was as gray and almost as solitary as the empty sweep of the clouds above it.

Here Rodney stopped the carriage and helped Katharine to alight. Henry, too, gave her his hand, and fancied that she pressed it very slightly in parting as if she sent him a message. But the carriage rolled on immediately, without wakening Mrs. Hilbery, and left the couple standing by the obelisk. That Rodney was angry with her and had made this opportunity for speaking to her, Katharine knew very well; she was neither glad nor sorry that the time had come, nor, indeed, knew what to expect, and thus remained silent. The carriage grew smaller and smaller upon the dusky road, and still Rodney did not speak. Perhaps, she thought, he waited until the last sign of the carriage had disappeared beneath the curve of the road and they were left entirely alone. To cloak their silence she read the writing on the obelisk, to do which she had to walk completely round it. She was murmuring a word to two of the pious lady's thanks above her breath when Rodney joined her. In silence they set out along the cart-track which skirted the verge of the trees.

To break the silence was exactly what Rodney wished to do, and yet could not do to his own satisfaction. In company it was far easier to approach Katharine; alone with her, the aloofness and force of her character checked all his natural methods of attack. He believed that she had behaved very badly to him, but each separate instance of unkindness seemed too petty to be advanced when they were alone together.

"There's no need for us to race," he complained at last; upon which she immediately slackened her pace, and walked too slowly to suit him. In desperation he said the first thing he thought of, very peevishly and without the dignified prelude which he had intended.

"I've not enjoyed my holiday."

"No?"

"No. I shall be glad to get back to work again."

"Saturday, Sunday, Monday—there are only three days more," she counted.

"No one enjoys being made a fool of before other people," he blurted out, for his irritation rose as she spoke, and got the better of his awe of her, and was inflamed by that awe.

"That refers to me, I suppose," she said calmly.

"Every day since we've been here you've done something to make me appear ridiculous," he went on. "Of course, so long as it amuses you, you're welcome; but we have to remember that we are going to spend our lives together. I asked you, only this morning, for example, to come out and take a turn with me in the garden. I was waiting for you ten minutes, and you never came. Every one saw me waiting. The stable-boys saw me. I was so ashamed that I went in. Then, on the drive you hardly spoke to me. Henry noticed it. Every one notices it. . . . You find no difficulty in talking to Henry, though."

She noted these various complaints and determined philosophically to answer none of them, although the last stung her to considerable irritation. She wished to find out how deep his grievance lay.

"None of these things seem to me to matter," she said.

"Very well, then. I may as well hold my tongue," he replied.

"In themselves they don't seem to me to matter; if they hurt you, of course they matter," she corrected herself scrupulously. Her tone of consideration touched him, and he walked on in silence for a space.

"And we might be so happy, Katharine!" he exclaimed impulsively, and drew her arm through his. She withdrew it directly.

"As long as you let yourself feel like this we shall never be happy," she said.

The harshness, which Henry had noticed, was again unmistakable in her manner. William flinched and was silent. Such severity, accompanied by something indescribably cold and impersonal in her manner, had constantly been meted out to him during the last few days, always in the company of others. He had recouped himself by some ridiculous display of vanity which, as he knew, put him still more at her mercy. Now that he was alone with her there was no stimulus from outside to draw his attention from his injury. By a considerable effort of self-control he forced himself to remain silent, and to make himself distinguish what part of his pain was due to vanity, what part to the certainty that no woman really loving him could speak thus.

"What do I feel about Katharine?" he thought to himself. It was clear that she had been a very desirable and distinguished figure, the mistress of her little section of the world; but more than that, she was the person of all others who seemed to him the arbitress of life, the woman whose judgment was naturally right and steady, as his had never been in spite of all his culture. And then he could not see her come into a room without a sense of the flowing of robes, of the flowering of blossoms, of the purple waves of the sea, of all things that are lovely and mutable on the surface but still and passionate in their heart.

"If she were callous all the time and had only led me on to laugh at me I couldn't have felt that about her," he thought. "I'm not a fool, after all. I can't have been utterly mistaken all these years. And yet, when she speaks to me like that! The truth of it is," he thought, "that I've got such despicable faults that no one could help speaking to me like that. Katharine is quite right. And yet those are not my serious feelings, as she knows quite well. How can I change myself? What would make her care for me?" He was terribly tempted here to break the silence by asking Katharine in what respects he could change himself to suit her; but he sought consolation instead by running over the list of his gifts and acquirements, his knowledge of Greek and Latin, his knowledge of art and literature, his skill in the management of meters, and his ancient west-country blood. But the feeling that underlay all these feelings and puzzled him profoundly and kept him silent was the certainty that he loved Katharine as sincerely as he had it in him to love any one. And yet she could speak to him like that! In a sort of bewilderment he lost all desire to speak, and would quite readily have taken up some different topic of conversation if Katharine had started one. This, however, she did not do.

He glanced at her, in case her expression might help him to understand her behavior. As usual, she had quickened her pace unconsciously, and was now walking a little in front of him; but he could gain little information from her eyes, which looked steadily at the brown heather, or from the lines drawn seriously upon her forehead. Thus to lose touch with her, for he had no idea what she was thinking, was so unpleasant to him that he began to talk about his grievances again, without, however, much conviction in his voice.

"If you have no feeling for me, wouldn't it be kinder to say so to me in private?"

"Oh, William," she burst out, as if he had interrupted some absorbing train of thought, "how you go on about feelings! Isn't it better not to talk so much, not to be worrying always about small things that don't really matter?"

"That's the question precisely," he exclaimed. "I only want you to tell me that they don't matter. There are times when you seem indifferent to everything. I'm vain, I've a thousand faults; but you know they're not everything; you know I care for you."

"And if I say that I care for you, don't you believe me?"

"Say it, Katharine! Say it as if you meant it! Make me feel that you care for me!"

She could not force herself to speak a word. The heather was growing dim around them, and the horizon was blotted out by white mist. To ask her for passion or for certainty seemed like asking that damp prospect for fierce blades of fire, or the faded sky for the intense blue vault of June.

He went on now to tell her of his love for her, in words which bore, even to her critical senses, the stamp of truth; but none of this touched her, until, coming to a gate whose hinge was rusty, he heaved it open with his shoulder, still talking and taking no account of his effort. The virility of this deed impressed her; and yet, normally, she attached no value to the power of opening gates. The strength of muscles has nothing to do on the face of it with the strength of affections; nevertheless, she felt a sudden concern for this power running to waste on her account, which, combined with a desire to keep possession of that strangely attractive masculine power, made her rouse herself from her torpor.

Why should she not simply tell him the truth—which was that she had accepted him in a misty state of mind when nothing had its right shape or size? that it was deplorable, but that with clearer eyesight marriage was out of the question? She did not want to marry any one. She wanted to go away by herself, preferably to some bleak northern moor, and there study mathematics and the science of astronomy. Twenty words would explain the whole situation to him. He had ceased to speak; he had told her once more how he loved her and why. She summoned her courage, fixed her eyes upon a lightning-splintered ash-tree, and, almost as if she were reading a writing fixed to the trunk, began:

"I was wrong to get engaged to you. I shall never make you happy. I have never loved you."

"Katharine!" he protested.

"No, never," she repeated obstinately. "Not rightly. Don't you see, I didn't know what I was doing?"

"You love some one else?" he cut her short.

"Absolutely no one."

"Henry?" he demanded.

"Henry? I should have thought, William, even you——"

"There is some one," he persisted. "There has been a change in the last few weeks. You owe it to me to be honest, Katharine."

"If I could, I would," she replied.

"Why did you tell me you would marry me, then?" he demanded.

Why, indeed? A moment of pessimism, a sudden conviction of the undeniable prose of life, a lapse of the illusion which sustains youth midway between heaven and earth, a desperate attempt to reconcile herself with facts—she could only recall a moment, as of waking from a dream, which now seemed to her a moment of surrender. But who could give reasons such as these for doing what she had done? She shook her head very sadly.

"But you're not a child—you're not a woman of moods,"

Rodney persisted. "You couldn't have accepted me if you hadn't loved me!" he cried.

A sense of her own misbehavior, which she had succeeded in keeping from her by sharpening her consciousness of Rodney's faults, now swept over her and almost overwhelmed her. What were his faults in comparison with the fact that he cared for her? What were her virtues in comparison with the fact that she did not care for him? In a flash the conviction that not to care is the uttermost sin of all stamped itself upon her inmost thought; and she felt herself branded for ever.

He had taken her arm, and held her hand firmly in his, nor had she the force to resist what now seemed to her his enormously superior strength. Very well; she would submit, as her mother and her aunt and most women, perhaps, had submitted; and yet she knew that every second of such submission to his strength was a second of treachery to him.

"I did say I would marry you, but it was wrong," she forced herself to say, and she stiffened her arm as if to annul even the seeming submission of that separate part of her; "for I don't love you, William; you've noticed it, every one's noticed it; why should we go on pretending? When I told you I loved you, I was wrong. I said what I knew to be untrue."

As none of her words seemed to her at all adequate to represent what she felt, she repeated them, and emphasized them without realizing the effect that they might have upon a man who cared for her. She was completely taken aback by finding her arm suddenly dropped; then she saw his face most strangely contorted; was he laughing, it flashed across her? In another moment she saw that he was in tears. In her bewilderment at this apparition she stood aghast for a second. With a desperate sense that this horror must, at all costs, be stopped, she then put her arms about him, drew his head for a moment upon her shoulder, and led him on, murmuring words of consolation, until he heaved a great sigh. They held fast to each other; her tears, too, ran down her cheeks; and were both quite silent. Noticing the difficulty with which he walked, and feeling the same extreme lassitude in her own limbs, she proposed that they should rest for a moment where the bracken was brown and shriveled beneath an oak-tree. He assented. Once more he gave a great sigh, and wiped his eyes with a childlike unconsciousness, and began to speak without a trace of his previous anger. The idea came to her that they were like the children in the fairy tale who were lost in a wood, and with this in her mind she noticed the scattering of dead leaves all round them which had been blown by the wind into heaps, a foot or two deep, here and there.

"When did you begin to feel this, Katharine?" he said; "for it isn't true to say that you've always felt it. I admit I was unreasonable the first night when you found that your clothes had been left behind. Still, where's the fault in that? I could promise you never to interfere with your clothes again. I admit I was cross when I found you upstairs with Henry. Perhaps I showed it too openly. But that's not unreasonable either when one's engaged. Ask your mother. And now this terrible thing——" He broke off, unable for the moment to proceed any further. "This decision you say you've come to—have you discussed it with any one? Your mother, for example, or Henry?"

"No, no, of course not," she said, stirring the leaves with her hand. "But you don't understand me, William——"

"Help me to understand you——"

"You don't understand, I mean, my real feelings; how could you? I've only now faced them myself. But I haven't got the sort of feeling—love, I mean—I don't know what to call it"—she looked vaguely towards the horizon sunk under mist—"but, anyhow, without it our marriage would be a farce——"

"How a farce?" he asked. "But this kind of analysis is disastrous!" he exclaimed.

"I should have done it before," she said gloomily.

"You make yourself think things you don't think," he

continued, becoming demonstrative with his hands, as his manner was. "Believe me, Katharine, before we came here we were perfectly happy. You were full of plans for our house—the chair-covers, don't you remember?—like any other woman who is about to be married. Now, for no reason whatever, you begin to fret about your feeling and about my feeling, with the usual result. I assure you, Katharine, I've been through it all myself. At one time I was always asking myself absurd questions which came to nothing either. What you want, if I may say so, is some occupation to take you out of yourself when this morbid mood comes on. If it hadn't been for my poetry, I assure you, I should often have been very much in the same state myself. To let you into a secret," he continued, with his little chuckle, which now sounded almost assured, "I've often gone home from seeing you in such a state of nerves that I had to force myself to write a page or two before I could get you out of my head. Ask Denham; he'll tell you how he met me one night; he'll tell you what a state he found me in."

Katharine started with displeasure at the mention of Ralph's name. The thought of the conversation in which her conduct had been made a subject for discussion with Denham roused her anger; but, as she instantly felt, she had scarcely the right to grudge William any use of her name, seeing what her fault against him had been from first to last. And yet Denham! She had a view of him as a judge. She figured him sternly weighing instances of her levity in this masculine court of inquiry into feminine morality and gruffly dismissing both her and her family with some half-sarcastic, half-tolerant phrase which sealed her doom, as far as he was concerned, for ever. Having met him so lately, the sense of his character was strong in her. The thought was not a pleasant one for a proud woman, but she had yet to learn the art of subduing her expression. Her eyes fixed upon the ground, her brows drawn together, gave William a very fair picture of the resentment that she was forcing herself to control. A certain degree of apprehension, occasionally culminating in a kind of fear, had always entered into his love for her, and had increased, rather to his surprise, in the greater intimacy of their engagement. Beneath her steady, exemplary surface ran a vein of passion which seemed to him now perverse, now completely irrational, for it never took the normal channel of glorification of him and his doings; and, indeed, he almost preferred the steady good sense, which had always marked their relationship, to a more romantic bond. But passion she had, he could not deny it, and hitherto he had tried to see it employed in his thoughts upon the lives of the children who were to be born to them.

"She will make a perfect mother—a mother of sons," he thought; but seeing her sitting there, gloomy and silent, he began to have his doubts on this point. "A farce, a farce," he thought to himself. "She said that our marriage would be a farce," and he became suddenly aware of their situation, sitting upon the ground, among the dead leaves, not fifty yards from the main road, so that it was quite possible for some one passing to see and recognize them. He brushed off his face any trace that might remain of that unseemly exhibition of emotion. But he was more troubled by Katharine's appearance, as she sat rapt in thought upon the ground, than by his own; there was something improper to him in her self-forgetfulness. A man naturally alive to the conventions of society, he was strictly conventional where women were concerned, and especially if the women happened to be in any way connected with him. He noticed with distress the long strand of dark hair touching her shoulder and two or three dead beech-leaves attached to her dress; but to recall her mind in their present circumstances to a sense of these details was impossible. She sat there, seeming unconscious of everything. He suspected that in her silence she was reproaching herself; but he wished that she would think of her hair and of the dead beech-leaves, which were of more immediate importance to him than anything else. Indeed, these trifles drew his attention strangely from his own doubtful and uneasy state of mind; for relief, mixing itself with pain, stirred up a most curious hurry and tumult in his breast, almost concealing his first sharp sense of bleak and overwhelming disappointment. In order to relieve this restlessness and close a distressingly ill-ordered scene, he rose abruptly and helped Katharine to her feet. She smiled a little at the minute care with which he tidied her and yet, when he brushed the dead leaves from his own coat, she flinched, seeing in that action the gesture of a lonely man.

"William," she said, "I will marry you. I will try to make you happy."

CHAPTER XIX

THE afternoon was already growing dark when the two other wayfarers, Mary and Ralph Denham, came out on the high road beyond the outskirts of Lincoln. The high road, as they both felt, was better suited to this return journey than the open country, and for the first mile or so of the way they spoke little. In his own mind Ralph was following the passage of the Otway carriage over the heath; he then went back to the five or ten minutes that he had spent with Katharine, and examined each word with the care that a scholar displays upon the irregularities of an ancient text. He was determined that the glow, the romance, the atmosphere of this meeting should not paint what he must in future regard as sober facts. On her side Mary was silent, not because her thoughts took much handling, but because her mind seemed empty of thought as her heart of feeling. Only Ralph's presence, as she knew, preserved this numbness, for she could foresee a time of loneliness when many varieties of pain would beset her. At the present moment her effort was to preserve what she could of the wreck of her self-respect, for such she deemed that momentary glimpse of her love so involuntarily revealed to Ralph. In the light of reason it did not much matter, perhaps, but it was her instinct to be careful of that vision of herself which keeps pace so evenly beside every one of us, and had been damaged by her confession. The gray night coming down over the country was kind to her; and she thought that one of these days she would find comfort in sitting upon the earth, alone, beneath a tree. Looking through the darkness, she marked the swelling ground and the tree. Ralph made her start by saying abruptly:

"What I was going to say when we were interrupted at

lunch was that if you go to America I shall come, too. It
can't be harder to earn a living there than it is here. However, that's not the point. The point is, Mary, that I want
to marry you. Well, what do you say?" He spoke firmly,
waited for no answer, and took her arm in his. "You know
me by this time, the good and the bad," he went on. "You
know my tempers. I've tried to let you know my faults.
Well, what do you say, Mary?"

She said nothing, but this did not seem to strike him.

"In most ways, at least in the important ways, as you
said, we know each other and we think alike. I believe you
are the only person in the world I could live with happily.
And if you feel the same about me—as you do, don't you,
Mary?—we should make each other happy." Here he paused,
and seemed to be in no hurry for an answer; he seemed,
indeed, to be continuing his own thoughts.

"Yes, but I'm afraid I couldn't do it," Mary said at last.
The casual and rather hurried way in which she spoke, together with the fact that she was saying the exact opposite
of what he expected her to say, baffled him so much that he
instinctively loosened his clasp upon her arm and she withdrew it quietly.

"You couldn't do it?" he asked.

"No, I couldn't marry you," she replied.

"You don't care for me?"

She made no answer.

"Well, Mary," he said, with a curious laugh, "I must be
an arrant fool, for I thought you did." They walked for a
minute or two in silence, and suddenly he turned to her,
looked at her, and exclaimed: "I don't believe you, Mary.
You're not telling me the truth."

"I'm too tired to argue, Ralph," she replied, turning her
head away from him. "I ask you to believe what I say. I
can't marry you; I don't want to marry you."

The voice in which she stated this was so evidently the
voice of one in some extremity of anguish that Ralph had
no course but to obey her. And as soon as the tone of her

voice had died out, and the surprise faded from his mind, he found himself believing that she had spoken the truth, for he had but little vanity, and soon her refusal seemed a natural thing to him. He slipped through all the grades of despondency until he reached a bottom of absolute gloom. Failure seemed to mark the whole of his life; he had failed with Katharine, and now he had failed with Mary. Up at once sprang the thought of Katharine, and with it a sense of exulting freedom, but this he checked instantly. No good had ever come to him from Katharine; his whole relationship with her had been made up of dreams; and as he thought of the little substance there had been in his dreams he began to lay the blame of the present catastrophe upon his dreams.

"Haven't I always been thinking of Katharine while I was with Mary? I might have loved Mary if it hadn't been for that idiocy of mine. She cared for me once, I'm certain of that, but I tormented her so with my humors that I let my chances slip, and now she won't risk marrying me. And this is what I've made of my life—nothing, nothing, nothing."

The tramp of their boots upon the dry road seemed to asseverate nothing, nothing, nothing. Mary thought that this silence was the silence of relief; his depression she ascribed to the fact that he had seen Katharine and parted from her, leaving her in the company of William Rodney. She could not blame him for loving Katharine, but that, when he loved another, he should ask her to marry him— that seemed to her the cruellest treachery. Their old friendship and its firm base upon indestructible qualities of character crumbled, and her whole past seemed foolish, herself weak and credulous, and Ralph merely the shell of an honest man. Oh, the past—so much made up of Ralph; and now, as she saw, made up of something strange and false and other than she had thought it. She tried to recapture a saying she had made to help herself that morning, as Ralph paid the bill for luncheon; but she could see him paying the bill more vividly than she could remember the phrase.

Something about truth was in it; how to see the truth is our great chance in this world.

"If you don't want to marry me," Ralph now began again, without abruptness, with diffidence rather, "there is no need why we should cease to see each other, is there? Or would you rather that we should keep apart for the present?"

"Keep apart? I don't know—I must think about it."

"Tell me one thing, Mary," he resumed; "have I done anything to make you change your mind about me?"

She was immensely tempted to give way to her natural trust in him, revived by the deep and now melancholy tones of his voice, and to tell him of her love, and of what had changed it. But although it seemed likely that she would soon control her anger with him, the certainty that he did not love her, confirmed by every word of his proposal, forbade any freedom of speech. To hear him speak and to feel herself unable to reply, or constrained in her replies, was so painful that she longed for the time when she should be alone. A more pliant woman would have taken this chance of an explanation, whatever risks attached to it; but to one of Mary's firm and resolute temperament there was degradation in the idea of self-abandonment; let the waves of emotion rise ever so high, she could not shut her eyes to what she conceived to be the truth. Her silence puzzled Ralph. He searched his memory for words or deeds that might have made her think badly of him. In his present mood instances came but too quickly, and on top of them this culminating proof of his baseness—that he had asked her to marry him when his reasons for such a proposal were selfish and half-hearted.

"You needn't answer," he said grimly. "There are reasons enough, I know. But must they kill our friendship, Mary? Let me keep that, at least."

"Oh," she thought to herself, with a sudden rush of anguish which threatened disaster to her self-respect, "it has

come to this—to this—when I could have given him everything!"

"Yes, we can still be friends," she said, with what firmness she could muster.

"I shall want your friendship," he said. He added, "If
you find it possible, let me see you as often as you can. The
oftener the better. I shall want your help."

She promised this, and they went on to talk calmly of
things that had no reference to their feelings—a talk which,
in its constraint, was infinitely sad to both of them.

One more reference was made to the state of things between them late that night, when Elizabeth had gone to her
room, and the two young men had stumbled off to bed in
such a state of sleep that they hardly felt the floor beneath
their feet after a day's shooting.

Mary drew her chair a little nearer to the fire, for the
logs were burning low, and at this time of night it was
hardly worth while to replenish them. Ralph was reading,
but she had noticed for some time that his eyes instead of
following the print were fixed rather above the page with
an intensity of gloom that came to weigh upon her mind.
She had not weakened in her resolve not to give way, for
reflection had only made her more bitterly certain that, if
she gave way, it would be to her own wish and not to his.
But she had determined that there was no reason why he
should suffer if her reticence were the cause of his suffering.
Therefore, although she found it painful, she spoke:

"You asked me if I had changed my mind about you,
Ralph," she said. "I think there's only one thing. When
you asked me to marry you, I don't think you meant it.
That made me angry—for the moment. Before, you'd always spoken the truth."

Ralph's book slid down upon his knee and fell upon the
floor. He rested his forehead on his hand and looked into
the fire. He was trying to recall the exact words in which
he had made his proposal to Mary.

"I never said I loved you," he said at last.

She winced; but she respected him for saying what he did, for this, after all, was a fragment of the truth which she had vowed to live by.

"And to me marriage without love doesn't seem worth while," she said.

"Well, Mary, I'm not going to press you," he said. "I see you don't want to marry me. But love—don't we all talk a great deal of nonsense about it? What does one mean? I believe I care for you more genuinely than nine men out of ten care for the women they're in love with. It's only a story one makes up in one's mind about another person, and one knows all the time it isn't true. Of course one knows; why, one's always taking care not to destroy the illusion. One takes care not to see them too often, or to be alone with them for too long together. It's a pleasant illusion, but if you're thinking of the risks of marriage, it seems to me that the risk of marrying a person you're in love with is something colossal."

"I don't believe a word of that, and what's more you don't, either," she replied with anger. "However, we don't agree; I only wanted you to understand." She shifted her position, as if she were about to go. An instinctive desire to prevent her from leaving the room made Ralph rise at this point and begin pacing up and down the nearly empty kitchen, checking his desire, each time he reached the door, to open it and step out into the garden. A moralist might have said that at this point his mind should have been full of self-reproach for the suffering he had caused. On the contrary, he was extremely angry, with the confused impotent anger of one who finds himself unreasonably but efficiently frustrated. He was trapped by the illogicality of human life. The obstacles in the way of his desire seemed to him purely artificial, and yet he could see no way of removing them. Mary's words, the tone of her voice even, angered him, for she would not help him. She was part of the insanely jumbled muddle of a world which impedes the sensible life. He would have liked to slam the door or break the hind legs of a chair, for the obstacles had taken some such curiously substantial shape in his mind.

"I doubt that one human being ever understands another," he said, stopping in his march and confronting Mary at a distance of a few feet.

"Such damned liars as we all are, how can we? But we can try. If you don't want to marry me, don't; but the position you take up about love, and not seeing each other—isn't that mere sentimentality? You think I've behaved very badly," he continued, as she did not speak. "Of course I behave badly; but you can't judge people by what they do. You can't go through life measuring right and wrong with a foot-rule. That's what you're always doing, Mary; that's what you're doing now."

She saw herself in the Suffrage Office, delivering judgment, meting out right and wrong, and there seemed to her to be some justice in the charge, although it did not affect her main position.

"I'm not angry with you," she said slowly. "I will go on seeing you, as I said I would."

It was true that she had promised that much already, and it was difficult for him to say what more it was that he wanted—some intimacy, some help against the ghost of Katharine, perhaps, something that he knew he had no right to ask; and yet, as he sank into his chair and looked once more at the dying fire it seemed to him that he had been defeated, not so much by Mary as by life itself. He felt himself thrown back to the beginning of life again, where everything has yet to be won; but in extreme youth one has an ignorant hope. He was no longer certain that he would triumph.

CHAPTER XX

HAPPILY for Mary Datchet she returned to the office to find that by some obscure Parliamentary maneuver the vote had once more slipped beyond the attainment of women. Mrs. Seal was in a condition bordering upon frenzy. The duplicity of Ministers, the treachery of mankind, the insult to womanhood, the setback to civilization, the ruin of her life's work, the feelings of her father's daughter—all these topics were discussed in turn, and the office was littered with newspaper cuttings branded with the blue, if ambiguous, marks of her displeasure. She confessed herself at fault in her estimate of human nature.

"The simple elementary acts of justice," she said, waving her hand towards the window, and indicating the foot-passengers and omnibuses then passing down the far side of Russell Square, "are as far beyond them as they ever were. We can only look upon ourselves, Mary, as pioneers in a wilderness. We can only go on patiently putting the truth before them. It isn't *them*," she continued, taking heart from her sight of the traffic, "it's their leaders. It's those gentlemen sitting in Parliament and drawing four hundred a year of the people's money. If we had to put our case to the people, we should soon have justice done to us. I have always believed in the people, and I do so still. But——" She shook her head and implied that she would give them one more chance, and if they didn't take advantage of that she couldn't answer for the consequences.

Mr. Clacton's attitude was more philosophical and better supported by statistics. He came into the room after Mrs. Seal's outburst and pointed out, with historical illustrations, that such reverses had happened in every political campaign

255

of any importance. If anything, his spirits were improved by the disaster. The enemy, he said, had taken the offensive; and it was now up to the Society to outwit the enemy. He gave Mary to understand that he had taken the measure of their cunning, and had already bent his mind to the task which, so far as she could make out, depended solely upon him. It depended, so she came to think, when invited into his room for a private conference, upon a systematic revision of the card-index, upon the issue of certain new lemon-colored leaflets, in which the facts were marshaled once more in a very striking way, and upon a large scale map of England dotted with little pins tufted with differently colored plumes of hair according to their geographical position. Each district, under the new system, had its flag, its bottle of ink, its sheaf of documents tabulated and filed for reference in a drawer, so that by looking under M or S, as the case might be, you had all the facts with respect to the Suffrage organizations of that county at your fingers' ends. This would require a great deal of work, of course.

"We must try to consider ourselves rather in the light of a telephone exchange—for the exchange of ideas, Miss Datchet," he said; and taking pleasure in his image, he continued it. "We should consider ourselves the center of an enormous system of wires, connecting us up with every district of the country. We must have our fingers upon the pulse of the community; we want to know what people all over England are thinking; we want to put them in the way of thinking rightly." The system, of course, was only roughly sketched so far—jotted down, in fact, during the Christmas holidays.

"When you ought to have been taking a rest, Mr. Clacton," said Mary dutifully, but her tone was flat and tired.

"We learn to do without holidays, Miss Datchet," said Mr. Clacton, with a spark of satisfaction in his eye.

He wished particularly to have her opinion of the lemon-colored leaflet. According to his plan, it was to be distributed in immense quantities immediately, in order to stimulate and generate, "to generate and stimulate," he repeated, "right thoughts in the country before the meeting of Parliament."

"We have to take the enemy by surprise," he said. "They don't let the grass grow under their feet. Have you seen Bingham's address to his constituents? That's a hint of the sort of thing we've got to meet, Miss Datchet."

He handed her a great bundle of newspaper cuttings, and, begging her to give him her views upon the yellow leaflet before lunch-time, he turned with alacrity to his different sheets of paper and his different bottles of ink.

Mary shut the door, laid the documents upon her table, and sank her head on her hands. Her brain was curiously empty of any thought. She listened, as if, perhaps, by listening she would become merged again in the atmosphere of the office. From the next room came the rapid spasmodic sounds of Mrs. Seal's erratic typewriting; she, doubtless, was already hard at work helping the people of England, as Mr. Clacton put it, to think rightly; "generating and stimulating," those were his words. She was striking a blow against the enemy, no doubt, who didn't let the grass grow beneath their feet. Mr. Clacton's words repeated themselves accurately in her brain. She pushed the papers wearily over to the farther side of the table. It was no use, though; something or other had happened to her brain—a change of focus so that near things were indistinct again. The same thing had happened to her once before, she remembered, after she had met Ralph in the gardens of Lincoln's Inn Fields; she had spent the whole of a committee meeting in thinking about sparrows and colors, until, almost at the end of the meeting, her old convictions had all come back to her. But they had only come back, she thought with scorn at her feebleness, because she wanted to use them to fight against Ralph. They weren't, rightly speaking, convictions at all. She could not see the world divided into separate compartments of good people and bad people, any more than she could believe so implicitly in the rightness of her own thought as to wish to bring the population of the British Isles into agreement with it. She looked at the lemon-colored leaflet, and thought almost enviously of the faith which could find comfort in the issue of such documents; for herself she would be content to remain silent for ever if a share of personal happiness were granted her. She read Mr. Clacton's statement with a curious division of judgment, noting its weak and pompous verbosity on the one hand, and, at the same time, feeling that faith, faith in an illusion, perhaps, but, at any rate, faith in something, was of all gifts the most to be envied. An illusion it was, no doubt. She looked curiously round her at the furniture of the office, at the machinery in which she had taken so much pride, and marveled to think that once the copying-presses, the card-index, the files of documents, had all been shrouded, wrapped in some mist which gave them a unity and a general dignity and purpose independently of their separate significance. The ugly cumbersomeness of the furniture alone impressed her now. Her attitude had become very lax and despondent when the typewriter stopped in the next room. Mary immediately drew up to the table, laid hands on an unopened envelope, and adopted an expression which might hide her state of mind from Mrs. Seal. Some instinct of decency required that she should not allow Mrs. Seal to see her face. Shading her eyes with her fingers, she watched Mrs. Seal pull out one drawer after another in her search for some envelope or leaflet. She was tempted to drop her fingers and exclaim:

"Do sit down, Sally, and tell me how you manage it—how you manage, that is, to bustle about with perfect confidence in the necessity of your own activities, which to me seem as futile as the buzzing of a belated blue-bottle." She said nothing of the kind, however, and the pretence of industry which she preserved so long as Mrs. Seal was in the room served to set her brain in motion, so that she dispatched her morning's work much as usual. At one o'clock she was surprised to find how efficiently she had dealt with the morning. As she put her hat on she determined to lunch at a shop in the Strand, so as to set that other piece of mechanism, her body, into action. With a brain working and a body working one could keep step with the crowd and never be found out for the hollow machine, lacking the essential thing, that one was conscious of being.

She considered her case as she walked down the Charing Cross Road. She put to herself a series of questions. Would she mind, for example, if the wheels of that motor-omnibus passed over her and crushed her to death? No, not in the least; or an adventure with that disagreeable-looking man hanging about the entrance of the Tube station? No; she could not conceive fear or excitement. Did suffering in any form appal her? No, suffering was neither good nor bad. And this essential thing? In the eyes of every single person she detected a flame; as if a spark in the brain ignited spontaneously at contact with the things they met and drove them on. The young women looking into the milliners' windows had that look in their eyes; and elderly men turning over books in the second-hand book-shops, and eagerly waiting to hear what the price was—the very lowest price—they had it, too. But she cared nothing at all for clothes or for money either. Books she shrank from, for they were connected too closely with Ralph. She kept on her way resolutely through the crowd of people, among whom she was so much of an alien, feeling them cleave and give way before her.

Strange thoughts are bred in passing through crowded streets should the passenger, by chance, have no exact destination in front of him, much as the mind shapes all kinds of forms, solutions, images when listening inattentively to music. From an acute consciousness of herself as an individual, Mary passed to a conception of the scheme of things in which, as a human being, she must have her share. She half held a vision; the vision shaped and dwindled. She wished she had a pencil and a piece of paper to help her to give a form to this conception which composed itself as

she walked down the Charing Cross Road. But if she talked
to any one, the conception might escape her. Her vision
seemed to lay out the lines of her life until death in a way
which satisfied her sense of harmony. It only needed a
persistent effort of thought, stimulated in this strange way
by the crowd and the noise, to climb the crest of existence
and see it all laid out once and for ever. Already her suffering as an individual was left behind her. Of this process,
which was to her so full of effort, which comprised infinitely
swift and full passages of thought, leading from one crest
to another, as she shaped her conception of life in this world,
only two articulate words escaped her, muttered beneath her
breath—"Not happiness—not happiness."

She sat down on a seat opposite the statue of one of
London's heroes upon the Embankment, and spoke the
words aloud. To her they represented the rare flower or
splinter of rock brought down by a climber in proof that he
has stood for a moment, at least, upon the highest peak of
the mountain. She had been up there and seen the world
spread to the horizon. It was now necessary to alter her
course to some extent, according to her new resolve. Her
post should be in one of those exposed and desolate stations
which are shunned naturally by happy people. She arranged
the details of the new plan in her mind, not without a grim
satisfaction.

"Now," she said to herself, rising from her seat, "I'll
think of Ralph."

Where was he to be placed in the new scale of life? Her
exalted mood seemed to make it safe to handle the question.
But she was dismayed to find how quickly her passions leapt
forward the moment she sanctioned this line of thought.
Now she was identified with him and rethought his thoughts
with complete self-surrender; now, with a sudden cleavage
of spirit, she turned upon him and denounced him for his
cruelty.

"But I refuse—I refuse to hate any one," she said aloud;
chose the moment to cross the road with circumspection,

and ten minutes later lunched in the Strand, cutting her meat
firmly into small pieces, but giving her fellow-diners no
further cause to judge her eccentric.   Her soliloquy crystal-
ized itself into little fragmentary phrases emerging suddenly
from the turbulence of her thought, particularly when she
had to exert herself in any way, either to move, to count
money, or to choose a turning.   "To know the truth—to
accept without bitterness"—those, perhaps, were the most
articulate of her utterances, for no one could have made
head or tail of the queer gibberish murmured in front of the
statue of Francis, Duke of Bedford, save that the name of
Ralph occurred frequently in very strange connections, as if,
having spoken it, she wished, superstitiously, to cancel it by
adding some other word that robbed the sentence with his
name in it of any meaning.

Those champions of the cause of women, Mr. Clacton
and Mrs. Seal, did not perceive anything strange in Mary's
behavior, save that she was almost half an hour later than
usual in coming back to the office.   Happily, their own affairs kept them busy, and she was free from their inspection.
If they had surprised her they would have found her lost,
apparently, in admiration of the large hotel across the
square, for, after writing a few words, her pen rested upon
the paper, and her mind pursued its own journey among
the sun-blazoned windows and the drifts of purplish smoke
which formed her view.   And, indeed, this background was
by no means out of keeping with her thoughts.   She saw to
the remote spaces behind the strife of the foreground, en-
abled now to gaze there, since she had renounced her own
demands, privileged to see the larger view, to share the vast
desires and sufferings of the mass of mankind.   She had
been too lately and too roughly mastered by facts to take an
easy pleasure in the relief of renunciation; such satisfaction
as she felt came only from the discovery that, having renounced everything that made life happy, easy, splendid,
individual, there remained a hard reality, unimpaired by

one's personal adventures, remote as the stars, unquenchable as they are.

While Mary Datchet was undergoing this curious transformation from the particular to the universal, Mrs. Seal remembered her duties with regard to the kettle and the gas-fire. She was a little surprised to find that Mary had drawn her chair to the window, and, having lit the gas, she raised herself from a stooping posture and looked at her. The most obvious reason for such an attitude in a secretary was some kind of indisposition. But Mary, rousing herself with an effort, denied that she was indisposed.

"I'm frightfully lazy this afternoon," she added, with a glance at her table. "You must really get another secretary, Sally."

The words were meant to be taken lightly, but something in the tone of them roused a jealous fear which was always dormant in Mrs. Seal's breast. She was terribly afraid that one of these days Mary, the young woman who typified so many rather sentimental and enthusiastic ideas, who had some sort of visionary existence in white with a sheaf of lilies in her hand, would announce, in a jaunty way, that she was about to be married.

"You don't mean that you're going to leave us?" she said.

"I've not made up my mind about anything," said Mary— a remark which could be taken as a generalization.

Mrs. Seal got the teacups out of the cupboard and set them on the table.

"You're not going to be married, are you?" she asked, pronouncing the words with nervous speed.

"Why are you asking such absurd questions this afternoon, Sally?" Mary asked, not very steadily. "Must we all get married?"

Mrs. Seal emitted a most peculiar chuckle. She seemed for one moment to acknowledge the terrible side of life which is concerned with the emotions, the private lives, of the sexes, and then to sheer off from it with all possible speed into the shades of her own shivering virginity. She was made so uncomfortable by the turn the conversation had taken, that she plunged her head into the cupboard, and endeavored to abstract some very obscure piece of china.

"We have our work," she said, withdrawing her head, displaying cheeks more than usually crimson, and placing a jam-pot emphatically upon the table. But, for the moment, she was unable to launch herself upon one of those enthusiastic, but inconsequent, tirades upon liberty, democracy, the rights of the people, and the iniquities of the Government, in which she delighted. Some memory from her own past or from the past of her sex rose to her mind and kept her abashed. She glanced furtively at Mary, who still sat by the window with her arm upon the sill. She noticed how young she was and full of the promise of womanhood. The sight made her so uneasy that she fidgeted the cups upon their saucers.

"Yes—enough work to last a lifetime," said Mary, as if concluding some passage of thought.

Mrs. Seal brightened at once. She lamented her lack of scientific training, and her deficiency in the processes of logic, but she set her mind to work at once to make the prospects of the cause appear as alluring and important as she could. She delivered herself of an harangue in which she asked a great many rhetorical questions and answered them with a little bang of one fist upon another.

"To last a lifetime? My dear child, it will last all our lifetimes. As one falls another steps into the breach. My father, in his generation, a pioneer—I, coming after him, do my little best. What, alas! can one do more? And now it's you young women—we look to you—the future looks to you. Ah, my dear, if I'd a thousand lives, I'd give them all to our cause. The cause of women, d'you say? I say the cause of humanity. And there are some"—she glanced fiercely at the window—"who don't see it! There are some who are satisfied to go on, year after year, refusing to admit the truth. And we who have the vision—the kettle boiling over? No, no, let me see to it—we who know the truth," she continued, gesticulating with the kettle and the teapot. Owing to these encumbrances, perhaps, she lost the thread of her discourse, and concluded, rather wistfully, "It's all so *simple.*" She referred to a matter that was a perpetual source of bewilderment to her—the extraordinary incapacity of the human race, in a world where the good is so unmistakably divided from the bad, of distinguishing one from the other, and embodying what ought to be done in a few large, simple Acts of Parliament, which would, in a very short time, completely change the lot of humanity.

"One would have thought," she said, "that men of University training, like Mr. Asquith—one would have thought than an appeal to reason would not be unheard by them. But reason," she reflected, "what is reason without Reality?"

Doing homage to the phrase, she repeated it once more, and caught the ear of Mr. Clacton, as he issued from his room; and he repeated it a third time, giving it, as he was in the habit of doing with Mrs. Seal's phrases, a dryly humorous intonation. He was well pleased with the world, however, and he remarked, in a flattering manner, that he would like to see that phrase in large letters at the head of a leaflet.

"But, Mrs. Seal, we have to aim at a judicious combination of the two," he added in his magisterial way to check the unbalanced enthusiasm of the women. "Reality has to be voiced by reason before it can make itself felt. The weak point of all these movements, Miss Datchet," he continued, taking his place at the table and turning to Mary as usual when about to deliver his more profound cogitations, "is that they are not based upon sufficiently intellectual grounds. A mistake, in my opinion. The British public likes a pellet of reason in its jam of eloquence—a pill of reason in its pudding of sentiment," he said, sharpening the phrase to a satisfactory degree of literary precision.

His eyes rested, with something of the vanity of an author, upon the yellow leaflet which Mary held in her hand.

She rose, took her seat at the head of the table, poured out
tea for her colleagues, and gave her opinion upon the leaflet.
So she had poured out tea, so she had criticized Mr. Clacton's leaflets a hundred times already; but now it seemed to
her that she was doing it in a different spirit; she had en-
listed in the army, and was a volunteer no longer. She had
renounced something and was now—how could she express
it?—not quite "in the running" for life. She had always
known that Mr. Clacton and Mrs. Seal were not in the running, and across the gulf that separated them she had seen
them in the guise of shadow people, flitting in and out of
the ranks of the living—eccentrics, undeveloped human beings, from whose substance some essential part had been cut
away. All this had never struck her so clearly as it did this
afternoon, when she felt that her lot was cast with them for
ever. One view of the world plunged in darkness, so a more
volatile temperament might have argued after a season of
despair, let the world turn again and show another, more
splendid, perhaps. No, Mary thought, with unflinching
loyalty to what appeared to her to be the true view, having
lost what is best, I do not mean to pretend that any other
view does instead. Whatever happens, I mean to have no
pretences in my life. Her very words had a sort of distinctness which is sometimes produced by sharp, bodily pain.
To Mrs. Seal's secret jubilation the rule which forbade discussion of shop at tea-time was overlooked. Mary and Mr.
Clacton argued with a cogency and a ferocity which made
the little woman feel that something very important—she
hardly knew what—was taking place. She became much excited; one crucifix became entangled with another, and she
dug a considerable hole in the table with the point of her
pencil in order to emphasize the most striking heads of the
discourse; and how any combination of Cabinet Ministers
could resist such discourse she really did not know.

She could hardly bring herself to remember her own private instrument of justice—the typewriter. The telephone-
bell rang, and as she hurried off to answer a voice which

always seemed a proof of importance by itself, she felt that it was at this exact spot on the surface of the globe that all the subterranean wires of thought and progress came together. When she returned, with a message from the printer, she found that Mary was putting on her hat firmly; there was something imperious and dominating in her attitude altogether.

"Look, Sally," she said, "these letters want copying. These I've not looked at. The question of the new census will have to be gone into carefully. But I'm going home now. Good night, Mr. Clacton; good night, Sally."

"We are very fortunate in our secretary, Mr. Clacton," said Mrs. Seal, pausing with her hand on the papers, as the door shut behind Mary. Mr. Clacton himself had been vaguely impressed by something in Mary's behavior towards him. He envisaged a time even when it would become necessary to tell her that there could not be two masters in one office—but she was certainly able, very able, and in touch with a group of very clever young men. No doubt they had suggested to her some of her new ideas.

He signified his assent to Mrs. Seal's remark, but observed, with a glance at the clock, which showed only half an hour past five:

"If she takes the work seriously, Mrs. Seal—but that's just what some of your clever young ladies don't do." So saying he returned to his room, and Mrs. Seal, after a moment's hesitation, hurried back to her labors.

CHAPTER XXI

MARY walked to the nearest station and reached home in an incredibly short space of time, just so much, indeed, as was needed for the intelligent understanding of the news of the world as the *Westminster Gazette* reported it. Within a few minutes of opening her door, she was in trim for a hard evening's work. She unlocked a drawer and took out a manuscript, which consisted of a very few pages, entitled, in a forcible hand, "Some Aspects of the Democratic State." The aspects dwindled out in a criss-cross of blotted lines in the very middle of a sentence, and suggested that the author had been interrupted, or convinced of the futility of proceeding, with her pen in the air. . . . Oh, yes, Ralph had come in at that point. She scored that sheet very effectively, and, choosing a fresh one, began at a great rate with a generalization upon the structure of human society, which was a good deal bolder than her custom. Ralph had told her once that she couldn't write English, which accounted for those frequent blots and insertions; but she put all that behind her, and drove ahead with such words as came her way, until she had accomplished half a page of generalization and might legitimately draw breath. Directly her hand stopped her brain stopped too, and she began to listen. A paper-boy shouted down the street; an omnibus ceased and lurched on again with the heave of duty once more shouldered; the dullness of the sounds suggested that a fog had risen since her return, if, indeed, a fog has power to deaden sound, of which fact, she could not be sure at the present moment. It was the sort of fact Ralph Denham knew. At any rate, it was no concern of hers, and she was about to dip a pen when her

ear was caught by the sound of a step upon the stone staircase. She followed it past Mr. Chippen's chambers; past
Mr. Gibson's; past Mr. Turner's; after which it became her
sound. A postman, a washerwoman, a circular, a bill—she
presented herself with each of these perfectly natural possibilities; but, to her surprise, her mind rejected each one
of them impatiently, even apprehensively. The step became
slow, as it was apt to do at the end of the steep climb, and
Mary, listening for the regular sound, was filled with an
intolerable nervousness. Leaning against the table, she felt
the knock of her heart push her body perceptibly backwards
and forwards—a state of nerves astonishing and reprehensible in a stable woman. Grotesque fancies took shape. Alone,
at the top of the house, an unknown person approaching
nearer and nearer—how could she escape? There was no
way of escape. She did not even know whether that oblong
mark on the ceiling was a trap-door to the roof or not. And
if she got on to the roof—well, there was a drop of sixty
feet or so on to the pavement. But she sat perfectly still,
and when the knock sounded, she got up directly and opened
the door without hesitation. She saw a tall figure outside,
with something ominous to her eyes in the look of it.

"What do you want?" she said, not recognizing the face
in the fitful light of the staircase.

"Mary? I'm Katharine Hilbery!"

Mary's self-possession returned almost excessively, and
her welcome was decidedly cold, as if she must recoup herself for this ridiculous waste of emotion. She moved her
green-shaded lamp to another table, and covered "Some
Aspects of the Democratic State" with a sheet of blotting-
paper.

"Why can't they leave me alone?" she thought bitterly,
connecting Katharine and Ralph in a conspiracy to take
from her even this hour of solitary study, even this poor
little defence against the world. And, as she smoothed
down the sheet of blotting-paper over the manuscript, she
braced herself to resist Katharine, whose presence struck

her, not merely by its force, as usual, but as something in the nature of a menace.

"You're working?" said Katharine, with hesitation, perceiving that she was not welcome.

"Nothing that matters," Mary replied, drawing forward the best of the chairs and poking the fire.

"I didn't know you had to work after you had left the office," said Katharine, in a tone which gave the impression that she was thinking of something else, as was, indeed, the case.

She had been paying calls with her mother, and in between the calls Mrs. Hilbery had rushed into shops and bought pillow-cases and blotting-books on no perceptible method for the furnishing of Katharine's house. Katharine had a sense of impedimenta accumulating on all sides of her. She had left her at length, and had come on to keep an engagement to dine with Rodney at his rooms. But she did not mean to get to him before seven o'clock, and so had plenty of time to walk all the way from Bond Street to the Temple if she wished it. The flow of faces streaming on either side of her had hypnotized her into a mood of profound despondency, to which her expectation of an evening alone with Rodney contributed. They were very good friends again, better friends, they both said, than ever before. So far as she was concerned this was true. There were many more things in him than she had guessed until emotion brought them forth—strength, affection, sympathy. And she thought of them and looked at the faces passing, and thought how much alike they were, and how distant, nobody feeling anything as she felt nothing, and distance, she thought, lay inevitably between the closest, and their intimacy was the worst pretence of all. For, "Oh dear," she thought, looking into a tobacconist's window, "I don't care for any of them, and I don't care for William, and people say this is the thing that matters most, and I can't see what they mean by it."

She looked desperately at the smooth-bowled pipes, and

wondered—should she walk on by the Strand or by the Embankment? It was not a simple question, for it concerned not different streets so much as different streams of thought. If she went by the Strand she would force herself to think out the problem of the future, or some mathematical problem; if she went by the river she would certainly begin to think about things that didn't exist—the forest, the ocean beach, the leafy solitudes, the magnanimous hero. No, no, no! A thousand times no!—it wouldn't do; there was something repulsive in such thoughts at present; she must take something else; she was out of that mood at present. And then she thought of Mary; the thought gave her confidence, even pleasure of a sad sort, as if the triumph of Ralph and Mary proved that the fault of her failure lay with herself and not with life. An indistinct idea that the sight of Mary might be of help, combined with her natural trust in her, suggested a visit; for, surely, her liking was of a kind that implied liking upon Mary's side also. After a moment's hesitation she decided, although she seldom acted upon impulse, to act upon this one, and turned down a side street and found Mary's door. But her reception was not encouraging; clearly Mary didn't want to see her, had no help to impart, and the half-formed desire to confide in her was quenched immediately. She was slightly amused at her own delusion, looked rather absent-minded, and swung her gloves to and fro, as if doling out the few minutes accurately before she could say good-by.

Those few minutes might very well be spent in asking for information as to the exact position of the Suffrage Bill, or in expounding her own very sensible view of the situation. But there was a tone in her voice, or a shade in her opinions, or a swing of her gloves which served to irritate Mary Datchet, whose manner became increasingly direct, abrupt, and even antagonistic. She became conscious of a wish to make Katharine realize the importance of this work, which she discussed so coolly, as though she, too, had sacrificed what Mary herself had sacrificed. The swinging of the gloves

ceased, and Katharine, after ten minutes, began to make
movements preliminary to departure. At the sight of this,
Mary was aware—she was abnormally aware of things to-
night—of another very strong desire; Katharine was not to
be allowed to go, to disappear into the free, happy world of
irresponsible individuals. She must be made to realize—to
feel.

"I don't quite see," she said, as if Katharine had challenged her explicitly, "how, things being as they are, any
one can help trying, at least, to do something."

"No. But how *are* things?"

Mary pressed her lips, and smiled ironically; she had
Katharine at her mercy; she could, if she liked, discharge
upon her head wagon-loads of revolting proof of the state
of things ignored by the casual, the amateur, the looker-on,
the cynical observer of life at a distance. And yet she hesitated. As usual, when she found herself in talk with Katharine, she began to feel rapid alternations of opinion about
her, arrows of sensation striking strangely through the envelope of personality, which shelters us so conveniently from
our fellows. What an egoist, how aloof she was! And yet,
not in her words, perhaps, but in her voice, in her face, in
her attitude, there were signs of a soft brooding spirit, of
a sensibility unblunted and profound, playing over her
thoughts and deeds, and investing her manner with an habitual gentleness. The arguments and phrases of Mr. Clacton fell flat against such armor.

"You'll be married, and you'll have other things to think
of," she said inconsequently, and with an accent of con-
descension. She was not going to make Katharine understand in a second, as she would, all she herself had learnt
at the cost of such pain. No. Katharine was to be happy;
Katharine was to be ignorant; Mary was to keep this knowledge of the impersonal life for herself. The thought of her
morning's renunciation stung her conscience, and she tried
to expand once more into that impersonal condition which
was so lofty and so painless. She must check this desire to

be an individual again, whose wishes were in conflict with those of other people. She repented of her bitterness.

Katharine now renewed her signs of leave-taking; she had drawn on one of her gloves, and looked about her as if in search of some trivial saying to end with. Wasn't there some picture, or clock, or chest of drawers which might be singled out for notice? something peaceable and friendly to end the uncomfortable interview? The green-shaded lamp burnt in the corner, and illumined books and pens and blotting-paper. The whole aspect of the place started another train of thought and struck her as enviably free; in such a room one could work—one could have a life of one's own.

"I think you're very lucky," she observed. "I envy you, living alone and having your own things"—and engaged in this exalted way, which had no recognition or engagement-ring, she added in her own mind.

Mary's lips parted slightly. She could not conceive in what respects Katharine, who spoke sincerely, could envy her.

"I don't think you've got any reason to envy me," she said.

"Perhaps one always envies other people," Katharine observed vaguely.

"Well, but you've got everything that any one can want."

Katharine remained silent. She gazed into the fire quietly, and without a trace of self-consciousness. The hostility which she had divined in Mary's tone had completely disappeared, and she forgot that she had been upon the point of going.

"Well, I suppose I have," she said at length. "And yet I sometimes think——" She paused; she did not know how to express what she meant.

"It came over me in the Tube the other day," she resumed, with a smile; "what is it that makes these people go one way rather than the other? It's not love; it's not reason; I think it must be some idea. Perhaps, Mary, our affections are the shadow of an idea. Perhaps there isn't any such thing as affection in itself. . . ." She spoke half-mockingly, asking her question, which she scarcely troubled to frame, not of Mary, or of any one in particular.

But the words seemed to Mary Datchet shallow, supercilious, cold-blooded, and cynical all in one. All her natural instincts were roused in revolt against them.

"I'm the opposite way of thinking, you see," she said.

"Yes; I know you are," Katharine replied, looking at her as if now she were about, perhaps, to explain something very important.

Mary could not help feeling the simplicity and good faith that lay behind Katharine's words.

"I think affection is the only reality," she said.

"Yes," said Katharine, almost sadly. She understood that Mary was thinking of Ralph, and she felt it impossible to press her to reveal more of this exalted condition; she could only respect the fact that, in some few cases, life arranged itself thus satisfactorily and pass on. She rose to her feet accordingly. But Mary exclaimed, with unmistakable earnestness, that she must not go; that they met so seldom; that she wanted to talk to her so much. . . . Katharine was surprised at the earnestness with which she spoke. It seemed to her that there could be no indiscretion in mentioning Ralph by name.

Seating herself "for ten minutes," she said: "By the way, Mr. Denham told me he was going to give up the Bar and live in the country. Has he gone? He was beginning to tell me about it, when we were interrupted."

"He thinks of it," said Mary briefly. The color at once came to her face.

"It would be a very good plan," said Katharine in her decided way.

"You think so?"

"Yes, because he would do something worth while; he would write a book. My father always says that he's the most remarkable of the young men who write for him."

Mary bent low over the fire and stirred the coal between

the bars with a poker. Katharine's mention of Ralph had roused within her an almost irresistible desire to explain to her the true state of the case between herself and Ralph. She knew, from the tone of her voice, that in speaking of Ralph she had no desire to probe Mary's secrets, or to insinuate any of her own. Moreover, she liked Katharine; she trusted her; she felt a respect for her. The first step of confidence was comparatively simple; but a further confidence had revealed itself, as Katharine spoke, which was not so simple, and yet it impressed itself upon her as a necessity; she must tell Katharine what it was clear that she had no conception of—she must tell Katharine that Ralph was in love with her.

"I don't know what he means to do," she said hurriedly, seeking time against the pressure of her own conviction. "I've not seen him since Christmas."

Katharine reflected that this was odd; perhaps, after all, she had misunderstood the position. She was in the habit of assuming, however, that she was rather unobservant of the finer shades of feeling, and she noted her present failure as another proof that she was a practical, abstract-minded person, better fitted to deal with figures than with the feelings of men and women. Anyhow, William Rodney would say so.

"And now——" she said.

"Oh, please stay!" Mary exclaimed, putting out her hand to stop her. Directly Katharine moved she felt, inarticulately and violently, that she could not bear to let her go. If Katharine went, her only chance of speaking was lost; her only chance of saying something tremendously important was lost. Half a dozen words were sufficient to wake Katharine's attention, and put flight and further silence beyond her power. But although the words came to her lips, her throat closed upon them and drove them back. After all, she considered, why should she speak? Because it is right, her instinct told her; right to expose oneself without reservations to other human beings. She flinched from the thought. It asked too much of one already stripped bare. Something she must keep of her own. But if she did keep something of her own? Immediately she figured an immured life, continuing for an immense period, the same feelings living for ever, neither dwindling nor changing within the ring of a thick stone wall. The imagination of this loneliness frightened her, and yet to speak—to lose her loneliness, for it had already become dear to her, was beyond her power.

Her hand went down to the hem of Katharine's skirt, and, fingering a line of fur, she bent her head as if to examine it.

"I like this fur," she said, "I like your clothes. And you mustn't think that I'm going to marry Ralph," she continued, in the same tone, "because he doesn't care for me at all. He cares for some one else." Her head remained bent, and her hand still rested upon the skirt.

"It's a shabby old dress," said Katharine, and the only sign that Mary's words had reached her was that she spoke with a little jerk.

"You don't mind my telling you that?" said Mary, raising herself.

"No, no," said Katharine; "but you're mistaken, aren't you?" She was, in truth, horribly uncomfortable, dismayed, indeed, disillusioned. She disliked the turn things had taken quite intensely. The indecency of it afflicted her. The suffering implied by the tone appalled her. She looked at Mary furtively, with eyes that were full of apprehension. But if she had hoped to find that these words had been spoken without understanding of their meaning, she was at once disappointed. Mary lay back in her chair, frowning slightly, and looking, Katharine thought, as if she had lived fifteen years or so in the space of a few minutes.

"There are some things, don't you think, that one can't be mistaken about?" Mary said, quietly and almost coldly. "That is what puzzles me about this question of being in love. I've always prided myself upon being reasonable," she added. "I didn't think I could have felt this—I mean if the other person didn't. I was foolish. I let myself pretend." Here she paused. "For, you see, Katharine," she proceeded, rousing herself and speaking with greater energy, "I *am* in love. There's no doubt about that. . . . I'm tremendously in love . . . with Ralph." The little forward shake of her head, which shook a lock of hair, together with her brighter color, gave her an appearance at once proud and defiant.

Katharine thought to herself, "That's how it feels then." She hesitated, with a feeling that it was not for her to speak; and then said, in a low tone, "You've got that."

"Yes," said Mary; "I've got that. One wouldn't *not* be in love. . . . But I didn't mean to talk about that; I only wanted you to know. There's another thing I want to tell you . . ." She paused. "I haven't any authority from Ralph to say it; but I'm sure of this—he's in love with you."

Katharine looked at her again, as if her first glance must have been deluded, for, surely, there must be some outward sign that Mary was talking in an excited, or bewildered, or fantastic manner. No; she still frowned, as if she sought her way through the clauses of a difficult argument, but she still looked more like one who reasons than one who feels.

"That proves that you're mistaken—utterly mistaken," said Katharine, speaking reasonably, too. She had no need to verify the mistake by a glance at her own recollections, when the fact was so clearly stamped upon her mind that if Ralph had any feeling towards her it was one of critical hostility. She did not give the matter another thought, and Mary, now that she had stated the fact, did not seek to prove it, but tried to explain to herself, rather than to Katharine, her motives in making the statement.

She had nerved herself to do what some large and imperious instinct demanded her doing; she had been swept on the breast of a wave beyond her reckoning.

"I've told you," she said, "because I want you to help me. I don't want to be jealous of you. And I am—I'm fearfully jealous. The only way, I thought, was to tell you."

She hesitated, and groped in her endeavor to make her feelings clear to herself.

"If I tell you, then we can talk; and when I'm jealous, I can tell you. And if I'm tempted to do something frightfully mean, I can tell you; you could make me tell you. I find talking so difficult; but loneliness frightens me. I should shut it up in my mind. Yes, that's what I'm afraid of. Going about with something in my mind all my life that never changes. I find it so difficult to change. When I think a thing's wrong I never stop thinking it wrong, and Ralph was quite right, I see, when he said that there's no such thing as right and wrong; no such thing, I mean, as judging people——"

"Ralph Denham said that?" said Katharine, with considerable indignation. In order to have produced such suffering in Mary, it seemed to her that he must have behaved with extreme callousness. It seemed to her that he had discarded the friendship, when it suited his convenience to do so, with some falsely philosophical theory which made his conduct all the worse. She was going on to express herself thus, had not Mary at once interrupted her.

"No, no," she said; "you don't understand. If there's any fault it's mine entirely; after all, if one chooses to run risks——"

Her voice faltered into silence. It was borne in upon her how completely in running her risk she had lost her prize, lost it so entirely that she had no longer the right, in talking of Ralph, to presume that her knowledge of him supplanted all other knowledge. She no longer completely possessed her love, since his share in it was doubtful; and now, to make things yet more bitter, her clear vision of the way to face life was rendered tremulous and uncertain, because another was witness of it. Feeling her desire for the old unshared intimacy too great to be borne without tears, she rose, walked to the farther end of the room, held the curtains apart, and stood there mastered for a moment. The grief itself was not ignoble; the sting of it lay in the fact that she had been led to this act of treachery against herself. Trapped, cheated, robbed, first by Ralph and then by Katharine, she seemed all dissolved in humiliation, and bereft of anything she could call her own. Tears of weakness welled up and rolled down her cheeks. But tears, at least, she could control, and would this instant, and then, turning, she would face Katharine, and retrieve what could be retrieved of the collapse of her courage.

She turned. Katharine had not moved; she was leaning a little forward in her chair and looking into the fire. Something in the attitude reminded Mary of Ralph. So he would sit, leaning forward, looking rather fixedly in front of him, while his mind went far away, exploring, speculating, until he broke off with his, "Well, Mary?"—and the silence, that had been so full of romance to her, gave way to the most delightful talk that she had ever known.

Something unfamiliar in the pose of the silent figure, something still, solemn, significant about it, made her hold her breath. She paused. Her thoughts were without bitterness. She was surprised by her own quiet and confidence. She came back silently, and sat once more by Katharine's side. Mary had no wish to speak. In the silence she seemed to have lost her isolation; she was at once the sufferer and the pitiful spectator of suffering; she was happier than she had ever been; she was more bereft; she was rejected, and she was immensely beloved. Attempt to express these sensations was vain, and, moreover, she could not help believing that, without any words on her side, they were shared. Thus for some time longer they sat silent, side by side, while Mary fingered the fur on the skirt of the old dress.

CHAPTER XXII

THE fact that she would be late in keeping her engagement with William was not the only reason which sent Katharine almost at racing speed along the Strand in the direction of his rooms. Punctuality might have been achieved by taking a cab, had she not wished the open air to fan into flame the glow kindled by Mary's words. For among all the impressions of the evening's talk one was of the nature of a revelation and subdued the rest to insignificance. Thus one looked; thus one spoke; such was love.

"She sat up straight and looked at me, and then she said, 'I'm in love,' " Katharine mused, trying to set the whole scene in motion. It was a scene to dwell on with so much wonder that not a grain of pity occurred to her; it was a flame blazing suddenly in the dark; by its light Katharine perceived far too vividly for her comfort the mediocrity, indeed the entirely fictitious character of her own feelings so far as they pretended to correspond with Mary's feelings. She made up her mind to act instantly upon the knowledge thus gained, and cast her mind in amazement back to the scene upon the heath, when she had yielded, heaven knows why, for reasons which seemed now imperceptible. So in broad daylight one might revisit the place where one has groped and turned and succumbed to utter bewilderment in a fog.

"It's all so simple," she said to herself. "There can't be any doubt. I've only got to speak now. I've only got to speak," she went on saying, in time to her own footsteps, and completely forgot Mary Datchet.

William Rodney, having come back earlier from the office than he expected, sat down to pick out the melodies in "The Magic Flute" upon the piano. Katharine was late, but that was nothing new, and, as she had no particular liking for music, and he felt in the mood for it, perhaps it was as well. This defect in Katharine was the more strange, William reflected, because, as a rule, the women of her family were unusually musical. Her cousin, Cassandra Otway, for example, had a very fine taste in music, and he had charming recollections of her in a light fantastic attitude, playing the flute in the morning-room at Stogdon House. He recalled with pleasure the amusing way in which her nose, long like all the Otway noses, seemed to extend itself into the flute, as if she were some inimitably graceful species of musical mole. The little picture suggested very happily her melodious and whimsical temperament. The enthusiasms of a young girl of distinguished upbringing appealed to William, and suggested a thousand ways in which, with his training and accomplishments, he could be of service to her. She ought to be given the chance of hearing good‹ music, as it is played by those who have inherited the great tradition. Moreover, from one or two remarks let fall in the course of conversation, he thought it possible that she had what Katharine professed to lack, a passionate, if untaught, appreciation of literature. He had lent her his play. Meanwhile, as Katharine was certain to be late, and "The Magic Flute" is nothing without a voice, he felt inclined to spend the time of waiting in writing a letter to Cassandra, exhorting her to read Pope in preference to Dostoevsky, until her feeling for form was more highly developed. He set himself down to compose this piece of advice in a shape which was light and playful, and yet did no injury to a cause which he had near at heart, when he heard Katharine upon the stairs. A moment later it was plain that he had been mistaken, it was not Katharine; but he could not settle himself to his letter. His temper had changed from one of urbane contentment—indeed of delicious expansion—to one of uneasiness and expectation. The dinner was brought in, and had to be set by the fire to keep hot. It was now a quarter of an hour beyond the specified time. He bethought him of a piece of news which had depressed him in the earlier part of the day. Owing to the illness of one of his fellow-clerks, it was likely that he would get no holiday until later in the year, which would mean the postponement of their marriage. But this possibility, after all, was not so disagreeable as the probability which forced itself upon him with every tick of the clock that Katharine had completely forgotten her engagement. Such things had happened less frequently since Christmas, but what if they were going to begin to happen again? What if their marriage should turn out, as she had said, a farce? He acquitted her of any wish to hurt him wantonly, but there was something in her character which made it impossible for her to help hurting people. Was she cold? Was she self-absorbed? He tried to fit her with each of these descriptions, but he had to own that she puzzled him.

"There are so many things that she doesn't understand," he reflected, glancing at the letter to Cassandra which he had begun and laid aside. What prevented him from finishing the letter which he had so much enjoyed beginning? The reason was that Katharine might, at any moment, enter the room. The thought, implying his bondage to her, irritated him acutely. It occurred to him that he would leave the letter lying open for her to see, and he would take the opportunity of telling her that he had sent his play to Cassandra for her to criticize. Possibly, but not by any means certainly, this would annoy her—and as he reached the doubtful comfort of this conclusion, there was a knock on the door and Katharine came in. They kissed each other coldly and she made no apology for being late. Nevertheless, her mere presence moved him strangely; but he was determined that this should not weaken his resolution to make some kind of stand against her; to get at the truth about her. He let her make her own disposition of clothes and busied himself with the plates.

"I've got a piece of news for you, Katharine," he said directly they sat down to table; "I shan't get my holiday in April. We shall have to put off our marriage."

He rapped the words out with a certain degree of brisk-ness. Katharine started a little, as if the announcement disturbed her thoughts.

"That won't make any difference, will it? I mean the lease isn't signed," she replied. "But why? What has hap-pened?"

He told her, in an off-hand way, how one of his fellow-clerks had broken down, and might have to be away for months, six months even, in which case they would have to think over their position. He said it in a way which struck her, at last, as oddly casual. She looked at him. There was no outward sign that he was annoyed with her. Was she well dressed? She thought sufficiently so. Perhaps she was late? She looked for a clock.

"It's a good thing we didn't take the house then," she re-peated thoughtfully.

"It'll mean, too, I'm afraid, that I shan't be as free for a considerable time as I have been," he continued. She had time to reflect that she gained something by all this, though it was too soon to determine what. But the light which had been burning with such intensity as she came along was suddenly overclouded, as much by his manner as by his news. She had been prepared to meet opposition, which is simple to encounter compared with—she did not know what it was that she had to encounter. The meal passed in quiet, well-controlled talk about indifferent things. Music was not a subject about which she knew anything, but she liked him to tell her things; and could, she mused, as he talked, fancy the evenings of married life spent thus, over the fire; spent thus, or with a book, perhaps, for then she would have time to read her books, and to grasp firmly with every muscle of her unused mind what she longed to know. The atmos-phere was very free. Suddenly William broke off. She looked up apprehensively, brushing aside these thoughts with annoyance.

"Where should I address a letter to Cassandra?" he asked

her. It was obvious again that William had some meaning or other to-night, or was in some mood. "We've struck up a friendship," he added.

"She's at home, I think," Katharine replied.

"They keep her too much at home," said William. "Why don't you ask her to stay with you, and let her hear a little good music? I'll just finish what I was saying, if you don't mind, because I'm particularly anxious that she should hear to-morrow."

Katharine sank back in her chair, and Rodney took the paper on his knees, and went on with his sentence. "Style, you know, is what we tend to neglect———"; but he was far more conscious of Katharine's eye upon him than of what he was saying about style. He knew that she was looking at him, but whether with irritation or indifference he could not guess.

In truth, she had fallen sufficiently into his trap to feel uncomfortably roused and disturbed and unable to proceed on the lines laid down for herself. This indifferent, if not hostile, attitude on William's part made it impossible to break off without animosity, largely and completely. Infinitely preferable was Mary's state, she thought, where there was a simple thing to do and one did it. In fact, she could not help supposing that some littleness of nature had a part in all the refinements, reserves, and subtleties of feeling for which her friends and family were so distinguished. For example, although she liked Cassandra well enough, her fantastic method of life struck her as purely frivolous; now it was socialism, now it was silkworms, now it was music— which last she supposed was the cause of William's sudden interest in her. Never before had William wasted the minutes of her presence in writing his letters. With a curious sense of light opening where all, hitherto, had been opaque, it dawned upon her that, after all, possibly, yes, probably, nay, certainly, the devotion which she had almost wearily taken for granted existed in a much slighter degree than she had suspected, or existed no longer. She looked at him attentively as if this discovery of hers must show traces in his face. Never had she seen so much to respect in his appearance, so much that attracted her by its sensitiveness and intelligence, although she saw these qualities as if they were those one responds to, dumbly, in the face of a stranger. The head bent over the paper, thoughtful as usual, had now a composure which seemed somehow to place it at a distance, like a face seen talking to some one else behind glass.

He wrote on, without raising his eyes. She would have spoken, but could not bring herself to ask him for signs of affection which she had no right to claim. The conviction that he was thus strange to her filled her with despondency, and illustrated quite beyond doubt the infinite loneliness of human beings. She had never felt the truth of this so strongly before. She looked away into the fire; it seemed to her that even physically they were now scarcely within speaking distance; and spiritually there was certainly no human being with whom she could claim comradeship; no dream that satisfied her as she was used to be satisfied; nothing remained in whose reality she could believe, save those abstract ideas—figures, laws, stars, facts, which she could hardly hold to for lack of knowledge and a kind of shame.

When Rodney owned to himself the folly of this prolonged silence, and the meanness of such devices, and looked up ready to seek some excuse for a good laugh, or opening for a confession, he was disconcerted by what he saw. Katharine seemed equally oblivious of what was bad or of what was good in him. Her expression suggested concentration upon something entirely remote from her surroundings. The carelessness of her attitude seemed to him rather masculine than feminine. His impulse to break up the constraint was chilled, and once more the exasperating sense of his own impotency returned to him. He could not help contrasting Katharine with his vision of the engaging, whimsical Cassandra; Katharine undemonstrative, inconsiderate, silent, and yet so notable that he could never do without her good opinion.

She veered round upon him a moment later, as if, when her train of thought was ended, she became aware of his presence.

"Have you finished your letter?" she asked. He thought he heard faint amusement in her tone, but not a trace of jealousy.

"No, I'm not going to write any more to-night," he said. "I'm not in the mood for it for some reason. I can't say what I want to say."

"Cassandra won't know if it's well written or badly written," Katharine remarked.

"I'm not so sure about that. I should say she has a good deal of literary feeling."

"Perhaps," said Katharine indifferently. "You've been neglecting my education lately, by the way. I wish you'd read something. Let me choose a book." So speaking, she went across to his bookshelves and began looking in a desultory way among his books. Anything, she thought, was better than bickering or the strange silence which drove home to her the distance between them. As she pulled one book forward and then another she thought ironically of her own certainty not an hour ago; how it had vanished in a moment, how she was merely marking time as best she could, not knowing in the least where they stood, what they felt, or whether William loved her or not. More and more the condition of Mary's mind seemed to her wonderful and enviable—if, indeed, it could be quite as she figured it—if, indeed, simplicity existed for any one of the daughters of women.

"Swift," she said, at last, taking out a volume at haphazard to settle this question at least. "Let us have some Swift."

Rodney took the book, held it in front of him, inserted one finger between the pages, but said nothing. His face wore a queer expression of deliberation, as if he were weighing one thing with another, and would not say anything until his mind were made up.

Katharine, taking her chair beside him, noted his silence and looked at him with sudden apprehension. What she hoped or feared, she could not have said; a most irrational and indefensible desire for some assurance of his affection was, perhaps, uppermost in her mind. Peevishness, complaints, exacting cross-examination she was used to, but this attitude of composed quiet, which seemed to come from the consciousness of power within, puzzled her. She did not know what was going to happen next.

At last William spoke.

"I think it's a little odd, don't you?" he said, in a voice of detached reflection. "Most people, I mean, would be seriously upset if their marriage was put off for six months or so. But we aren't; now how do you account for that?"

She looked at him and observed his judicial attitude as of one holding far aloof from emotion.

"I attribute it," he went on, without waiting for her to answer, "to the fact that neither of us is in the least romantic about the other. That may be partly, no doubt, because we've known each other so long; but I'm inclined to think there's more in it than that. There's something temperamental. I think you're a trifle cold, and I suspect I'm a trifle self-absorbed. If that were so it goes a long way to explaining our odd lack of illusion about each other. I'm not saying that the most satisfactory marriages aren't founded upon this sort of understanding. But certainly it struck me as odd this morning, when Wilson told me, how little upset I felt. By the way, you're sure we haven't committed ourselves to that house?"

"I've kept the letters, and I'll go through them to-morrow; but I'm certain we're on the safe side."

"Thanks. As to the psychological problem," he continued, as if the question interested him in a detached way, "there's no doubt, I think, that either of us is capable of feeling what, for reasons of simplicity, I call romance for a third person—at least, I've little doubt in my own case."

It was, perhaps, the first time in all her knowledge of him that Katharine had known William enter thus deliberately and without sign of emotion upon a statement of his own feelings. He was wont to discourage such intimate discussions by a little laugh or turn of the conversation, as much as to say that men, or men of the world, find such topics a little silly, or in doubtful taste. His obvious wish to explain something puzzled her, interested her, and neutralized the wound to her vanity. For some reason, too, she felt more at ease with him than usual; or her ease was more the ease of equality—she could not stop to think of that at the moment though. His remarks interested her too much for the light that they threw upon certain problems of her own.

"What is this romance?" she mused.

"Ah, that's the question. I've never come across a definition that satisfied me, though there are some very good ones" —he glanced in the direction of his books.

"It's not altogether knowing the other person, perhaps— it's ignorance," she hazarded.

"Some authorities say it's a question of distance—romance in literature, that is——"

"Possibly, in the case of art. But in the case of people it may be ——" she hesitated.

"Have you no personal experience of it?" he asked, letting his eyes rest upon her swiftly for a moment.

"I believe it's influenced me enormously," she said, in the tone of one absorbed by the possibilities of some view just presented to them; "but in my life there's so little scope for it," she added. She reviewed her daily task, the perpetual demands upon her for good sense, self-control, and accuracy in a house containing a romantic mother. Ah, but her romance wasn't *that* romance. It was a desire, an echo, a sound; she could drape it in color, see it in form, hear it in music, but not in words; no, never in words. She sighed, teased by desires so incoherent, so incommunicable.

"But isn't it curious," William resumed, "that you should neither feel it for me, nor I for you?"

Katharine agreed that it was curious—very; but even more curious to her was the fact that she was discussing the question with William. It revealed possibilities which opened a prospect of a new relationship altogether. Somehow it seemed to her that he was helping her to understand what she had never understood; and in her gratitude she was conscious of a most sisterly desire to help him, too—sisterly, save for one pang, not quite to be subdued, that for him she was without romance.

"I think you might be very happy with some one you loved in that way," she said.

"You assume that romance survives a closer knowledge of the person one loves?"

He asked the question formally, to protect himself from the sort of personality which he dreaded. The whole situation needed the most careful management lest it should degenerate into some degrading and disturbing exhibition such as the scene, which he could never think of without shame, upon the heath among the dead leaves. And yet each sentence brought him relief. He was coming to understand something or other about his own desires hitherto undefined by him, the source of his difficulty with Katharine. The wish to hurt her, which had urged him to begin, had completely left him, and he felt that it was only Katharine now who could help him to be sure. He must take his time. There were so many things that he could not say without the greatest difficulty—that name, for example, Cassandra. Nor could he move his eyes from a certain spot, a fiery glen surrounded by high mountains, in the heart of the coals. He waited in suspense for Katharine to continue. She had said that he might be very happy with some one he loved in that way.

"I don't see why it shouldn't last with you," she resumed. "I can imagine a certain sort of person——" she paused; she was aware that he was listening with the greatest intentness, and that his formality was merely the cover for an extreme anxiety of some sort. There *was* some person then—some woman—who could it be? Cassandra? Ah, possibly——

"A person," she added, speaking in the most matter-of-fact tone she could command, "like Cassandra Otway, for instance. Cassandra is the most interesting of the Otways —with the exception of Henry. Even so, I like Cassandra better. She has more than mere cleverness. She is a character—a person by herself."

"Those dreadful insects!" burst from William, with a nervous laugh, and a little spasm went through him as Katharine noticed. It *was* Cassandra then. Automatically and dully she replied, "You could insist that she confined herself to—to—something else. . . . But she cares for music; I believe she writes poetry; and there can be no doubt that she has a peculiar charm——"

She ceased, as if defining to herself this peculiar charm After a moment's silence William jerked out:

"I thought her affectionate?"

"Extremely affectionate. She worships Henry. When you think what a house that is—Uncle Francis always in one mood or another——"

"Dear, dear, dear," William muttered.

"And you have so much in common."

"My dear Katharine!" William exclaimed, flinging himself back in his chair, and uprooting his eyes from the spot in the fire. "I really don't know what we're talking about. . . . I assure you. . . ."

He was covered with an extreme confusion.

He withdrew the finger that was still thrust between the pages of Gulliver, opened the book, and ran his eye down the list of chapters, as though he were about to select the one most suitable for reading aloud. As Katharine watched him, she was seized with preliminary symptoms of his own panic. At the same time she was convinced that, should he find the right page, take out his spectacles, clear his throat, and open his lips, a chance that would never come again in all their lives would be lost to them both.

"We're talking about things that interest us both very much," she said. "Shan't we go on talking, and leave Swift for another time? I don't feel in the mood for Swift, and it's a pity to read any one when that's the case—particularly Swift."

The pretence of wise literary speculation, as she calculated, restored William's confidence in his security, and he replaced the book in the bookcase, keeping his back turned to her as he did so, and taking advantage of this circumstance to summon his thoughts together.

But a second of introspection had the alarming result of showing him that his mind, when looked at from within, was no longer familiar ground. He felt, that is to say, what he had never consciously felt before; he was revealed to himself as other than he was wont to think him; he was afloat upon a sea of unknown and tumultuous possibilities. He paced once up and down the room, and then flung himself impetuously into the chair by Katharine's side. He had never felt anything like this before; he put himself entirely into her hands; he cast off all responsibility. He very nearly exclaimed aloud:

"You've stirred up all these odious and violent emotions, and now you must do the best you can with them."

Her near presence, however, had a calming and reassuring effect upon his agitation, and he was conscious only of an implicit trust that, somehow, he was safe with her, that she would see him through, find out what it was that he wanted, and procure it for him.

"I wish to do whatever you tell me to do," he said. "I put myself entirely in your hands, Katharine."

"You must try to tell me what you feel," she said.

"My dear, I feel a thousand things every second. I don't know, I'm sure, what I feel. That afternoon on the heath —it was then—then———" He broke off; he did not tell her what had happened then. "Your ghastly good sense, as usual, has convinced me—for the moment—but what the truth is, Heaven only knows!" he exclaimed.

"Isn't it the truth that you are, or might be, in love with Cassandra?" she said gently.

William bowed his head. After a moment's silence he murmured:

"I believe you're right, Katharine."

She sighed, involuntarily. She had been hoping all this time, with an intensity that increased second by second against the current of her words, that it would not in the end come to this. After a moment of surprising anguish, she summoned her courage to tell him how she wished only that she might help him, and had framed the first words of her speech when a knock, terrific and startling to people in their overwrought condition, sounded upon the door.

"Katharine, I worship you," he urged, half in a whisper.

"Yes," she replied, withdrawing with a little shiver, "but you must open the door."

CHAPTER XXIII

WHEN Ralph Denham entered the room and saw Katharine seated with her back to him, he was conscious of a change in the grade of the atmosphere such as a traveler meets with sometimes upon the roads, particularly after sunset, when, without warning, he runs from clammy chill to a hoard of unspent warmth in which the sweetness of hay and beanfield is cherished, as if the sun still shone although the moon is up. He hesitated; he shuddered; he walked elaborately to the window and laid aside his coat. He balanced his stick most carefully against the folds of the curtain. Thus occupied with his own sensations and preparations, he had little time to observe what either of the other two was feeling. Such symptoms of agitation as he might perceive (and they had left their tokens in brightness of eye and pallor of cheeks) seemed to him well befitting the actors in so great a drama as that of Katharine Hilbery's daily life. Beauty and passion were the breath of her being, he thought.

She scarcely noticed his presence, or only as it forced her to adopt a manner of composure, which she was certainly far from feeling. William, however, was even more agitated than she was, and her first instalment of promised help took the form of some commonplace upon the age of the building or the architect's name, which gave him an excuse to fumble in a drawer for certain designs, which he laid upon the table between the three of them.

Which of the three followed the designs most carefully it would be difficult to tell, but it is certain that not one of the three found for the moment anything to say. Years of training in a drawing-room came at length to Katharine's

help, and she said something suitable, at the same moment
withdrawing her hand from the table because she perceived
that it trembled.   William agreed effusively; Denham corroborated him, speaking in rather high-pitched tones; they
thrust aside the plans, and drew nearer to the fireplace.

"I'd rather live here than anywhere in the whole of London," said Denham.

("And I've got nowhere to live") Katharine thought, as
she agreed aloud.

"You could get rooms here, no doubt, if you wanted to,"
Rodney replied.

"But I'm just leaving London for good—I've taken that
cottage I was telling you about." The announcement seemed
to convey very little to either of his hearers.

"Indeed?—that's sad. . . . You must give me your
address.   But you won't cut yourself off altogether, surely——"

"You'll be moving, too, I suppose," Denham remarked.

William showed such visible signs of floundering that
Katharine collected herself and asked:

"Where is the cottage you've taken?"

In answering her, Denham turned and looked at her.   As
their eyes met, she realized for the first time that she was
talking to Ralph Denham, and she remembered, without
recalling any details, that she had been speaking of him
quite lately, and that she had reason to think ill of him.
What Mary had said she could not remember, but she felt
that there was a mass of knowledge in her mind which she
had not had time to examine—knowledge now lying on the
far side of a gulf.   But her agitation flashed the queerest
lights upon her past.   She must get through the matter in
hand, and then think it out in quiet.   She bent her mind to
follow what Ralph was saying.   He was telling her that he
had taken a cottage in Norfolk, and she was saying that she
knew, or did not know, that particular neighborhood.   But
after a moment's attention her mind flew to Rodney, and
she had an unusual, indeed unprecedented, sense that they

were in touch and shared each other's thoughts. If only Ralph were not there, she would at once give way to her desire to take William's hand, then to bend his head upon her shoulder, for this was what she wanted to do more than anything at the moment, unless, indeed, she wished more than anything to be alone—yes, that was what she wanted. She was sick to death of these discussions; she shivered at the effort to reveal her feelings. She had forgotten to answer. William was speaking now.

"But what will you find to do in the country?" she asked at random, striking into a conversation which she had only half heard, in such a way as to make both Rodney and Denham look at her with a little surprise. But directly she took up the conversation, it was William's turn to fall silent. He at once forgot to listen to what they were saying, although he interposed nervously at intervals, "Yes, yes, yes." As the minutes passed, Ralph's presence became more and more intolerable to him, since there was so much that he must say to Katharine; the moment he could not talk to her, terrible doubts, unanswerable questions accumulated, which he must lay before Katharine, for she alone could help him now. Unless he could see her alone, it would be impossible for him ever to sleep, or to know what he had said in a moment of madness, which was not altogether mad, or was it mad? He nodded his head, and said, nervously, "Yes, yes," and looked at Katharine, and thought how beautiful she looked; there was no one in the world that he admired more. There was an emotion in her face which lent it an expression he had never seen there. Then, as he was turning over means by which he could speak to her alone, she rose, and he was taken by surprise, for he had counted on the fact that she would outstay Denham. His only chance, then, of saying something to her in private, was to take her downstairs and walk with her to the street. While he hesitated, however, overcome with the difficulty of putting one simple thought into words when all his thoughts were scattered about, and all were too strong for utterance, he was struck silent by something that was still more unexpected. Denham got up from his chair, looked at Katharine, and said:

"I'm going, too. Shall we go together?"

And before William could see any way of detaining him —or would it be better to detain Katharine?—he had taken his hat, stick, and was holding the door open for Katharine to pass out. The most that William could do was to stand at the head of the stairs and say good-night. He could not offer to go with them. He could not insist that she should stay. He watched her descend, rather slowly, owing to the dusk of the staircase, and he had a last sight of Denham's head and of Katharine's head near together, against the panels, when suddenly a pang of acute jealousy overcame him, and had he not remained conscious of the slippers upon his feet, he would have run after them or cried out. As it was he could not move from the spot. At the turn of the staircase Katharine turned to look back, trusting to this last glance to seal their compact of good friendship. Instead of returning her silent greeting, William grinned back at her a cold stare of sarcasm or of rage.

She stopped dead for a moment, and then descended slowly into the court. She looked to the right and to the left, and once up into the sky. She was only conscious of Denham as a block upon her thoughts. She measured the distance that must be traversed before she would be alone. But when they came to the Strand no cabs were to be seen, and Denham broke the silence by saying:

"There seem to be no cabs. Shall we walk on a little?"

"Very well," she agreed, paying no attention to him.

Aware of her preoccupation, or absorbed in his own thoughts, Ralph said nothing further; and in silence they walked some distance along the Strand. Ralph was doing his best to put his thoughts into such order that one came before the rest, and the determination that when he spoke he should speak worthily, made him put off the moment of speaking till he had found the exact words and even the place that best suited him. The Strand was too busy. There was too much risk, also, of finding an empty cab. Without a word of explanation he turned to the left, down one of the side streets leading to the river. On no account must they part until something of the very greatest importance had happened. He knew perfectly well what he wished to say, and had arranged not only the substance, but the order in which he was to say it. Now, however, that he was alone with her, not only did he find the difficulty of speaking almost insurmountable, but he was aware that he was angry with her for thus disturbing him, and casting, as it was so easy for a person of her advantages to do, these phantoms and pitfalls across his path. He was determined that he would question her as severely as he would question himself; and make them both, once and for all, either justify her dominance or renounce it. But the longer they walked thus alone, the more he was disturbed by the sense of her actual presence. Her skirt blew; the feathers in her hat waved; sometimes he saw her a step or two ahead of him, or had to wait for her to catch him up.

The silence was prolonged, and at length drew her attention to him. First she was annoyed that there was no cab to free her from his company; then she recalled vaguely something that Mary had said to make her think ill of him; she could not remember what, but the recollection, combined with his masterful ways—why did he walk so fast down this side street?—made her more and more conscious of a person of marked, though disagreeable, force by her side. She stopped and, looking round her for a cab, sighted one in the distance. He was thus precipitated into speech.

"Should you mind if we walked a little farther?" he asked. "There's something I want to say to you."

"Very well," she replied, guessing that his request had something to do with Mary Datchet.

"It's quieter by the river," he said, and instantly he crossed over. "I want to ask you merely this," he began. But he paused so long that she could see his head against the sky; the slope of his thin cheek and his large, strong nose were clearly marked against it. While he paused, words that were quite different from those he intended to use presented themselves.

"I've made you my standard ever since I saw you. I've dreamt about you; I've thought of nothing but you; you represent to me the only reality in the world."

His words, and the queer strained voice in which he spoke them, made it appear as if he addressed some person who was not the woman beside him, but some one far away.

"And now things have come to such a pass that, unless I can speak to you openly, I believe I shall go mad. I think of you as the most beautiful, the truest thing in the world," he continued, filled with a sense of exaltation, and feeling that he had no need now to choose his words with pedantic accuracy, for what he wanted to say was suddenly become plain to him.

"I see you everywhere, in the stars, in the river; to me you're everything that exists; the reality of everything. Life, I tell you, would be impossible without you. And now I want——"

She had heard him so far with a feeling that she had dropped some material word which made sense of the rest. She could hear no more of this unintelligible rambling without checking him. She felt that she was overhearing what was meant for another.

"I don't understand," she said. "You're saying things that you don't mean."

"I mean every word I say," he replied, emphatically. He turned his head towards her. She recovered the words she was searching for while he spoke. "Ralph Denham is in love with you." They came back to her in Mary Datchet's voice. Her anger blazed up in her.

"I saw Mary Datchet this afternoon," she exclaimed.

He made a movement as if he were surprised or taken aback, but answered in a moment:

"She told you that I had asked her to marry me, I suppose?"

"No!" Katharine exclaimed, in surprise.

"I did though. It was the day I saw you at Lincoln," he continued. "I had meant to ask her to marry me, and then I looked out of the window and saw you. After that I didn't want to ask any one to marry me. But I did it; and she knew I was lying, and refused me. I thought then, and still think, that she cares for me. I behaved very badly. I don't defend myself."

"No," said Katharine, "I should hope not. There's no defence that I can think of. If any conduct is wrong, that is." She spoke with an energy that was directed even more against herself than against him. "It seems to me," she continued, with the same energy, "that people are bound to be honest. There's no excuse for such behavior." She could now see plainly before her eyes the expression on Mary Datchet's face.

After a short pause, he said:

"I am not telling you that I am in love with you. I am not in love with you."

"I didn't think that," she replied, conscious of some bewilderment.

"I have not spoken a word to you that I do not mean," he added.

"Tell me then what it is that you mean," she said at length.

As if obeying a common instinct, they both stopped and, bending slightly over the balustrade of the river, looked into the flowing water.

"You say that we've got to be honest," Ralph began. "Very well. I will try to tell you the facts; but I warn you, you'll think me mad. It's a fact, though, that since I first saw you four or five months ago I have made you, in an utterly absurd way, I expect, my ideal. I'm almost ashamed to tell you what lengths I've gone to. It's become the thing that matters most in my life." He checked himself. "Without knowing you, except that you're beautiful, and all that, I've come to believe that we're in some sort of agreement; that we're after something together; that we see something. . . . I've got into the habit of imagining you; I'm always thinking what you'd say or do; I walk along the street talking to you; I dream of you. It's merely a bad habit, a schoolboy habit, day-dreaming; it's a common experience; half one's friends do the same; well, those are the facts."

Simultaneously, they both walked on very slowly.

"If you were to know me you would feel none of this," she said. "We don't know each other—we've always been —interrupted. . . . Were you going to tell me this that day my aunts came?" she asked, recollecting the whole scene.

He bowed his head.

"The day you told me of your engagement," he said.

She thought, with a start, that she was no longer engaged.

"I deny that I should cease to feel this if I knew you," he went on. "I should feel it more reasonably—that's all. I shouldn't talk the kind of nonsense I've talked to-night. . . . But it wasn't nonsense. It was the truth," he said doggedly. "It's the important thing. You can force me to talk as if this feeling for you were an hallucination, but all our feelings are that. The best of them are half illusions. Still," he added, as if arguing to himself, "if it weren't as real a feeling as I'm capable of, I shouldn't be changing my life on your account."

"What do you mean?" she inquired.

"I told you. I'm taking a cottage. I'm giving up my profession."

"On my account?" she asked, in amazement.

"Yes, on your account," he replied. He explained his meaning no further.

"But I don't know you or your circumstances," she said at last, as he remained silent.

"You have no opinion about me one way or the other?"

"Yes, I suppose I have an opinion——" she hesitated.

He controlled his wish to ask her to explain herself, and

much to his pleasure she went on, appearing to search her mind.

"I thought that you criticized me—perhaps disliked me. I thought of you as a person who judges——"

"No; I'm a person who feels," he said, in a low voice.

"Tell me, then, what has made you do this?" she asked, after a break.

He told her in an orderly way, betokening careful preparation, all that he had meant to say at first; how he stood with regard to his brothers and sisters; what his mother had said, and his sister Joan had refrained from saying; exactly how many pounds stood in his name at the bank; what prospect his brother had of earning a livelihood in America; how much of their income went on rent, and other details known to him by heart. She listened to all this, so that she could have passed an examination in it by the time Waterloo Bridge was in sight; and yet she was no more listening to it than she was counting the paving-stones at her feet. She was feeling happier than she had felt in her life. If Denham could have seen how visibly books of algebraic symbols, pages all speckled with dots and dashes and twisted bars, came before her eyes as they trod the Embankment, his secret joy in her attention might have been dispersed. She went on, saying, "Yes, I see. . . . But how would that help you? . . . Your brother has passed his examination?" so sensibly, that he had constantly to keep his brain in check; and all the time she was in fancy looking up through a telescope at white shadow-cleft disks which were other worlds, until she felt herself possessed of two bodies, one walking by the river with Denham, the other concentrated to a silver globe aloft in the fine blue space above the scum of vapors that was covering the visible world. She looked at the sky once, and saw that no star was keen enough to pierce the flight of watery clouds now coursing rapidly before the west wind. She looked down hurriedly again. There was no reason, she assured herself, for this feeling of happiness; she was not free; she was not alone; she was still bound to earth by a million fibres; every step took her nearer home. Nevertheless, she exulted as she had never exulted before. The air was fresher, the lights more distinct, the cold stone of the balustrade colder and harder, when by chance or purpose she struck her hand against it. No feeling of annoyance with Denham remained; he certainly did not hinder any flight she might choose to make, whether in the direction of the sky or of her home; but that her condition was due to him, or to anything that he had said, she had no consciousness at all.

They were now within sight of the stream of cabs and omnibuses crossing to and from the Surrey side of the river; the sound of the traffic, the hooting of motor-horns, and the light chime of tram-bells sounded more and more distinctly, and, with the increase of noise, they both became silent. With a common instinct they slackened their pace, as if to lengthen the time of semi-privacy allowed them. To Ralph, the pleasure of these last yards of the walk with Katharine was so great that he could not look beyond the present moment to the time when she should have left him. He had no wish to use the last moments of their companionship in adding fresh words to what he had already said. Since they had stopped talking, she had become to him not so much a real person, as the very woman he dreamt of; but his solitary dreams had never produced any such keenness of sensation as that which he felt in her presence. He himself was also strangely transfigured. He had complete mastery of all his faculties. For the first time he was in possession of his full powers. The vistas which opened before him seemed to have no perceptible end. But the mood had none of the restlessness or feverish desire to add one delight to another which had hitherto marked, and somewhat spoilt, the most rapturous of his imaginings. It was a mood that took such clear-eyed account of the conditions of human life that he was not disturbed in the least by the gliding presence of a taxicab, and without agitation he perceived that Katharine was conscious of it also, and turned her head in that direction. Their halting steps acknowledged the desirability of engaging the cab; and they stopped simultaneously, and signed to it.

"Then you will let me know your decision as soon as you can?" he asked, with his hand on the door.

She hesitated for a moment. She could not immediately recall what the question was that she had to decide.

"I will write," she said vaguely. "No," she added, in a second, bethinking her of the difficulties of writing anything decided upon a question to which she had paid no attention, "I don't see how to manage.it."

She stood looking at Denham, considering and hesitating, with her foot upon the step. He guessed her difficulties; he knew in a second that she had heard nothing; he knew everything that she felt.

"There's only one place to discuss things satisfactorily that I know of," he said quickly; "that's Kew."

"Kew?"

"Kew," he repeated, with immense decision. He shut the door and gave her address to the driver. She instantly was conveyed away from him, and her cab joined the knotted stream of vehicles, each marked by a light, and indistinguishable one from the other. He stood watching for a moment, and then, as if swept by some fierce impulse, from the spot where they had stood, he turned, crossed the road at a rapid pace, and disappeared.

He walked on upon the impetus of this last mood of almost supernatural exaltation until he reached a narrow street, at this hour empty of traffic and passengers. Here, whether it was the shops with their shuttered windows, the smooth and silvered curve of the wood pavement, or a natural ebb of feeling, his exaltation slowly oozed and deserted him. He was now conscious of the loss that follows any revelation; he had lost something in speaking to Katharine, for, after all, was the Katharine whom he loved the same as the real Katharine? She had transcended her entirely at moments; her skirt had blown, her feather waved, her voice spoken; yes, but how terrible sometimes the pause between the voice of one's dreams and the voice that comes from the object of one's dreams! He felt a mixture of disgust and pity at the figure cut by human beings when they try to carry out, in practice, what they have the power to con- ceive. How small both he and Katharine had appeared when they issued from the cloud of thought that enveloped them! He recalled the small, inexpressive, commonplace words in which they had tried to communicate with each other; he repeated them over to himself. By repeating Katharine's words, he came in a few moments to such a sense of her presence that he worshipped her more than ever. But she was engaged to be married, he remembered with a start. The strength of his feeling was revealed to him instantly, and he gave himself up to an irresistible rage and sense of frustration. The image of Rodney came before him with every circumstance of folly and indignity. That little pink-cheeked dancing-master to marry Katharine? that gibbering ass with the face of a monkey on an organ? that posing, vain, fantastical fop? with his tragedies and his comedies, his innumerable spites and prides and pettinesses? Lord! marry Rodney! She must be as great a fool as he was. His bitterness took possession of him, and as he sat in the corner of the underground carriage, he looked as stark an image of unapproachable severity as could be imagined. Directly he reached home he sat down at his table, and began to write Katharine a long, wild, mad letter, begging her for both their sakes to break with Rodney, imploring her not to do what would destroy for ever the one beauty, the one truth, the one hope; not to be a traitor, not to be a deserter, for if she were—and he wound up with a quiet and brief assertion that, whatever she did or left undone, he would believe to be the best, and accept from her with gratitude. He covered sheet after sheet, and heard the early carts start- ing for London before he went to bed.

CHAPTER XXIV

THE first signs of spring, even such as make themselves felt towards the middle of February, not only produce little white and violet flowers in the more sheltered corners of woods and gardens, but bring to birth thoughts and desires comparable to those faintly colored and sweetly scented petals in the minds of men and women. Lives frozen by age, so far as the present is concerned, to a hard surface, which neither reflects nor yields, at this season become soft and fluid, reflecting the shapes and colors of the present, as well as the shapes and colors of the past. In the case of Mrs. Hilbery, these early spring days were chiefly upsetting inasmuch as they caused a general quickening of her emotional powers, which, as far as the past was concerned, had never suffered much diminution. But in the spring her desire for expression invariably increased. She was haunted by the ghosts of phrases. She gave herself up to a sensual delight in the combinations of words. She sought them in the pages of her favorite authors. She made them for herself on scraps of paper, and rolled them on her tongue when there seemed no occasion for such eloquence. She was upheld in these excursions by the certainty that no language could outdo the splendor of her father's memory, and although her efforts did not notably further the end of his biography, she was under the impression of living more in his shade at such times than at others. No one can escape the power of language, let alone those of English birth brought up from childhood, as Mrs. Hilbery had been, to disport themselves now in the Saxon plainness, now in the Latin splendor of the tongue, and stored with memories, as

she was, of old poets exuberating in an infinity of vocables.
Even Katharine was slightly affected against her better
judgment by her mother's enthusiasm.   Not that her judgment could altogether acquiesce in the necessity for a study
of Shakespeare's sonnets as a preliminary to the fifth chapter of her grandfather's biography.   Beginning with a perfectly frivolous jest, Mrs. Hilbery had evolved a theory
that Anne Hathaway had a way, among other things, of
writing Shakespeare's sonnets; the idea, struck out to en-
liven a party of professors, who forwarded a number of
privately printed manuals within the next few days for her
instruction, had submerged her in a flood of Elizabethan
literature; she had come half to believe in her joke, which
was, she said, at least as good as other people's facts, and
all her fancy for the time being centered upon Stratford-
on-Avon.   She had a plan, she told Katharine, when, rather
later than usual, Katharine came into the room the morning
after her walk by the river, for visiting Shakespeare's tomb.
Any fact about the poet had become, for the moment, of far
greater interest to her than the immediate present, and the
certainty that there was existing in England a spot of
ground where Shakespeare had undoubtedly stood, where
his very bones lay directly beneath one's feet, was so absorbing to her on this particular occasion that she greeted her
daughter with the exclamation:

"D'you think he ever passed this house?"

The question, for the moment, seemed to Katharine to
have reference to Ralph Denham.

"On his way to Blackfriars, I mean," Mrs. Hilbery continued, "for you know the latest discovery is that he owned
a house there."

Katharine still looked about her in perplexity, and Mrs.
Hilbery added:

"Which is a proof that he wasn't as poor as they've sometimes said.   I should like to think that he had enough,
though I don't in the least want him to be rich."

Then, perceiving her daughter's expression of perplexity, Mrs. Hilbery burst out laughing.

"My dear, I'm not talking about *your* William, though that's another reason for liking him. I'm talking, I'm thinking, I'm dreaming of *my* William—William Shakespeare, of course, Isn't it odd," she mused, standing at the window and tapping gently upon the pane, "that for all one can see, that dear old thing in the blue bonnet, crossing the road with her basket on her arm, has never heard that there was such a person? Yet it all goes on: lawyers hurrying to their work, cabmen squabbling for their fares, little boys rolling their hoops, little girls throwing bread to the gulls, as if there weren't a Shakespeare in the world. I should like to stand at that crossing all day long and say: 'People, read Shakespeare!'"

Katharine sat down at her table and opened a long dusty envelope. As Shelley was mentioned in the course of the letter as if he were alive, it had, of course, considerable value. Her immediate task was to decide whether the whole letter should be printed, or only the paragraph which mentioned Shelley's name, and she reached out for a pen and held it in readiness to do justice upon the sheet. Her pen, however, remained in the air. Almost surreptitiously she slipped a clean sheet in front of her, and her hand, descending, began drawing square boxes halved and quartered by straight lines, and then circles which underwent the same process of dissection.

"Katharine! I've hit upon a brilliant idea!" Mrs. Hilbery exclaimed—"to lay out, say, a hundred pounds or so on copies of Shakespeare, and give them to working men. Some of your clever friends who get up meetings might help us, Katharine. And that might lead to a playhouse, where we could all take parts. You'd be Rosalind—but you've a dash of the old nurse in you. Your father's Hamlet, come to years of discretion; and I'm—well, I'm a bit of them all; I'm quite a large bit of the fool, but the fools in Shakespeare say all the clever things. Now who shall

William be? A hero? Hotspur? Henry the Fifth? No, William's got a touch of Hamlet in him, too. I can fancy that William talks to himself when he's alone. Ah, Katharine, you must say very beautiful things when you're together!" she added wistfully, with a glance at her daughter, who had told her nothing about the dinner the night before.

"Oh, we talk a lot of nonsense," said Katharine, hiding her slip of paper as her mother stood by her, and spreading the old letter about Shelley in front of her.

"It won't seem to you nonsense in ten years' time," said Mrs. Hilbery. "Believe me, Katharine, you'll look back on these days afterwards; you'll remember all the silly things you've said; and you'll find that your life has been built on them. The best of life is built on what we say when we're in love. It isn't nonsense, Katharine," she urged, "it's the truth, it's the only truth."

Katharine was on the point of interrupting her mother, and then she was on the point of confiding in her. They came strangely close together sometimes. But, while she hesitated and sought for words not too direct, her mother had recourse to Shakespeare, and turned page after page, set upon finding some quotation which said all this about love far, far better than she could. Accordingly, Katharine did nothing but scrub one of her circles an intense black with her pencil, in the midst of which process the telephone-bell rang, and she left the room to answer it.

When she returned, Mrs. Hilbery had found not the passage she wanted, but another of exquisite beauty as she justly observed, looking up for a second to ask Katharine who that was?

"Mary Datchet," Katharine replied briefly.

"Ah—I half wish I'd called you Mary, but it wouldn't have gone with Hilbery, and it wouldn't have gone with Rodney. Now this isn't the passage I wanted. (I never can find what I want.) But it's spring; it's the daffodils; it's the green fields; it's the birds."

She was cut short in her quotation by another imperative telephone-bell. Once more Katharine left the room.

"My dear child, how odious the triumphs of science are!" Mrs. Hilbery exclaimed on her return. "They'll be linking us with the moon next—but who was that?"

"William," Katharine replied yet more briefly.

"I'll forgive William anything, for I'm certain that there aren't any Williams in the moon. I hope he's coming to luncheon?"

"He's coming to tea."

"Well, that's better than nothing, and I promise to leave you alone."

"There's no need for you to do that," said Katharine.

She swept her hand over the faded sheet, and drew herself up squarely to the table as if she refused to waste time any longer. The gesture was not lost upon her mother. It hinted at the existence of something stern and unapproachable in her daughter's character, which struck chill upon her, as the sight of poverty, or drunkenness, or the logic with which Mr. Hilbery sometimes thought good to demolish her certainty of an approaching millennium struck chill upon her. She went back to her own table, and putting on her spectacles with a curious expression of quiet humility, addressed herself for the first time that morning to the task before her. The shock with an unsympathetic world had a sobering effect on her. For once, her industry surpassed her daughter's. Katharine could not reduce the world to that particular perspective in which Harriet Martineau, for instance, was a figure of solid importance, and possessed of a genuine relationship to this figure or to that date. Singularly enough, the sharp call of the telephone-bell still echoed in her ear, and her body and mind were in a state of tension, as if, at any moment, she might hear another summons of greater interest to her than the whole of the nineteenth century. She did not clearly realize what this call was to be; but when the ears have got into the habit of listening,

they go on listening involuntarily, and thus Katharine spent
the greater part of the morning in listening to a variety of
sounds in the back streets of Chelsea. For the first time in
her life, probably, she wished that Mrs. Hilbery would not
keep so closely to her work. A quotation from Shakespeare
would not have come amiss. Now and again she heard a
sigh from her mother's table, but that was the only proof
she gave of her existence, and Katharine did not think of
connecting it with the square aspect of her own position at
the table, or, perhaps, she would have thrown her pen down
and told her mother the reason of her restlessness. The
only writing she managed to accomplish in the course of
the morning was one letter, addressed to her cousin, Cassandra Otway—a rambling letter, long, affectionate, playful
and commanding all at once. She bade Cassandra put her
creatures in the charge of a groom, and come to them for a
week or so. They would go and hear some music together.
Cassandra's dislike of rational society, she said, was an af-
fectation fast hardening into a prejudice, which would, in
the long run, isolate her from all interesting people and pur-
suits. She was finishing the sheet when the sound she was
anticipating all the time actually struck upon her ears. She
jumped up hastily, and slammed the door with a sharpness
which made Mrs. Hilbery start. Where was Katharine off
to? In her preoccupied state she had not heard the bell.

The alcove on the stairs, in which the telephone was
placed, was screened for privacy by a curtain of purple velvet. It was a pocket for superfluous possessions, such as
exist in most houses which harbor the wreckage of three
generations. Prints of great-uncles, famed for their prowess
in the East, hung above Chinese teapots, whose sides were
riveted by little gold stitches, and the precious teapots, again,
stood upon bookcases containing the complete works of
William Cowper and Sir Walter Scott. The thread of
sound, issuing from the telephone, was always colored by
the surroundings which received it, so it seemed to Kath-

arine. Whose voice was now going to combine with them, or to strike a discord?

"Whose voice?" she asked herself, hearing a man inquire, with great determination, for her number. The unfamiliar voice now asked for Miss Hilbery. Out of all the welter of voices which crowd round the far end of the telephone, out of the enormous range of possibilities, whose voice, what possibility, was this? A pause gave her time to ask herself this question. It was solved next moment.

"I've looked out the train. . . . Early on Saturday afternoon would suit me best. . . . I'm Ralph Denham. . . . But I'll write it down. . . ."

With more than the usual sense of being impinged upon the point of a bayonet, Katharine replied:

"I think I could come. I'll look at my engagements. . . . Hold on."

She dropped the machine, and looked fixedly at the print of the great-uncle who had not ceased to gaze, with an air of amiable authority, into a world which, as yet, beheld no symptoms of the Indian Mutiny. And yet, gently swinging against the wall, within the black tube, was a voice which recked nothing of Uncle James, of China teapots, or of red velvet curtains. She watched the oscillation of the tube, and at the same moment became conscious of the individuality of the house in which she stood; she heard the soft domestic sounds of regular existence upon staircases and floors above her head, and movements through the wall in the house next door. She had no very clear vision of Denham himself, when she lifted the telephone to her lips and replied that she thought Saturday would suit her. She hoped that he would not say good-bye at once, although she felt no particular anxiety to attend to what he was saying, and began, even while he spoke, to think of her own upper room, with its books, its papers pressed between the leaves of dictionaries, and the table that could be cleared for work. She replaced the instrument, thoughtfully; her restlessness was assuaged; she finished her letter to Cassandra without difficulty, addressed the envelope, and fixed the stamp with her usual quick decision.

A bunch of anemones caught Mrs. Hilbery's eye when they had finished luncheon. The blue and purple and white of the bowl, standing in a pool of variegated light on a polished Chippendale table in the drawing-room window, made her stop dead with an exclamation of pleasure.

"Who is lying ill in bed, Katharine?" she demanded. "Which of our friends wants cheering up? Who feels that they've been forgotten and passed over, and that nobody wants them? Whose water rates are overdue, and the cook leaving in a temper without waiting for her wages? There was somebody I know——" she concluded, but for the moment the name of this desirable acquaintance escaped her. The best representative of the forlorn company whose day would be brightened by a bunch of anemones was, in Katharine's opinion, the widow of a general living in the Cromwell Road. In default of the actually destitute and starving, whom she would much have preferred, Mrs. Hilbery was forced to acknowledge her claims, for though in comfortable circumstances, she was extremely dull, unattractive, connected in some oblique fashion with literature, and had been touched to the verge of tears, on one occasion, by an afternoon call.

It happened that Mrs. Hilbery had an engagement elsewhere, so that the task of taking the flowers to the Cromwell Road fell upon Katharine. She took her letter to Cassandra with her, meaning to post it in the first pillar-box she came to. When, however, she was fairly out of doors, and constantly invited by pillar-boxes and post-offices to slip her envelope down their scarlet throats, she forbore. She made absurd excuses, as that she did not wish to cross the road, or that she was certain to pass another post-office in a more central position a little farther on. The longer she held the letter in her hand, however, the more persistently certain questions pressed upon her, as if from a collection of voices in the air. These invisible people wished

NIGHT AND DAY

to be informed whether she was engaged to William Rodney, or was the engagement broken off? Was it right, they asked, to invite Cassandra for a visit, and was William Rodney in love with her, or likely to fall in love? Then the questioners paused for a moment, and resumed as if another side of the problem had just come to their notice. What did Ralph Denham mean by what he said to you last night? Do you consider that he is in love with you? Is it right to consent to a solitary walk with him, and what advice are you going to give him about his future? Has William Rodney cause to be jealous of your conduct, and what do you propose to do about Mary Datchet? What are you going to do? What does honor require you to do? they repeated.

"Good Heavens!" Katharine exclaimed, after listening to all these remarks, "I suppose I ought to make up my mind."

But the debate was a formal skirmishing, a pastime to gain breathing-space. Like all people brought up in a tradition, Katharine was able, within ten minutes or so, to reduce any moral difficulty to its traditional shape and solve it by the traditional answers. The book of wisdom lay open, if not upon her mother's knee, upon the knees of many uncles and aunts. She had only to consult them, and they would at once turn to the right page and read out an answer exactly suited to one in her position. The rules which should govern the behavior of an unmarried woman are written in red ink, graved upon marble, if, by some freak of nature, it should fall out that the unmarried woman has not the same writing scored upon her heart. She was ready to believe that some people are fortunate enough to reject, accept, resign, or lay down their lives at the bidding of traditional authority; she could envy them; but in her case the questions became phantoms directly she tried seriously to find an answer, which proved that the traditional answer would be of no use to her individually. Yet it had served so many people, she thought, glancing at the rows of houses on either side of her, where families, whose incomes must be between

a thousand and fifteen-hundred a year lived, and kept, perhaps, three servants, and draped their windows with curtains which were always thick and generally dirty, and must,
she thought, since you could only see a looking-glass gleaming above a sideboard on which a dish of apples was set,
keep the room inside very dark.   But she turned her head
away, observing that this was not a method of thinking
the matter out.

The only truth which she could discover was the truth of
what she herself felt—a frail beam when compared with the
broad illumination shed by the eyes of all the people who
are in agreement to see together; but having rejected the
visionary voices, she had no choice but to make this her
guide through the dark masses which confronted her.   She
tried to follow her beam, with an expression upon her face
which would have made any passer-by think her reprehensi-
bly and almost ridiculously detached from the surrounding
scene.   One would have felt alarmed lest this young and
striking woman were about to do something eccentric.   But
her beauty saved her from the worst fate that can befall a
pedestrian; people looked at her, but they did not laugh.
To seek a true feeling among the chaos of the unfeelings or
half-feelings of life, to recognize it when found, and to accept the consequences of the discovery, draws lines upon the
smoothest brow, while it quickens the light of the eyes; it
is a pursuit which is alternately bewildering, debasing, and
exalting, and, as Katharine speedily found, her discoveries
gave her equal cause for surprise, shame, and intense anxiety.   Much depended, as usual, upon the interpretation of
the word love; which word came up again and again,
whether she considered Rodney, Denham, Mary Datchet, or
herself; and in each case it seemed to stand for something
different, and yet for something unmistakable and something not to be passed by.   For the more she looked into the
confusion of lives which, instead of running parallel, had
suddenly intersected each other, the more distinctly she
seemed to convince herself that there was no other light on

them than was shed by this strange illumination, and no other path save the one upon which it threw its beams. Her blindness in the case of Rodney, her attempt to match his true feeling with her false feeling, was a failure never to be sufficiently condemned; indeed, she could only pay it the tribute of leaving it a black and naked landmark unburied by attempt at oblivion or excuse.

With this to humiliate there was much to exalt. She thought of three different scenes; she thought of Mary sitting upright and saying, "I'm in love—I'm in love"; she thought of Rodney losing his self-consciousness among the dead leaves, and speaking with the abandonment of a child; she thought of Denham leaning upon the stone parapet and talking to the distant sky, so that she thought him mad. Her mind, passing from Mary to Denham, from William to Cassandra, and from Denham to herself—if, as she rather doubted, Denham's state of mind was connected with herself—seemed to be tracing out the lines of some symmetrical pattern, some arrangement of life, which invested, if not herself, at least the others, not only with interest, but with a kind of tragic beauty. She had a fantastic picture of them upholding splendid palaces upon their bent backs. They were the lantern-bearers, whose lights, scattered among the crowd, wove a pattern, dissolving, joining, meeting again in combination. Half forming such conceptions as these in her rapid walk along the dreary streets of South Kensington, she determined that, whatever else might be obscure, she must further the objects of Mary, Denham, William, and Cassandra. The way was not apparent. No course of action seemed to her indubitably right. All she achieved by her thinking was the conviction that, in such a cause, no risk was too great; and that, far from making any rules for herself or others, she would let difficulties accumulate unsolved, situations widen their jaws unsatiated, while she maintained a position of absolute and fearless independence. So she could best serve the people who loved.

Read in the light of this exaltation, there was a new meaning in the words which her mother had penciled upon the card attached to the bunch of anemones. The door of the house in the Cromwell Road opened; gloomy vistas of passage and staircase were revealed; such light as there was seemed to be concentrated upon a silver salver of visiting-cards, whose black borders suggested that the widow's friends had all suffered the same bereavement. The parlor-maid could hardly be expected to fathom the meaning of the grave tone in which the young lady proffered the flowers, with Mrs. Hilbery's love; and the door shut upon the offering.

The sight of a face, the slam of a door, are both rather destructive of exaltation in the abstract; and, as she walked back to Chelsea, Katharine had her doubts whether anything would come of her resolves. If you cannot make sure of people, however, you can hold fairly fast to figures, and in some way or other her thought about such problems as she was wont to consider worked in happily with her mood as to her friends' lives. She reached home rather late for tea.

On the ancient Dutch chest in the hall she perceived one, or two hats, coats, and walking-sticks, and the sound of voices reached her as she stood outside the drawing-room door. Her mother gave a little cry as she came in; a cry which conveyed to Katharine the fact that she was late, that the teacups and milk-jugs were in a conspiracy of disobedience, and that she must immediately take her place at the head of the table and pour out tea for the guests. Augustus Pelham, the diarist, liked a calm atmosphere in which to tell his stories; he liked attention; he liked to elicit little facts, little stories, about the past and the great dead, from such distinguished characters as Mrs. Hilbery for the nourishment of his diary, for whose sake he frequented tea-tables and ate yearly an enormous quantity of buttered toast. He, therefore, welcomed Katharine with relief, and she had merely to shake hands with Rodney and to greet the American lady who had come to be shown the relics, before the talk started again on the broad lines of reminiscence and discussion which were familiar to her.

Yet, even with this thick veil between them, she could not help looking at Rodney, as if she could detect what had happened to him since they met. It was in vain. His clothes, even the white slip, the pearl in his tie, seemed to intercept her quick glance, and to proclaim the futility of such inquiries of a discreet, urbane gentleman, who balanced his cup of tea and poised a slice of bread and butter on the edge of the saucer. He would not meet her eye, but that could be accounted for by his activity in serving and helping, and the polite alacrity with which he was answering the questions of the American visitor.

It was certainly a sight to daunt any one coming in with a head full of theories about love. The voices of the invisible questioners were reinforced by the scene round the table, and sounded with a tremendous self-confidence, as if they had behind them the common sense of twenty generations, together with the immediate approval of Mr. Augustus Pelham, Mrs. Vermont Bankes, William Rodney, and, possibly, Mrs. Hilbery herself. Katharine set her teeth, not entirely in the metaphorical sense, for her hand, obeying the impulse towards definite action, laid firmly upon the table beside her an envelope which she had been grasping all this time in complete forgetfulness. The address was uppermost, and a moment later she saw William's eye rest upon it as he rose to fulfil some duty with a plate. His expression instantly changed. He did what he was on the point of doing, and then looked at Katharine with a look which revealed enough of his confusion to show her that he was not entirely represented by his appearance. In a minute or two he proved himself at a loss with Mrs. Vermont Bankes, and Mrs. Hilbery, aware of the silence with her usual quickness, suggested that, perhaps, it was now time that Mrs. Bankes should be shown "our things."

Katharine accordingly rose, and led the way to the little

inner room with the pictures and the books. Mrs. Bankes
and Rodney followed her.

She turned on the lights, and began directly in her low,
pleasant voice: "This table is my grandfather's writing-
table. Most of the later poems were written at it. And
this is his pen—the last pen he ever used." She took it in
her hand and paused for the right number of seconds.
"Here," she continued, "is the original manuscript of the
'Ode to Winter.' The early manuscripts are far less corrected than the later ones, as you will see directly. . . . Oh,
do take it yourself," she added, as Mrs. Bankes asked, in an
awestruck tone of voice, for that privilege, and began a
preliminary unbuttoning of her white kid gloves.

"You are wonderfully like your grandfather, Miss Hilbery," the American lady observed, gazing from Katharine
to the portrait, "especially about the eyes. Come, now, I
expect she writes poetry herself, doesn't she?" she asked in
a jocular tone, turning to William. "Quite one's ideal of a
poet, is it not, Mr. Rodney? I cannot tell you what a privilege I feel it to be standing just here with the poet's granddaughter. You must know we think a great deal of your
grandfather in America, Miss Hilbery. We have societies
for reading him aloud. What! His very own slippers!"
Laying aside the manuscript, she hastily grasped the old
shoes, and remained for a moment dumb in contemplation
of them.

While Katharine went on steadily with her duties as
show-woman, Rodney examined intently a row of little
drawings which he knew by heart already. His disordered
state of mind made it necessary for him to take advantage
of these little respites, as if he had been out in a high wind
and must straighten his dress in the first shelter he reached.
His calm was only superficial, as he knew too well; it did
not exist much below the surface of tie, waistcoat, and white
slip.

On getting out of bed that morning he had fully made
up his mind to ignore what had been said the night before;

he had been convinced, by the sight of Denham, that his love for Katharine was passionate, and when he addressed her early that morning on the telephone, he had meant his cheerful but authoritative tones to convey to her the fact that, after a night of madness, they were as indissolubly engaged as ever. But when he reached his office his torments began. He found a letter from Cassandra waiting for him. She had read his play, and had taken the very first opportunity to write and tell him what she thought of it. She knew, she wrote, that her praise meant absolutely nothing; but still, she had sat up all night; she thought this, that, and the other; she was full of enthusiasm most elaborately scratched out in places, but enough was written plain to gratify William's vanity exceedingly. She was quite intelligent enough to say the right things, or, even more charmingly, to hint at them. In other ways, too, it was a very charming letter. She told him about her music, and about a Suffrage meeting to which Henry had taken her, and she asserted, half seriously, that she had learnt the Greek alphabet, and found it "fascinating." The word was underlined. Had she laughed when she drew that line? Was she ever serious? Didn't the letter show the most engaging compound of enthusiasm and spirit and whimsicality, all tapering into a flame of girlish freakishness, which flitted, for the rest of the morning, as a will-o'-the-wisp, across Rodney's landscape. He could not resist beginning an answer to her there and then. He found it particularly delightful to shape a style which should express the bowing and curtsying, advancing and retreating, which are characteristic of one of the many million partnerships of men and women. Katharine never trod that particular measure, he could not help reflecting; Katharine—Cassandra; Cassandra—Katharine—they alternated in his consciousness all day long. It was all very well to dress oneself carefully, compose one's face, and start off punctually at half-past four to a tea-party in Cheyne Walk, but Heaven only knew what would come of it all, and when Katharine, after sitting silent with her usual immobility, wantonly drew from her pocket and slapped down on the table beneath his eyes a letter addressed to Cassandra herself, his composure deserted him. What did she mean by her behavior?

He looked up sharply from his row of little pictures. Katharine was disposing of the American lady in far too arbitrary a fashion. Surely the victim herself must see how foolish her enthusiasms appeared in the eyes of the poet's granddaughter. Katharine never made any attempt to spare people's feelings, he reflected; and, being himself very sensitive to all shades of comfort and discomfort, he cut short the auctioneer's catalog, which Katharine was reeling off more and more absent-mindedly, and took Mrs. Vermont Bankes, with a queer sense of fellowship in suffering, under his own protection.

But within a few minutes the American lady had completed her inspection, and inclining her head in a little nod of reverential farewell to the poet and his shoes, she was escorted downstairs by Rodney. Katharine stayed by herself in the little room. The ceremony of ancestor-worship had been more than usually oppressive to her. Moreover, the room was becoming crowded beyond the bounds of order. Only that morning a heavily insured proof-sheet had reached them from a collector in Australia, which recorded a change of the poet's mind about a very famous phrase, and, therefore, had claims to the honor of glazing and framing. But was there room for it? Must it be hung on the staircase, or should some other relic give place to do it honor? Feeling unable to decide the question, Katharine glanced at the portrait of her grandfather, as if to ask his opinion. The artist who had painted it was now out of fashion, and by dint of showing it to visitors, Katharine had almost ceased to see anything but a glow of faintly pleasing pink and brown tints, enclosed within a circular scroll of gilt laurel-leaves. The young man who was her grandfather looked vaguely over her head. The sensual lips were slighty parted, and gave the face an expression of beholding something lovely or miraculous vanishing or just rising upon the rim of the distance. The expression repeated itself curiously upon Katharine's face as she gazed up into his. They were the same age, or very nearly so. She wondered what he was looking for; were there waves beating upon a shore for him, too, she wondered, and heroes riding through the leaf-hung forests? For perhaps the first time in her life she thought of him as a man, young, unhappy, tempestuous, full of desires and faults; for the first time she realized him for herself, and not from her mother's memory. He might have been her brother, she thought. It seemed to her that they were akin, with the mysterious kinship of blood which makes it seem possible to interpret the sights which the eyes of the dead behold so intently, or even to believe that they look with us upon our present joys and sorrows. He would have understood, she thought, suddenly; and instead of laying her withered flowers upon his shrine, she brought him her own perplexities—perhaps a gift of greater value, should the dead be conscious of gifts, than flowers and incense and adoration. Doubts, questionings, and despondencies she felt, as she looked up, would be more welcome to him than homage, and he would hold them but a very small burden if she gave him, also, some share in what she suffered and achieved. The depth of her own pride and love were not more apparent to her than the sense that the dead asked neither flowers nor regrets, but a share in the life which they had given her, the life which they had lived.

Rodney found her a moment later sitting beneath her grandfather's portrait. She laid her hand on the seat next her in a friendly way, and said:

"Come and sit down, William. How glad I was you were here! I felt myself getting ruder and ruder."

"You are not good at hiding your feelings," he returned dryly.

"Oh, don't scold me—I've had a horrid afternoon." She told him how she had taken the flowers to Mrs. McCormick, and how South Kensington impressed her as the preserve of officers' widows. She described how the door had opened, and what gloomy avenues of busts and palm-trees and umbrellas had been revealed to her. She spoke lightly, and succeeded in putting him at his ease. Indeed, he rapidly became too much at his ease to persist in a condition of cheerful neutrality. He felt his composure slipping from him. Katharine made it seem so natural to ask her to help him, or advise him, to say straight out what he had in his mind. The letter from Cassandra was heavy in his pocket. There was also the letter to Cassandra lying on the table in the next room. The atmosphere seemed charged with Cassandra. But, unless Katharine began the subject of her own accord, he could not even hint—he must ignore the whole affair; it was the part of a gentleman to preserve a bearing that was, as far as he could make it, the bearing of an undoubting lover. At intervals he sighed deeply. He talked rather more quickly than usual about the possibility that some of the operas of Mozart would be played in the summer. He had received a notice, he said, and at once produced a pocket-book stuffed with papers, and began shuffling them in search. He held a thick envelope between his finger and thumb, as if the notice from the opera company had become in some way inseparably attached to it.

"A letter from Cassandra?" said Katharine, in the easiest voice in the world, looking over his shoulder. "I've just written to ask her to come here, only I forgot to post it."

He handed her the envelope in silence. She took it, extracted the sheets, and read the letter through.

The reading seemed to Rodney to take an intolerably long time.

"Yes," she observed at length, "a very charming letter."

Rodney's face was half turned away, as if in bashfulness. Her view of his profile almost moved her to laughter. She glanced through the pages once more.

"I see no harm," William blurted out, "in helping her—

with Greek, for example—if she really cares for that sort of thing."

"There's no reason why she shouldn't care," said Katharine, consulting the pages once more. "In fact—ah, here it is—'The Greek alphabet is absolutely *fascinating*.' Obviously she does care."

"Well, Greek may be rather a large order. I was thinking chiefly of English. Her criticisms of my play, though they're too generous, evidently immature—she can't be more than twenty-two, I suppose?—they certainly show the sort of thing one wants: real feeling for poetry, understanding, not formed, of course, but it's at the root of everything after all. There'd be no harm in lending her books?"

"No. Certainly not."

"But if it—hum—led to a correspondence? I mean, Katharine, I take it, without going into matters which seem to me a little morbid, I mean," he floundered, "you, from your point of view, feel that there's nothing disagreeable to you in the notion? If so, you've only to speak, and I never think of it again."

She was surprised by the violence of her desire that he never should think of it again. For an instant it seemed to her impossible to surrender an intimacy, which might not be the intimacy of love, but was certainly the intimacy of true friendship, to any woman in the world. Cassandra would never understand him—she was not good enough for him. The letter seemed to her a letter of flattery—a letter addressed to his weakness, which it made her angry to think was known to another. For he was not weak; he had the rare strength of doing what he promised—she had only to speak, and he would never think of Cassandra again.

She paused. Rodney guessed the reason. He was amazed.

"She loves me," he thought. The woman he admired more than any one in the world, loved him, as he had given up hope that she would ever love him. And now that for the first time he was sure of her love, he resented it. He felt it as a fetter, an encumbrance, something which made them both, but him in particular, ridiculous. He was in her power completely, but his eyes were open and he was no longer her slave or her dupe. He would be her master in future. The instant prolonged itself as Katharine realized the strength of her desire to speak the words that should keep William for ever, and the baseness of the temptation which assailed her to make the movement, or speak the word, which he had often begged her for, which she was now near enough to feeling. She held the letter in her hand. She sat silent.

At this moment there was a stir in the other room; the voice of Mrs. Hilbery was heard talking of proof-sheets rescued by miraculous providence from butcher's ledgers in Australia; the curtain separating one room from the other was drawn apart, and Mrs. Hilbery and Augustus Pelham stood in the doorway. Mrs. Hilbery stopped short. She looked at her daughter, and at the man her daughter was to marry, with her peculiar smile that always seemed to tremble on the brink of satire.

"The best of all my treasures, Mr. Pelham!" she exclaimed. "Don't move, Katharine. Sit still, William. Mr. Pelham will come another day."

Mr. Pelham looked, smiled, bowed, and, as his hostess had moved on, followed her without a word. The curtain was drawn again either by him or by Mrs. Hilbery.

But her mother had settled the question somehow. Katharine doubted no longer.

"As I told you last night," she said, "I think it's your duty, if there's a chance that you care for Cassandra, to discover what your feeling is for her now. It's your duty to her, as well as to me. But we must tell my mother. We can't go on pretending."

"That is entirely in your hands, of course," said Rodney, with an immediate return to the manner of a formal man of honor.

"Very well," said Katharine.

Directly he left her she would go to her mother, and

explain that the engagement was at an end—or it might be better that they should go together?

"But, Katharine," Rodney began, nervously attempting to stuff Cassandra's sheets back into their envelope; "if Cassandra—should Cassandra—you've asked Cassandra to stay with you."

"Yes; but I've not posted the letter."

He crossed his knees in a discomfited silence. By all his codes it was impossible to ask a woman with whom he had just broken off his engagement to help him to become acquainted with another woman with a view to his falling in love with her. If it was announced that their engagement was over, a long and complete separation would inevitably follow; in those circumstances, letters and gifts were returned; after years of distance the severed couple met, perhaps at an evening party, and touched hands uncomfortably with an indifferent word or two. He would be cast off completely; he would have to trust to his own resources. He could never mention Cassandra to Katharine again; for months, and doubtless years, he would never see Katharine again; anything might happen to her in his absence.

Katharine was almost as well aware of his perplexities as he was. She knew in what direction complete generosity pointed the way; but pride—for to remain engaged to Rodney and to cover his experiments hurt what was nobler in her than mere vanity—fought for its life.

"I'm to give up my freedom for an indefinite time," she thought, "in order that William may see Cassandra here at his ease. He's not the courage to manage it without my help—he's too much of a coward to tell me openly what he wants. He hates the notion of a public breach. He wants to keep us both."

When she reached this point, Rodney pocketed the letter and elaborately looked at his watch. Although the action meant that he resigned Cassandra, for he knew his own incompetence and distrusted himself entirely, and lost Katharine, for whom his feeling was profound though unsatisfactory, still it appeared to him that there was nothing else left for him to do. He was forced to go, leaving Katharine free, as he had said, to tell her mother that the engagement was at an end. But to do what plain duty required of an honorable man, cost an effort which only a day or two ago would have been inconceivable to him. That a relationship such as he had glanced at with desire could be possible between him and Katharine, he would have been the first, two days ago, to deny with indignation. But now his life had changed; his attitude had changed; his feelings were different; new aims and possibilities had been shown him, and they had an almost irresistible fascination and force. The training of a life of thirty-five years had not left him defenceless; he was still master of his dignity; he rose, with a mind made up to an irrevocable farewell.

"I leave you, then," he said, standing up and holding out his hand with an effort that left him pale, but lent him dignity, "to tell your mother that our engagement is ended by your desire."

She took his hand and held it.

"You don't trust me?" she said.

"I do, absolutely," he replied.

"No. You don't trust me to help you. . . . I could help you?"

"I'm hopeless without your help!" he exclaimed passionately, but withdrew his hand and turned his back. When he faced her, she thought that she saw him for the first time without disguise.

"It's useless to pretend that I don't understand what you're offering, Katharine. I admit what you say. Speaking to you perfectly frankly, I believe at this moment that I *do* love your cousin; there is a chance that, with your help, I might—but no," he broke off, "it's impossible, it's wrong —I'm infinitely to blame for having allowed this situation to arise."

"Sit beside me. Let's consider sensibly——"

"Your sense has been our undoing——" he groaned.

"I accept the responsibility."

"Ah, but can I allow that?" he exclaimed. "It would mean—for we must face it, Katharine—that we let our engagement stand for the time nominally; in fact, of course, your freedom would be absolute."

"And yours too."

"Yes, we should both be free. Let us say that I saw Cassandra once, twice, perhaps, under these conditions; and then if, as I think certain, the whole thing proves a dream, we tell your mother instantly. Why not tell her now, indeed, under pledge of secrecy?"

"Why not? It would be over London in ten minutes, besides, she would never even remotely understand."

"Your father, then? This secrecy is detestable—it's dishonorable."

"My father would understand even less than my mother."

"Ah, who could be expected to understand?" Rodney groaned; "but it's from your point of view that we must look at it. It's not only asking too much, it's putting you into a position—a position in which I could not endure to see my own sister."

"We're not brothers and sisters," she said impatiently, "and if we can't decide, who can? I'm not talking nonsense," she proceeded. "I've done my best to think this out from every point of view, and I've come to the conclusion that there are risks which have to be taken,—though I don't deny that they hurt horribly."

"Katharine, you mind? You'll mind too much."

"No I shan't," she said stoutly. "I shall mind a good deal, but I'm prepared for that; I shall get through it, because you will help me. You'll both help me. In fact, we'll help each other. That's a Christian doctrine, isn't it?"

"It sounds more like Paganism to me," Rodney groaned, as he reviewed the situation into which her Christian doctrine was plunging them.

And yet he could not deny that a divine relief possessed him, and that the future, instead of wearing a lead-colored mask, now blossomed with a thousand varied gaieties and excitements. He was actually to see Cassandra within a week or perhaps less, and he was more anxious to know the date of her arrival than he could own even to himself. It seemed base to be so anxious to pluck this fruit of Katharine's unexampled generosity and of his own contemptible baseness. And yet, though he used these words automatically, they had now no meaning. He was not debased in his own eyes by what he had done, and as for praising Katharine, were they not partners, conspirators, people bent upon the same quest together, so that to praise the pursuit of a common end as an act of generosity was meaningless. He took her hand and pressed it, not in thanks so much as in an ecstasy of comradeship.

"We will help each other," he said, repeating her words, seeking her eyes in an enthusiasm of friendship.

Her eyes were grave but dark with sadness as they rested on him. "He's already gone," she thought, "far away— he thinks of me no more." And the fancy came to her that, as they sat side by side, hand in hand, she could hear the earth pouring from above to make a barrier between them, so that, as they sat, they were separated second by second by an impenetrable wall. The process, which affected her as that of being sealed away and for ever from all companionship with the person she cared for most, came to an end at last, and by common consent they unclasped their fingers, Rodney touching hers with his lips, as the curtain parted, and Mrs. Hilbery peered through the opening with her benevolent and sarcastic expression to ask whether Katharine could remember was it Tuesday or Wednesday, and did she dine in Westminster?

"Dearest William," she said, pausing, as if she could not resist the pleasure of encroaching for a second upon this wonderful world of love and confidence and romance. "Dearest children," she added, disappearing with an impulsive gesture, as if she forced herself to draw the curtain upon a scene which she refused all temptation to interrupt.

CHAPTER XXV

AT a quarter-past three in the afternoon of the following Saturday Ralph Denham sat on the bank of the
lake in Kew Gardens, dividing the dial-plate of his watch
into sections with his forefinger. The just and inexorable
nature of time itself was reflected in his face. He might
have been composing a hymn to the unhasting and unrest-
ing march of that divinity. He seemed to greet the lapse of
minute after minute with stern acquiescence in the inevitable
order. His expression was so severe, so serene, so immobile,
that it seemed obvious that for him at least there was a
grandeur in the departing hour which no petty irritation
on his part was to mar, although the wasting time wasted
also high private hopes of his own.

His face was no bad index to what went on within him.
He was in a condition of mind rather too exalted for the
trivialities of daily life. He could not accept the fact that
a lady was fifteen minutes late in keeping her appointment
without seeing in that accident the frustration of his entire
life. Looking at his watch, he seemed to look deep into the
springs of human existence, and by the light of what he
saw there altered his course towards the north and the midnight. . . . Yes, one's voyage must be made absolutely without companions through ice and black water—towards what
goal? Here he laid his finger upon the half-hour, and decided that when the minute-hand reached that point he
would go, at the same time answering the question put by
another of the many voices of consciousness with the reply
that there was undoubtedly a goal, but that it would need
the most relentless energy to keep anywhere in its direction.
Still, still, one goes on, the ticking seconds seemed to assure

him, with dignity, with open eyes, with determination not to
accept the second-rate, not to be tempted by the unworthy,
not to yield, not to compromise.   Twenty-five minutes
past three were now marked upon the face of the watch.
The world, he assured himself, since Katharine Hilbery
was now half an hour behind her time, offers no happiness,
no rest from struggle, no certainty.   In a scheme of things
utterly bad from the start the only unpardonable folly is
that of hope.   Raising his eyes for a moment from the face
of his watch, he rested them upon the opposite bank, reflectively and not without a certain wistfulness, as if the sternness of their gaze were still capable of mitigation.   Soon
a look of the deepest satisfaction filled them, though, for a
moment, he did not move.   He watched a lady who came
rapidly, and yet with a trace of hesitation, down the broad
grass-walk towards him.   She did not see him.   Distance
lent her figure an indescribable height, and romance seemed
to surround her from the floating of a purple veil which
the light air filled and curved from her shoulders.

"Here she comes, like a ship in full sail," he said to himself, half remembering some line from a play or poem
where the heroine bore down thus with feathers flying and
airs saluting her.   The greenery and the high presences of
the trees surrounded her as if they stood forth at her coming.   He rose, and she saw him; her little exclamation
proved that she was glad to find him, and then that she
blamed herself for being late.

"Why did you never tell me?   I didn't know there was
this," she remarked, alluding to the lake, the broad green
space, the vista of trees, with the ruffled gold of the Thames
in the distance and the Ducal castle standing in its meadows.
She paid the rigid tail of the Ducal lion the tribute of in-
credulous laughter.

"You've never been to Kew?" Denham remarked.

But it appeared that she had come once as a small child,
when the geography of the place was entirely different, and
the fauna included certainly flamingoes and, possibly,

camels. They strolled on, refashioning these legendary gardens. She was, as he felt, glad merely to stroll and loiter and let her fancy touch upon anything her eyes encountered —a bush, a park-keeper, a decorated goose—as if the relaxation soothed her. The warmth of the afternoon, the first of spring, tempted them to sit upon a seat in a glade of beech-trees, with forest drives striking green paths this way and that around them. She sighed deeply.

"It's so peaceful," she said, as if in explanation of her sigh. Not a single person was in sight, and the stir of the wind in the branches, that sound so seldom heard by Londoners, seemed to her as if wafted from fathomless oceans of sweet air in the distance.

While she breathed and looked, Denham was engaged in uncovering with the point of his stick a group of green spikes half smothered by the dead leaves. He did this with the peculiar touch of the botanist. In naming the little green plant to her he used the Latin name, thus disguising some flower familiar even to Chelsea, and making her exclaim, half in amusement, at his knowledge. Her own ignorance was vast, she confessed. What did one call that tree opposite, for instance, supposing one condescended to call it by its English name? Beech or elm or sycamore? It chanced, by the testimony of a dead leaf, to be oak; and a little attention to a diagram which Denham proceeded to draw upon an envelope soon put Katharine in possession of some of the fundamental distinctions between our British trees. She then asked him to inform her about flowers. To her they were variously shaped and colored petals, poised, at different seasons of the year, upon very similar green stalks; but to him they were, in the first instance, bulbs or seeds, and later, living things endowed with sex, and pores, and susceptibilities which adapted themselves by all manner of ingenious devices to live and beget life, and could be fashioned squat or tapering, flame-colored or pale, pure or spotted, by processes which might reveal the secrets of human existence. Denham spoke with increasing ardor of a hobby which had long been his in secret. No discourse could have worn a more welcome sound in Katharine's ears. For weeks she had heard nothing that made such pleasant music in her mind. It wakened echoes in all those remote fastnesses of her being where loneliness had brooded so long undisturbed.

She wished he would go on for ever talking of plants, and showing her how science felt not quite blindly for the law that ruled their endless variations. A law that might be inscrutable but was certainly omnipotent appealed to her at the moment, because she could find nothing like it in possession of human lives. Circumstances had long forced her, as they force most women in the flower of youth, to consider, painfully and minutely, all that part of life which is conspicuously without order; she had had to consider moods and wishes, degrees of liking or disliking, and their effect upon the destiny of people dear to her; she had been forced to deny herself any contemplation of that other part of life where thought constructs a destiny which is independent of human beings. As Denham spoke, she followed his words and considered their bearing with an easy vigor which spoke of a capacity long hoarded and unspent. The very trees and the green merging into the blue distance became symbols of the vast external world which recks so little of the happiness, of the marriages or deaths of individuals. In order to give her examples of what he was saying, Denham led the way, first to the Rock Garden, and then to the Orchid House.

For him there was safety in the direction which the talk had taken. His emphasis might come from feelings more personal than those science roused in him, but it was disguised, and naturally he found it easy to expound and explain. Nevertheless, when he saw Katharine among the orchids, her beauty strangely emphasized by the fantastic plants, which seemed to peer and gape at her from striped hoods and fleshy throats, his ardor for botany waned, and a more complex feeling replaced it. She fell silent. The orchids seemed to suggest absorbing reflections. In defiance of the rules she stretched her ungloved hand and touched one. The sight of the rubies upon her finger affected him so disagreeably that he started and turned away. But next moment he controlled himself; he looked at her taking in one strange shape after another with the contemplative, considering gaze of a person who sees not exactly what is before him, but gropes in regions that lie beyond it. The far-away look entirely lacked self-consciousness. Denham doubted whether she remembered his presence. He could recall himself, of course, by a word or a movement—but why? She was happier thus. She needed nothing that he could give her. And for him, too, perhaps, it was best to keep aloof, only to know that she existed, to preserve what he already had—perfect, remote, and unbroken. Further, her still look, standing among the orchids in that hot atmosphere, strangely illustrated some scene that he had imagined in his room at home. The sight, mingling with his recollection, kept him silent when the door was shut and they were walking on again.

But though she did not speak, Katharine had an uneasy sense that silence on her part was selfishness. It was selfish of her to continue, as she wished to do, a discussion of subjects not remotely connected with any human beings. She roused herself to consider their exact position upon the turbulent map of the emotions. Oh yes—it was a question whether Ralph Denham should live in the country and write a book; it was getting late; they must waste no more time; Cassandra arrived to-night for dinner; she flinched and roused herself, and discovered that she ought to be holding something in her hands. But they were empty. She held them out with an exclamation.

"I've left my bag somewhere—where?" The gardens had no points of the compass, so far as she was concerned. She had been walking for the most part on grass—that was all she knew. Even the road to the Orchid House had now split itself into three. But there was no bag in the Orchid

House. It must, therefore, have been left upon the seat. They retraced their steps in the preoccupied manner of people who have to think about something that is lost. What did this bag look like? What did it contain?

"A purse—a ticket—some letters, papers," Katharine counted, becoming more agitated as she recalled the list. Denham went on quickly in advance of her, and she heard him shout that he had found it before she reached the seat. In order to make sure that all was safe she spread the contents on her knee. It was a queer collection, Denham thought, gazing with the deepest interest. Loose gold coins were tangled in a narrow strip of lace; there were letters which somehow suggested the extreme of intimacy; there were two or three keys, and lists of commissions against which crosses were set at intervals. But she did not seem satisfied until she had made sure of a certain paper so folded that Denham could not judge what it contained. In her relief and gratitude she began at once to say that she had been thinking over what Denham had told her of his plans.

He cut her short. "Don't let's discuss that dreary business."

"But I thought——"

"It's a dreary business. I ought never to have bothered you——"

"Have you decided, then?"

He made an impatient sound. "It's not a thing that matters."

She could only say rather flatly, "Oh!"

"I mean it matters to me, but it matters to no one else. Anyhow," he continued, more amiably, "I see no reason why you should be bothered with other people's nuisances."

She supposed that she had let him see too clearly her weariness of this side of life.

"I'm afraid I've been absent-minded," she began, remembering how often William had brought this charge against her.

334 NIGHT AND DAY

"You have a good deal to make you absent-minded," he replied.

"Yes," she replied, flushing. "No," she contradicted herself. "Nothing particular, I mean. But I was thinking about plants. I was enjoying myself. In fact, I've seldom enjoyed an afternoon more. But I want to hear what you've settled, if you don't mind telling me."

"Oh, it's all settled," he replied. "I'm going to this infernal cottage to write a worthless book."

"How I envy you," she replied, with the utmost sincerity.

"Well, cottages are to be had for fifteen shillings a week."

"Cottages are to be had—yes," she replied. "The question is——" She checked herself. "Two rooms are all I should want," she continued, with a curious sigh; "one for eating, one for sleeping. Oh, but I should like another, a large one at the top, and a little garden where one could grow flowers. A path—so—down to a river, or up to a wood, and the sea not very far off, so that one could hear the waves at night. Ships just vanishing on the horizon——" She broke off. "Shall you be near the sea?"

"My notion of perfect happiness," he began, not replying to her question, "is to live as you've said."

"Well, now you can. You will work, I suppose," she continued; "you'll work all the morning and again after tea and perhaps at night. You won't have people always coming about you to interrupt."

"How far can one live alone?" he asked. "Have you tried ever?"

"Once for three weeks," she replied. "My father and mother were in Italy, and something happened so that I couldn't join them. For three weeks I lived entirely by myself, and the only person I spoke to was a stranger in a shop where I lunched—a man with a beard. Then I went back to my room by myself and—well, I did what I liked. It doesn't make me out an amiable character, I'm afraid," she added, "but I can't endure living with other people. An occasional man with a beard is interesting; he's detached;

he lets me go my way, and we know we shall never meet again. Therefore, we are perfectly sincere—a thing not possible with one's friends."

"Nonsense," Denham replied abruptly.

"Why 'nonsense'?" she inquired.

"Because you don't mean what you say," he expostulated.

"You're very positive," she said, laughing and looking at him. How arbitrary, hot-tempered, and imperious he was! He had asked her to come to Kew to advise him; he then told her that he had settled the question already; he then proceeded to find fault with her. He was the very opposite of William Rodney, she thought; he was shabby, his clothes were badly made, he was ill versed in the amenities of life; he was tongue-tied and awkward to the verge of obliterating his real character. He was awkwardly silent; he was awkwardly emphatic. And yet she liked him.

"I don't mean what I say," she repeated good-humoredly. "Well——?"

"I doubt whether you make absolute sincerity your standard in life," he answered significantly.

She flushed. He had penetrated at once to the weak spot —her engagement, and had reason for what he said. He was not altogether justified now, at any rate, she was glad to remember; but she could not enlighten him and must bear his insinuations, though from the lips of a man who had behaved as he had behaved their force should not have been sharp. Nevertheless, what he said had its force, she mused; partly because he seemed unconscious of his own lapse in the case of Mary Datchet, and thus baffled her insight; partly because he always spoke with force, for what reason she did not yet feel certain.

"Absolute sincerity is rather difficult, don't you think?" she inquired, with a touch of irony.

"There are people one credits even with that," he replied a little vaguely. He was ashamed of his savage wish to hurt her, and yet it was not for the sake of hurting her, who was beyond his shafts, but in order to mortify his own incredibly reckless impulse of abandonment to the spirit which seemed, at moments, about to rush him to the uttermost ends of the earth. She affected him beyond the scope of his wildest dreams. He seemed to see that beneath the quiet surface of her manner, which was almost pathetically at hand and within reach for all the trivial demands of daily life, there was a spirit which she reserved or repressed for some reason either of loneliness or—could it be possible—of love. Was it given to Rodney to see her unmasked, unrestrained, unconscious of her duties? a creature of uncalculating passion and instinctive freedom? No; he refused to believe it. It was in her loneliness that Katharine was unreserved. "I went back to my room by myself and I did—what I liked." She had said that to him, and in saying it had given him a glimpse of possibilities, even of confidences, as if he might be the one to share her loneliness, the mere hint of which made his heart beat faster and his brain spin. He checked himself as brutally as he could. He saw her redden, and in the irony of her reply he heard her resentment.

He began slipping his smooth, silver watch in his pocket, in the hope that somehow he might help himself back to that calm and fatalistic mood which had been his when he looked at its face upon the bank of the lake, for that mood must, at whatever cost, be the mood of his intercourse with Katharine. He had spoken of gratitude and acquiescence in the letter which he had never sent, and now all the force of his character must make good those vows in her presence.

She, thus challenged, tried meanwhile to define her points. She wished to make Denham understand.

"Don't you see that if you have no relations with people it's easier to be honest with them?" she inquired. "That is what I meant. One needn't cajole them; one's under no obligation to them. Surely you must have found with your own family that it's impossible to discuss what matters to you most because you're all herded together, because you're in a conspiracy, because the position is false——" Her reasoning suspended itself a little inconclusively, for the subject was complex, and she found herself in ignorance whether Denham had a family or not. Denham was agreed with her as to the destructiveness of the family system, but he did not wish to discuss the problem at that moment.

He turned to a problem which was of greater interest to him.

"I'm convinced," he said, "that there are cases in which perfect sincerity is possible—cases where there's no relationship, though the people live together, if you like, where each is free, where there's no obligation upon either side."

"For a time—perhaps," she agreed, a little despondently. "But obligations always grow up. There are feelings to be considered. People aren't simple, and though they may mean to be reasonable, they end"—in the condition in which she found herself, she meant, but added lamely—"in a muddle."

"Because," Denham instantly intervened, "they don't make themselves understood at the beginning. I could undertake, at this instant," he continued, with a reasonable intonation which did much credit to his self-control, "to lay down terms for a friendship which should be perfectly sincere and perfectly straightforward."

She was curious to hear them, but, besides feeling that the topic concealed dangers better known to her than to him, she was reminded by his tone of his curious abstract declaration upon the Embankment. Anything that hinted at love for the moment alarmed her; it was as much an infliction to her as the rubbing of a skinless wound.

But he went on, without waiting for her invitation.

"In the first place, such a friendship must be unemotional," he laid it down emphatically. "At least, on both sides it must be understood that if either chooses to fall in love, he or she does so entirely at his own risk. Neither is under any obligation to the other. They must be at liberty to break or to alter at any moment. They must be able to say whatever they wish to say. All this must be understood."

"And they gain something worth having?" she asked.

"It's a risk—of course it's a risk," he replied. The word was one that she had been using frequently in her arguments with herself of late.

"But it's the only way—if you think friendship worth having," he concluded.

"Perhaps under those conditions it might be," she said reflectively.

"Well," he said, "those are the terms of the friendship I wish to offer you." She had known that this was coming, but, none the less, felt a little shock, half of pleasure, half of reluctance, when she heard the formal statement.

"I should like it," she began, "but——"

"Would Rodney mind?"

"Oh no," she replied quickly.

"No, no, it isn't that," she went on, and again came to an end. She had been touched by the unreserved and yet ceremonious way in which he had made what he called his offer of terms, but if he was generous it was the more necessary for her to be cautious. They would find themselves in difficulties, she speculated; but, at this point, which was not very far, after all, upon the road of caution, her foresight deserted her. She sought for some definite catastrophe into which they must inevitably plunge. But she could think of none. It seemed to her that these catastrophes were fictitious; life went on and on—life was different altogether from what people said. And not only was she at an end of her stock of caution, but it seemed suddenly altogether superfluous. Surely if any one could take care of himself, Ralph Denham could; he had told her that he did not love her. And, further, she meditated, walking on beneath the beech-trees and swinging her umbrella, as in her thought she was accustomed to complete freedom, why should she perpetually apply so different a standard to her behavior in practice? Why, she reflected, should there be this perpetual disparity between the thought and the action, between the life of solitude and the life of society, this astonishing precipice on one side of which the soul was active and in broad daylight, on the other side of which it was contemplative and dark as night? Was it not possible to step from one to the other, erect, and without essential change? Was this not the chance he offered her—the rare and wonderful chance of friendship? At any rate, she told Denham, with a sigh in which he heard both impatience and relief, that she agreed; she thought him right; she would accept his terms of friendship.

"Now," she said, "let's go and have tea."

In fact, these principles having been laid down, a great lightness of spirit showed itself in both of them. They were both convinced that something of profound importance had been settled, and could now give their attention to their tea and the Gardens. They wandered in and out of glass-houses, saw lilies swimming in tanks, breathed in the scent of thousands of carnations, and compared their respective tastes in the matter of trees and lakes. While talking ex-clusively of what they saw, so that any one might have overheard them, they felt that the compact between them was made firmer and deeper by the number of people who passed them and suspected nothing of the kind. The ques-tion of Ralph's cottage and future was not mentioned again

CHAPTER XXVI

ALTHOUGH the old coaches, with their gay panels and the guard's horn, and the humors of the box and the vicissitudes of the road, have long moldered into dust so far as they were matter, and are preserved in the printed pages of our novelists so far as they partook of the spirit, a journey to London by express train can still be a very pleasant and romantic adventure. Cassandra Otway, at the age of twenty-two, could imagine few things more pleasant. Satiated with months of green fields as she was, the first row of artisans' villas on the outskirts of London seemed to have something serious about it, which positively increased the importance of every person in the railway carriage, and even, to her impressionable mind, quickened the speed of the train and gave a note of stern authority to the shriek of the engine-whistle. They were bound for London; they must have precedence of all traffic not similarly destined. A different demeanor was necessary directly one stepped out upon Liverpool Street platform, and became one of those preoccupied and hasty citizens for whose needs innumerable taxi-cabs, motor-omnibuses, and underground railways were in waiting. She did her best to look dignified and preoccupied too, but as the cab carried her away, with a determination which alarmed her a little, she became more and more forgetful of her station as a citizen of London, and turned her head from one window to another, picking up eagerly a building on this side or a street scene on that to feed her intense curiosity. And yet, while the drive lasted no one was real, nothing was ordinary; the crowds, the Government buildings, the tide of men and women washing the base of the great glass windows, were all generalized, and affected her as if she saw them on the stage.

All these feelings were sustained and partly inspired by
the fact that her journey took her straight to the center of
her most romantic world. A thousand times in the midst of
her pastoral landscape her thoughts took this precise road,
were admitted to the house in Chelsea, and went directly
upstairs to Katharine's room, where, invisible themselves,
they had the better chance of feasting upon the privacy of
the room's adorable and mysterious mistress. Cassandra
adored her cousin; the adoration might have been foolish,
but was saved from that excess and lent an engaging charm
by the volatile nature of Cassandra's temperament. She had
adored a great many things and people in the course of
twenty-two years; she had been alternately the pride and the
desperation of her teachers. She had worshipped architecture and music, natural history and humanity, literature and
art, but always at the height of her enthusiasm, which was
accompanied by a brilliant degree of accomplishment, she
changed her mind and bought, surreptitiously, another grammar. The terrible results which governesses had predicted
from such mental dissipation were certainly apparent now
that Cassandra was twenty-two, and had never passed an
examination, and daily showed herself less and less capable
of passing one. The more serious prediction that she could
never possibly earn her living was also verified. But from
all these short strands of different accomplishments Cassandra wove for herself an attitude, a cast of mind, which, if
useless, was found by some people to have the not despicable virtues of vivacity and freshness. Katharine, for example, thought her a most charming companion. The cousins seemed to assemble between them a great range of qualities which are never found united in one person and seldom
in half a dozen people. Where Katharine was simple,
Cassandra was complex; where Katharine was solid and
direct, Cassandra was vague and evasive. In short, they
represented very well the manly and the womanly sides of
the feminine nature, and, for foundation, there was the profound unity of common blood between them. If Cassandra

adored Katharine she was incapable of adoring any one
without refreshing her spirit with frequent draughts of
raillery and criticism, and Katharine enjoyed her laughter
at least as much as her respect.

Respect was certainly uppermost in Cassandra's mind at
the present moment. Katharine's engagement had appealed
to her imagination as the first engagement in a circle of
contemporaries is apt to appeal to the imaginations of the
others; it was solemn, beautiful, and mysterious; it gave
both parties the important air of those who have been initi-
ated into some rite which is still concealed from the rest of
the group. For Katharine's sake Cassandra thought William a most distinguished and interesting character, and
welcomed first his conversation and then his manuscript as
the marks of a friendship which it flattered and delighted
her to inspire.

Katharine was still out when she arrived at Cheyne Walk.
After greeting her uncle and aunt and receiving, as usual,
a present of two sovereigns for "cab fares and dissipation"
from Uncle Trevor, whose favorite niece she was, she
changed her dress and wandered into Katharine's room to
await her. What a great looking-glass Katharine had, she
thought, and how mature all the arrangements upon the
dressing-table were compared to what she was used to at
home. Glancing round, she thought that the bills stuck
upon a skewer and stood for ornament upon the mantelpiece
were astonishingly like Katharine, There wasn't a photograph of William anywhere to be seen. The room, with
its combination of luxury and bareness, its silk dressing-
gowns and crimson slippers, its shabby carpet and bare
walls, had a powerful air of Katharine herself; she stood
in the middle of the room and enjoyed the sensation; and
then, with a desire to finger what her cousin was in the
habit of fingering, Cassandra began to take down the books
which stood in a row upon the shelf above the bed. In
most houses this shelf is the ledge upon which the last relics
of religious belief lodge themselves as if, late at night, in the

heart of privacy, people, skeptical by day, find solace in sipping one draught of the old charm for such sorrows or perplexities as may steal from their hiding-places in the dark. But there was no hymn-book here. By their battered covers and enigmatical contents, Cassandra judged them to be old school-books belonging to Uncle Trevor, and piously, though eccentrically, preserved by his daughter. There was no end, she thought, to the unexpectedness of Katharine. She had once had a passion for geometry herself, and, curled upon Katharine's quilt, she became absorbed in trying to remember how far she had forgotten what she once knew. Katharine, coming in a little later, found her deep in this characteristic pursuit.

"My dear," Cassandra exclaimed, shaking the book at her cousin, "my whole life's changed from this moment! I must write the man's name down at once, or I shall forget——"

Whose name, what book, which life was changed Katharine proceeded to ascertain. She began to lay aside her clothes hurriedly, for she was very late.

"May I sit and watch you?" Cassandra asked, shutting up her book. "I got ready on purpose."

"Oh, you're ready, are you?" said Katharine, half turning in the midst of her operations, and looking at Cassandra, who sat, clasping her knees, on the edge of the bed.

"There are people dining here," she said, taking in the effect of Cassandra from a new point of view. After an interval, the distinction, the irregular charm, of the small face with its long tapering nose and its bright oval eyes were very notable. The hair rose up off the forehead rather stiffly, and, given a more careful treatment by hairdressers and dressmakers, the light angular figure might possess a likeness to a French lady of distinction in the eighteenth century.

"Who's coming to dinner?" Cassandra asked, anticipating further possibilities of rapture.

"There's William, and, I believe, Aunt Eleanor and Uncle Aubrey."

"I'm so glad William is coming. Did he tell you that he sent me his manuscript? I think it's wonderful—I think he's almost good enough for you, Katharine."

"You shall sit next to him and tell him what you think of him."

"I shan't dare do that," Cassandra asserted.

"Why? You're not afraid of him, are you?"

"A little—because he's connected with you."

Katharine smiled.

"But then, with your well-known fidelity, considering that you're staying here at least a fortnight, you won't have any illusions left about me by the time you go. I give you a week, Cassandra. I shall see my power fading day by day. Now it's at the climax; but to-morrow it'll have begun to fade. What am I to wear, I wonder? Find me a blue dress, Cassandra, over there in the long wardrobe."

She spoke disconnectedly, handling brush and comb, and pulling out the little drawers in her dressing-table and leaving them open. Cassandra, sitting on the bed behind her, saw the reflection of her cousin's face in the looking-glass. The face in the looking-glass was serious and intent, apparently occupied with other things besides the straightness of the parting which, however, was being driven as straight as a Roman road through the dark hair. Cassandra was impressed again by Katharine's maturity; and, as she enveloped herself in the blue dress which filled almost the whole of the long looking-glass with blue light and made it the frame of a picture, holding not only the slightly moving effigy of the beautiful woman, but shapes and colors of objects reflected from the background, Cassandra thought that no sight had ever been quite so romantic. It was all in keeping with the room and the house, and the city round them; for her ears had not yet ceased to notice the hum of distant wheels.

They went downstairs rather late, in spite of Katharine's

extreme speed in getting ready. To Cassandra's ears the buzz of voices inside the drawing-room was like the tuning up of the instruments of the orchestra. It seemed to her that there were numbers of people in the room, and that they were strangers, and that they were beautiful and dressed with the greatest distinction, although they proved to be mostly her relations, and the distinction of their clothing was confined, in the eyes of an impartial observer, to the white waistcoat which Rodney wore. But they all rose simultaneously, which was by itself impressive, and they all exclaimed, and shook hands, and she was introduced to Mr. Peyton, and the door sprang open, and dinner was announced, and they filed off, William Rodney offering her his slightly bent black arm, as she had secretly hoped he would. In short, had the scene been looked at only through her eyes, it must have been described as one of magical brilliancy. The pattern of the soup-plates, the stiff folds of the napkins, which rose by the side of each plate in the shape of arum lilies, the long sticks of bread tied with pink ribbon, the silver dishes and the sea-colored champagne glasses, with the flakes of gold congealed in their stems— all these details, together with a curiously pervasive smell of kid gloves, contributed to her exhilaration, which must be repressed, however, because she was grown up, and the world held no more for her to marvel at.

The world held no more for her to marvel at, it is true; but it held other people, and each other person possessed in Cassandra's mind some fragment of what privately she called "reality." It was a gift that they would impart if you asked them for it, and thus no dinner-party could possibly be dull, and little Mr. Peyton on her right and William Rodney on her left were in equal measure endowed with the quality which seemed to her so unmistakable and so precious that the way people neglected to demand it was a constant source of surprise to her. She scarcely knew, indeed, whether she was talking to Mr. Peyton or to William Rodney. But to one who, by degrees, assumed the shape of an elderly man with a mustache, she described how she had arrived in London that very afternoon, and how she had taken a cab and driven through the streets. Mr. Peyton, an editor of fifty years, bowed his bald head repeatedly, with apparent understanding. At least, he understood that she was very young and pretty, and saw that she was excited, though he could not gather at once from her words or remember from his own experience what there was to be excited about. "Were there any buds on the trees?" he asked. "Which line did she travel by?"

He was cut short in these amiable inquiries by her desire to know whether he was one of those who read, or one of those who look out of the window? Mr. Peyton was by no means sure which he did. He rather thought he did both. He was told that he had made a most dangerous confession. She could deduce his entire history from that one fact. He challenged her to proceed; and she proclaimed him a Liberal Member of Parliament.

William, nominally engaged in a desultory conversation with Aunt Eleanor, heard every word, and taking advantage of the fact that elderly ladies have little continuity of conversation, at least with those whom they esteem for their youth and their sex, he asserted his presence by a very nervous laugh.

Cassandra turned to him directly. She was enchanted to find that, instantly and with such ease, another of these fascinating beings was offering untold wealth for her extraction.

"There's no doubt what *you* do in a railway carriage, William," she said, making use in her pleasure of his first name. "You never *once* look out of the window; you read *all* the time."

"And what facts do you deduce from that?" Mr. Peyton asked.

"Oh, that he's a poet, of course," said Cassandra. "But I must confess that I knew that before, so it isn't fair. I've got your manuscript with me," she went on, disregarding Mr. Peyton in a shameless way. "I've got all sorts of things I want to ask you about it."

William inclined his head and tried to conceal the pleasure that her remark gave him. But the pleasure was not unalloyed. However susceptible to flattery William might be, he would never tolerate it from people who showed a gross or emotional taste in literature, and if Cassandra erred even slightly from what he considered essential in this respect he would express his discomfort by flinging out his hands and wrinkling his forehead; he would find no pleasure in her flattery after that.

"First of all," she proceeded, "I want to know why you chose to write a play?"

"Ah! You mean it's not dramatic?"

"I mean that I don't see what it would gain by being acted. But then does Shakespeare gain? Henry and I are always arguing about Shakespeare. I'm certain he's wrong, but I can't prove it because I've only seen Shakespeare acted once in Lincoln. But I'm quite positive," she insisted, "that Shakespeare wrote for the stage."

"You're perfectly right," Rodney exclaimed. "I was hoping you were on that side. Henry's wrong—entirely wrong. Of course, I've failed, as all the moderns fail. Dear, dear, I wish I'd consulted you before."

From this point they proceeded to go over, as far as memory served them, the different aspects of Rodney's drama. She said nothing that jarred upon him, and untrained daring had the power to stimulate experience to such an extent that Rodney was frequently seen to hold his fork suspended before him, while he debated the first principles of the art. Mrs. Hilbery thought to herself that she had never seen him to such advantage; yes, he was somehow different; he reminded her of some one who was dead, some one who was distinguished—she had forgotten his name.

Cassandra's voice rose high in its excitement.

"You've not read 'The Idiot'!" she exclaimed.

"I've read 'War and Peace'," William replied, a little testily.

" '*War and Peace*'!" she echoed, in a tone of derision.

"I confess I don't understand the Russians."

"Shake hands! Shake hands!" boomed Uncle Aubrey from across the table. "Neither do I. And I hazard the opinion that they don't themselves."

The old gentleman had ruled a large part of the Indian Empire, but he was in the habit of saying that he had rather have written the works of Dickens. The table now took possession of a subject much to its liking. Aunt Eleanor showed premonitory signs of pronouncing an opinion. Although she had blunted her taste upon some form of philanthropy for twenty-five years, she had a fine natural instinct for an upstart or a pretender, and knew to a hairbreadth what literature should be and what it should not be. She was born to the knowledge, and scarcely thought it a matter to be proud of.

"Insanity is not a fit subject for fiction," she announced positively.

"There's the well-known case of Hamlet," Mr. Hilbery interposed, in his leisurely, half-humorous tones.

"Ah, but poetry's different, Trevor," said Aunt Eleanor, as if she had special authority from Shakespeare to say so. "Different altogether. And I've never thought, for my part, that Hamlet was as mad as they make out. What is your opinion, Mr. Peyton?" For, as there was a minister of literature present in the person of the editor of an esteemed review, she deferred to him.

Mr. Peyton leant a little back in his chair, and, putting his head rather on one side, observed that that was a question that he had never been able to answer entirely to his satisfaction. There was much to be said on both sides, but as he considered upon which side he should say it, Mrs. Hilbery broke in upon his judicious meditations.

"Lovely, lovely Ophelia!" she exclaimed. "What a wonderful power it is—poetry! I wake up in the morning all bedraggled; there's a yellow fog outside; little Emily turns on the electric light when she brings me my tea, and says, 'Oh, ma'am, the water's frozen in the cistern, and cook's cut her finger to the bone.' And then I open a little green book, and the birds are singing, the stars shining, the flowers twinkling——" She looked about her as if these presences had suddenly manifested themselves round her dining-room table.

"Has the cook cut her finger badly?" Aunt Eleanor demanded, addressing herself naturally to Katharine.

"Oh, the cook's finger is only my way of putting it," said Mrs. Hilbery. "But if she had cut her arm off, Katharine would have sewn it on again," she remarked, with an affectionate glance at her daughter, who looked, she thought, a little sad. "But what horrid, horrid thoughts," she wound up, laying down her napkin and pushing her chair back. "Come, let us find something more cheerful to talk about upstairs."

Upstairs in the drawing-room Cassandra found fresh sources of pleasure, first in the distinguished and expectant look of the room, and then in the chance of exercising her divining-rod upon a new assortment of human beings. But the low tones of the women, their meditative silences, the beauty which, to her at least, shone even from black satin and the knobs of amber which encircled elderly necks, changed her wish to chatter to a more subdued desire merely to watch and to whisper. She entered with delight into an atmosphere in which private matters were being interchanged freely, almost in monosyllables, by the older women who now accepted her as one of themselves. Her expression became very gentle and sympathetic, as if she, too, were full of solicitude for the world which was somehow being cared for, managed and deprecated by Aunt Maggie and Aunt Eleanor. After a time she perceived that Katharine was outside the community in some way, and, suddenly, she threw aside her wisdom and gentleness and concern and began to laugh.

"What are you laughing at?" Katharine asked.

A joke so foolish and unfilial wasn't worth explaining.

"It was nothing—ridiculous—in the worst of taste, but still, if you half shut your eyes and looked——" Katharine half shut her eyes and looked, but she looked in the wrong direction, and Cassandra laughed more than ever, and was still laughing and doing her best to explain in a whisper that Aunt Eleanor, through half-shut eyes, was like the parrot in the cage at Stogdon House, when the gentlemen came in and Rodney walked straight up to them and wanted to know what they were laughing at.

"I utterly refuse to tell you!" Cassandra replied, standing up straight, clasping her hands in front of her, and facing him. Her mockery was delicious to him. He had not even for a second the fear that she had been laughing at him. She was laughing because life was so adorable, so enchanting.

"Ah, but you're cruel to make me feel the barbarity of my sex," he replied, drawing his feet together and pressing his finger-tips upon an imaginary opera-hat or malacca cane. "We've been discussing all sorts of dull things, and now I shall never know what I want to know more than anything in the world."

"You don't deceive us for a minute!" she cried. "Not for a second. We both know that you've been enjoying yourself immensely. Hasn't he, Katharine?"

"No," she replied, "I think he's speaking the truth. He doesn't care much for politics."

Her words, though spoken simply, produced a curious change in the light, sparkling atmosphere. William at once lost his look of animation and said seriously:

"I detest politics."

"I don't think any man has the right to say that," said Cassandra, almost severely.

"I agree. I mean that I detest politicians," he corrected himself quickly.

"You see, I believe Cassandra is what they call a Feminist," Katharine went on. "Or rather, she was a Feminist six months ago, but it's no good supposing that she is now what she was then. That is one of her greatest charms in my eyes. One never can tell." She smiled at her as an elder sister might smile.

"Katharine, you make one feel so horribly small!" Cassandra exclaimed.

"No, no, that's not what she means," Rodney interposed. "I quite agree that women have an immense advantage over us there. One misses a lot by attempting to know things thoroughly."

"He knows Greek thoroughly," said Katharine. "But then he also knows a good deal about painting, and a certain amount about music. He's very cultivated—perhaps the most cultivated person I know."

"And poetry," Cassandra added.

"Yes, I was forgetting his play," Katharine remarked, and turning her head as though she saw something that needed her attention in a far corner of the room, she left them.

For a moment they stood silent, after what seemed a deliberate introduction to each other, and Cassandra watched her crossing the room.

"Henry," she said next moment, "would say that a stage ought to be no bigger than this drawing-room. He wants there to be singing and dancing as well as acting—only all the opposite of Wagner—you understand?"

They sat down, and Katharine, turning when she reached the window, saw William with his hand raised in gesticulation and his mouth open, as if ready to speak the moment Cassandra ceased.

Katharine's duty, whether it was to pull a curtain or move a chair, was either forgotten or discharged, but she continued to stand by the window without doing anything. The elderly people were all grouped together round the fire. They seemed an independent, middle-aged community busy with its own concerns. They were telling stories very well and

listening to them very graciously. But for her there was
no obvious employment.

"If anybody says anything, I shall say that I'm looking
at the river," she thought, for in her slavery to her family
traditions, she was ready to pay for her transgression with
some plausible falsehood. She pushed aside the blind and
looked at the river. But it was a dark night and the water
was barely visible. Cabs were passing, and couples were
loitering slowly along the road, keeping as close to the
railings as possible, though the trees had as yet no leaves
to cast shadow upon their embraces. Katharine, thus withdrawn, felt her loneliness. The evening had been one of
pain, offering her, minute after minute, plainer proof that
things would fall out as she had foreseen. She had faced
tones, gestures, glances; she knew, with her back to them,
that William, even now, was plunging deeper and deeper into the delight of unexpected understanding with Cassandra.
He had almost told her that he was finding it infinitely
better than he could have believed. She looked out of the
window, sternly determined to forget private misfortunes,
to forget herself, to forget individual lives. With her eyes
upon the dark sky, voices reached her from the room in
which she was standing. She heard them as if they came
from people in another world, a world antecedent to her
world, a world that was the prelude, the antechamber to
reality; it was as if, lately dead, she heard the living talking.
The dream nature of our life had never been more apparent
to her, never had life been more certainly an affair of four
walls, whose objects existed only within the range of lights
and fires, beyond which lay nothing, or nothing more than
darkness. She seemed physically to have stepped beyond
the region where the light of illusion still makes it desirable
to possess, to love, to struggle. And yet her melancholy
brought her no serenity. She still heard the voices within
the room. She was still tormented by desires. She wished
to be beyond their range. She wished inconsistently enough
that she could find herself driving rapidly through the

streets; she was even anxious to be with some one who, after a moment's groping, took a definite shape and solidified into the person of Mary Datchet. She drew the curtains so that the draperies met in deep folds in the middle of the window.

"Ah, there she is," said Mr. Hilbery, who was standing swaying affably from side to side, with his back to the fire. "Come here, Katharine. I couldn't see where you'd got to —our children," he observed parenthetically, "have their uses—I want you to go to my study, Katharine; go to the third shelf on the right-hand side of the door; take down 'Trelawny's Recollections of Shelley'; bring it to me. Then, Peyton, you will have to admit to the assembled company that you have been mistaken."

" 'Trelawny's Recollections of Shelley.' The third shelf on the right of the door," Katharine repeated. After all, one does not check children in their play, or rouse sleepers from their dreams. She passed William and Cassandra on her way to the door.

"Stop, Katharine," said William, speaking almost as if he were conscious of her against his will. "Let me go." He rose, after a second's hesitation, and she understood that it cost him an effort. She knelt one knee upon the sofa where Cassandra sat, looking down at her cousin's face, which still moved with the speed of what she had been saying.

"Are you—happy?" she asked.

"Oh, my dear!" Cassandra exclaimed, as if no further words were needed. "Of course, we disagree about every subject under the sun," she exclaimed, "but I think he's the cleverest man I've ever met—and you're the most beautiful woman," she added, looking at Katharine, and as she looked her face lost its animation and became almost melancholy in sympathy with Katharine's melancholy, which seemed to Cassandra the last refinement of her distinction.

"Ah, but it's only ten o'clock," said Katharine darkly.

"As late as that! Well——?" She did not understand.

"At twelve my horses turn into rats and off I go. The illusion fades. But I accept my fate. I make hay while the sun shines." Cassandra looked at her with a puzzled expression.

"Here's Katharine talking about rats, and hay, and all sorts of odd things," she said, as William returned to them. He had been quick. "Can you make her out?"

Katharine perceived from his little frown and hesitation that he did not find that particular problem to his taste at present. She stood upright at once and said in a different tone:

"I really am off, though. I wish you'd explain if they say anything, William. I shan't be late, but I've got to see some one."

"At this time of night?" Cassandra exclaimed.

"Whom have you got to see?" William demanded.

"A friend," she remarked, half turning her head towards him. She knew that he wished her to stay, not, indeed, with them, but in their neighborhood, in case of need.

"Katharine has a great many friends," said William rather lamely, sitting down once more, as Katharine left the room.

She was soon driving quickly, as she had wished to drive, through the lamp-lit streets. She liked both light and speed, and the sense of being out of doors alone, and the knowledge that she would reach Mary in her high, lonely room at the end of the drive. She climbed the stone steps quickly, remarking the queer look of her blue silk skirt and blue shoes upon the stone, dusty with the boots of the day, under the light of an occasional jet of flickering gas.

The door was opened in a second by Mary herself, whose face showed not only surprise at the sight of her visitor, but some degree of embarrassment. She greeted her cordially, and, as there was no time for explanations, Katharine walked straight into the sitting-room, and found herself in the presence of a young man who was lying back in a chair and holding a sheet of paper in his hand, at which he was

looking as if he expected to go on immediately with what he
was in the middle of saying to Mary Datchet. The apparition of an unknown lady in full evening dress seemed to disturb him. He took his pipe from his mouth, rose stiffly,
and sat down again with a jerk.

"Have you been dining out?" Mary asked.

"Are you working?" Katharine inquired simultaneously.

The young man shook his head, as if he disowned his
share in the question with some irritation.

"Well, not exactly," Mary replied. "Mr. Basnett had
brought some papers to show me. We were going through
them, but we'd almost done. . . . Tell us about your party."

Mary had a ruffled appearance, as if she had been running
her fingers through her hair in the course of her conversation; she was dressed more or less like a Russian peasant
girl. She sat down again in a chair which looked as if it
had been her seat for some hours; the saucer which stood
upon the arm contained the ashes of many cigarettes. Mr.
Basnett, a very young man with a fresh complexion and a
high forehead from which the hair was combed straight
back, was one of that group of "very able young men" suspected by Mr. Clacton, justly as it turned out, of an influence
upon Mary Datchet. He had come down from one of the
Universities not long ago, and was now charged with the
reformation of society. In connection with the rest of the
group of very able young men he had drawn up a scheme
for the education of labor, for the amalgamation of the
middle class and the working class, and for a joint assault
of the two bodies, combined in the Society for the Education
of Democracy, upon Capital. The scheme had already
reached the stage in which it was permissible to hire an
office and engage a secretary, and he had been deputed to
expound the scheme to Mary, and make her an offer of the
Secretaryship, to which, as a matter of principle, a small
salary was attached. Since seven o'clock that evening he
had been reading out loud the document in which the faith
of the new reformers was expounded, but the reading was

so frequently interrupted by discussion, and it was so often necessary to inform Mary "in strictest confidence" of the private characters and evil designs of certain individuals and societies that they were still only half-way through the manuscript. Neither of them realized that the talk had already lasted three hours. In their absorption they had forgotten even to feed the fire, and yet both Mr. Basnett in his exposition, and Mary in her interrogation, carefully preserved a kind of formality calculated to check the desire of the human mind for irrelevant discussion. Her questions frequently began, "Am I to understand—" and his deplies invariably represented the views of some one called "we."

By this time Mary was almost persuaded that she, too, was included in the "we," and agreed with Mr. Basnett in believing that "our" views, "our" society, "our" policy, stood for something quite definitely segregated from the main body of society in a circle of superior illumination.

The appearance of Katharine in this atmosphere was extremely incongruous, and had the effect of making Mary remember all sorts of things that she had been glad to forget.

"You've been dining out?" she asked again, looking, with a little smile, at the blue silk and the pearl-sewn shoes.

"No, at home. Are you starting something new?" Katharine hazarded, rather hesitatingly, looking at the papers.

"We are," Mr. Basnett replied. He said no more.

"I'm thinking of leaving our friends in Russell Square," Mary explained.

"I see. And then you will do something else."

"Well, I'm afraid I like working," said Mary.

"Afraid," said Mr. Basnett, conveying the impression that, in his opinion, no sensible person could be afraid of liking to work.

"Yes," said Katharine, as if he had stated this opinion aloud. "I should like to start something—something off one's own bat—that's what I should like."

"Yes, that's the fun," said Mr. Basnett, looking at her for the first time rather keenly, and refilling his pipe.

"But you can't limit work—that's what I mean," said Mary. "I mean there are other sorts of work. No one works harder than a woman with little children."

"Quite so," said Mr. Basnett. "It's precisely the women with babies we want to get hold of." He glanced at his document, rolled it into a cylinder between his fingers, and gazed into the fire. Katharine felt that in this company anything that one said would be judged upon its merits; one had only to say what one thought, rather barely and tersely, with a curious assumption that the number of things that could properly be thought about was strictly limited. And Mr. Basnett was only stiff upon the surface; there was an intelligence in his face which attracted her intelligence.

"When will the public know?" she asked.

"What d'you mean—about us?" Mr. Basnett asked, with a little smile.

"That depends upon many things," said Mary. The conspirators looked pleased, as if Katharine's question, with the belief in their existence which it implied, had a warming effect upon them.

"In starting a society such as we wish to start (we can't say any more at present)," Mr. Basnett began, with a little jerk of his head, "there are two things to remember—the Press and the public. Other societies, which shall be nameless, have gone under because they've appealed only to cranks. If you don't want a mutual admiration society, which dies as soon as you've all discovered each other's faults, you must nobble the Press. You must appeal to the public."

"That's the difficulty," said Mary thoughtfully.

"That's where she comes in," said Mr. Basnett, jerking his head in Mary's direction. "She's the only one of us who's a capitalist. She can make a whole-time job of it. I'm tied to an office; I can only give my spare time. Are you, by any chance, on the look-out for a job?" he asked

Katharine, with a queer mixture of distrust and deference.

"Marriage is her job at present," Mary replied for her.

"Oh, I see," said Mr. Basnett. He made allowances for that; he and his friends had faced the question of sex, along with all others, and assigned it an honorable place in their scheme of life. Katharine felt this beneath the roughness of his manner; and a world entrusted to the guardianship of Mary Datchet and Mr. Basnett seemed to her a good world, although not a romantic or beautiful place or, to put it figuratively, a place where any line of blue mist softly linked tree to tree upon the horizon. For a moment she thought she saw in his face, bent now over the fire, the features of that original man whom we still recall every now and then, although we know only the clerk, barrister, Governmental official, or workingman variety of him. Not that Mr. Basnett, giving his days to commerce and his spare time to social reform, would long carry about him any trace of his possibilities of completeness; but, for the moment, in his youth and ardor, still speculative, still uncramped, one might imagine him the citizen of a nobler state than ours. Katharine turned over her small stock of information, and wondered what their society might be going to attempt. Then she remembered that she was hindering their business, and rose, still thinking of this society, and thus thinking, she said to Mr. Basnett:

"Well, you'll ask me to join when the time comes, I hope."

He nodded, and took his pipe from his mouth, but, being unable to think of anything to say, he put it back again, although he would have been glad if she had stayed.

Against her wish, Mary insisted upon taking her downstairs, and then, as there was no cab to be seen, they stood in the street together, looking about them.

"Go back," Katharine urged her, thinking of Mr. Basnett with his papers in his hand.

"You can't wander about the streets alone in those clothes," said Mary, but the desire to find a cab was not her true reason for standing beside Katharine for a minute or two. Unfortunately for her composure, Mr. Basnett and his papers seemed to her an incidental diversion of life's serious purpose compared with some tremendous fact which manifested itself as she stood alone with Katharine. It may have been their common womanhood.

"Have you seen Ralph?" she asked suddenly, without preface.

"Yes," said Katharine directly, but she did not remember when or where she had seen him. It took her a moment or two to remember why Mary should ask her if she had seen Ralph.

"I believe I'm jealous," said Mary.

"Nonsense, Mary," said Katharine, rather distractedly, taking her arm and beginning to walk up the street in the direction of the main road. "Let me see; we went to Kew, and we agreed to be friends. Yes, that's what happened." Mary was silent, in the hope that Katharine would tell her more. But Katharine said nothing.

"It's not a question of friendship," Mary exclaimed, her anger rising, to her own surprise. "You know it's not. How can it be? I've no right to interfere——" She stopped. "Only I'd rather Ralph wasn't hurt," she concluded.

"I think he seems able to take care of himself," Katharine observed. Without either of them wishing it, a feeling of hostility had risen between them.

"Do you really think it's worth it?" said Mary, after a pause.

"How can one tell?" Katharine asked.

"Have you ever cared for any one?" Mary demanded rashly and foolishly.

"I can't wander about London discussing my feelings— Here's a cab—no, there's some one in it."

"We don't want to quarrel," said Mary.

"Ought I to have told him that I wouldn't be his friend?" Katharine asked. "Shall I tell him that? If so, what reason shall I give him?"

"Of course you can't tell him that," said Mary, controlling herself.

"I believe I shall, though," said Katharine suddenly.

"I lost my temper, Katharine; I shouldn't have said what I did."

"The whole thing's foolish," said Katharine, peremptorily. "That's what I say. It's not worth it." She spoke with unnecessary vehemence, but it was not directed against Mary Datchet. Their animosity had completely disappeared, and upon both of them a cloud of difficulty and darkness rested, obscuring the future, in which they had both to find a way.

"No, no, it's not worth it," Katharine repeated. "Suppose, as you say, it's out of the question—this friendship; he falls in love with me. I don't want that. Still," she added, "I believe you exaggerate; love's not everything; marriage itself is only one of the things——" They had reached the main thoroughfare, and stood looking at the omnibuses and passers-by, who seemed, for the moment, to illustrate what Katharine had said of the diversity of human interests. For both of them it had become one of those moments of extreme detachment, when it seems unnecessary ever again to shoulder the burden of happiness and self-assertive existence. Their neighbors were welcome to their possessions.

"I don't lay down any rules," said Mary, recovering herself first, as they turned after a long pause of this description. "All I say is that you should know what you're about —for certain; but," she added, "I expect you do."

At the same time she was profoundly perplexed, not only by what she knew of the arrangements for Katharine's marriage, but by the impression which she had of her, there on her arm, dark and inscrutable.

They walked back again and reached the steps which led up to Mary's flat. Here they stopped and paused for a moment, saying nothing.

"You must go in," said Katharine, rousing herself. "He's

waiting all this time to go on with his reading." She glanced up at the lighted window near the top of the house, and they both looked at it and waited for a moment. A flight of semicircular steps ran up to the hall, and Mary slowly mounted the first two or three, and paused, looking down upon Katharine.

"I think you underrate the value of that emotion," she said slowly, and a little awkwardly. She climbed another step and looked down once more upon the figure that was only partly lit up, standing in the street with a colorless face turned upwards. As Mary hesitated, a cab came by and Katharine turned and stopped it, saying as she opened the door:

"Remember, I want to belong to your society—remember," she added, having to raise her voice a little, and shutting the door upon the rest of her words.

Mary mounted the stairs step by step, as if she had to lift her body up an extremely steep ascent. She had had to wrench herself forcibly away from Katharine, and every step vanquished her desire. She held on grimly, encouraging herself as though she were actually making some great physical effort in climbing a height. She was conscious that Mr. Basnett, sitting at the top of the stairs with his documents, offered her solid footing if she were capable of reaching it. The knowledge gave her a faint sense of exaltation.

Mr. Basnett raised his eyes as she opened the door.

"I'll go on where I left off," he said. "Stop me if you want anything explained."

He had been re-reading the document, and making pencil notes in the margin while he waited, and he went on again as if there had been no interruption. Mary sat down among the flat cushions, lit another cigarette, and listened with a frown upon her face.

Katharine leant back in the corner of the cab that carried her to Chelsea, conscious of fatigue, and conscious, too, of the sober and satisfactory nature of such industry as she had just witnessed. The thought of it composed and calmed her. When she reached home she let herself in as quietly as she could, in the hope that the household was already gone to bed. But her excursion had occupied less time than she thought, and she heard sounds of unmistakable liveliness upstairs. A door opened, and she drew herself into a ground-floor room in case the sound meant that Mr. Peyton were taking his leave. From where she stood she could see the stairs, though she was herself invisible. Some one was coming down the stairs, and now she saw that it was William Rodney. He looked a little strange, as if he were walking in his sleep; his lips moved as if he were acting some part to himself. He came down very slowly, step by step, with one hand upon the banisters to guide himself. She thought he looked as if he were in some mood of high exaltation, which it made her uncomfortable to witness any longer unseen. She stepped into the hall. He gave a great start upon seeing her and stopped.

"Katharine!" he exclaimed. "You've been out?" he asked.

"Yes. . . . Are they still up?"

He did not answer, and walked into the ground-floor room through the door which stood open.

"It's been more wonderful than I can tell you," he said, "I'm incredibly happy——"

He was scarcely addressing her, and she said nothing. For a moment they stood at opposite sides of a table saying nothing. Then he asked her quickly, "But tell me, how did it seem to you? What did you think, Katharine? Is there a chance that she likes me? Tell me, Katharine!"

Before she could answer a door opened on the landing above and disturbed them. It disturbed William excessively. He started back, walked rapidly into the hall, and said in a loud and ostentatiously ordinary tone:

"Good night, Katharine. Go to bed now. I shall see you soon. I hope I shall be able to come to-morrow."

Next moment he was gone. She went upstairs and found

Cassandra on the landing. She held two or three books in her hand, and she was stooping to look at others in a little bookcase. She said that she could never tell which book she wanted to read in bed, poetry, biography, or metaphysics.

"What do you read in bed, Katharine?" she asked, as they walked upstairs side by side.

"Sometimes one thing—sometimes another," said Katharine vaguely. Cassandra looked at her.

"D'you know, you're extraordinarily queer," she said. "Every one seems to me a little queer. Perhaps it's the effect of London"

"Is William queer, too?" Katharine asked.

"Well, I think he is a little," Cassandra replied. "Queer, but very fascinating. I shall read Milton to-night. It's been one of the happiest nights of my life, Katharine," she added, looking with shy devotion at her cousin's beautiful face.

CHAPTER XXVII

LONDON, in the first days of spring, has buds that open and flowers that suddenly shake their petals—white, purple, or crimson—in competition with the display in the garden beds, although these city flowers are merely so many doors flung wide in Bond Street and the neighborhood, inviting you to look at a picture, or hear a symphony, or merely crowd and crush yourself among all sorts of vocal, excitable, brightly colored human beings. But, all the same, it is no mean rival to the quieter process of vegetable florescence. Whether or not there is a generous motive at the root, a desire to share and impart, or whether the animation is purely that of insensate fervor and friction, the effect, while it lasts, certainly encourages those who are young, and those who are ignorant, to think the world one great bazaar, with banners fluttering and divans heaped with spoils from every quarter of the globe for their delight.

As Cassandra Otway went about London provided with shillings that opened turnstiles, or more often with large white cards that disregarded turnstiles, the city seemed to her the most lavish and hospitable of hosts. After visiting the National Gallery, or Hertford House, or hearing Brahms or Beethoven at the Bechstein Hall, she would come back to find a new person awaiting her, in whose soul were imbedded some grains of the invaluable substance which she still called reality, and still believed that she could find. The Hilberys, as the saying is, "knew every one," and that arrogant claim was certainly upheld by the number of houses which, within a certain area, lit their lamps at night, opened their doors after 3 p. m., and admitted the Hilberys to their dining-rooms, say, once a month. An indefinable freedom

and authority of manner, shared by most of the people who
lived in these houses, seemed to indicate that whether it was
a question of art, music, or government, they were well
within the gates, and could smile indulgently at the vast
mass of humanity which is forced to wait and struggle, and
pay for entrance with common coin at the door. The gates
opened instantly to admit Cassandra. She was naturally
critical of what went on inside, and inclined to quote what
Henry would have said; but she often succeeded in contra-
dicting Henry, in his absence, and invariably paid her part-
ner at dinner, or the kind old lady who remembered her
grandmother, the compliment of believing that there was
meaning in what they said. For the sake of the light in her
eager eyes, much crudity of expression and some untidiness
of person were forgiven her. It was generally felt that,
given a year or two of experience, introduced to good dressmakers, and preserved from bad influences, she would be an
acquisition. Those elderly ladies, who sit on the edge of
ballrooms sampling the stuff of humanity between finger and
thumb and breathing so evenly that the necklaces, which
rise and fall upon their breasts, seem to represent some ele-
mental force, such as the waves upon the ocean of humanity,
concluded, a little smilingly, that she would do. They meant
that she would in all probability marry some young man
whose mother they respected.

William Rodney was fertile in suggestions. He knew of
little galleries, and select concerts, and private performances,
and somehow made time to meet Katharine and Cassandra,
and to give them tea or dinner or supper in his rooms afterwards. Each one of her fourteen days thus promised to
bear some bright illumination in its sober text. But Sunday
approached. The day is usually dedicated to Nature. The
weather was almost kindly enough for an expedition. But
Cassandra rejected Hampton Court, Greenwich, Richmond,
and Kew in favor of the Zoological Gardens. She had once
trifled with the psychology of animals, and still knew something about inherited characteristics. On Sunday afternoon,

therefore, Katharine, Cassandra, and William Rodney drove off to the Zoo. As their cab approached the entrance, Katharine bent forward and waved her hand to a young man who was walking rapidly in the same direction.

"There's Ralph Denham!" she exclaimed. "I told him to meet us here," she added. She had even come provided with a ticket for him. William's objection that he would not be admitted was, therefore, silenced directly. But the way in which the two men greeted each other was significant of what was going to happen. As soon as they had admired the little birds in the large cage William and Cassandra lagged behind, and Ralph and Katharine pressed on rather in advance. It was an arrangement in which William took his part, and one that suited his convenience, but he was annoyed all the same. He thought that Katharine should have told him that she had invited Denham to meet them.

"One of Katharine's friends," he said rather sharply. It was clear that he was irritated, and Cassandra felt for his annoyance. They were standing by the pen of some Oriental hog, and she was prodding the brute gently with the point of her umbrella, when a thousand little observations seemed, in some way, to collect in one center. The center was one of intense and curious emotion. Were they happy? She dismissed the question as she asked it, scorning herself for applying such simple measures to the rare and splendid emotions of so unique a couple. Nevertheless, her manner became immediately different, as if, for the first time, she felt consciously womanly, and as if William might conceivably wish later on to confide in her. She forgot all about the psychology of animals, and the recurrence of blue eyes and brown, and became instantly engrossed in her feelings as a woman who could administer consolation, and she hoped that Katharine would keep ahead with Mr. Denham, as a child who plays at being grown-up hopes that her mother won't come in just yet, and spoil the game. Or was it not rather that she had ceased to play at being grown-up, and was conscious, suddenly, that she was alarmingly mature and in earnest?

There was still unbroken silence between Katharine and Ralph Denham, but the occupants of the different cages served instead of speech.

"What have you been doing since we met?" Ralph asked at length.

"Doing?" she pondered. "Walking in and out of other people's houses. I wonder if these animals are happy?" she speculated, stopping before a gray bear, who was philosophically playing with a tassel which once, perhaps, formed part of a lady's parasol.

"I'm afraid Rodney didn't like my coming," Ralph remarked.

"No. But he'll soon get over that," she replied. The detachment expressed by her voice puzzled Ralph, and he would have been glad if she had explained her meaning further. But he was not going to press her for explanations. Each moment was to be, as far as he could make it, complete in itself, owing nothing of its happiness to explanations, borrowing neither bright nor dark tints from the future.

"The bears seem happy," he remarked. "But we must buy them a bag of something. There's the place to buy buns. Let's go and get them." They walked to the counter piled with little paper bags, and each simultaneously produced a shilling and pressed it upon the young lady, who did not know whether to oblige the lady or the gentleman, but decided, from conventional reasons, that it was the part of the gentleman to pay.

"I wish to pay," said Ralph peremptorily, refusing the coin which Katharine tendered. "I have a reason for what I do," he added, seeing her smile at his tone of decision.

"I believe you have a reason for everything," she agreed, breaking the bun into parts and tossing them down the bears' throats, "but I can't believe it's a good one this time. What is your reason?"

He refused to tell her. He could not explain to her that he was offering up consciously all his happiness to her, and wished, absurdly enough, to pour every possession he had upon the blazing pyre, even his silver and gold. He wished to keep this distance between them—the distance which separates the devotee from the image in the shrine.

Circumstances conspired to make this easier than it would have been, had they been seated in a drawing-room, for example, with a tea-tray between them. He saw her against a background of pale grottos and sleek hides; camels slanted their heavy-lidded eyes at her, giraffes fastidiously observed her from their melancholy eminence, and the pink-lined trunks of elephants cautiously abstracted buns from her outstretched hands. Then there were the hothouses. He saw her bending over pythons coiled upon the sand, or considering the brown rock breaking the stagnant water of the alligators' pool, or searching some minute section of tropical forest for the golden eye of a lizard or the indrawn movement of the green frogs' flanks. In particular, he saw her outlined against the deep green waters, in which squadrons of silvery fish wheeled incessantly, or ogled her for a moment, pressing their distorted mouths against the glass, quivering their tails straight out behind them. Again, there was the insect house, where she lifted the blinds of the little cages, and marveled at the purple circles marked upon the rich tussore wings of some lately emerged and semi-conscious butterfly, or at caterpillars immobile like the knobbed twigs of a pale-skinned tree, or at slim green snakes stabbing the glass wall again and again with their flickering cleft tongues. The heat of the air, and the bloom of heavy flowers, which swam in water or rose stiffly from great red jars, together with the display of curious patterns and fantastic shapes, produced an atmosphere in which human beings tended to look pale and to fall silent.

Opening the door of a house which rang with the mocking and profoundly unhappy laughter of monkeys, they discovered William and Cassandra. William appeared to be

tempting some small reluctant animal to descend from an
upper perch to partake of half an apple. Cassandra was
reading out, in her high-pitched tones, an account of this
creature's secluded disposition and nocturnal habits. She
saw Katharine and exclaimed:

"Here you are! Do prevent William from torturing this
unfortunate aye-aye."

"We thought we'd lost you," said William. He looked
from one to the other, and seemed to take stock of Denham's
unfashionable appearance. He seemed to wish to find some
outlet for malevolence, but, failing one, he remained silent.
The glance, the slight quiver of the upper lip, were not lost
upon Katharine.

"William isn't kind to animals," she remarked. "He
doesn't know what they like and what they don't like."

"I take it you're well versed in these matters, Denham,"
said Rodney, withdrawing his hand with the apple.

"It's mainly a question of knowing how to stroke them,"
Denham replied.

"Which is the way to the Reptile House?" Cassandra
asked him, not from a genuine desire to visit the reptiles,
but in obedience to her new-born feminine susceptibility,
which urged her to charm and conciliate the other sex.
Denham began to give her directions, and Katharine and
William moved on together.

"I hope you've had a pleasant afternoon," William remarked.

"I like Ralph Denham," she replied.

"Ça se voit," William returned, with superficial urbanity.

Many retorts were obvious, but wishing, on the whole,
for peace, Katharine merely inquired:

"Are you coming back to tea?"

"Cassandra and I thought of having tea at a little shop
in Portland Place," he replied. "I don't know whether you
and Denham would care to join us."

"I'll ask him," she replied, turning her head to look for

him. But he and Cassandra were absorbed in the aye-aye once more.

William and Katharine watched them for a moment, and each looked curiously at the object of the other's preference. But resting his eye upon Cassandra, to whose elegance the dressmakers had now done justice, William said sharply:

"If you come, I hope you won't do your best to make me ridiculous."

"If that's what you're afraid of I certainly shan't come," Katharine replied.

They were professedly looking into the enormous central cage of monkeys, and being thoroughly annoyed by William, she compared him to a wretched misanthropical ape, huddled in a scrap of old shawl at the end of a pole, darting peevish glances of suspicion and distrust at his companions. Her tolerance was deserting her. The events of the past week had worn it thin. She was in one of those moods, perhaps not uncommon with either sex, when the other becomes very clearly distinguished, and of contemptible baseness, so that the necessity of association is degrading, and the tie, which at such moments is always extremely close, drags like a halter round the neck. William's exacting demands and his jealousy had pulled her down into some horrible swamp of her nature where the primeval struggle between man and woman still rages.

"You seem to delight in hurting me," William persisted. "Why did you say that just now about my behavior to animals?" As he spoke he rattled his stick against the bars of the cage, which gave his words an accompaniment peculiarly exasperating to Katharine's nerves.

"Because it's true. You never see what any one feels," she said. "You think of no one but yourself."

"That is not true," said William. By his determined rattling he had now collected the animated attention of some half-dozen apes. Either to propitiate them, or to show his consideration for their feelings, he proceeded to offer them the apple which he held.

The sight, unfortunately, was so comically apt in its illustration of the picture in her mind, the ruse was so transparent, that Katharine was seized with laughter. She laughed uncontrollably. William flushed red. No display of anger could have hurt his feelings more profoundly. It was not only that she was laughing at him; the detachment of the sound was horrible.

"I don't know what you're laughing at," he muttered, and, turning, found that the other couple had rejoined them. As if the matter had been privately agreed upon, the couples separated once more, Katharine and Denham passing out of the house without more than a perfunctory glance round them. Denham obeyed what seemed to be Katharine's wish in thus making haste. Some change had come over her. He connected it with her laughter, and her few words in private with Rodney; he felt that she had become unfriendly to him. She talked, but her remarks were indifferent, and when he spoke her attention seemed to wander. This change of mood was at first extremely disagreeable to him; but soon he found it salutary. The pale drizzling atmosphere of the day affected him, also. The charm, the insidious magic in which he had luxuriated, were suddenly gone; his feeling had become one of friendly respect, and to his great pleasure he found himself thinking spontaneously of the relief of finding himself alone in his room that night. In his surprise at the suddenness of the change, and at the extent of his freedom, he bethought him of a daring plan, by which the ghost of Katharine could be more effectually exorcised than by mere abstinence. He would ask her to come home with him to tea. He would force her through the mill of family life; he would place her in a light unsparing and revealing. His family would find nothing to admire in her, and she, he felt certain, would despise them all, and this, too, would help him. He felt himself becoming more and more merciless towards her. By such courageous measures any one, he thought, could end the absurd passions which were the cause of so much pain and waste. He could foresee a time when his experiences, his discovery, and his triumph were made available for younger brothers who found themselves in the same predicament. He looked at his watch, and remarked that the gardens would soon be closed.

"Anyhow," he added, "I think we've seen enough for one afternoon. Where have the others got to?" He looked over his shoulder, and, seeing no trace of them, remarked at once:

"We'd better be independent of them. The best plan will be for you to come back to tea with me."

"Why shouldn't you come with me?" she asked.

"Because we're next door to Highgate here," he replied promptly.

She assented, having very little notion whether Highgate was next door to Regent's Park or not. She was only glad to put off her return to the family tea-table in Chelsea for an hour or two. They proceeded with dogged determination through the winding roads of Regent's Park, and the Sunday-stricken streets of the neighborhood, in the direction of the Tube station. Ignorant of the way, she resigned herself entirely to him, and found his silence a convenient cover beneath which to continue her anger with Rodney.

When they stepped out of the train into the still grayer gloom of Highgate, she wondered, for the first time, where he was taking her. Had he a family, or did he live alone in rooms? On the whole she was inclined to believe that he was the only son of an aged, and possibly invalid, mother. She sketched lightly, upon the blank vista down which they walked, the little white house and the tremulous old lady rising from behind her tea-table to greet her with faltering words about "my son's friends," and was on the point of asking Ralph to tell her what she might expect, when he jerked open one of the infinite number of identical wooden doors, and led her up a tiled path to a porch in the Alpine style of architecture. As they listened to the shaking of the bell in the basement, she could summon no vision to replace the one so rudely destroyed.

"I must warn you to expect a family party," said Ralph. "They're mostly in on Sundays. We can go to my room afterwards."

"Have you many brothers and sisters?" she asked, without concealing her dismay.

"Six or seven," he replied grimly, as the door opened.

While Ralph took off his coat, she had time to notice the ferns and photographs and draperies, and to hear a hum, or rather a babble, of voices talking each other down, from the sound of them. The rigidity of extreme shyness came over her. She kept as far behind Denham as she could, and walked stiffly after him into a room blazing with unshaded lights, which fell upon a number of people, of different ages, sitting round a large dining-room table untidily strewn with food, and unflinchingly lit up by incandescent gas. Ralph walked straight to the far end of the table.

"Mother, this is Miss Hilbery," he said.

A large elderly lady, bent over an unsatisfactory spirit-lamp, looked up with a little frown, and observed:

"I beg your pardon. I thought you were one of my own girls. Dorothy," she continued on the same breath, to catch the servant before she left the room, "we shall want some more methylated spirits—unless the lamp itself is out of order. If one of you could invent a good spirit-lamp——" she sighed, looking generally down the table, and then began seeking among the china before her for two clean cups for the new-comers.

The unsparing light revealed more ugliness than Katharine had seen in one room for a very long time. It was the ugliness of enormous folds of brown material, looped and festooned, of plush curtains, from which depended balls and fringes, partially concealing bookshelves swollen with black school-texts. Her eye was arrested by crossed scabbards of fretted wood upon the dull green wall, and wherever there was a high flat eminence, some fern waved from a pot of crinkled china, or a bronze horse reared so high that the stump of a tree had to sustain his forequarters.

The waters of family life seemed to rise and close over her head, and she munched in silence.

At length Mrs. Denham looked up from her teacups and remarked:

"You see, Miss Hilbery, my children all come in at different hours and want different things. (The tray should go up if you've done, Johnnie.) My boy Charles is in bed with a cold. What else can you expect?—standing in the wet playing football. We did try drawing-room tea, but it didn't do."

A boy of sixteen, who appeared to be Johnnie, grumbled derisively both at the notion of drawing-room tea and at the necessity of carrying a tray up to his brother. But he took himself off, being enjoined by his mother to mind what he was doing, and shut the door after him.

"It's much nicer like this," said Katharine, applying herself with determination to the dissection of her cake; they had given her too large a slice. She knew that Mrs. Denham suspected her of critical comparisons. She knew that she was making poor progress with her cake. Mrs. Denham had looked at her sufficiently often to make it clear to Katharine that she was asking who this young woman was, and why Ralph had brought her to tea with them. There was an obvious reason, which Mrs. Denham had probably reached by this time. Outwardly, she was behaving with rather rusty and laborious civility. She was making conversation about the amenities of Highgate, its development and situation.

"When I first married," she said, "Highgate was quite separate from London, Miss Hilbery, and this house, though you wouldn't believe it, had a view of apple orchards. That was before the Middletons built their house in front of us."

"It must be a great advantage to live at the top of a hill," said Katharine. Mrs. Denham agreed effusively, as if her opinion of Katharine's sense had risen.

"Yes, indeed, we find it very healthy," she said, and she went on, as people who live in the suburbs so often do, to prove that it was healthier, more convenient, and less spoilt than any suburb round London. She spoke with such emphasis that it was quite obvious that she expressed unpopular views, and that her children disagreed with her.

"The ceiling's fallen down in the pantry again," said Hester, a girl of eighteen, abruptly.

"The whole house will be down one of these days," James muttered.

"Nonsense," said Mrs. Denham. "It's only a little bit of plaster—I don't see how any house could be expected to stand the wear and tear you give it." Here some family joke exploded, which Katharine could not follow. Even Mrs. Denham laughed against her will.

"Miss Hilbery's thinking us all so rude," she added reprovingly. Miss Hilbery smiled and shook her head, and was conscious that a great many eyes rested upon her, for a moment, as if they would find pleasure in discussing her when she was gone. Owing, perhaps, to this critical glance, Katharine decided that Ralph Denham's family was commonplace, unshapely, lacking in charm, and fitly expressed by the hideous nature of their furniture and decorations. She glanced along a mantelpiece ranged with bronze chariots, silver vases, and china ornaments that were either facetious or eccentric.

She did not apply her judgment consciously to Ralph, but when she looked at him, a moment later, she rated him lower than at any other time of their acquaintanceship.

He had made no effort to tide over the discomforts of her introduction, and now, engaged in argument with his brother, apparently forgot her presence. She must have counted upon his support more than she realized, for this indifference, emphasized, as it was, by the insignificant commonplace of his surroundings, awoke her, not only to that ugliness, but to her own folly. She thought of one scene after another in a few seconds, with that shudder which is almost a blush. She had believed him when he spoke of friendship. She had believed in a spiritual light burning steadily and steadfastly behind the erratic disorder and incoherence of life. The light was now gone out, suddenly, as if a sponge had blotted it. The litter of the table and the tedious but exacting conversation of Mrs. Denham remained: they struck, indeed, upon a mind bereft of all defences, and, keenly conscious of the degradation which is the result of strife whether victorious or not, she thought gloomily of her loneliness, of life's futility, of the barren prose of reality, of William Rodney, of her mother, and the unfinished book.

Her answers to Mrs. Denham were perfunctory to the verge of rudeness, and to Ralph, who watched her narrowly, she seemed further away than was compatible with her physical closeness. He glanced at her, and ground out further steps in his argument, determined that no folly should remain when this experience was over. Next moment, a silence, sudden and complete, descended upon them all. The silence of all these people round the untidy table was enormous and hideous; something horrible seemed about to burst from it, but they endured it obstinately. A second later the door opened and there was a stir of relief; cries of "Hullo, Joan! There's nothing left for you to eat," broke up the oppressive concentration of so many eyes upon the table-cloth, and set the waters of family life dashing in brisk little waves again. It was obvious that Joan had some mysterious and beneficent power upon her family. She went up to Katharine as if she had heard of her, and was very glad to see her at last. She explained that she had been visiting an uncle who was ill, and that had kept her. No, she hadn't had any tea, but a slice of bread would do. Some one handed up a hot cake, which had been keeping warm in the fender; she sat down by her mother's side, Mrs. Denham's anxieties seemed to relax, and every one began eating and drinking, as if tea had begun over again. Hester voluntarily explained to Katharine that she was reading to pass some examination, because she wanted more than anything in the whole world to go to Newnham.

"Now, just let me hear you decline *amo*—I love," Johnnie demanded.

"No, Johnnie, no Greek at meal-times," said Joan, over-hearing him instantly. "She's up at all hours of the night over her books, Miss Hilbery, and I'm sure that's not the way to pass examinations," she went on, smiling at Katharine, with the worried humorous smile of the elder sister whose younger brothers and sisters have become almost like children of her own.

"Joan, you don't really think that *amo* is Greek?" Ralph asked.

"Did I say Greek? Well, never mind. No dead languages at tea-time. My dear boy, don't trouble to make me any toast——"

"Or if you do, surely there's the toasting-fork some-where?" said Mrs. Denham, still cherishing the belief that the bread-knife could be spoilt. "Do one of you ring and ask for one," she said, without any conviction that she would be obeyed. "But is Ann coming to be with Uncle Joseph?" she continued. "If so, surely they had better send Amy to us——" and in the mysterious delight of learning further details of these arrangements, and suggesting more sensible plans of her own, which, from the aggrieved way in which she spoke, she did not seem to expect any one to adopt, Mrs. Denham completely forgot the presence of a well-dressed visitor, who had to be informed about the amenities of Highgate. As soon as Joan had taken her seat, an argu-ment had sprung up on either side of Katharine, as to whether the Salvation Army has any right to play hymns at street corners on Sunday mornings, thereby making it impossible for James to have his sleep out, and tampering with the rights of individual liberty.

"You see, James likes to lie in bed and sleep like a hog," said Johnnie, explaining himself to Katharine, whereupon James fired up and, making her his goal, also exclaimed:

"Because Sundays are my one chance in the week of

having my sleep out. Johnnie messes with stinking chemicals in the pantry——"

They appealed to her, and she forgot her cake and began to laugh and talk and argue with sudden animation. The large family seemed to her so warm and various that she forgot to censure them for their taste in pottery. But the personal question between James and Johnnie merged into some argument already, apparently, debated, so that the parts had been distributed among the family, in which Ralph took the lead; and Katharine found herself opposed to him and the champion of Johnnie's cause, who, it appeared, always lost his head and got excited in argument with Ralph.

"Yes, yes, that's what I mean. She's got it right," he exclaimed, after Katharine had restated his case, and made it more precise. The debate was left almost solely to Katharine and Ralph. They looked into each other's eyes fixedly, like wrestlers trying to see what movement is coming next, and while Ralph spoke, Katharine bit her lower lip, and was always ready with her next point as soon as he had done. They were very well matched, and held the opposite views.

But at the most exciting stage of the argument, for no reason that Katharine could see, all chairs were pushed back, and one after another the Denham family got up and went out of the door, as if a bell had summoned them. She was not used to the clockwork regulations of a large family. She hesitated in what she was saying, and rose. Mrs. Denham and Joan had drawn together and stood by the fireplace, slightly raising their skirts above their ankles, and discussing something which had an air of being very serious and very private. They appeared to have forgotten her presence among them. Ralph stood holding the door open for her.

"Won't you come up to my room?" he said. And Katharine, glancing back at Joan, who smiled at her in a preoccupied way, followed Ralph upstairs. She was thinking of their argument, and when, after the long climb, he opened his door, she began at once.

"The question is, then, at what point is it right for the

individual to assert his will against the will of the State."

For some time they continued the argument, and then the intervals between one statement and the next became longer and longer, and they spoke more speculatively and less pugnaciously, and at last fell silent. Katharine went over the argument in her mind, remembering how, now and then, it had been set conspicuously on the right course by some remark offered either by James or by Johnnie.

"Your brothers are very clever," she said. "I suppose you're in the habit of arguing?"

"James and Johnnie will go on like that for hours," Ralph replied. "So will Hester, if you start her upon Elizabethan dramatists."

"And the little girl with the pigtail?"

"Molly? She's only ten. But they're always arguing among themselves."

He was immensely pleased by Katharine's praise of his brothers and sisters. He would have liked to go on telling her about them, but he checked himself.

"I see that it must be difficult to leave them," Katharine continued. His deep pride in his family was more evident to him, at that moment, than ever before, and the idea of living alone in a cottage was ridiculous. All that brotherhood and sisterhood, and a common childhood in a common past mean, all the stability, the unambitious comradeship, and tacit understanding of family life at its best, came to his mind, and he thought of them as a company, of which he was the leader, bound on a difficult, dreary, but glorious voyage. And it was Katharine who had opened his eyes to this, he thought.

A little dry chirp from the corner of the room now roused her attention.

"My tame rook," he explained briefly. "A cat had bitten one of its legs." She looked at the rook, and her eyes went from one object to another.

"You sit here and read?" she said, her eyes resting upon his books. He said that he was in the habit of working there at night.

"The great advantage of Highgate is the view over London. At night the view from my window is splendid." He was extremely anxious that she should appreciate his view, and she rose to see what was to be seen. It was already dark enough for the turbulent haze to be yellow with the light of street lamps, and she tried to determine the quarters of the city beneath her. The sight of her gazing from his window gave him a peculiar satisfaction. When she turned, at length, he was still sitting motionless in his chair.

"It must be late," she said. "I must be going." She settled upon the arm of the chair irresolutely, thinking that she had no wish to go home. William would be there, and he would find some way of making things unpleasant for her, and the memory of their quarrel came back to her. She had noticed Ralph's coldness, too. She looked at him, and from his fixed stare she thought that he must be working out some theory, some argument. He had thought, perhaps, of some fresh point in his position, as to the bounds of personal liberty. She waited, silently, thinking about liberty.

"You've won again," he said at last, without moving.

"I've won?" she repeated, thinking of the argument.

"I wish to God I hadn't asked you here," he burst out.

"What do you mean?"

"When you're here, it's different—I'm happy. You've only to walk to the window—you've only to talk about liberty. When I saw you down there among them all——" He stopped short.

"You thought how ordinary I was."

"I tried to think so. But I thought you more wonderful than ever."

An immense relief, and a reluctance to enjoy that relief, conflicted in her heart.

She slid down into the chair.

"I thought you disliked me," she said.

"God knows I tried," he replied. "I've done my best to see you as you are, without any of this damned romantic nonsense. That was why I asked you here, and it's increased my folly. When you're gone I shall look out of that window and think of you. I shall waste the whole evening thinking of you. I shall waste my whole life, I believe."

He spoke with such vehemence that her relief disappeared; she frowned; and her tone changed to one almost of severity.

"This is what I foretold. We shall gain nothing but unhappiness. Look at me, Ralph." He looked at her "I assure you that I'm far more ordinary than I appear. Beauty means nothing whatever. In fact, the most beautiful women are generally the most stupid. I'm not that, but I'm a matter-of-fact, prosaic, rather ordinary character; I order the dinner, I pay the bills, I do the accounts, I wind up the clock, and I never look at a book."

"You forget——" he began, but she would not let him speak.

"You come and see me among flowers and pictures, and think me mysterious, romantic, and all the rest of it. Being yourself very inexperienced and very emotional, you go home and invent a story about me, and now you can't separate me from the person you've imagined me to be. You call that, I suppose, being in love; as a matter of fact it's being in delusion. All romantic people are the same," she added. "My mother spends her life in making stories about the people she's fond of. But I won't have you do it about me, if I can help it."

"You can't help it," he said.

"I warn you it's the source of all evil."

"And of all good," he added.

"You'll find out that I'm not what you think me."

"Perhaps. But I shall gain more than I lose."

"If such gain's worth having."

They were silent for a space.

"That may be what we have to face," he said. "There may be nothing else. Nothing but what we imagine."

"The reason of our loneliness," she mused, and they were silent for a time.

"When are you to be married?" he asked abruptly, with a change of tone.

"Not till September, I think. It's been put off."

"You won't be lonely then," he said. "According to what people say, marriage is a very queer business. They say it's different from anything else. It may be true. I've known one or two cases where it seems to be true." He hoped that she would go on with the subject. But she made no reply. He had done his best to master himself, and his voice was sufficiently indifferent, but her silence tormented him. She would never speak to him of Rodney of her own accord, and her reserve left a whole continent of her soul in darkness.

"It may be put off even longer than that," she said, as if by an afterthought. "Some one in the office is ill, and William has to take his place. We may put it off for some time in fact."

"That's rather hard on him, isn't it?" Ralph asked.

"He has his work," she replied. "He has lots of things that interests him. . . . I know I've been to that place," she broke off, pointing to a photograph. "But I can't remember where it is—oh, of course—it's Oxford. Now, what about your cottage?"

"I'm not going to take it."

"How you change your mind!" she smiled.

"It's not that," he said impatiently. "It's that I want to be where I can see you."

"Our compact is going to hold in spite of all I've said?" she asked.

"For ever, so far as I'm concerned," he replied.

"You're going to go on dreaming and imagining and

making up stories about me as you walk along the street, and pretending that we're riding in a forest, or landing on an island——"

"No. I shall think of you ordering dinner, paying bills, doing the accounts, showing old ladies the relics——"

"That's better," she said. "You can think of me to-morrow morning looking up dates in the 'Dictionary of National Biography.' "

"And forgetting your purse," Ralph added.

At this she smiled, but in another moment her smile faded, either because of his words or of the way in which he spoke them. She was capable of forgetting things. He saw that. But what more did he see? Was he not looking at something she had never shown to anybody? Was it not something so profound that the notion of his seeing it almost shocked her? Her smile faded, and for a moment she seemed upon the point of speaking, but looking at him in silence, with a look that seemed to ask what she could not put into words, she turned and bade him good night.

CHAPTER XXVIII

L IKE a strain of music, the effect of Katharine's presence slowly died from the room in which Ralph sat alone. The music had ceased in the rapture of its melody. He strained to catch the faintest lingering echoes; for a moment the memory lulled him into peace; but soon it failed, and he paced the room so hungry for the sound to come again that he was conscious of no other desire left in life. She had gone without speaking; abruptly a chasm had been cut in his course, down which the tide of his being plunged in disorder; fell upon rocks; flung itself to destruction. The distress had an effect of physical ruin and disaster. He trembled; he was white; he felt exhausted, as if by a great physical effort. He sank at last into a chair standing opposite her empty one, and marked, mechanically, with his eye upon the clock, how she went farther and farther from him, was home now, and now, doubtless, again with Rodney. But it was long before he could realize these facts; the immense desire for her presence churned his senses into foam, into froth, into a haze of emotion that removed all facts from his grasp, and gave him a strange sense of distance, even from the material shapes of wall and window by which he was surrounded. The prospect of the future, now that the strength of his passion was revealed to him, appalled him.

The marriage would take place in September, she had said; that allowed him, then, six full months in which to undergo these terrible extremes of emotion. Six months of torture, and after that the silence of the grave, the isolation of the insane, the exile of the damned; at best, a life from which the chief good was knowingly and for ever excluded. An impartial judge might have assured him that

384

his chief hope of recovery lay in this mystic temper, which identified a living woman with much that no human beings long possess in the eyes of each other; she would pass, and the desire for her vanish, but his belief in what she stood for, detached from her, would remain. This line of thought offered, perhaps, some respite, and possessed of a brain that had its station considerably above the tumult of the senses, he tried to reduce the vague and wandering incoherency of his emotions to order. The sense of self-preservation was strong in him, and Katharine herself had strangely revived it by convincing him that his family deserved and needed all his strength. She was right, and for their sake, if not for his own, this passion, which could bear no fruit, must be cut off, uprooted, shown to be as visionary and baseless as she had maintained. The best way of achieving this was not to run away from her, but to face her, and having steeped himself in her qualities, to convince his reason that they were, as she assured him, not those that he imagined. She was a practical woman, a domestic wife for an inferior poet, endowed with romantic beauty by some freak of unintelligent Nature. No doubt her beauty itself would not stand examination. He had the means of settling this point at least. He possessed a book of photographs from the Greek statues; the head of a goddess, if the lower part were concealed, had often given him the ecstasy of being in Katharine's presence. He took it down from the shelf and found the picture. To this he added a note from her, bidding him meet her at the Zoo. He had a flower which he had picked at Kew to teach her botany. Such were his relics. He placed them before him, and set himself to visualize her so clearly that no deception or delusion was possible. In a second he could see her, with the sun slanting across her dress, coming towards him down the green walk at Kew. He made her sit upon the seat beside him. He heard her voice, so low and yet so decided in its tone; she spoke reasonably of indifferent matters. He could see her faults, and analyze her virtues. His pulse became quieter, and his brain increased in clarity. This time she could not escape him. The illusion of her presence became more and more complete. They seemed to pass in and out of each other's minds, questioning and answering. The utmost fullness of communion seemed to be theirs. Thus united, he felt himself raised to an eminence, exalted, and filled with a power of achievement such as he had never known in singleness. Once more he told over conscientiously her faults, both of face and character; they were clearly known to him; but they merged themselves in the flawless union that was born of their association. They surveyed life to its uttermost limits. How deep it was when looked at from this height! How sublime! How the commonest things moved him almost to tears! Thus, he forgot the inevitable limitations; he forgot her absence, he thought it of no account whether she married him or another; nothing mattered, save that she should exist, and that he should love her. Some words of these reflections were uttered aloud, and it happened that among them were the words, "I love her." It was the first time that he had used the word "love" to describe his feeling; madness, romance, hallucination— he had called it by these names before; but having, apparently by accident, stumbled upon the word "love," he repeated it again and again with a sense of revelation.

"But I'm in love with you!" he exclaimed, with something like dismay. He leant against the window-sill, looking over the city as she had looked. Everything had become miraculously different and completely distinct. His feelings were justified and needed no further explanation. But he must impart them to some one, because his discovery was so important that it concerned other people too. Shutting the book of Greek photographs, and hiding his relics, he ran downstairs, snatched his coat, and passed out of doors.

The lamps were being lit, but the streets were dark enough and empty enough to let him walk his fastest, and to talk aloud as he walked. He had no doubt where he was going. He was going to find Mary Datchet. The desire to share what he felt, with some one who understood it, was so imperious that he did not question it. He was soon in her street. He ran up the stairs leading to her flat two steps at a time, and it never crossed his mind that she might not be at home. As he rang her bell, he seemed to himself to be announcing the presence of something wonderful that was separate from himself, and gave him power and authority over all other people. Mary came to the door after a moment's pause. He was perfectly silent, and in the dusk his face looked completely white. He followed her into her room.

"Do you know each other?" she said, to his extreme surprise, for he had counted on finding her alone. A young man rose, and said that he knew Ralph by sight.

"We were just going through some papers," said Mary. "Mr. Basnett has to help me, because I don't know much about my work yet. It's the new society," she explained. "I'm the secretary. I'm no longer at Russell Square."

The voice in which she gave this information was so constrained as to sound almost harsh.

"What are your aims?" said Ralph. He looked neither at Mary nor at Mr. Basnett. Mr. Basnett thought he had seldom seen a more disagreeable or formidable man than this friend of Mary's, this sarcastic-looking, white-faced Mr. Denham, who seemed to demand, as if by right, an account of their proposals, and to criticize them before he had heard them. Nevertheless, he explained his projects as clearly as he could, and knew that he wished Mr. Denham to think well of them.

"I see," said Ralph, when he had done. "D'you know, Mary," he suddenly remarked, "I believe I'm in for a cold. Have you any quinine?" The look which he cast at her frightened her; it expressed mutely, perhaps without his own consciousness, something deep, wild, and passionate. She left the room at once. Her heart beat fast at the knowledge of Ralph's presence; but it beat with pain, and with

an extraordinary fear. She stood listening for a moment
to the voices in the next room.

"Of course, I agree with you," she heard Ralph say, in
this strange voice, to Mr. Basnett. "But there's more that
might be done. Have you seen Judson, for instance? You
should make a point of getting him."

Mary returned with the quinine.

"Judson's address?" Mr. Basnett inquired, pulling out
his notebook and preparing to write. For twenty minutes,
perhaps, he wrote down names, addresses, and other suggestions that Ralph dictated to him. Then, when Ralph fell
silent, Mr. Basnett felt that his presence was not desired,
and thanking Ralph for his help, with a sense that he was
very young and ignorant compared with him, he said good-
bye.

"Mary," said Ralph, directly Mr. Basnett had shut the
door and they were alone together. "Mary," he repeated.
But the old difficulty of speaking to Mary without reserve
prevented him from continuing. His desire to proclaim
his love for Katharine was still strong in him, but he had
felt, directly he saw Mary, that he could not share it with
her. The feeling increased as he sat talking to Mr. Basnett.
And yet all the time he was thinking of Katharine, and
marveling at his love. The tone in which he spoke Mary's
name was harsh.

"What is it, Ralph?" she asked, startled by his tone. She
looked at him anxiously, and her little frown showed that
she was trying painfully to understand him, and was puzzled. He could feel her groping for his meaning, and he
was annoyed with her, and thought how he had always
found her slow, painstaking, and clumsy. He had behaved
badly to her, too, which made his irritation the more acute.
Without waiting for him to answer, she rose as if his answer were indifferent to her, and began to put in order
some papers that Mr. Basnett had left on the table. She
hummed a scrap of a tune under her breath, and moved

about the room as if she were occupied in making things tidy, and had no other concern.

"You'll stay and dine?" she said casually, returning to her seat.

"No," Ralph replied. She did not press him further. They sat side by side without speaking, and Mary reached her hand for her work basket, and took out her sewing and threaded a needle.

"That's a clever young man," Ralph observed, referring to Mr. Basnett.

"I'm glad you thought so. It's tremendously interesting work, and considering everything, I think we've done very well. But I'm inclined to agree with you; we ought to try to be more conciliatory. We're absurdly strict. It's difficult to see that there may be sense in what one's opponents say, though they are one's opponents. Horace Basnett is certainly too uncompromising. I mustn't forget to see that he writes that letter to Judson. You're too busy, I suppose, to come on to our committee?" She spoke in the most impersonal manner.

"I may be out of town," Ralph replied, with equal distance of manner.

"Our executive meets every week, of course," she observed. "But some of our members don't come more than once a month. Members of Parliament are the worst; it was a mistake, I think, to ask them."

She went on sewing in silence.

"You've not taken your quinine," she said, looking up and seeing the tabloids upon the mantelpiece.

"I don't want it," said Ralph shortly.

"Well, you know best," she replied tranquilly.

"Mary, I'm a brute!" he exclaimed. "Here I come and waste your time, and do nothing but make myself disagreeable."

"A cold coming on does make one feel wretched," she replied.

"I've not got a cold. That was a lie. There's nothing

the matter with me. I'm mad, I suppose. I ought to have
had the decency to keep away. But I wanted to see you—
I wanted to tell you—I'm in love, Mary." He spoke the
word, but, as he spoke it, it seemed robbed of substance.

"In love, are you?" she said quietly. "I'm glad, Ralph."

"I suppose I'm in love. Anyhow, I'm out of my mind.
I can't think, I can't work, I don't care a hang for anything
in the world. Good Heavens, Mary! I'm in torment! One
moment I'm happy; next I'm miserable. I hate her for half
an hour; then I'd give my whole life to be with her for
ten minutes; all the time I don't know what I feel, or why
I feel it; it's insanity, and yet it's perfectly reasonable. Can
you make any sense of it? Can you see what's happened?
I'm raving, I know; don't listen, Mary; go on with your
work."

He rose and began, as usual, to pace up and down the
room. He knew that what he had just said bore very little
resemblance to what he felt, for Mary's presence acted upon him like a very strong magnet, drawing from him certain expressions which were not those he made use of when
he spoke to himself, nor did they represent his deepest feelings. He felt a little contempt for himself at having spoken
thus; but somehow he had been forced into speech.

"Do sit down," said Mary suddenly. "You make me
so——" She spoke with unusual irritability, and Ralph,
noticing it with surprise, sat down at once.

"You haven't told me her name—you'd rather not, I
suppose?"

"Her name? Katharine Hilbery."

"But she's engaged——"

"To Rodney. They're to be married in September."

"I see," said Mary. But in truth the calm of his manner,
now that he was sitting down once more, wrapt her in the
presence of something which she felt to be so strong, so
mysterious, so incalculable, that she scarcely dared to attempt to intercept it by any word or question that she was
able to frame. She looked at Ralph blankly, with a kind of

awe in her face, her lips slightly parted, and her brows raised. He was apparently quite unconscious of her gaze. Then, as if she could look no longer, she leant back in her chair, and half closed her eyes. The distance between them hurt her terribly; one thing after another came into her mind, tempting her to assail Ralph with questions, to force him to confide in her, and to enjoy once more his intimacy. But she rejected every impulse, for she could not speak without doing violence to some reserve which had grown between them, putting them a little far from each other, so that he seemed to her dignified and remote, like a person she no longer knew well.

"Is there anything that I could do for you?" she asked gently, and even with courtesy, at length.

"You could see her—no, that's not what I want; you mustn't bother about me, Mary." He, too, spoke very gently.

"I'm afraid no third person can do anything to help," she added.

"No," he shook his head. "Katharine was saying to-day how lonely we are." She saw the effort with which he spoke Katharine's name, and believed that he forced himself to make amends now for his concealment in the past. At any rate, she was conscious of no anger against him; but rather of a deep pity for one condemned to suffer as she had suffered. But in the case of Katharine it was different; she was indignant with Katharine.

"There's always work," she said, a little aggressively.

Ralph moved directly.

"Do you want to be working now?" he asked.

"No, no. It's Sunday," she replied. "I was thinking of Katharine. She doesn't understand about work. She's never had to. She doesn't know what work is. I've only found out myself quite lately. But it's the thing that saves one—I'm sure of that."

"There are other things, aren't there?" he hesitated.

"Nothing that one can count upon," she returned. "After

all, other people—" she stopped, but forced herself to go on. "Where should I be now if I hadn't got to go to my office every day? Thousands of people would tell you the same thing—thousands of women. I tell you, work is the only thing that saved me, Ralph." He set his mouth, as if her words rained blows on him; he looked as if he had made up his mind to bear anything she might say, in silence. He had deserved it, and there would be relief in having to bear it. But she broke off, and rose as if to fetch something from the next room. Before she reached the door she turned back, and stood facing him, self-possessed, and yet defiant and formidable in her composure.

"It's all turned out splendidly for me," she said. "It will for you, too. I'm sure of that. Because, after all, Katharine is worth it."

"Mary—!" he exclaimed. But her head was turned away, and he could not say what he wished to say. "Mary, you're splendid," he concluded. She faced him as he spoke, and gave him her hand. She had suffered and relinquished, she had seen her future turned from one of infinite promise to one of barrenness, and yet, somehow, over what she scarcely knew, and with what results she could hardly foretell, she had conquered. With Ralph's eyes upon her, smiling straight back at him serenely and proudly, she knew, for the first time, that she had conquered. She let him kiss her hand.

The streets were empty enough on Sunday night, and if the Sabbath, and the domestic amusements proper to the Sabbath, had not kept people indoors, a high strong wind might very probably have done so. Ralph Denham was aware of a tumult in the street much in accordance with his own sensations. The gusts, sweeping along the Strand, seemed at the same time to blow a clear space across the sky in which stars appeared, and for a short time the quick-speeding silver moon riding through clouds, as if they were waves of water surging round her and over her. They swamped her, but she emerged; they broke over her and covered her again; she issued forth indomitable. In the country fields all the wreckage of winter was being dispersed; the dead leaves, the withered bracken, the dry and discolored grass, but no bud would be broken, nor would the new stalks that showed above the earth take any harm, and perhaps to-morrow a line of blue or yellow would show through a slit in their green. But the whirl of the atmosphere alone was in Denham's mood, and what of star or blossom appeared was only as a light gleaming for a second upon heaped waves fast following each other. He had not been able to speak to Mary, though for a moment he had come near enough to be tantalized by a wonderful possibility of understanding. But the desire to communicate something of the very greatest importance possessed him completely; he still wished to bestow this gift upon some other human being; he sought their company. More by instinct than by conscious choice, he took the direction which led to Rodney's rooms. He knocked loudly upon his door; but no one answered. He rang the bell. It took him some time to accept the fact that Rodney was out. When he could no longer pretend that the sound of the wind in the old building was the sound of some one rising from his chair, he ran downstairs again, as if his goal had been altered and only just revealed to him. He walked in the direction of Chelsea.

But physical fatigue, for he had not dined and had tramped both far and fast, made him sit for a moment upon a seat on the Embankment. One of the regular occupants of those seats, an elderly man who had drunk himself, probably, out of work and lodging, drifted up, begged a match, and sat down beside him. It was a windy night, he said; times were hard; some long story of bad luck and injustice followed, told so often that the man seemed to be talking to himself, or, perhaps, the neglect of his audience had long made any attempt to catch their attention seem scarcely worth while. When he began to speak Ralph had a wild desire to talk to him; to question him; to make him understand. He did, in fact, interrupt him at one point; but it was useless. The ancient story of failure, ill-luck, undeserved disaster, went down the wind, disconnected syllables flying past Ralph's ears with a queer alternation of loudness and faintness as if, at certain moments, the man's memory of his wrongs revived and then flagged, dying down at last into a grumble of resignation, which seemed to represent a final lapse into the accustomed despair. The unhappy voice afflicted Ralph, but it also angered him. And when the elderly man refused to listen and mumbled on, an odd image came to his mind of a lighthouse besieged by the flying bodies of lost birds, who were dashed senseless, by the gale, against the glass. He had a strange sensation that he was both lighthouse and bird; he was steadfast and brilliant; and at the same time he was whirled, with all other things, senseless against the glass. He got up, left his tribute of silver, and pressed on, with the wind against him. The image of the lighthouse and the storm full of birds persisted, taking the place of more definite thoughts, as he walked past the Houses of Parliament and down Grosvenor Road, by the side of the river. In his state of physical fatigue, details merged themselves in the vaster prospect, of which the flying gloom and the intermittent lights of lamp-posts and private houses were the outward token, but he never lost his sense of walking in the direction of Katharine's house. He took it for granted that something would then happen, and, as he walked on, his mind became more and more full of pleasure and expectancy. Within a certain radius of her house the streets came under the influence of her presence. Each house had an individuality known to Ralph, because of the tremendous individuality of the house in which she lived. For some yards before reaching the Hilberys' door he walked in a trance of pleasure, but when he reached it, and pushed the gate of the little garden open, he hesitated. He did not know what to do next. There was no hurry, however, for the outside of the house held pleasure enough to last him some time longer. He crossed the road, and leant against the balustrade of the Embankment, fixing his eyes upon the house.

Lights burnt in the three long windows of the drawing-room. The space of the room behind became, in Ralph's vision, the center of the dark, flying wilderness of the world; the justification for the welter of confusion surrounding it; the steady light which cast its beams, like those of a lighthouse, with searching composure over the trackless waste. In this little sanctuary were gathered together several different people, but their identity was dissolved in a general glory of something that might, perhaps, be called civilization; at any rate, all dryness, all safety, all that stood up above the surge and preserved a consciousness of its own, was centered in the drawing-room of the Hilberys. Its purpose was beneficent; and yet so far above his level as to have something austere about it, a light that cast itself out and yet kept itself aloof. Then he began, in his mind, to distinguish different individuals within, consciously refusing as yet to attack the figure of Katharine. His thoughts lingered over Mrs. Hilbery and Cassandra; and then he turned to Rodney and Mr. Hilbery. Physically, he saw them bathed in that steady flow of yellow light which filled the long oblongs of the windows; in their movements they were beautiful; and in their speech he figured a reserve of meaning, unspoken, but understood. At length, after all this half-conscious selection and arrangement, he allowed himself to approach the figure of Katharine herself; and instantly the scene was flooded with excitement. He did not see her in the body; he seemed curiously to see her as a shape of light, the light itself; he seemed, simplified and exhausted as he was, to be like one of those lost birds fascinated by the lighthouse and held to the glass by the splendor of the blaze.

These thoughts drove him to tramp a beat up and down the pavement before the Hilberys' gate. He did not trouble himself to make any plans for the future. Something of an unknown kind would decide both the coming year and

the coming hour. Now and again, in his vigil, he sought
the light in the long windows, or glanced at the ray which
gilded a few leaves and a few blades of grass in the little
garden. For a long time the light burnt without changing
He had just reached the limit of his beat and was turning,
when the front door opened, and the aspect of the house
was entirely changed. A black figure came down the little
pathway and paused at the gate. Denham understood instantly that it was Rodney. Without hesitation, and conscious only of a great friendliness for any one coming from
that lighted room, he walked straight up to him and stopped
him. In the flurry of the wind Rodney was taken aback,
and for the moment tried to press on, muttering something,
as if he suspected a demand upon his charity.

"Goodness, Denham, what are you doing here?" he exclaimed, recognizing him.

Ralph mumbled something about being on his way home.
They walked on together, though Rodney walked quick
enough to make it plain that he had no wish for company.

He was very unhappy. That afternoon Cassandra had
repulsed him; he had tried to explain to her the difficulties
of the situation, and to suggest the nature of his feelings
for her without saying anything definite or anything offensive to her. But he had lost his head; under the goad of
Katharine's ridicule he had said too much, and Cassandra,
superb in her dignity and severity, had refused to hear another word, and threatened an immediate return to her
home. His agitation, after an evening spent between the
two women, was extreme. Moreover, he could not help
suspecting that Ralph was wandering near the Hilberys'
house, at this hour, for reasons connected with Katharine.
There was probably some understanding between them—
not that anything of the kind mattered to him now. He
was convinced that he had never cared for any one save
Cassandra, and Katharine's future was no concern of his.
Aloud, he said, shortly, that he was very tired and wished
to find a cab. But on Sunday night, on the Embankment,

cabs were hard to come by, and Rodney found himself constrained to walk some distance, at any rate, in Denham's
company. Denham maintained his silence. Rodney's irritation lapsed. He found the silence oddly suggestive of
the good masculine qualities which he much respected, and
had at this moment great reason to need. After the mystery, difficulty, and uncertainty of dealing with the other
sex, intercourse with one's own is apt to have a composing
and even ennobling influence, since plain speaking is possible and subterfuges of no avail. Rodney, too, was much
in need of a confidant; Katharine, despite her promises of
help, had failed him at the critical moment; she had gone
off with Denham; she was, perhaps, tormenting Denham as
she had tormented him. How grave and stable he seemed,
speaking little, and walking firmly, compared with what
Rodney knew of his own torments and indecisions! He
began to cast about for some way of telling the story of his
relations with Katharine and Cassandra that would not
lower him in Denham's eyes. It then occurred to him that,
perhaps, Katharine herself had confided in Denham; they
had something in common; it was likely that they had discussed him that very afternoon. The desire to discover
what they had said of him now came uppermost in his mind.
He recalled Katharine's laugh; he remembered that she had
gone, laughing, to walk with Denham.

"Did you stay long after we'd left?" he asked abruptly.

"No. We went back to my house."

This seemed to confirm Rodney's belief that he had been
discussed. He turned over the unpalatable idea for a while,
in silence.

"Women are incomprehensible creatures, Denham!" he
then exclaimed.

"Um," said Denham, who seemed to himself possessed of
complete understanding, not merely of women, but of the
entire universe. He could read Rodney, too, like a book.
He knew that he was unhappy, and he pitied him, and
wished to help him.

"You say something and they—fly into a passion. Or
for no reason at all, they laugh. I take it that no amount
of education will——" The remainder of the sentence was
lost in the high wind, against which they had to struggle;
but Denham understood that he referred to Katharine's
laughter, and that the memory of it was still hurting him.
In comparison with Rodney, Denham felt himself very secure; he saw Rodney as one of the lost birds dashed senseless against the glass; one of the flying bodies of which the
air was full. But he and Katharine were alone together,
aloft, splendid, and luminous with a twofold radiance. He
pitied the unstable creature beside him; he felt a desire to
protect him, exposed without the knowledge which made
his own way so direct. They were united as the adventur-
ous are united, though one reaches the goal and the other
perishes by the way.

"You couldn't laugh at some one you cared for."

This sentence, apparently addressed to no other human
being, reached Denham's ears. The wind seemed to muffle
it and fly away with it directly. Had Rodney spoken those
words?

"You love her." Was that his own voice, which seemed
to sound in the air several yards in front of him?

"I've suffered tortures, Denham, tortures!"

"Yes, yes, I know that."

"She's laughed at me."

"Never—to me."

The wind blew a space between the words—blew them
so far away that they seemed unspoken.

"How I've loved her!"

This was certainly spoken by the man at Denham's side.
The voice had all the marks of Rodney's character, and recalled, with strange vividness, his personal appearance.
Denham could see him against the blank buildings and towers of the horizon. He saw him dignified, exalted, and
tragic, as he might have appeared thinking of Katharine
alone in his rooms at night.

"I am in love with Katharine myself. That is why I am here to-night."

Ralph spoke distinctly and deliberately, as if Rodney's confession had made this statement necessary.

Rodney exclaimed something inarticulate.

"Ah, I've always known it," he cried, "I've known it from the first. You'll marry her!"

The cry had a note of despair in it. Again the wind intercepted their words. They said no more. At length they drew up beneath a lamp-post, simultaneously.

"My God, Denham, what fools we both are!" Rodney exclaimed. They looked at each other, queerly, in the light of the lamp. Fools! They seemed to confess to each other the extreme depths of their folly. For the moment, under the lamp-post, they seemed to be aware of some common knowledge which did away with the possibility of rivalry, and made them feel more sympathy for each other than for any one else in the world. Giving simultaneously a little nod, as if in confirmation of this understanding, they parted without speaking again.

CHAPTER XXIX

BETWEEN twelve and one that Sunday night Katharine lay in bed, not asleep, but in that twilight region where a detached and humorous view of our own lot is possible; or if we must be serious, our seriousness is tempered by the swift oncome of slumber and oblivion. She saw the forms of Ralph, William, Cassandra, and herself, as if they were all equally unsubstantial, and, in putting off reality, had gained a kind of dignity which rested upon each impartially. Thus rid of any uncomfortable warmth of partisanship or load of obligation, she was dropping off to sleep when a light tap sounded upon her door. A moment later Cassandra stood beside her, holding a candle and speaking in the low tones proper to the time of night.

"Are you awake, Katharine?"

"Yes, I'm awake. What is it?"

She roused herself, sat up, and asked what in Heaven's name Cassandra was doing?

"I couldn't sleep, and I thought I'd come and speak to you—only for a moment, though. I'm going home to-morrow."

"Home? Why, what has happened?"

"Something happened to-day which makes it impossible for me to stay here."

Cassandra spoke formally, almost solemnly; the announcement was clearly prepared and marked a crisis of the utmost gravity. She continued what seemed to be part of a set speech.

"I have decided to tell you the whole truth, Katharine. William allowed himself to behave in a way which made me extremely uncomfortable to-day."

Katharine seemed to waken completely, and at once to be in control of herself.

"At the Zoo?" she asked.

"No, on the way home. When we had tea."

As if foreseeing that the interview might be long, and the night chilly, Katharine advised Cassandra to wrap herself in a quilt. Cassandra did so with unbroken solemnity.

"There's a train at eleven," she said. "I shall tell Aunt Maggie that I have to go suddenly. . . . I shall make Violet's visit an excuse. But, after thinking it over, I don't see how I can go without telling you the truth."

She was careful to abstain from looking in Katharine's direction. There was a slight pause.

"But I don't see the least reason why you should go," said Katharine eventually. Her voice sounded so astonishingly equable that Cassandra glanced at her. It was impossible to suppose that she was either indignant or surprised; she seemed, on the contrary, sitting up in bed, with her arms clasped round her knees and a little frown on her brow, to be thinking closely upon a matter of indifference to her.

"Because I can't allow any man to behave to me in that way," Cassandra replied, and she added, "particularly when I know that he is engaged to some one else."

"But you like him, don't you?" Katharine inquired.

"That's got nothing to do with it," Cassandra exclaimed indignantly. "I consider his conduct, under the circumstances, most disgraceful."

This was the last of the sentences of her premeditated speech; and having spoken it she was left unprovided with any more to say in that particular style. When Katharine remarked:

"I should say it had everything to do with it," Cassandra's self-possession deserted her.

"I don't understand you in the least, Katharine. How can you behave as you behave? Ever since I came here I've been amazed by you!"

"You've enjoyed yourself, haven't you?" Katharine asked.

"Yes, I have," Cassandra admitted.

"Anyhow, my behavior hasn't spoiled your visit."

"No," Cassandra allowed once more. She was completely at a loss. In her forecast of the interview she had taken it for granted that Katharine, after an outburst of incredulity, would agree that Cassandra must return home as soon as possible. But Katharine, on the contrary, accepted her statement at once, seemed neither shocked nor surprised, and merely looked rather more thoughtful than usual. From being a mature woman charged with an important mission, Cassandra shrunk to the stature of an inexperienced child.

"Do you think I've been very foolish about it?" she asked.

Katharine made no answer, but still sat deliberating silently, and a certain feeling of alarm took possession of Cassandra. Perhaps her words had struck far deeper than she had thought, into depths beyond her reach, as so much of Katharine was beyond her reach. She thought suddenly that she had been playing with very dangerous tools.

Looking at her at length, Katharine asked slowly, as if she found the question very difficult to ask.

"But do you care for William?"

She marked the agitation and bewilderment of the girl's expression, and how she looked away from her.

"Do you mean, am I in love with him?" Cassandra asked, breathing quickly, and nervously moving her hands.

"Yes, in love with him," Katharine repeated.

"How can I love the man you're engaged to marry?" Cassandra burst out.

"He may be in love with you."

"I don't think you've any right to say such things, Katharine," Cassandra exclaimed. "Why do you say them? Don't you mind in the least how William behaves to other women? If I were engaged, I couldn't bear it!"

"We're not engaged," said Katharine, after a pause.

"Katharine!" Cassandra cried.

"No, we're not engaged," Katharine repeated. "But no one knows it but ourselves."

"But why—I don't understand—you're not engaged!" Cassandra said again. "Oh, that explains it! You're not in love with him! You don't want to marry him!"

"We aren't in love with each other any longer," said Katharine, as if disposing of something for ever and ever.

"How queer, how strange, how unlike other people you are, Katharine," Cassandra said, her whole body and voice seeming to fall and collapse together, and no trace of anger or excitement remaining, but only a dreamy quietude.

"You're not in love with him?"

"But I love him," said Katharine.

Cassandra remained bowed, as if by the weight of the revelation, for some little while longer. Nor did Katharine speak. Her attitude was that of some one who wishes to be concealed as much as possible from observation. She sighed profoundly; she was absolutely silent, and apparently overcome by her thoughts.

"D'you know what time it is?" she said at length, and shook her pillow, as if making ready for sleep.

Cassandra rose obediently, and once more took up her candle. Perhaps the white dressing-gown, and the loosened hair, and something unseeing in the expression of the eyes gave her a likeness to a woman walking in her sleep. Katharine, at least, thought so.

"There's no reason why I should go home, then?" Cassandra said, pausing. "Unless you want me to go, Katharine? What *do* you want me to do?"

For the first time their eyes met.

"You wanted us to fall in love," Cassandra exclaimed, as if she read the certainty there. But as she looked she saw a sight that surprised her. The tears rose slowly in Katharine's eyes and stood there, brimming but contained—the tears of some profound emotion, happiness, grief, renunciation; an emotion so complex in its nature that to express it was impossible, and Cassandra, bending her head and receiving the tears upon her cheek, accepted them in silence as the consecration of her love.

"Please, miss," said the maid, about eleven o'clock on the following morning, "Mrs. Milvain is in the kitchen."

A long wicker basket of flowers and branches had arrived from the country, and Katharine, kneeling upon the floor of the drawing-room, was sorting them while Cassandra watched her from an arm-chair, and absent-mindedly made spasmodic offers of help which were not accepted. The maid's message had a curious effect upon Katharine.

She rose, walked to the window, and, the maid being gone, said emphatically and even tragically:

"You know what that means."

Cassandra had understood nothing.

"Aunt Celia is in the kitchen," Katharine repeated.

"Why in the kitchen?" Cassandra asked, not unnaturally.

"Probably because she's discovered something," Katharine replied.   Cassandra's thoughts flew to the subject of her preoccupation.

"About us?" she inquired.

"Heaven knows," Katharine replied.   "I shan't let her stay in the kitchen, though.   I shall bring her up here."

The sternness with which this was said suggested that to bring Aunt Celia upstairs was, for some reason, a disciplinary measure.

"For goodness' sake, Katharine," Cassandra exclaimed, jumping from her chair and showing signs of agitation, "don't be rash.   Don't let her suspect.   Remember, nothing's certain——"

Katharine assured her by nodding her head several times, but the manner in which she left the room was not calculated to inspire complete confidence in her diplomacy.

Mrs. Milvain was sitting, or rather perching, upon the edge of a chair in the servants' room.   Whether there was any sound reason for her choice of a subterranean chamber, or whether it corresponded with the spirit of her quest, Mrs. Milvain invariably came in by the back door and sat in the servants' room when she was engaged in confidential family transactions. The ostensible reason she gave was that neither Mr. nor Mrs. Hilbery should be disturbed. But, in truth, Mrs. Milvain depended even more than most elderly women of her generation upon the delicious emotions of intimacy, agony, and secrecy, and the additional thrill provided by the basement was one not lightly to be forfeited. She protested almost plaintively when Katharine proposed to go upstairs.

"I've something that I want to say to you in *private*," she said, hesitating reluctantly upon the threshold of her ambush.

"The drawing-room is empty——"

"But we might meet your mother upon the stairs. We might disturb your father," Mrs. Milvain objected, taking tne precaution to speak in a whisper already.

But as Katharine's presence was absolutely necessary to the success of the interview, and as Katharine obstinately receded up the kitchen stairs, Mrs. Milvain had no course but to follow her. She glanced furtively about her as she proceeded upstairs, drew her skirts together, and stepped with circumspection past all doors, whether they were open or shut.

"Nobody will overhear us?" she murmured, when the comparative sanctuary of the drawing-room had been reached. "I see that I have interrupted you," she added, glancing at the flowers strewn upon the floor. A moment later she inquired, "Was some one sitting with you?" noticing a handkerchief that Cassandra had dropped in her flight.

"Cassandra was helping me to put the flowers in water," said Katharine, and she spoke so firmly and clearly that Mrs. Milvain glanced nervously at the main door and then at the curtain which divided the little room with the relics from the drawing-room.

"Ah, Cassandra is still with you," she remarked. "And did William send you those lovely flowers?"

Katharine sat down opposite her aunt and said neither yes nor no. She looked past her, and it might have been thought that she was considering very critically the pattern of the curtains. Another advantage of the basement, from Mrs. Milvain's point of view, was that it made it necessary to sit very close together, and the light was dim compared with that which now poured through three windows upon Katharine and the basket of flowers, and gave even the slight angular figure of Mrs. Milvain herself a halo of gold.

"They're from Stogdon House," said Katharine abruptly, with a little jerk of her head.

Mrs. Milvain felt that it would be easier to tell her niece what she wished to say if they were actually in physical contact, for the spiritual distance between them was formidable. Katharine, however, made no overtures, and Mrs. Milvain, who was possessed of rash but heroic courage, plunged without preface:

"People are talking about you, Katharine. That is why I have come this morning. You forgive me for saying what I'd much rather not say? What I say is only for your own sake, my child."

"There's nothing to forgive yet, Aunt Celia," said Katharine, with apparent good humor.

"People are saying that William goes everywhere with you and Cassandra, and that he is always paying her attentions. At the Markhams' dance he sat out five dances with her. At the Zoo they were seen alone together. They left together. They never came back here till seven in the evening. But that is not all. They say his manner is very marked—he is quite different when she is there."

Mrs. Milvain, whose words had run themselves together, and whose voice had raised its tone almost to one of protest, here ceased, and looked intently at Katharine, as if to judge the effect of her communication. A slight rigidity had passed over Katharine's face. Her lips were pressed together; her eyes were contracted, and they were still fixed upon the curtain. These superficial changes covered an extreme inner loathing such as might follow the display of some hideous or indecent spectacle. The indecent spectacle was her own action beheld for the first time from the outside; her aunt's words made her realize how infinitely repulsive the body of life is without its soul.

"Well?" she said at length.

Mrs. Milvain made a gesture as if to bring her closer, but it was not returned.

"We all know how good you are—how unselfish—how you sacrifice yourself to others. But you've been too unselfish, Katharine. You have made Cassandra happy, and she has taken advantage of your goodness."

"I don't understand, Aunt Celia," said Katharine. "What has Cassandra done?"

"Cassandra has behaved in a way that I could not have thought possible," said Mrs. Milvain warmly. "She has been utterly selfish—utterly heartless. I must speak to her before I go."

"I don't understand," Katharine persisted.

Mrs. Milvain looked at her. Was it possible that Katharine really doubted? That there was something that Mrs. Milvain herself did not understand? She braced herself, and pronounced the tremendous words:

"Cassandra has stolen William's love."

Still the words seemed to have curiously little effect.

"Do you mean," said Katharine, "that he has fallen in love with her?"

"There are ways of *making* men fall in love with one, Katharine."

Katharine remained silent. The silence alarmed Mrs. Milvain, and she began hurriedly:

"Nothing would have made me say these things but your own good. I have not wished to interfere; I have not wished to give you pain. I am a useless old woman. I have no children of my own. I only want to see you happy, Katharine."

Again she stretched forth her arms, but they remained empty.

"You are not going to say these things to Cassandra," said Katharine suddenly. "You've said them to me; that's enough."

Katharine spoke so low and with such restraint that Mrs. Milvain had to strain to catch her words, and when she heard them she was dazed by them.

"I've made you angry! I knew I should!" she exclaimed: She quivered, and a kind of sob shook her; but even to have made Katharine angry was some relief, and allowed her to feel some of the agreeable sensations of martyrdom.

"Yes," said Katharine, standing up, "I'm so angry that I don't want to say anything more. I think you'd better go, Aunt Celia. We don't understand each other."

At these words Mrs. Milvain looked for a moment terribly apprehensive; she glanced at her niece's face, but read no pity there, whereupon she folded her hands upon a black velvet bag which she carried in an attitude that was almost one of prayer. Whatever divinity she prayed to, if pray she did, at any rate she recovered her dignity in a singular way and faced her niece.

"Married love," she said slowly and with emphasis upon every word, "is the most sacred of all loves. The love of husband and wife is the most holy we know. That is the lesson Mamma's children learnt from her; that is what they can never forget. I have tried to speak as she would have wished her daughter to speak. You are her grandchild."

Katharine seemed to judge this defence upon its merits, and then to convict it of falsity.

"I don't see that there is any excuse for your behavior," she said.

At these words Mrs. Milvain rose and stood for a moment beside her niece. She had never met with such treatment before, and she did not know with what weapons to break down the terrible wall of resistance offered her by one who, by virtue of youth and beauty and sex, should have been all tears and supplications. But Mrs. Milvain herself was obstinate; upon a matter of this kind she could not admit that she was either beaten or mistaken. She beheld herself the champion of married love in its purity and supremacy; what her niece stood for she was quite unable to say, but she was filled with the gravest suspicions. The old woman and the young woman stood side by side in unbroken silence. Mrs. Milvain could not make up her mind to withdraw while her principles trembled in the balance and her curiosity remained unappeased. She ransacked her mind for some question that should force Katharine to enlighten her, but the supply was limited, the choice difficult, and while she hesitated the door opened and William Rodney came in. He carried in his hand an enormous and splendid bunch of white and purple flowers, and, either not seeing Mrs. Milvain, or disregarding her, he advanced straight to Katharine, and presented the flowers with the words:

"These are for you, Katharine."

Katharine took them with a glance that Mrs. Milvain did not fail to intercept. But with all her experience, she did not know what to make of it. She watched anxiously for further illumination. William greeted her without obvious sign of guilt, and, explaining that he had a holiday, both he and Katharine seemed to take it for granted that his holiday should be celebrated with flowers and spent in Cheyne Walk. A pause followed; that, too, was natural; and Mrs. Milvain began to feel that she laid herself open to a charge of selfishness if she stayed. The mere presence of a young man had altered her disposition curiously, and filled her with a desire for a scene which should end in an emotional forgiveness. She would have given much to clasp both nephew and niece in her arms. But she could not flatter herself that any hope of the customary exaltation remained.

"I must go," she said, and she was conscious of an extreme flatness of spirit.

Neither of them said anything to stop her. William politely escorted her downstairs, and somehow, amongst her protests and embarrassments, Mrs. Milvain forgot to say good-bye to Katharine. She departed, murmuring words about masses of flowers and a drawing-room always beautiful even in the depths of winter.

William came back to Katharine; he found her standing where he had left her.

"I've come to be forgiven," he said. "Our quarrel was perfectly hateful to me. I've not slept all night. You're not angry with me, are you, Katharine?"

She could not bring herself to answer him until she had rid her mind of the impression that her aunt had made on her. It seemed to her that the very flowers were contaminated, and Cassandra's pocket-handkerchief, for Mrs. Milvain had used them for evidence in her investigations.

"She's been spying upon us," she said, "following us about London, overhearing what people are saying——"

"Mrs. Milvain?" Rodney exclaimed. "What has she told you?"

His air of open confidence entirely vanished.

"Oh, people are saying that you're in love with Cassandra, and that you don't care for me."

"They have seen us?" he asked.

"Everything we've done for a fortnight has been seen."

"I told you that would happen!" he exclaimed.

He walked to the window in evident perturbation. Katharine was too indignant to attend to him. She was swept away by the force of her own anger. Clasping Rodney's flowers, she stood upright and motionless.

Rodney turned away from the window.

"It's all been a mistake," he said. "I blame myself for it. I should have known better. I let you persuade me in a moment of madness. I beg you to forget my insanity, Katharine."

"She wished even to persecute Cassandra!" Katharine burst out, not listening to him. "She threatened to speak to her. She's capable of it—she's capable of anything!"

"Mrs. Milvain is not tactful, I know, but you exaggerate, Katharine. People are talking about us. She was right to tell us. It only confirms my own feeling—the position is monstrous."

At length Katharine realized some part of what he meant.

"You don't mean that this influences you, William?" she asked in amazement.

"It does," he said, flushing. "It's intensely disagreeable to me. I can't endure that people should gossip about us. And then there's your cousin—Cassandra——" He paused in embarrassment.

"I came here this morning, Katharine," he resumed, with a change of voice, "to ask you to forget my folly, my bad temper, my inconceivable behavior. I came, Katharine, to ask whether we can't return to the position we were in before this—this season of lunacy. Will you take me back, Katharine, once more and for ever?"

No doubt her beauty, intensified by emotion and enhanced by the flowers of bright color and strange shape which she carried wrought upon Rodney, and had its share in bestowing upon her the old romance. But a less noble passion worked in him, too; he was inflamed by jealousy. His tentative offer of affection had been rudely and, as he thought, completely repulsed by Cassandra on the preceding day. Denham's confession was in his mind. And ultimately, Katharine's dominion over him was of the sort that the fevers of the night cannot exorcise.

"I was as much to blame as you were yesterday," she said gently, disregarding his question. "I confess, William, the sight of you and Cassandra together made me jealous, and I couldn't control myself. I laughed at you, I know."

"You jealous!" William exclaimed. "I assure you, Katharine, you've not the slightest reason to be jealous. Cassandra dislikes me, so far as she feels about me at all. I was foolish enough to try to explain the nature of our relationship. I couldn't resist telling her what I supposed myself to feel for her. She refused to listen, very rightly. But she left me in no doubt of her scorn."

Katharine hesitated. She was confused, agitated, physically tired, and had already to reckon with the violent feeling of dislike aroused by her aunt which still vibrated through all the rest of her feelings. She sank into a chair and dropped her flowers upon her lap.

"She charmed me," Rodney continued. "I thought I loved her. But that's a thing of the past. It's all over, Katharine. It was a dream—an hallucination. We were both equally to blame, but no harm's done if you believe how truly I care for you. Say you believe me!"

He stood over her, as if in readiness to seize the first sign of her assent. Precisely at that moment, owing, perhaps, to her vicissitudes of feeling, all sense of love left her, as in a moment a mist lifts from the earth. And when the mist departed a skeleton world and blankness alone remained—a terrible prospect for the eyes of the living to behold. He saw the look of terror in her face, and without understanding its origin, took her hand in his. With the sense of companionship returned a desire, like that of a child for shelter, to accept what he had to offer her—and at that moment it seemed that he offered her the only thing that could make it tolerable to live. She let him press his lips to her cheek, and leant her head upon his arm. It was the moment of his triumph. It was the only moment in which she belonged to him and was dependent upon his protection.

"Yes, yes, yes," he murmured, "you accept me, Katharine. You love me."

For a moment she remained silent. He then heard her murmur:

"Cassandra loves you more than I do."

"Cassandra?" he whispered.

"She loves you," Katharine repeated. She raised herself

and repeated the sentence yet a third time. "She loves you."

William slowly raised himself. He believed instinctively what Katharine said, but what it meant to him he was unable to understand. Could Cassandra love him? Could she have told Katharine that she loved him? The desire to know the truth of this was urgent, unknown though the consequences might be. The thrill of excitement associated with the thought of Cassandra once more took possession of him. No longer was it the excitement of anticipation and ignorance; it was the excitement of something greater than a possibility, for now he knew her and had measure of the sympathy between them. But who could give him certainty? Could Katharine, Katharine who had lately lain in his arms, Katharine herself the most admired of women? He looked at her, with doubt, and with anxiety, but said nothing.

"Yes, yes," she said, interpreting his wish for assurance, "it's true. I know what she feels for you."

"She loves me?"

Katharine nodded.

"Ah, but who knows what I feel? How can I be sure of my feeling myself? Ten minutes ago I asked you to marry me. I still wish it—I don't know what I wish——"

He clenched his hands and turned away. He suddenly faced her and demanded: "Tell me what you feel for Denham."

"For Ralph Denham?" she asked. "Yes!" she exclaimed, as if she had found the answer to some momentarily perplexing question. "You're jealous of me, William; but you're not in love with me. I'm jealous of you. Therefore, for both our sakes, I say, speak to Cassandra at once."

He tried to compose himself. He walked up and down the room; he paused at the window and surveyed the flowers strewn upon the floor. Meanwhile his desire to have Katharine's assurance confirmed became so insistent that he could no longer deny the overmastering strength of his feeling for Cassandra.

"You're right," he exclaimed, coming to a standstill and rapping his knuckles sharply upon a small table carrying one slender vase. "I love Cassandra."

As he said this, the curtains hanging at the door of the little room parted, and Cassandra herself stepped forth.

"I have overheard every word!" she exclaimed.

A pause succeeded this announcement. Rodney made a step forward and said:

"Then you know what I wish to ask you. Give me your answer——"

She put her hands before her face; she turned away and seemed to shrink from both of them.

"What Katharine said," she murmured. "But," she added, raising her head with a look of fear from the kiss with which he greeted her admission, "how frightfully difficult it all is! Our feelings, I mean—yours and mine and Katharine's. Katharine, tell me, are we doing right?"

"Right—of course we're doing right," William answered her, "if, after what you've heard, you can marry a man of such incomprehensible confusion, such deplorable——"

"Don't, William," Katharine interposed; "Cassandra has heard us; she can judge what we are; she knows better than we could tell her."

But, still holding William's hand, questions and desires welled up in Cassandra's heart. Had she done wrong in listening? Why did Aunt Celia blame her? Did Katharine think her right? Above all, did William really love her, for ever and ever, better than any one?

"I must be first with him, Katharine!" she exclaimed. "I can't share him even with you."

"I shall never ask that," said Katharine. She moved a little away from where they sat and began half-consciously sorting her flowers.

"But you've shared with me," Cassandra said. "Why can't I share with you? Why am I so mean? I know why

it is," she added. "We understand each other, William and
I. You've never understood each other. You're too different."

"I've never admired anybody more," William interposed.

"It's not that"—Cassandra tried to enlighten him—"it's
understanding."

"Have I never understood you, Katharine? Have I been
very selfish?"

"Yes," Cassandra interposed. "You've asked her for
sympathy, and she's not sympathetic; you've wanted her to
be practical, and she's not practical. You've been selfish;
you've been exacting—and so has Katharine—but it wasn't
anybody's fault."

Katharine had listened to this attempt at analysis with
keen attention. Cassandra's words seemed to rub the old
blurred image of life and freshen it so marvelously that it
looked new again. She turned to William.

"It's quite true," she said. "It was nobody's fault."

"There are many things that he'll always come to you
for," Cassandra continued, still reading from her invisible
book. "I accept that, Katharine. I shall never dispute it.
I want to be generous as you've been generous. But being
in love makes it more difficult for me."

They were silent. At length William broke the silence.

"One thing I beg of you both, he said, and the old nervousness of manner returned as he glanced at Katharine.
"We will never discuss these matters again. It's not that
I'm timid and conventional, as you think, Katharine. It's
that it spoils things to discuss them; it unsettles people's
minds; and now we're all so happy——"

Cassandra ratified this conclusion so far as she was concerned, and William, after receiving the exquisite pleasure
of her glance, with its absolute affection and trust, looked
anxiously at Katharine.

"Yes, I'm happy," she assured him. "And I agree. We
will never talk about it again."

"Oh, Katharine, Katharine!" Cassandra cried, holding
out her arms while the tears ran down her cheeks.

CHAPTER XXX

THE day was so different from other days to three people
in the house that the common routine of household
life—the maid waiting at table, Mrs. Hilbery writing a letter, the clock striking, and the door opening, and all the
other signs of long-established civilization appeared suddenly to have no meaning save as they lulled Mr. and Mrs.
Hilbery into the belief that nothing unusual had taken place.
It chanced that Mrs. Hilbery was depressed without visible
cause, unless a certain crudeness verging upon coarseness
in the temper of her favorite Elizabethans could be held
responsible for the mood. At any rate, she had shut up
"The Duchess of Malfi" with a sigh, and wished to know,
so she told Rodney at dinner, whether there wasn't some
young writer with a touch of the great spirit—somebody
who made you believe that life was *beautiful?* She got
little help from Rodney, and after singing her plaintive re-
quiem for the death of poetry by herself, she charmed herself into good spirits again by remembering the existence
of Mozart. She begged Cassandra to play to her, and when
they went upstairs Cassandra opened the piano directly, and
did her best to create an atmosphere of unmixed beauty. At
the sound of the first notes Katharine and Rodney both felt
an enormous sense of relief at the license which the music
gave them to loosen their hold upon the mechanism of behavior. They lapsed into the depths of thought. Mrs.
Hilbery was soon spirited away into a perfectly congenial
mood, that was half reverie and half slumber, half delicious
melancholy and half pure bliss. Mr. Hilbery alone attended. He was extremely musical, and made Cassandra
aware that he listened to every note. She played her best,

and won his approval. Leaning slightly forward in his chair, and turning his little green stone, he weighed the intention of her phrases approvingly, but stopped her suddenly to complain of a noise behind him. The window was unhasped. He signed to Rodney, who crossed the room immediately to put the matter right. He stayed a moment longer by the window than was, perhaps, necessary, and having done what was needed, drew his chair a little closer than before to Katharine's side. The music went on. Under cover of some exquisite run of melody, he leant towards her and whispered something. She glanced at her father and mother, and a moment later left the room, almost unobserved, with Rodney.

"What is it?" she asked, as soon as the door was shut.

Rodney made no answer, but led her downstairs into the dining-room on the ground floor. Even when he had shut the door he said nothing, but went straight to the window and parted the curtains. He beckoned to Katharine.

"There he is again," he said. "Look, there—under the lamp-post."

Katharine looked. She had no idea what Rodney was talking about. A vague feeling of alarm and mystery possessed her. She saw a man standing on the opposite side of the road facing the house beneath a lamp-post. As they looked the figure turned, walked a few steps, and came back again to his old position. It seemed to her that he was looking fixedly at her, and was conscious of her gaze on him. She knew, in a flash, who the man was who was watching them. She drew the curtain abruptly.

"Denham," said Rodney. "He was there last night too." He spoke sternly. His whole manner had become full of authority. Katharine felt almost as if he accused her of some crime. She was pale and uncomfortably agitated, as much by the strangeness of Rodney's behavior as by the sight of Ralph Denham.

"If he chooses to come——" she said defiantly.

"You can't let him wait out there. I shall tell him to

come in." Rodney spoke with such decision that when he raised his arm Katharine expected him to draw the curtain instantly. She caught his hand with a little exclamation.

"Wait!" she cried. "I don't allow you."

"You can't wait," he replied. "You've gone too far." His hand remained upon the curtain. "Why don't you admit, Katharine," he broke out, looking at her with an expression of contempt as well as of anger, "that you love him? Are you going to treat him as you treated me?"

She looked at him, wondering, in spite of all her perplexity, at the spirit that possessed him.

"I forbid you to draw the curtain," she said.

He reflected, and then took his hand away.

"I've no right to interfere," he concluded. "I'll leave you. Or, if you like, we'll go back to the drawing-room."

"No. I can't go back," she said, shaking her head. She bent her head in thought.

"You love him, Katharine," Rodney said suddenly. His tone had lost something of its sternness, and might have been used to urge a child to confess its fault. She raised her eyes and fixed them upon him.

"I love him?" she repeated. He nodded. She searched his face, as if for further confirmation of his words, and, as he remained silent and expectant, turned away once more and continued her thoughts. He observed her closely, but without stirring, as if he gave her time to make up her mind to fulfil her obvious duty. The strains of Mozart reached them from the room above.

"Now," she said suddenly, with a sort of desperation, rising from her chair and seeming to command Rodney to fulfil his part. He drew the curtain instantly, and she made no attempt to stop him. Their eyes at once sought the same spot beneath the lamp-post.

"He's not there!" she exclaimed.

No one was there. William threw the window up and looked out. The wind rushed into the room, together with the sound of distant wheels, footsteps hurrying along the pavement, and the cries of sirens hooting down the river.

"Denham!" William cried.

"Ralph!" said Katharine, but she spoke scarcely louder than she might have spoken to some one in the same room. With their eyes fixed upon the opposite side of the road, they did not notice a figure close to the railing which divided the garden from the street. But Denham had crossed the road and was standing there. They were startled by his voice close at hand.

"Rodney!"

"There you are! Come in, Denham." Rodney went to the front door and opened it. "Here he is," he said, bringing Ralph with him into the dining-room where Katharine stood, with her back to the open window. Their eyes met for a second. Denham looked half dazed by the strong light, and, buttoned in his overcoat, with his hair ruffled across his forehead by the wind, he seemed like somebody rescued from an open boat out at sea. William promptly shut the window and drew the curtains. He acted with a cheerful decision as if he were master of the situation, and knew exactly what he meant to do.

"You're the first to hear the news, Denham," he said. "Katharine isn't going to marry me, after all."

"Where shall I put——" Ralph began vaguely, holding out his hat and glancing about him; he balanced it carefully against a silver bowl that stood upon the sideboard. He then sat himself down rather heavily at the head of the oval dinner-table. Rodney stood on one side of him and Katharine on the other. He appeared to be presiding over some meeting from which most of the members were absent. Meanwhile, he waited, and his eyes rested upon the glow of the beautifully polished mahogany table.

"William is engaged to Cassandra," said Katharine briefly.

At that Denham looked up quickly at Rodney. Rodney's expression changed. He lost his self-possession. He smiled a little nervously, and then his attention seemed to be caught by a fragment of melody from the floor above. He seemed for a moment to forget the presence of the others. He glanced towards the door.

"I congratulate you," said Denham.

"Yes, yes. We're all mad—quite out of our minds, Denham," he said. "It's partly Katharine's doing—partly mine." He looked oddly round the room as if he wished to make sure that the scene in which he played a part had some real existence. "Quite mad," he repeated. "Even Katharine—" His gaze rested upon her finally, as if she, too, had changed from his old view of her. He smiled at her as if to encourage her. "Katharine shall explain," he said, and giving a little nod to Denham, he left the room.

Katharine sat down at once, and leant her chin upon her hands. So long as Rodney was in the room the proceedings of the evening had seemed to be in his charge, and had been marked by a certain unreality. Now that she was alone with Ralph she felt at once that a constraint had been taken from them both. She felt that they were alone at the bottom of the house, which rose, story upon story, upon the top of them.

"Why were you waiting out there?" she asked.

"For the chance of seeing you," he replied.

"You would have waited all night if it hadn't been for William. It's windy too. You must have been cold. What could you see? Nothing but our windows."

"It was worth it. I heard you call me."

"I called you?" She had called unconsciously.

"They were engaged this morning," she told him, after a pause.

"You're glad?" he asked.

She bent her head. "Yes, yes," she sighed. "But you don't know how good he is—what he's done for me—" Ralph made a sound of understanding. "You waited there last night too?" she asked.

"Yes. I can wait," Denham replied.

The words seemed to fill the room with an emotion which

Katharine connected with the sound of distant wheels, the
footsteps hurrying along the pavement, the cries of sirens
hooting down the river, the darkness and the wind. She
saw the upright figure standing beneath the lamp-post.

"Waiting in the dark," she said, glancing at the window,
as if he saw what she was seeing. "Ah, but it's different—"
She broke off. "I'm not the person you think me. Until
you realize that it's impossible——"

Placing her elbows on the table, she slid her ruby ring
up and down her finger abstractedly. She frowned at the
rows of leather-bound books opposite her. Ralph looked
keenly at her. Very pale, but sternly concentrated upon
her meaning, beautiful but so little aware of herself as to
seem remote from him also, there was something distant
and abstract about her which exalted him and chilled him
at the same time.

"No, you're right," he said. "I don't know you. I've
never known you."

"Yet perhaps you know me better than any one else,"
she mused.

Some detached instinct made her aware that she was
gazing at a book which belonged by rights to some other
part of the house. She walked over to the shelf, took it
down, and returned to her seat, placing the book on the table
between them. Ralph opened it and looked at the portrait
of a man with a voluminous white shirt-collar, which
formed the frontispiece.

"I say I do know you, Katharine," he affirmed, shutting
the book. "It's only for moments that I go mad."

"Do you call two whole nights a moment?"

"I swear to you that now, at this instant, I see you precisely as you are. No one has ever known you as I know
you. . . . Could you have taken down that book just now
if I hadn't known you?"

"That's true," she replied, "but you can't think how I'm
divided—how I'm at my ease with you, and how I'm bewildered. The unreality—the dark—the waiting outside

in the wind—yes, when you look at me, not seeing me, and
I don't see you either. . . . But I do see," she went on
quickly, changing her position and frowning again, "heaps
of things, only not you."

"Tell me what you see," he urged.

But she could not reduce her vision to words, since it
was no single shape colored upon the dark, but rather a
general excitement, an atmosphere, which, when she tried
to visualize it, took form as a wind scouring the flanks of
northern hills and flashing light upon cornfields and pools.

"Impossible," she sighed, laughing at the ridiculous notion of putting any part of this into words.

"Try, Katharine," Ralph urged her.

"But I can't—I'm talking a sort of nonsense—the sort
of nonsense one talks to oneself." She was dismayed by
the expression of longing and despair upon his face. "I
was thinking about a mountain in the North of England,"
she attempted. "It's too silly—I won't go on."

"We were there together?" he pressed her.

"No. I was alone." She seemed to be disappointing the
desire of a child. His face fell.

"You're always alone there?"

"I can't explain." She could not explain that she was
essentially alone there. "It's not a mountain in the North
of England. It's an imagination—a story one tells oneself.
You have yours too?"

"You're with me in mine. You're the thing I make up,
you see."

"Oh, I see," she sighed. "That's why it's so impossible."
She turned upon him almost fiercely. "You must try to
stop it," she said.

"I won't," he replied roughly, "because I—" He stopped.
He realized that the moment had come to impart that news
of the utmost importance which he had tried to impart to
Mary Datchet, to Rodney upon the Embankment, to the
drunken tramp upon the seat. How should he offer it to
Katharine? He looked quickly at her. He saw that she

was only half attentive to him; only a section of her was exposed to him. The sight roused in him such desperation that he had much ado to control his impulse to rise and leave the house. Her hand lay loosely curled upon the table. He seized it and grasped it firmly as if to make sure of her existence and of his own. "Because I love you, Katharine," he said.

Some roundness or warmth essential to that statement was absent from his voice, and she had merely to shake her head very slightly for him to drop her hand and turn away in shame at his own impotence. He thought that she had detected his wish to leave her. She had discerned the break in his resolution, the blankness in the heart of his vision. It was true that he had been happier out in the street, thinking of her, than now that he was in the same room with her. He looked at her with a guilty expression on his face. But her look expressed neither disappointment nor reproach. Her pose was easy, and she seemed to give effect to a mood of quiet speculation by the spinning of her ruby ring upon the polished table. Denham forgot his despair in wondering what thoughts now occupied her.

"You don't believe me?" he said. His tone was humble, and made her smile at him.

"As far as I understand you—but what should you advise me to do with this ring?" she asked, holding it out.

"I should advise you to let me keep it for you," he replied, in the same tone of half-humorous gravity.

"After what you've said, I can hardly trust you—unless you'll unsay what you've said?"

"Very well. I'm not in love with you."

"But I think you *are* in love with me. . . . As I am with you," she added casually enough. "At least," she said slipping her ring back to its old position, "what other word describes the state we're in?"

She looked at him gravely and inquiringly, as if in search of help.

"It's when I'm with you that I doubt it, not when I'm alone," he stated.

"So I thought," she replied.

In order to explain to her his state of mind, Ralph recounted his experience with the photograph, the letter, and the flower picked at Kew. She listened very seriously.

"And then you went raving about the streets," she mused. "Well, it's bad enough. But my state is worse than yours, because it hasn't anything to do with facts. It's an hallucination, pure and simple—an intoxication. . . . One can be in love with pure reason?" she hazarded. "Because if you're in love with a vision, I believe that that's what I'm in love with."

This conclusion seemed fantastic and profoundly unsatisfactory to Ralph, but after the astonishing variations of his own sentiments during the past half-hour he could not accuse her of fanciful exaggeration.

"Rodney seems to know his own mind well enough," he said almost bitterly. The music, which had ceased, had now begun again, and the melody of Mozart seemed to express the easy and exquisite love of the two upstairs.

"Cassandra never doubted for a moment. But we—" she glanced at him as if to ascertain his position, "we see each other only now and then——"

"Like lights in a storm——"

"In the midst of a hurricane," she concluded, as the window shook beneath the pressure of the wind. They listened to the sound in silence.

Here the door opened with considerable hesitation, and Mrs. Hilbery's head appeared, at first with an air of caution, but having made sure that she had admitted herself to the dining-room and not to some more unusual region, she came completely inside and seemed in no way taken aback by the sight she saw. She seemed, as usual, bound on some quest of her own which was interrupted pleasantly but strangely by running into one of those queer, unnecessary ceremonies that other people thought fit to indulge in.

"Please don't let me interrupt you, Mr.——" she was at a loss, as usual, for the name, and Katharine thought that she did not recognize him. "I hope you've found something nice to read," she added, pointing to the book upon the table. "Byron—ah, Byron. I've known people who knew Lord Byron," she said.

Katharine, who had risen in some confusion, could not help smiling at the thought that her mother found it perfectly natural and desirable that her daughter should be reading Byron in the dining-room late at night alone with a strange young man. She blessed a disposition that was so convenient, and felt tenderly towards her mother and her mother's eccentricities. But Ralph observed that although Mrs. Hilbery held the book so close to her eyes she was not reading a word.

"My dear mother, why aren't you in bed?" Katharine exclaimed, changing astonishingly in the space of a minute to her usual condition of authoritative good sense. "Why are you wandering about?"

"I'm sure I should like your poetry better than I like Lord Byron's," said Mrs. Hilbery, addressing Ralph Denham.

"Mr. Denham doesn't write poetry; he has written articles for father, for the Review," Katharine said, as if prompting her memory.

"Oh dear! How dull!" Mrs. Hilbery exclaimed, with a sudden laugh that rather puzzled her daughter.

Ralph found that she had turned upon him a gaze that was at once very vague and very penetrating.

"But I'm sure you read poetry at night. I always judge by the expression of the eyes," Mrs. Hilbery continued. ("The windows of the soul," she added parenthetically.) "I don't know much about the law," she went on, "though many of my relations were lawyers. Some of them looked very handsome, too, in their wigs. But I think I do know a little about poetry," she added. "And all the things that aren't written down, but—but—" She waved her hand, as if to indicate the wealth of unwritten poetry all about them. "The night and the stars, the dawn coming up, the barges swimming past, the sun setting. . . . Ah dear," she sighed, "well, the sunset is very lovely too. I sometimes think that poetry isn't so much what we write as what we feel, Mr. Denham."

During this speech of her mother's Katharine had turned away, and Ralph felt that Mrs. Hilbery was talking to him apart, with a desire to ascertain something about him which she veiled purposely by the vagueness of her words. He felt curiously encouraged and heartened by the beam in her eye rather than by her actual words. From the distance of her age and sex she seemed to be waving to him, hailing him as a ship sinking beneath the horizon might wave its flag of greeting to another setting out upon the same voyage. He bent his head, saying nothing, but with a curious certainty that she had read an answer to her inquiry that satisfied her. At any rate, she rambled off into a description of the Law Courts which turned to a denunciation of English justice, which, according to her, imprisoned poor men who couldn't pay their debts. "Tell me, shall we ever do without it all?" she asked, but at this point Katharine gently insisted that her mother should go to bed. Looking back from half-way up the staircase, Katharine seemed to see Denham's eyes watching her steadily and intently with an expression that she had guessed in them when he stood looking at the windows across the road.

CHAPTER XXXI

THE tray which brought Katharine's cup of tea the next morning brought, also, a note from her mother, announcing that it was her intention to catch an early train to Stratford-on-Avon that very day.

"Please find out the best way of getting there," the note ran, "and wire to dear Sir John Burdett to expect me, with my love. I've been dreaming all night of you and Shakespeare, dearest Katharine."

This was no momentary impulse. Mrs. Hilbery had been dreaming of Shakespeare any time these six months, toying with the idea of an excursion to what she considered the heart of the civilized world. To stand six feet above Shakespeare's bones, to see the very stones worn by his feet, to reflect that the oldest man's oldest mother had very likely seen Shakespeare's daughter— such thoughts roused an emotion in her, which she expressed at unsuitable moments, and with a passion that would not have been unseemly in a pilgrim to a sacred shrine. The only strange thing was that she wished to go by herself. But, naturally enough, she was well provided with friends who lived in the neighborhood of Shakespeare's tomb, and were delighted to welcome her; and she left later to catch her train in the best of spirits. There was a man selling violets in the street. It was a fine day. She would remember to send Mr. Hilbery the first daffodil she saw. And, as she ran back into the hall to tell Katharine, she felt, she had always felt, that Shakespeare's command to leave his bones undisturbed applied only to odious curiosity-mongers—not to dear Sir John and herself. Leaving her daughter to cogitate the theory of Anne Hathaway's sonnets, and the buried manuscripts here referred to, with the implied menace to the safety of the heart of civilization itself, she briskly shut the door of her taxi-cab, and was whirled off upon the first stage of her pilgrimage.

The house was oddly different without her. Katharine found the maids already in possession of her room, which they meant to clean thoroughly during her absence. To Katharine it seemed as if they had brushed away sixty years or so with the first flick of their damp dusters. It seemed to her that the work she had tried to do in that room was being swept into a very insignificant heap of dust. The china shepherdesses were already shining from a bath of hot water. The writing-table might have belonged to a professional man of methodical habits.

Gathering together a few papers upon which she was at work, Katharine proceeded to her own room with the intention of looking through them, perhaps, in the course of the morning. But she was met on the stairs by Cassandra, who followed her up, but with such intervals between each step that Katharine began to feel her purpose dwindling before they had reached the door. Cassandra leant over the banisters, and looked down upon the Persian rug that lay on the floor of the hall.

"Doesn't everything look odd this morning?" she inquired. "Are you really going to spend the morning with those dull old letters, because if so——"

The dull old letters, which would have turned the heads of the most sober of collectors, were laid upon a table, and, after a moment's pause, Cassandra, looking grave all of a sudden, asked Katharine where she should find the "History of England" by Lord Macaulay. It was downstairs in Mr. Hilbery's study. The cousins descended together in search of it. They diverged into the drawing-room for the good reason that the door was open. The portrait of Richard Alardyce attracted their attention.

"I wonder what he was like?" It was a question that Katharine had often asked herself lately.

"Oh, a fraud like the rest of them—at least Henry says

so," Cassandra replied. "Though I don't believe everything Henry says," she added a little defensively.

Down they went into Mr. Hilbery's study, where they
began to look among his books. So desultory was this
examination that some fifteen minutes failed to discover
the work they were in search of.

"Must you read Macaulay's History, Cassandra?"
Katharine asked, with a stretch of her arms.

"I must," Cassandra replied briefly.

"Well, I'm going to leave you to look for it by yourself."

"Oh, no, Katharine. Please stay and help me. You
see—you see—I told William I'd read a little every day.
And I want to tell him that I've begun when he comes."

"When does William come?" Katharine asked, turning
to the shelves again.

"To tea, if that suits you?"

"If it suits me to be out, I suppose you mean."

"Oh, you're horrid. . . . Why shouldn't you——?"

"Yes?"

"Why shouldn't you be happy too?"

"I am quite happy," Katharine replied.

"I mean as I am. Katharine," she said impulsively, "do
let's be married on the same day."

"To the same man?"

"Oh, no, no. But why shouldn't you marry—some one
else?"

"Here's your Macaulay," said Katharine, turning round
with the book in her hand. "I should say you'd better
begin to read at once if you mean to be educated by tea-
time."

"Damn Lord Macaulay!" cried Cassandra, slapping the
book upon the table. "Would you rather not talk?"

"We've talked enough already," Katharine replied eva-
sively.

"I know I shan't be able to settle to Macaulay," said Cassandra, looking ruefully at the dull red cover of the pre-

scribed volume, which, however, possessed a talismanic property, since William admired it. He had advised a little serious reading for the morning hours.

"Have *you* read Macaulay?" she asked.

"No. William never tried to educate me." As she spoke she saw the light fade from Cassandra's face, as if she had implied some other, more mysterious, relationship. She was stung with compunction. She marveled at her own rashness in having influenced the life of another, as she had influenced Cassandra's life.

"We weren't serious," she said quickly.

"But I'm fearfully serious," said Cassandra, with a little shudder, and her look showed that she spoke the truth. She turned and glanced at Katharine as she had never glanced at her before. There was fear in her glance, which darted on her and then dropped guiltily. Oh, Katharine had everything—beauty, mind, character. She could never compete with Katharine; she could never be safe so long as Katharine brooded over her, dominating her, disposing of her. She called her cold, unseeing, unscrupulous, but the only sign she gave outwardly was a curious one—she reached out her hand and grasped the volume of history. At that moment the bell of the telephone rang and Katharine went to answer it. Cassandra, released from observation, dropped her book and clenched her hands. She suffered more fiery torture in those few minutes than she had suffered in the whole of her life; she learnt more of her capacities for feeling. But when Katharine reappeared she was calm, and had gained a look of dignity that was new to her.

"Was that him?" she asked.

"It was Ralph Denham," Katharine replied.

"I meant Ralph Denham."

"Why did you mean Ralph Denham? What has William told you about Ralph Denham?" The accusation that Katharine was calm, callous, and indifferent was not possible in face of her present air of animation. She gave

Cassandra no time to frame an answer. "Now, when are you and William going to be married?" she asked.

Cassandra made no reply for some moments. It was, indeed, a very difficult question to answer. In conversation the night before, William had indicated to Cassandra that, in his belief, Katharine was becoming engaged to Ralph Denham in the dining-room. Cassandra, in the rosy light of her own circumstances, had been disposed to think that the matter must be settled already. But a letter which she had received that morning from William, while ardent in its expression of affection, had conveyed to her obliquely that he would prefer the announcement of their engagement to coincide with that of Katharine's. This document Cassandra now produced, and read aloud, with considerable excisions and much hesitation.

". . . a thousand pities—ahem—I fear we shall cause a great deal of natural annoyance. If, on the other hand, what I have reason to think will happen, should happen—within reasonable time, and the present position is not in any way offensive to you, delay would, in my opinion, serve all our interests better than a premature explanation, which is bound to cause more surprise than is desirable——"

"Very like William," Katharine exclaimed, having gathered the drift of these remarks with a speed that, by itself, disconcerted Cassandra.

"I quite understand his feelings," Cassandra replied. "I quite agree with them. I think it would be much better, if you intend to marry Mr. Denham, that we should wait as William says."

"But, then, if I don't marry him for months—or, perhaps, not at all?"

Cassandra was silent. The prospect appalled her. Katharine had been telephoning to Ralph Denham; she looked queer, too; she must be, or about to become, engaged to him. But if Cassandra could have overheard the conversation upon the telephone, she would not have felt so cer-

tain that it tended in that direction. It was to this effect:

"I'm Ralph Denham speaking. I'm in my right senses
now."

"How long did you wait outside the house?"

"I went home and wrote you a letter. I tore it up."

"I shall tear up everything too."

"I shall come."

"Yes. Come to-day."

"I must explain to you——"

"Yes. We must explain——"

A long pause followed. Ralph began a sentence, which
he canceled with the word, "Nothing." Suddenly, together, at the same moment, they said good-bye. And yet,
if the telephone had been miraculously connected with some
higher atmosphere pungent with the scent of thyme and
the savor of salt, Katharine could hardly have breathed
in a keener sense of exhilaration. She ran downstairs on
the crest of it. She was amazed to find herself already
committed by William and Cassandra to marry the owner
of the halting voice she had just heard on the telephone.
The tendency of her spirit seemed to be in an altogether
different direction; and of a different nature. She had only
to look at Cassandra to see what the love that results in an
engagement and marriage means. She considered for a
moment, and then said: "If you don't want to tell people
yourselves, I'll do it for you. I know William has feelings
about these matters that make it very difficult for him to
do anything."

"Because he's fearfully sensitive about other people's
feelings," said Cassandra. "The idea that he could upset
Aunt Maggie or Uncle Trevor would make him ill for
weeks."

This interpretation of what she was used to call William's conventionality was new to Katharine. And yet she
felt it now to be the true one.

"Yes, you're right," she said.

"And then he worships beauty. He wants life to be beautiful in every part of it. Have you ever noticed how exquisitely he finishes everything? Look at the address on that envelope. Every letter is perfect."

Whether this applied also to the sentiments expressed in the letter, Katharine was not so sure; but when William's solicitude was spent upon Cassandra it not only failed to irritate her, as it had done when she was the object of it, but appeared, as Cassandra said, the fruit of his love of beauty.

"Yes," she said, "he loves beauty."

"I hope we shall have a great many children," said Cassandra. "He loves children."

This remark made Katharine realize the depths of their intimacy better than any other words could have done; she was jealous for one moment; but the next she was humiliated. She had known William for years, and she had never once guessed that he loved children. She looked at the queer glow of exaltation in Cassandra's eyes, through which she was beholding the true spirit of a human being, and wished that she would go on talking about William for ever. Cassandra was not unwilling to gratify her. She talked on. The morning slipped away. Katharine scarcely changed her position on the edge of her father's writing-table, and Cassandra never opened the "History of England."

And yet it must be confessed that there were vast lapses in the attention which Katharine bestowed upon her cousin. The atmosphere was wonderfully congenial for thoughts of her own. She lost herself sometimes in such deep reverie that Cassandra, pausing, could look at her for moments unperceived. What could Katharine be thinking about, unless it were Ralph Denham? She was satisfied, by certain random replies, that Katharine had wandered a little from the subject of William's perfections. But Katharine made no sign. She always ended these pauses by saying something so natural that Cassandra was deluded into

giving fresh examples of her absorbing theme. Then they
lunched, and the only sign that Katharine gave of abstraction was to forget to help the pudding. She looked so
like her mother, as she sat there oblivious of the tapioca,
that Cassandra was startled into exclaiming:

"How like Aunt Maggie you look!"

"Nonsense," said Katharine, with more irritation than
the remark seemed to call for.

In truth, now that her mother was away, Katharine did
feel less sensible than usual, but as she argued it to herself,
there was much less need for sense. Secretly, she was a
little shaken by the evidence which the morning had supplied of her immense capacity for—what could one call it?
—rambling over an infinite variety of thoughts that were
too foolish to be named. She was, for example, walking
down a road in Northumberland in the August sunset;
at the inn she left her companion, who was Ralph Denham,
and was transported, not so much by her own feet as by
some invisible means, to the top of a high hill. Here the
scents, the sounds among the dry heather-roots, the grass-
blades pressed upon the palm of her hand, were all so
perceptible that she could experience each one separately..
After this her mind made excursions into the dark of the
air, or settled upon the surface of the sea, which could be
discovered over there, or with equal unreason it returned
to its couch of bracken beneath the stars of midnight, and
visited the snow valleys of the moon. These fancies would
have been in no way strange, since the walls of every mind
are decorated with some such tracery, but she found herself suddenly pursuing such thoughts with an extreme ardor, which became a desire to change her actual condition
for something matching the conditions of her dream. Then
she started; then she awoke to the fact that Cassandra was
looking at her in amazement.

Cassandra would have liked to feel certain that, when
Katharine made no reply at all or one wide of the mark,
she was making up her mind to get married at once, but

it was difficult, if this were so, to account for some remarks
that Katharine let fall about the future. She recurred several times to the summer, as if she meant to spend that
season in solitary wandering. She seemed to have a plan
in her mind which required Bradshaws and the names of
inns.

Cassandra was driven finally, by her own unrest, to put
on her clothes and wander out along the streets of Chelsea,
on the pretence that she must buy something. But, in
her ignorance of the way, she became panic-stricken at
the thought of being late, and no sooner had she found the
shop she wanted, than she fled back again in order to be
at home when William came. He came, indeed, five minutes after she had sat down by the tea-table, and she had
the happiness of receiving him alone. His greeting put
her doubts of his affection at rest, but the first question he
asked was:

"Has Katharine spoken to you?"

"Yes. But she says she's not engaged. She doesn't
seem to think she's ever going to be engaged."

William frowned, and looked annoyed.

"They telephoned this morning, and she behaves very
oddly. She forgets to help the pudding," Cassandra added
by way of cheering him.

"My dear child, after what I saw and heard last night,
it's not a question of guessing or suspecting. Either she's
engaged to him—or——"

He left his sentence unfinished, for at this point Katharine herself appeared. With his recollections of the scene
the night before, he was too self-conscious even to look at
her, and it was not until she told him of her mother's visit
to Stratford-on-Avon that he raised his eyes. It was clear
that he was greatly relieved. He looked round him now,
as if he felt at his ease, and Cassandra exclaimed:

"Don't you think everything looks quite different?"

"You've moved the sofa?" he asked.

"No. Nothing's been touched," said Katharine. "Everything's exactly the same." But as she said this, with a decision which seemed to make it imply that more than the sofa was unchanged, she held out a cup into which she had forgotten to pour any tea. Being told of her forgetfulness, she frowned with annoyance, and said that Cassandra was demoralizing her. The glance she cast upon them, and the resolute way in which she plunged them into speech, made William and Cassandra feel like children who had been caught prying. They followed her obediently, making conversation. Any one coming in might have judged them acquaintances met, perhaps, for the third time. If that were so, one must have concluded that the hostess suddenly bethought her of an engagement pressing for fulfilment. First Katharine looked at her watch, and then she asked William to tell her the right time. When told that it was ten minutes to five she rose at once, and said:

"Then I'm afraid I must go."

She left the room, holding her unfinished bread and butter in her hand. William glanced at Cassandra.

"Well, she *is* queer!" Cassandra exclaimed.

William looked perturbed. He knew more of Katharine than Cassandra did, but even he could not tell——. In a second Katharine was back again dressed in outdoor things, still holding her bread and butter in her bare hand.

"If I'm late, don't wait for me," she said. "I shall have dined," and so saying, she left them.

"But she can't—" William exclaimed, as the door shut, "not without any gloves and bread and butter in her hand!" They ran to the window, and saw her walking rapidly along the street towards the City. Then she vanished.

"She must have gone to meet Mr. Denham," Cassandra exclaimed.

"Goodness knows!" William interjected.

The incident impressed them both as having something queer and ominous about it out of all proportion to its surface strangeness.

"It's the sort of way Aunt Maggie behaves," said Cassandra, as if in explanation.

William shook his head, and paced up and down the room looking extremely perturbed.

"This is what I've been foretelling," he burst out. "Once set the ordinary conventions aside— Thank Heaven Mrs. Hilbery is away. But there's Mr. Hilbery. How are we to explain it to him? I shall have to leave you."

"But Uncle Trevor won't be back for hours, William!" Cassandra implored.

"You never can tell. He may be on his way already. Or suppose Mrs. Milvain—your Aunt Celia—or Mrs. Cosham, or any other of your aunts or uncles should be shown in and find us alone together. You know what they're saying about us already."

Cassandra was equally stricken by the sight of William's agitation, and appalled by the prospect of his desertion.

"We might hide," she exclaimed wildly, glancing at the curtain which separated the room with the relics.

"I refuse entirely to get under the table," said William sarcastically.

She saw that he was losing his temper with the difficulties of the situation. Her instinct told her that an appeal to his affection, at this moment, would be extremely ill-judged. She controlled herself, sat down, poured out a fresh cup of tea, and sipped it quietly. This natural action, arguing complete self-mastery, and showing her in one of those feminine attitudes which William found adorable, did more than any argument to compose his agitation. It appealed to his chivalry. He accepted a cup. Next she asked for a slice of cake. By the time the cake was eaten and the tea drunk the personal question had lapsed, and they were discussing poetry. Insensibly they turned from the question of dramatic poetry in general, to the particular example which reposed in William's pocket, and when the maid came in to clear away the tea-things, William had asked permission to read a short passage aloud, "unless it bored her?"

Cassandra bent her head in silence, but she showed a little of what she felt in her eyes, and thus fortified, William felt confident that it would take more than Mrs. Milvain herself to rout him from his position. He read aloud.

Meanwhile Katharine walked rapidly along the street. If called upon to explain her impulsive action in leaving the tea-table, she could have traced it to no better cause than that William had glanced at Cassandra; Cassandra at William. Yet, because they had glanced, her position was impossible. If one forgot to pour out a cup of tea they rushed to the conclusion that she was engaged to Ralph Denham. She knew that in half an hour or so the door would open, and Ralph Denham would appear. She could not sit there and contemplate seeing him with William's and Cassandra's eyes upon them, judging their exact degree of intimacy, so that they might fix the wedding-day. She promptly decided that she would meet Ralph out of doors; she still had time to reach Lincoln's Inn Fields before he left his office. She hailed a cab, and bade it take her to a shop for selling maps which she remembered in Great Queen Street, since she hardly liked to be set down at his door. Arrived at the shop, she bought a large scale map of Norfolk, and thus provided, hurried into Lincoln's Inn Fields, and assured herself of the position of Messrs. Hoper and Grateley's office. The great gas chandeliers were alight in the office windows. She conceived that he sat at an enormous table laden with papers beneath one of them in the front room with the three tall windows. Having settled his position there, she began walking to and fro upon the pavement. Nobody of his build appeared. She scrutinized each male figure as it approached and passed her. Each male figure had, nevertheless, a look of him, due, perhaps, to the professional dress, the quick step, the keen glance which they cast upon her as they hastened home after the day's work. The square itself, with its immense houses all so fully occupied and stern of aspect, its atmosphere of industry and power, as if even the sparrows and the children were earning their daily bread, as if the sky itself, with its gray and scarlet clouds, reflected the serious intention of the city beneath it, spoke of him. Here was the fit place for their meeting, she thought; here was the fit place for her to walk thinking of him. She could not help comparing it with the domestic streets of Chelsea. With this comparison in her mind, she extended her range a little, and turned into the main road. The great torrent of vans and carts was sweeping down Kingsway; pedestrians were streaming in two currents along the pavements. She stood fascinated at the corner. The deep roar filled her ears; the changing tumult had the inexpressible fascination of varied life pouring ceaselessly with a purpose which, as she looked, seemed to her, somehow, the normal purpose for which life was framed; its complete indifference to the individuals, whom it swallowed up and rolled onwards, filled her with at least a temporary exaltation. The blend of daylight and of lamplight made her an invisible spectator, just as it gave the people who passed her a semi-transparent quality, and left the faces pale ivory ovals in which the eyes alone were dark. They tended the enormous rush of the current—the great flow, the deep stream, the unquenchable tide. She stood unobserved and absorbed, glorying openly in the rapture that had run subterraneously all day. Suddenly she was clutched, unwilling, from the outside, by the recollection of her purpose in coming there. She had come to find Ralph Denham. She hastily turned back into Lincoln's Inn Fields, and looked for her landmark—the light in the three tall windows. She sought in vain. The faces of the houses had now merged in the general darkness, and she had difficulty in determining which she sought. Ralph's three windows gave back on their ghostly glass panels only a reflection of the gray and greenish sky. She rang the bell, peremptorily, under the painted name of the firm. After some delay she was answered by a caretaker, whose pail and brush of themselves told her that the working day was over and the workers gone. Nobody, save perhaps Mr. Grateley himself, was left, she assured Katharine; every one else had been gone these ten minutes.

The news woke Katharine completely. Anxiety gained upon her. She hastened back into Kingsway, looking at people who had miraculously regained their solidity. She ran as far as the Tube station, overhauling clerk after clerk, solicitor after solicitor. Not one of them even faintly resembled Ralph Denham. More and more plainly did she see him; and more and more did he seem to her unlike any one else. At the door of the station she paused, and tried to collect her thoughts. He had gone to her house. By taking a cab she could be there probably in advance of him. But she pictured herself opening the drawing-room door, and William and Cassandra looking up, and Ralph's entrance a moment later, and the glances—the insinuations. No; she could not face it. She would write him a letter and take it at once to his house. She bought paper and pencil at the bookstall, and entered an A.B.C. shop, where, by ordering a cup of coffee, she secured an empty table, and began at once to write:

"I came to meet you and I have missed you. I could not face William and Cassandra. They want us——" here she paused. "They insist that we are engaged," she substituted, "and we couldn't talk at all, or explain anything. I want——" Her wants were so vast, now that she was in communication with Ralph, that the pencil was utterly inadequate to conduct them on to the paper; it seemed as if the whole torrent of Kingsway had to run down her pencil. She gazed intently at a notice hanging on the gold-encrusted wall opposite. ". . . to say all kinds of things," she added, writing each word with the painstaking of a child. But, when she raised her eyes again to meditate the next sentence, she was aware of a waitress, whose expression intimated that it was closing time, and, looking round, Katharine saw herself almost the last person left in the shop. She took up her letter, paid her bill, and found herself once more in the street. She would now take a cab to Highgate. But at that moment it flashed upon her that she could not remember the address. This check seemed to let fall a barrier across a very powerful current of desire. She ransacked her memory in desperation, hunting for the name, first by remembering the look of the house, and then by trying, in memory, to retrace the words she had written once, at least, upon an envelope. The more she pressed the farther the words receded. Was the house an Orchard Something, on the street a Hill? She gave it up. Never, since she was a child, had she felt anything like this blankness and desolation. There rushed in upon her, as if she were waking from some dream, all the consequences of her inexplicable indolence. She figured Ralph's face as he turned from her door without a word of explanation, receiving his dismissal as a blow from herself, a callous intimation that she did not wish to see him. She followed his departure from her door; but it was far more easy to see him marching far and fast in any direction for any length of time than to conceive that he would turn back to Highgate. Perhaps he would try once more to see her in Cheyne Walk? It was proof of the clearness with which she saw him, that she started forward as this possibility occurred to her, and almost raised her hand to beckon to a cab. No; he was too proud to come again; he rejected the desire and walked on and on, on and on— If only she could read the names of those visionary streets down which he passed! But her imagination betrayed her at this point, or mocked her with a sense of their strangeness, darkness, and distance. Indeed, instead of helping herself to any decision, she only filled her mind with the vast extent of London and the impossibility of finding any single figure that wandered off this way and that way, turned to the right and to the left, chose that dingy little back street where the children were playing in the road, and so—— She roused herself impatiently. She walked rapidly along Holborn. Soon she turned and walked as rapidly in the other direction. This indecision was not merely odious, but had something that alarmed her about it, as she had been alarmed slightly once or twice already that day; she felt unable to cope with the strength of her own desires. To a person controlled by habit, there was humiliation as well as alarm in this sudden release of what appeared to be a very powerful as well as an unreasonable force. An aching in the muscles of her right hand now showed her that she was crushing her gloves and the map of Norfolk in a grip sufficient to crack a more solid object. She relaxed her grasp; she looked anxiously at the faces of the passers-by to see whether their eyes rested on her for a moment longer than was natural, or with any curiosity. But having smoothed out her gloves, and done what she could to look as usual, she forgot spectators, and was once more given up to her desperate desire to find Ralph Denham. It was a desire now—wild, irrational, unexplained, resembling something felt in childhood. Once more she blamed herself bitterly for her carelessness. But finding herself opposite the Tube station, she pulled herself up and took counsel swiftly, as of old. It flashed upon her that she would go at once to Mary Datchet, and ask her to give her Ralph's address. The decision was a relief, not only in giving her a goal, but in providing her with a rational excuse for her own actions. It gave her a goal certainly, but the fact of having a goal led her to dwell exclusively upon her obsession; so that when she rang the bell of Mary's flat, she did not for a moment consider how this demand would strike Mary. To her extreme annoyance Mary was not at home; a charwoman opened the door. All Katharine could do was to accept the invitation to wait. She waited for, perhaps, fifteen minutes, and spent them in pacing from one end of the room to the other without intermission. When she heard Mary's key in the door she paused in front of the fireplace, and Mary found her standing upright, looking at once expectant and determined, like a person who has come on an errand of such importance that it must be broached without preface.

Mary exclaimed in surprise.

"Yes, yes," Katharine said, brushing these remarks aside, as if they were in the way.

"Have you had tea?"

"Oh yes," she said, thinking that she had had tea hundreds of years ago, somewhere or other.

Mary paused, took off her gloves, and, finding matches, proceeded to light the fire.

Katharine checked her with an impatient movement, and said:

"Don't light the fire for me. . . . I want to know Ralph Denham's address."

She was holding a pencil and preparing to write on the envelope. She waited with an imperious expression.

"The Apple Orchard, Mount Ararat Road, Highgate," Mary said, speaking slowly and rather strangely.

"Oh, I remember now!" Katharine exclaimed, with irritation at her own stupidity. "I suppose it wouldn't take twenty minutes to drive there?" She gathered up her purse and gloves and seemed about to go.

"But you won't find him," said Mary, pausing with a match in her hand. Katharine, who had already turned towards the door, stopped and looked at her.

"Why? Where is he?" she asked.

"He won't have left his office."

"But he has left the office," she replied. "The only question is will he have reached home yet? He went to see me at Chelsea; I tried to meet him and missed him. He will have found no message to explain. So I must find him—as soon as possible."

Mary took in the situation at her leisure.

"But why not telephone?" she said.

Katharine immediately dropped all that she was holding; her strained expression relaxed, and exclaiming, "Of course! Why didn't I think of that!" she seized the telephone receiver and gave her number. Mary looked at her steadily, and then left the room. At length Katharine heard, through all the superimposed weight of London, the mysterious sound of feet in her own house mounting to the little room, where she could almost see the pictures and the books; she listened with extreme intentness to the preparatory vibrations, and then established her identity.

"Has Mr. Denham called?"

"Yes, miss."

"Did he ask for me?"

"Yes. We said you were out, miss."

"Did he leave any message?"

"No. He went away. About twenty minutes ago, miss."

Katharine hung up the receiver. She walked the length of the room in such acute disappointment that she did not at first perceive Mary's absence. Then she called in a harsh and peremptory tone:

"Mary."

Mary was taking off her outdoor things in the bedroom. She heart Katharine call her. "Yes," she said, "I shan't be a moment." But the moment prolonged itself, as if for some reason Mary found satisfaction in making herself not only tidy, but seemly and ornamented. A stage in her life had been accomplished in the last months which left its traces for ever upon her bearing. Youth, and the bloom of youth, had receded, leaving the purpose of her face to show itself in the hollower cheeks, the firmer lips, the eyes no longer spontaneously observing at random, but narrowed upon an end which was not near at hand. This woman was now a serviceable human being, mistress of her own destiny, and thus, by some combination of ideas, fit to be adorned with the dignity of silver chains and glowing brooches. She came in at her leisure and asked:

"Well, did you get an answer?"

"He has left Chelsea already," Katharine replied.

"Still, he won't be home yet," said Mary.

Katharine was once more irresistibly drawn to gaze upon an imaginary map of London, to follow the twists and turns of unnamed streets.

"I'll ring up his home and ask whether he's back." Mary crossed to the telephone and, after a series of brief remarks, announced:

"No. His sister says he hasn't come back yet."

"Ah!" She applied her ear to the telephone once more. "They've had a message. He won't be back to dinner."

"Then what is he going to do?"

Very pale, and with her large eyes fixed not so much upon Mary as upon vistas of unresponding blankness, Katharine addressed herself also not so much to Mary as to the unrelenting spirit which now appeared to mock her from every quarter of her survey.

After waiting a little time Mary remarked indifferently:

"I really don't know." Slackly lying back in her armchair, she watched the little flames beginning to creep among the coals indifferently, as if they, too, were very distant and indifferent.

Katharine looked at her indignantly and rose.

"Possibly he may come here," Mary continued, without altering the abstract tone of her voice. "It would be worth your while to wait if you want to see him to-night." She bent forward and touched the wood, so that the flames slipped in between the interstices of the coal.

Katharine reflected. "I'll wait half an hour," she said.

Mary rose, went to the table, spread out her papers under the green-shaded lamp and, with an action that was becoming a habit, twisted a lock of hair round and round in her fingers. Once she looked unperceived at her visitor, who never moved, who sat so still, with eyes so intent, that you could almost fancy that she was watching something, some face that never looked up at her. Mary found herself unable to go on writing. She turned her eyes away, but only to be aware of the presence of what Katharine looked at. There were ghosts in the room, and one, strangely and sadly, was the ghost of herself. The minutes went by.

"What would be the time now?" said Katharine at last. The half-hour was not quite spent.

"I'm going to get dinner ready," said Mary, rising from her table.

"Then I'll go," said Katharine.

"Why don't you stay? Where are you going?"

Katharine looked round the room, conveying her uncertainty in her glance.

"Perhaps I might find him," she mused.

"But why should it matter? You'll see him another day."

Mary spoke, and intended to speak, cruelly enough.

"I was wrong to come here," Katharine replied.

Their eyes met with antagonism, and neither flinched.

"You had a perfect right to come here," Mary answered.

A loud knocking at the door interrupted them. Mary went to open it, and returning with some note or parcel, Katharine looked away so that Mary might not read her disappointment.

"Of course you had a right to come," Mary repeated, laying the note upon the table.

"No," said Katharine. "Except that when one's desperate one has a sort of right. I am desperate. How do I know what's happening to him now? He may do anything. He may wander about the streets all night. Anything may happen to him."

She spoke with a self-abandonment that Mary had never seen in her.

"You know you exaggerate; you're talking nonsense," she said roughly.

"Mary, I must talk—I must tell you——"

"You needn't tell me anything," Mary interrupted her. "Can't I see for myself?"

"No, no," Katharine exclaimed. "It's not that——"

Her look, passing beyond Mary, beyond the verge of the room and out beyond any words that came her way, wildly and passionately, convinced Mary that she, at any rate, could not follow such a glance to its end. She was baffled; she tried to think herself back again into the height of her love for Ralph. Pressing her fingers upon her eyelids, she murmured:

"You forget that I loved him too. I thought I knew him. I *did* know him."

And yet, what had she known? She could not remember it any more. She pressed her eyeballs until they struck stars and suns into her darkness. She convinced herself that she was stirring among ashes. She desisted. She was astonished at her discovery. She did not love Ralph any more. She looked back dazed into the room, and her eyes rested upon the table with its lamp-lit papers. The steady radiance seemed for a second to have its counterpart within her; she shut her eyes; she opened them and looked at the lamp again; another love burnt in the place of the old one, or so, in a momentary glance of amazement, she guessed before the revelation was over and the old surroundings asserted themselves. She leant in silence against the mantelpiece.

"There are different ways of loving," she murmured, half to herself, at length.

Katharine made no reply and seemed unaware of her words. She seemed absorbed in her own thoughts.

"Perhaps he's waiting in the street again to-night," she exclaimed. "I'll go now. I might find him."

"It's far more likely that he'll come here," said Mary, and Katharine, after considering for a moment, said:

"I'll wait another half-hour."

She sank down into her chair again, and took up the same position which Mary had compared to the position of one watching an unseeing face. She watched, indeed, not a face, but a procession, not of people, but of life itself: the good and bad; the meaning; the past, the present, and

the future. All this seemed apparent to her, and she
was not ashamed of her extravagance so much as exalted
to one of the pinnacles of existence, where it behoved the
world to do her homage. No one but she herself knew
what it meant to miss Ralph Denham on that particular
night; into this inadequate event crowded feelings that
the great crises of life might have failed to call forth.
She had missed him, and knew the bitterness of all failure;
she desired him, and knew the torment of all passion. It
did not matter what trivial accidents led to this culmination.
Nor did she care how extravagant she appeared, nor how
openly she showed her feelings.

When the dinner was ready Mary told her to come, and
she came submissively, as if she let Mary direct her movements for her. They ate and drank together almost in
silence, and when Mary told her to eat more, she ate more;
when she was told to drink wine, she drank it. Nevertheless, beneath this superficial obedience, Mary knew that
she was following her own thoughts unhindered. She
was not inattentive so much as remote; she looked at once
so unseeing and so intent upon some vision of her own
that Mary gradually felt more than protective—she became
actually alarmed at the prospect of some collision between
Katharine and the forces of the outside world. Directly
they had done, Katharine announced her intention of going.

"But where are you going to?" Mary asked, desiring
vaguely to hinder her.

"Oh, I'm going home—no, to Highgate perhaps."

Mary saw that it would be useless to try to stop her.
All she could do was to insist upon coming too, but she met
with no opposition; Katharine seemed indifferent to her
presence. In a few minutes they were walking along the
Strand. They walked so rapidly that Mary was deluded
into the belief that Katharine knew where she was going.
She herself was not attentive. She was glad of the movement along lamp-lit streets in the open air. She was fingering, painfully and with fear, yet with strange hope, too,

the discovery which she had stumbled upon unexpectedly that night. She was free once more at the cost of a gift, the best, perhaps, that she could offer, but she was, thank Heaven, in love no longer. She was tempted to spend the first instalment of her freedom in some dissipation; in the pit of the Coliseum, for example, since they were now passing the door. Why not go in and celebrate her independence of the tyranny of love? Or, perhaps, the top of an omnibus bound for some remote place such as Camberwell, or Sidcup, or the Welsh Harp would suit her better. She noticed these names painted on little boards for the first time for weeks. Or should she return to her room, and spend the night working out the details of a very enlightened and ingenious scheme? Of all possibilities this appealed to her most, and brought to mind the fire, the lamplight, the steady glow which had seemed lit in the place where a more passionate flame had once burnt.

Now Katharine stopped, and Mary woke to the fact that instead of having a goal she had evidently none. She paused at the edge of the crossing, and looked this way and that, and finally made as if in the direction of Haverstock Hill.

"Look here—where are you going?" Mary cried, catching her by the hand. "We must take that cab and go home." She hailed a cab and insisted that Katharine should get in, while she directed the driver to take them to Cheyne Walk.

Katharine submitted. "Very well," she said. "We may as well go there as anywhere else."

A gloom seemed to have fallen on her. She lay back in her corner, silent and apparently exhausted. Mary, in spite of her own preoccupation, was struck by her pallor and her attitude of dejection.

"I'm sure we shall find him," she said more gently than she had yet spoken.

"It may be too late," Katharine replied. Without understanding her, Mary began to pity her for what she was suffering.

"Nonsense," she said, taking her hand and rubbing it. "If we don't find him there we shall find him somewhere else."

"But suppose he's walking about the streets—for hours and hours?"

She leant forward and looked out of the window.

"He may refuse ever to speak to me again," she said in a low voice, almost to herself.

The exaggeration was so immense that Mary did not attempt to cope with it, save by keeping hold of Katharine's wrist. She half expected that Katharine might open the door suddenly and jump out. Perhaps Katharine perceived the purpose with which her hand was held.

"Don't be frightened," she said, with a little laugh. "I'm not going to jump out of the cab. It wouldn't do much good after all."

Upon this, Mary ostentatiously withdrew her hand.

"I ought to have apologized," Katharine continued, with an effort, "for bringing you into all this business; I haven't told you half, either. I'm no longer engaged to William Rodney. He is to marry Cassandra Otway. It's all arranged—all perfectly right. . . . And after he'd waited in the streets for hours and hours, William made me bring him in. He was standing under the lamp-post watching our windows. He was perfectly white when he came into the room. William left us alone, and we sat and talked. It seems ages and ages ago, now. Was it last night? Have I been out long? What's the time?" She sprang forward to catch sight of a clock, as if the exact time had some important bearing on her case.

"Only half-past eight!" she exclaimed. "Then he may be there still." She leant out of the window and told the cabman to drive faster.

"But if he's not there, what shall I do? Where could I find him? The streets are so crowded."

"We shall find him," Mary repeated.

Mary had no doubt but that somehow or other they
would find him. But suppose they did find him? She
began to think of Ralph with a sort of strangeness, in her
effort to understand how he could be capable of satisfying
this extraordinary desire. Once more she thought herself
back to her old view of him and could, with an effort,
recall the haze which surrounded his figure, and the sense
of confused, heightened exhilaration which lay all about
his neighborhood, so that for months at a time she had
never exactly heard his voice or seen his face—or so it now
seemed to her. The pain of her loss shot through her.
Nothing would ever make up—not success, or happiness,
or oblivion. But this pang was immediately followed by
the assurance that now, at any rate, she knew the truth;
and Katharine, she thought, stealing a look at her, did not
know the truth; yes, Katharine was immensely to be pitied.

The cab, which had been caught in the traffic, was now
liberated and sped on down Sloane Street. Mary was
conscious of the tension with which Katharine marked its
progress, as if her mind were fixed upon a point in front
of them, and marked, second by second, their approach
to it. She said nothing, and in silence Mary began to fix
her mind, in sympathy at first, and later in forgetfulness
of her companion, upon a point in front of them. She
imagined a point distant as a low star upon the horizon
of the dark. There for her too, for them both, was the
goal for which they were striving, and the end for the
ardors of their spirits was the same: but where it was,
or what it was, or why she felt convinced that they were
united in search of it, as they drove swiftly down the streets
of London side by side, she could not have said.

"At last," Katharine breathed, as the cab drew up at the
door. She jumped out and scanned the pavement on either
side. Mary, meanwhile, rang the bell. The door opened as
Katharine assured herself that no one of the people with-

in view had any likeness to Ralph. On seeing her, the maid said at once:

"Mr. Denham called again, miss. He has been waiting for you for some time."

Katharine vanished from Mary's sight. The door shut between them, and Mary walked slowly and thoughtfully up the street alone.

Katharine turned at once to the dining-room. But with her fingers upon the handle, she held back. Perhaps she realized that this was a moment which would never come again. Perhaps, for a second, it seemed to her that no reality could equal the imagination she had formed. Perhaps she was restrained by some vague fear or anticipation, which made her dread any exchange or interruption. But if these doubts and fears or this supreme bliss restrained her, it was only for a moment. In another second she had turned the handle and, biting her lip to control herself, she opened the door upon Ralph Denham. An extraordinary clearness of sight seemed to possess her on beholding him. So little, so single, so separate from all else he appeared, who had been the cause of these extreme agitations and aspirations. She could have laughed in his face. But, gaining upon this clearness of sight against her will, and to her dislike, was a flood of confusion, of relief, of certainty, of humility, of desire no longer to strive and to discriminate, yielding to which, she let herself sink within his arms and confessed her love.

CHAPTER XXXII

NOBODY asked Katharine any questions next day. If cross-examined she might have said that nobody spoke to her. She worked a little, wrote a little, ordered the dinner, and sat, for longer than she knew, with her head on her hand piercing whatever lay before her, whether it was a letter or a dictionary, as if it were a film upon the deep prospects that revealed themselves to her kindling and brooding eyes. She rose once, and going to the bookcase, took out her father's Greek dictionary and spread the sacred pages of symbols and figures before her. She smoothed the sheets with a mixture of affectionate amusement and hope. Would other eyes look on them with her one day? The thought, long intolerable, was now just bearable.

She was quite unaware of the anxiety with which her movements were watched and her expression scanned. Cassandra was careful not to be caught looking at her, and their conversation was so prosaic that were it not for certain jolts and jerks between the sentences, as if the mind were kept with difficulty to the rails, Mrs. Milvain herself could have detected nothing of a suspicious nature in what she overheard.

William, when he came in late that afternoon and found Cassandra alone, had a very serious piece of news to impart. He had just passed Katharine in the street and she had failed to recognize him.

"That doesn't matter with me, of course, but suppose it happened with somebody else? What would they think? They would suspect something merely from her expression. She looked—she looked"—he hesitated—"like some one walking in her sleep."

To Cassandra the significant thing was that Katharine

had gone out without telling her, and she interpreted this to mean that she had gone out to meet Ralph Denham. But to her surprise William drew no comfort from this probability.

"Once throw conventions aside," he began, "once do the things that people don't do——" and the fact that you are going to meet a young man is no longer proof of anything, except, indeed, that people will talk.

Cassandra saw, not without a pang of jealousy, that he was extremely solicitous that people should not talk about Katharine, as if his interest in her were still proprietary rather than friendly. As they were both ignorant of Ralph's visit the night before they had not that reason to comfort themselves with the thought that matters were hastening to a crisis. These absences of Katharine's, moreover, left them exposed to interruptions which almost destroyed their pleasure in being alone together.. The rainy evening made it impossible to go out; and, indeed, according to William's code, it was considerably more damning to be seen out of doors than surprised within. They were so much at the mercy of bells and doors that they could hardly talk of Macaulay with any conviction, and William preferred to defer the second act of his tragedy until another day.

Under these circumstances Cassandra showed herself at her best. She sympathized with William's anxieties and did her utmost to share them; but still, to be alone together, to be running risks together, to be partners in the wonderful conspiracy, was to her so enthralling that she was always forgetting discretion, breaking out into exclamations and admirations which finally made William believe that, although deplorable and upsetting, the situation was not without its sweetness.

When the door did open, he started, but braved the forthcoming revelation. It was not Mrs. Milvain, however, but Katharine herself who entered, closely followed by Ralph Denham. With a set expression which showed what an effort she was making, Katharine encountered their eyes, and saying, "We're not going to interrupt you," she led Denham behind the curtain which hung in front of the room with the relics. This refuge was none of her willing, but confronted with wet pavements and only some belated museum or Tube station for shelter, she was forced, for Ralph's sake, to face the discomforts of her own house. Under the street lamps she had thought him looking both tired and strained.

Thus separated, the two couples remained occupied for some time with their own affairs. Only the lowest murmurs penetrated from one section of the room to the other. At length the maid came in to bring a message that Mr. Hilbery would not be home for dinner. It was true that there was no need that Katharine should be informed, but William began to inquire Cassandra's opinion in such a way as to show that, with or without reason, he wished very much to speak to her.

From motives of her own Cassandra dissuaded him.

"But don't you think it's a little unsociable?" he hazarded. "Why not do something amusing?—go to the play, for instance? Why not ask Katharine and Ralph, eh?" The coupling of their names in this manner caused Cassandra's heart to leap with pleasure.

"Don't you think they must be——?" she began, but William hastily took her up.

"Oh, I know nothing about that. I only thought we might amuse ourselves, as your uncle's out."

He proceeded on his embassy with a mixture of excitement and embarrassment which caused him to turn aside with his hand on the curtain, and to examine intently for several moments the portrait of a lady, optimistically said by Mrs. Hilbery to be an early work of Sir Joshua Reynolds. Then, with some unnecessary fumbling, he drew aside the curtain, and with his eyes fixed upon the ground, repeated his message and suggested that they should all spend the evening at the play. Katharine accepted the suggestion with such cordiality that it was strange to find her of no clear mind as to the precise spectacle she wished to see. She left the choice entirely to Ralph and William, who, taking counsel fraternally over an evening paper, found themselves in agreement as to the merits of a music-hall. This being arranged, everything else followed easily and enthusiastically. Cassandra had never been to a music-hall. Katharine instructed her in the peculiar delights of an entertainment where Polar bears follow directly upon ladies in full evening dress, and the stage is alternately a garden of mystery, a milliner's band-box, and a fried-fish shop in the Mile End Road. Whatever the exact nature of the program that night, it fulfilled the highest purposes of dramatic art, so far, at least, as four of the audience were concerned.

No doubt the actors and the authors would have been surprised to learn in what shape their efforts reached those particular eyes and ears; but they could not have denied that the effect as a whole was tremendous. The hall resounded with brass and strings, alternately of enormous pomp and majesty, and then of sweetest lamentation. The reds and creams of the background, the lyres and harps and urns and skulls, the protuberances of plaster, the fringes of scarlet plush, the sinking and blazing of innumerable electric lights, could scarcely have been surpassed for decorative effect by any craftsman of the ancient or modern world.

Then there was the audience itself, bare-shouldered, tufted and garlanded in the stalls, decorous but festal in the balconies, and frankly fit for daylight and street life in the galleries. But, however they differed when looked at separately, they shared the same huge, lovable nature in the bulk, which murmured and swayed and quivered all the time the dancing and juggling and love-making went on in front of it, slowly laughed and reluctantly left off laughing, and applauded with a helter-skelter generosity which sometimes became unanimous and overwhelming. Once

William saw Katharine leaning forward and clapping her
hands with an abandonment that startled him. Her laugh
rang out with the laughter of the audience.

For a second he was puzzled, as if this laughter disclosed something that he had never suspected in her. But
then Cassandra's face caught his eye, gazing with aston-
ishment at the buffoon, not laughing, too deeply intent and
surprised to laugh at what she saw, and for some moments
he watched her as if she were a child.

The performance came to an end, the illusion dying out
first here and then there, as some rose to put on their
coats, others stood upright to salute "God Save the King,"
the musicians folded their music and encased their instruments, and the lights sank one by one until the house was
empty, silent, and full of great shadows. Looking back over
her shoulder as she followed Ralph through the swing
doors, Cassandra marveled to see how the stage was already entirely without romance. But, she wondered, did
they really cover all the seats in brown holland every
night?

The success of this entertainment was such that before
they separated another expedition had been planned for
the next day. The next day was Saturday; therefore both
William and Ralph were free to devote the whole afternoon to an expedition to Greenwich, which Cassandra had
never seen, and Katharine confused with Dulwich. On
this occasion Ralph was their guide. He brought them
without accident to Greenwich.

What exigencies of state or fantasies of imagination
first gave birth to the cluster of pleasant places by which
London is surrounded is matter of indifference now that
they have adapted themselves so admirably to the needs
of people between the ages of twenty and thirty with
Saturday afternoons to spend. Indeed, if ghosts have any
interest in the affections of those who succeed them they
must reap their richest harvests when the fine weather
comes again and the lovers, the sightseers, and the holiday-

makers pour themselves out of trains and omnibuses into their old pleasure-grounds. It is true that they go, for the most part, unthanked by name, although upon this occasion William was ready to give such discriminating praise as the dead architects and painters received seldom in the course of the year. They were walking by the river bank, and Katharine and Ralph, lagging a little behind, caught fragments of his lecture. Katharine smiled at the sound of his voice; she listened as if she found it a little unfamiliar, intimately though she knew it; she tested it. The note of assurance and happiness was new. William was very happy. She learnt every hour what sources of his happiness she had neglected. She had never asked him to teach her anything; she had never consented to read Macaulay; she had never expressed her belief that his play was second only to the works of Shakespeare. She followed dreamily in their wake, smiling and delighting in the sound which conveyed, she knew, the rapturous and yet not servile assent of Cassandra.

Then she murmured, "How can Cassandra—" but changed her sentence to the opposite of what she meant to say and ended, "how could she herself have been so blind?" But it was unnecessary to follow out such riddles when the presence of Ralph supplied her with more interesting problems, which somehow became involved with the little boat crossing the river, the majestic and careworn City, and the steamers homecoming with their treasury, or starting in search of it, so that infinite leisure would be necessary for the proper disentanglement of one from the other. He stopped, moreover, and began inquiring of an old boatman as to the tides and the ships. In thus talking he seemed different, and even looked different, she thought, against the river, with the steeples and towers for background. His strangeness, his romance, his power to leave her side and take part in the affairs of men, the possibility that they should together hire a boat and cross the river, the speed and wildness of this enterprise filled her mind and inspired her with such rapture, half of love and half of adventure, that William and Cassandra were startled from their talk, and Cassandra exclaimed, "She looks as if she were offering up a sacrifice! Very beautiful," she added quickly, though she repressed, in deference to William, her own wonder that the sight of Ralph Denham talking to a boatman on the banks of the Thames could move any one to such an attitude of adoration.

That afternoon, what with tea and the curiosities of the Thames tunnel and the unfamiliarity of the streets, passed so quickly that the only method of prolonging it was to plan another expedition for the following day. Hampton Court was decided upon, in preference to Hampstead, for though Cassandra had dreamt as a child of the brigands of Hampstead, she had now transferred her affections completely and for ever to William III. Accordingly, they arrived at Hampton Court about lunch-time on a fine Sunday morning. Such unity marked their expressions of admiration for the red-brick building that they might have come there for no other purpose than to assure each other that this palace was the stateliest palace in the world. They walked up and down the Terrace, four abreast, and fancied themselves the owners of the place, and calculated the amount of good to the world produced indubitably by such a tenancy.

"The only hope for us," said Katharine, "is that William shall die, and Cassandra shall be given rooms as the widow of a distinguished poet."

"Or——" Cassandra began, but checked herself from the liberty of envisaging Katharine as the widow of a distinguished lawyer. Upon this, the third day of junketing, it was tiresome to have to restrain oneself even from such innocent excursions of fancy. She dared not question William; he was inscrutable; he never seemed even to follow the other couple with curiosity when they separated, as they frequently did, to name a plant, or examine a fresco. Cassandra was constantly studying their backs. She noticed how sometimes the impulse to move came from Kath-arine, and sometimes from Ralph; how, sometimes, they walked slow, as if in profound intercourse, and sometimes fast, as if in passionate. When they came together again nothing could be more unconcerned than their manner.

"We have been wondering whether they ever catch a fish . . ." or, "We must leave time to visit the Maze." Then, to puzzle her further, William and Ralph filled in all interstices of meal-times or railway journeys with per-fectly good-tempered arguments; or they discussed politics, or they told stories, or they did sums together upon the backs of old envelopes to prove something. She suspected that Katharine was absent-minded, but it was impossible to tell. There were moments when she felt so young and inexperienced that she almost wished herself back with the silkworms at Stogdon House, and not embarked upon this bewildering intrigue.

These moments, however, were only the necessary shadow or chill which proved the substance of her bliss, and did not damage the radiance which seemed to rest equally upon the whole party. The fresh air of spring, the sky washed of clouds and already shedding warmth from its blue, seemed the reply vouchsafed by nature to the mood of her chosen spirits. These chosen spirits were to be found also among the deer, dumbly basking, and among the fish, set still in mid-stream, for they were mute sharers in a benignant state not needing any exposition by the tongue. No words that Cassandra could come by ex-pressed the stillness, the brightness, the air of expectancy which lay upon the orderly beauty of the grass walks and gravel paths down which they went walking four abreast that Sunday afternoon. Silently the shadows of the trees lay across the broad sunshine; silence wrapt her heart in its folds. The quivering stillness of the butterfly on the half-opened flower, the silent grazing of the deer in the sun, were the sights her eye rested upon and received as the images of her own nature laid open to happiness and trembling in its ecstasy.

But the afternoon wore on, and it became time to leave the gardens. As they drove from Waterloo to Chelsea, Katharine began to have some compunction about her father, which, together with the opening of offices and the need of working in them on Monday, made it difficult to plan another festival for the following day. Mr. Hilbery had taken their absence, so far, with paternal benevolence, but they could not trespass upon it indefinitely. Indeed, had they known it, he was already suffering from their absence, and longing for their return.

He had no dislike of solitude, and Sunday, in particular, was pleasantly adapted for letter-writing, paying calls, or a visit to his club. He was leaving the house on some such suitable expedition towards tea-time when he found himself stopped on his own doorstep by his sister, Mrs. Milvain. She should, on hearing that no one was at home, have withdrawn submissively, but instead she accepted his half-hearted invitation to come in, and he found himself in the melancholy position of being forced to order tea for her and sit in the drawing-room while she drank it. She speedily made it plain that she was only thus exacting because she had come on a matter of business. He was by no means exhilarated at the news.

"Katharine is out this afternoon," he remarked. "Why not come round later and discuss it with her—with us both, eh?"

"My dear Trevor, I have particular reasons for wishing to talk to you alone. . . . Where is Katharine?"

"She's out with her young man, naturally. Cassandra plays the part of chaperone very usefully. A charming young woman that—a great favorite of mine." He turned his stone between his fingers, and conceived different methods of leading Celia away from her obsession, which, he supposed, must have reference to the domestic affairs of Cyril as usual.

"With Cassandra," Mrs. Milvain repeated significantly.
"With Cassandra."

"Yes, with Cassandra," Mr. Hilbery agreed urbanely,
pleased at the diversion. "I think they said they were
going to Hampton Court, and I rather believe they were
taking a protégé of mine, Ralph Denham, a very clever
fellow, too, to amuse Cassandra. I thought the arrangement very suitable." He was prepared to dwell at some
length upon this safe topic, and trusted that Katharine
would come in before he had done with it.

"Hampton Court always seems to me an ideal spot for
engaged couples. There's the Maze, there's a nice place
for having tea—I forget what they call it—and then,
if the young man knows his business he contrives to take
his lady upon the river. Full of possibilities—full. Cake,
Celia?" Mr. Hilbery continued. "I respect my dinner too
much, but that can't possibly apply to you. You've never
observed that feast, so far as I can remember."

Her brother's affability did not deceive Mrs. Milvain;
it slightly saddened her; she well knew the cause of it.
Blind and infatuated as usual!

"Who is this Mr. Denham?" she asked.

"Ralph Denham?" said Mr. Hilbery, in relief that her
mind had taken this turn. "A very interesting young man.
I've a great belief in him. He's an authority upon our
mediæval institutions, and if he weren't forced to earn
his living he would write a book that very much wants
writing."

"He is not well off, then?" Mrs. Milvain interposed.

"Hasn't a penny, I'm afraid, and a family more or less
dependent on him."

"A mother and sisters?—His father is dead?"

"Yes, his father died some years ago," said Mr. Hilbery, who was prepared to draw upon his imagination,
if necessary, to keep Mrs. Milvain supplied with facts about
the private history of Ralph Denham since, for some inscrutable reason, the subject took her fancy.

"His father has been dead some time, and this young man had to take his place——"

"A legal family?" Mrs. Milvain inquired. "I fancy I've seen the name somewhere."

Mr. Hilbery shook his head. "I should be inclined to doubt whether they were altogether in that walk of life," he observed. "I fancy that Denham once told me that his father was a corn merchant. Perhaps he said a stock-broker. He came to grief, anyhow, as stockbrokers have a way of doing. I've a great respect for Denham," he added. The remark sounded to his ears unfortunately conclusive, and he was afraid that there was nothing more to be said about Denham. He examined the tips of his fingers carefully. "Cassandra's grown into a very charming young woman," he started afresh. "Charming to look at, and charming to talk to, though her historical knowledge is not altogether profound. Another cup of tea?"

Mrs. Milvain had given her cup a little push, which seemed to indicate some momentary displeasure. But she did not want any more tea.

"It is Cassandra that I have come about," she began. "I am very sorry to say that Cassandra is not at all what you think her, Trevor. She has imposed upon your and Maggie's goodness. She has behaved in a way that would have seemed incredible—in this house of all houses—were it not for other circumstances that are still more incredible."

Mr. Hilbery looked taken aback, and was silent for a second.

"It all sounds very black," he remarked urbanely, continuing his examination of his finger-nails. "But I own I am completely in the dark."

Mrs. Milvain became rigid, and emitted her message in little short sentences of extreme intensity.

"Who has Cassandra gone out with? William Rodney. Who has Katharine gone out with? Ralph Denham. Why are they for ever meeting each other round street corners, and going to music-halls, and taking cabs late at night?

Why will Katharine not tell me the truth when I question her? I understand the reason now. Katharine has entangled herself with this unknown lawyer; she has seen fit to condone Cassandra's conduct."

There was another slight pause.

"Ah, well, Katharine will no doubt have some explanation to give me," Mr. Hilbery replied imperturbably. "It's a little too complicated for me to take in all at once, I confess—and, if you won't think me rude, Celia, I think I'll be getting along towards Knightsbridge."

Mrs. Milvain rose at once.

"She has condoned Cassandra's conduct and entangled herself with Ralph Denham," she repeated. She stood very erect with the dauntless air of one testifying to the truth regardless of consequences. She knew from past discussions that the only way to counter her brother's indolence and indifference was to shoot her statements at him in a compressed form once finally upon leaving the room. Having spoken thus, she restrained herself from adding another word, and left the house with the dignity of one inspired by a great ideal.

She had certainly framed her remarks in such a way as to prevent her brother from paying his call in the region of Knightsbridge. He had no fears for Katharine, but there was a suspicion at the back of his mind that Cassandra might have been, innocently and ignorantly, led into some foolish situation in one of their unshepherded dissipations. His wife was an erratic judge of the conventions; he himself was lazy; and with Katharine absorbed, very naturally— Here he recalled, as well as he could, the exact nature of the charge. "She has condoned Cassandra's conduct and entangled herself with Ralph Denham." From which it appeared that Katharine was *not* absorbed, or which of them was it that had entangled herself with Ralph Denham? From this maze of absurdity Mr. Hilbery saw no way out until Katharine herself came to his help, so that he applied himself, very philosophically on the whole, to a book.

No sooner had he heard the young people come in and go upstairs than he sent a maid to tell Miss Katharine that he wished to speak to her in the study. She was slipping furs loosely onto the floor in the drawing-room in front of the fire. They were all gathered round, reluctant to part. The message from her father surprised Katharine, and the others caught from her look, as she turned to go, a vague sense of apprehension.

Mr. Hilbery was reassured by the sight of her. He congratulated himself, he prided himself, upon possessing a daughter who had a sense of responsibility and an understanding of life profound beyond her years. Moreover, she was looking to-day unusual; he had come to take her beauty for granted; now he remembered it and was surprised by it. He thought instinctively that he had interrupted some happy hour of hers with Rodney, and apologized.

"I'm sorry to bother you, my dear. I heard you come in, and thought I'd better make myself disagreeable at once— as it seems, unfortunately, that fathers are expected to make themselves disagreeable. Now, your Aunt Celia has been to see me; your Aunt Celia has taken it into her head apparently that you and Cassandra have been—let us say a little foolish. This going about together—these pleasant little parties—there's been some kind of misunderstanding. I told her I saw no harm in it, but I should just like to hear from yourself. Has Cassandra been left a little too much in the company of Mr. Denham?"

Katharine did not reply at once, and Mr. Hilbery tapped the coal encouragingly with the poker. Then she said, without embarrassment or apology:

"I don't see why I should answer Aunt Celia's questions. I've told her already that I won't."

Mr. Hilbery was relieved and secretly amused at the

thought of the interview, although he could not license such irreverence outwardly.

"Very good. Then you authorize me to tell her that she's been mistaken, and there was nothing but a little fun in it? You've no doubt, Katharine, in your own mind? Cassandra is in our charge, and I don't intend that people should gossip about her. I suggest that you should be a little more careful in future. Invite me to your next entertainment."

She did not respond, as he had hoped, with any affectionate or humorous reply. She meditated, pondering something or other, and he reflected that even his Katharine did not differ from other women in the capacity to let things be. Or had she something to say?

"Have you a guilty conscience?" he inquired lightly. "Tell me, Katharine," he said more seriously, struck by something in the expression of her eyes.

"I've been meaning to tell you for some time," she said. "I'm not going to marry William."

"You're not going—!" he exclaimed, dropping the poker in his immense surprise. "Why? When? Explain yourself, Katharine."

"Oh, some time ago—a week, perhaps more." Katharine spoke hurriedly and indifferently, as if the matter could no longer concern any one.

"But may I ask—why have I not been told of this—what do you mean by it?"

"We don't wish to be married—that's all."

"This is William's wish as well as yours?"

"Oh, yes. We agree perfectly."

Mr. Hilbery had seldom felt more completely at a loss. He thought that Katharine was treating the matter with curious unconcern; she scarcely seemed aware of the gravity of what she was saying; he did not understand the position at all. But his desire to smooth everything over comfortably came to his relief. No doubt there was some quarrel, some whimsey on the part of William, who, though a good fellow, was a little exacting sometimes—something that a woman could put right. But though he inclined to take the easiest view of his responsibilities, he cared too much for this daughter to let things be.

"I confess I find great difficulty in following you. I should like to hear William's side of the story," he said irritably. "I think he ought to have spoken to me in the first instance."

"I wouldn't let him," said Katharine. "I know it must seem to you very strange," she added. "But I assure you, if you'd wait a little—until mother comes back."

This appeal for delay was much to Mr. Hilbery's liking. But his conscience would not suffer it. People were talking. He could not endure that his daughter's conduct should be in any way considered irregular. He wondered whether, in the circumstances, it would be better to wire to his wife, to send for one of his sisters, to forbid William the house, to pack Cassandra off home—for he was vaguely conscious of responsibilities in her direction, too. His forehead was becoming more and more wrinkled by the multiplicity of his anxieties, which he was sorely tempted to ask Katharine to solve for him, when the door opened and William Rodney appeared. This necessitated a complete change, not only of manner, but of position also.

"Here's William," Katharine exclaimed, in a tone of relief. "I've told father we're not engaged," she said to him. "I've explained that I prevented you from telling him."

William's manner was marked by the utmost formality. He bowed very slightly in the direction of Mr. Hilbery, and stood erect, holding one lapel of his coat, and gazing into the center of the fire. He waited for Mr. Hilbery to speak.

Mr. Hilbery also assumed an appearance of formidable dignity. He had risen to his feet, and now bent the top part of his body slightly forward.

"I should like your account of this affair, Rodney—if Katharine no longer prevents you from speaking."

William waited two seconds at least.

"Our engagement is at an end," he said, with the utmost stiffness.

"Has this been arrived at by your joint desire?"

After a perceptible pause William bent his head, and Katharine said, as if by an afterthought:

"Oh, yes."

Mr. Hilbery swayed to and fro, and moved his lips as if to utter remarks which remained unspoken.

"I can only suggest that you should postpone any decision until the effect of this misunderstanding has had time to wear off. You have now known each other——" he began.

"There's been no misunderstanding," Katharine interposed. "Nothing at all." She moved a few paces across the room, as if she intended to leave them. Her preoccupied naturalness was in strange contrast to her father's pomposity and to William's military rigidity. He had not once raised his eyes. Katharine's glance, on the other hand, ranged past the two gentlemen, along the books, over the tables, towards the door. She was paying the least possible attention, it seemed, to what was happening. Her father looked at her with a sudden clouding and troubling of his expression. Somehow his faith in her stability and sense was queerly shaken. He no longer felt that he could ultimately entrust her with the whole conduct of her own affairs after a superficial show of directing them. He felt, for the first time in many years, responsible for her.

"Look here, we must get to the bottom of this," he said, dropping his formal manner and addressing Rodney as if Katharine were not present. "You've had some difference of opinion, eh? Take my word for it, most people go through this sort of thing when they're engaged. I've seen more trouble come from long engagements than from any other form of human folly. Take my advice and put the whole matter out of your minds—both of you. I prescribe a complete abstinence from emotion. Visit some cheerful seaside resort, Rodney."

He was struck by William's appearance, which seemed to
him to indicate profound feeling resolutely held in check.
No doubt, he reflected, Katharine had been very trying, unconsciously trying, and had driven him to take up a position
which was none of his willing. Mr. Hilbery certainly did
not overrate William's sufferings. No minutes in his life
had hitherto extorted from him such intensity of anguish.
He was now facing the consequences of his insanity. He
must confess himself entirely and fundamentally other than
Mr. Hilbery thought him. Everything was against him.
Even the Sunday evening and the fire and the tranquil
library scene were against him. Mr. Hilbery's appeal to
him as a man of the world was terribly against him. He
was no longer a man of any world that Mr. Hilbery cared
to recognize. But some power compelled him, as it had compelled him to come downstairs, to make his stand here and
now, alone and unhelped by any one, without prospect of
reward. He fumbled with various phrases; and then jerked
out:

"I love Cassandra."

Mr. Hilbery's face turned a curious dull purple. He
looked at his daughter. He nodded his head, as if to convey his silent command to her to leave the room; but either
she did not notice it or preferred not to obey.

"You have the impudence——" Mr. Hilbery began, in a
dull, low voice that he himself had never heard before, when
there was a scuffling and exclaiming in the hall, and Cassandra, who appeared to be insisting against some dissuasion
on the part of another, burst into the room.

"Uncle Trevor," she exclaimed, "I insist upon telling you
the truth!" She flung herself between Rodney and her
uncle, as if she sought to intercept their blows. As her
uncle stood perfectly still, looking very large and imposing,
and as nobody spoke, she shrank back a little, and looked
first at Katharine and then at Rodney. "You must know the
truth," she said, a little lamely.

"You have the impudence to tell me this in Katharine's

presence?" Mr. Hilbery continued, speaking with complete disregard of Cassandra's interruption.

"I am aware, quite aware——" Rodney's words, which were broken in sense, spoken after a pause, and with his eyes upon the ground, nevertheless expressed an astonishing amount of resolution. "I am quite aware what you must think of me," he brought out, looking Mr. Hilbery directly in the eyes for the first time.

"I could express my views on the subject more fully if we were alone," Mr. Hilbery returned.

"But you forget me," said Katharine. She moved a little towards Rodney, and her movement seemed to testify mutely to her respect for him, and her alliance with him. "I think William has behaved perfectly rightly, and, after all, it is I who am concerned—I and Cassandra."

Cassandra, too, gave an indescribably slight movement which seemed to draw the three of them into alliance together. Katharine's tone and glance made Mr. Hilbery once more feel completely at a loss, and in addition, painfully and angrily obsolete; but in spite of an awful inner hollowness he was outwardly composed.

"Cassandra and Rodney have a perfect right to settle their own affairs according to their own wishes; but I see no reason why they should do so either in my room or in my house. . . . I wish to be quite clear on this point, however; you are no longer engaged to Rodney."

He paused, and his pause seemed to signify that he was extremely thankful for his daughter's deliverance.

Cassandra turned to Katharine, who drew her breath as if to speak and checked herself; Rodney, too, seemed to await some movement on her part; her father glanced at her as if he half anticipated some further revelation. She remained perfectly silent. In the silence they heard distinctly steps descending the staircase, and Katharine went straight to the door.

"Wait," Mr. Hilbery commanded. "I wish to speak to you—alone," he added.

She paused, holding the door ajar.

"I'll come back," she said, and as she spoke she opened the door and went out. They could hear her immediately speak to some out outside, though the words were inaudible.

Mr. Hilbery was left confronting the guilty couple, who remained standing as if they did not accept their dismissal, and the disappearance of Katharine had brought some change into the situation. So, in his secret heart, Mr. Hilbery felt that it had, for he could not explain his daughter's behavior to his own satisfaction.

"Uncle Trevor," Cassandra exclaimed impulsively, "don't be angry, please. I couldn't help it; I do beg you to forgive me."

Her uncle still refused to acknowledge her identity, and still talked over her head as if she did not exist.

"I suppose you have communicated with the Otways," he said to Rodney grimly.

"Uncle Trevor, we wanted to tell you," Cassandra replied for him. "We waited——" she looked appealingly at Rodney, who shook his head ever so slightly.

"Yes? What were you waiting for?" her uncle asked sharply, looking at her at last.

The words died on her lips. It was apparent that she was straining her ears as if to catch some sound outside the room that would come to her help. He received no answer. He listened, too.

"This is a most unpleasant business for all parties," he concluded, sinking into his chair again, hunching his shoulders and regarding the flames. He seemed to speak to himself, and Rodney and Cassandra looked at him in silence.

"Why don't you sit down?" he said suddenly. He spoke gruffly, but the force of his anger was evidently spent, or some preoccupation had turned his mood to other regions. While Cassandra accepted his invitation, Rodney remained standing.

"I think Cassandra can explain matters better in my ab-

sence," he said, and left the room, Mr. Hilbery giving his
assent by a slight nod of the head.

Meanwhile, in the dining-room next door, Denham and
Katharine were once more seated at the mahogany table.
They seemed to be continuing a conversation broken off in
the middle, as if each remembered the precise point at which
they had been interrupted, and was eager to go on as quickly.
as possible. Katharine, having interposed a short account
of the interview with her father, Denham made no comment,
but said:

"Anyhow, there's no reason why we shouldn't see each
other."

"Or stay together. It's only marriage that's out of the
question," Katharine replied.

"But if I find myself coming to want you more and
more?"

"If our lapses come more and more often?"

He sighed impatiently, and said nothing for a moment.

"But at least," he renewed, "we've established the fact
that my lapses are still in some odd way connected with you;
yours have nothing to do with me. Katharine," he added,
his assumption of reason broken up by his agitation, "I assure you that we are in love—what other people call love.
Remember that night. We had no doubts whatever then.
We were absolutely happy for half an hour. You had no
lapse until the day after; I had no lapse until yesterday
morning. We've been happy at intervals all day until I—
went off my head, and you, quite naturally, were bored."

"Ah," she exclaimed, as if the subject chafed her, "I can't
make you understand. It's not boredom—I'm never bored.
Reality—reality," she ejaculated, tapping her finger upon
the table as if to emphasize and perhaps explain her isolated
utterance of this word. "I cease to be real to you. It's the
faces in a storm again—the vision in a hurricane. We come
together for a moment and we part. It's my fault, too. I'm
as bad as you are—worse, perhaps."

They were trying to explain, not for the first time, as

their weary gestures and frequent interruptions showed, what in their common language they had christened their "lapses"; a constant source of distress to them, in the past few days, and the immediate reason why Ralph was on his way to leave the house when Katharine, listening anxiously, heard him and prevented him. What was the cause of these lapses? Either because Katharine looked more beautiful, or more strange, because she wore something different, or said something unexpected, Ralph's sense of her romance welled up and overcame him either into silence or into inarticulate expressions, which Katharine, with unintentional but invariable perversity, interrupted or contradicted with some severity or assertion of prosaic fact. Then the vision disappeared, and Ralph expressed vehemently in his turn the conviction that he only loved her shadow and cared nothing for her reality. If the lapse was on her side it took the form of gradual detachment until she became completely absorbed in her own thoughts, which carried her away with such intensity that she sharply resented any recall to her companion's side. It was useless to assert that these trances were always originated by Ralph himself, however little in their later stages they had to do with him. The fact remained that she had no need of him and was very loath to be reminded of him. How, then, could they be in love? The fragmentary nature of their relationship was but too apparent.

Thus they sat depressed to silence at the dining-room table, oblivious of everything, while Rodney paced the drawing-room overhead in such agitation and exaltation of mind as he had never conceived possible, and Cassandra remained alone with her uncle. Ralph, at length, rose and walked gloomily to the window. He pressed close to the pane. Outside were truth and freedom and the immensity only to be apprehended by the mind in loneliness, and never communicated to another. What worse sacrilege was there than to attempt to violate what he perceived by seeking to impart it? Some movement behind him made him reflect that Katharine had the power, if she chose, to be in person what he dreamed of her spirit. He turned sharply to implore her help, when again he was struck cold by her look of distance, her expression of intentness upon some far object. As if conscious of his look upon her she rose and came to him, standing close by his side, and looking with him out into the dusky atmosphere. Their physical closeness was to him a bitter enough comment upon the distance between their minds. Yet distant as she was, her presence by his side transformed the world. He saw himself performing wonderful deeds of courage; saving the drowning, rescuing the forlorn. Impatient with this form of egotism, he could not shake off the conviction that somehow life was wonderful, romantic, a master worth serving so long as she stood there. He had no wish that she should speak; he did not look at her or touch her; she was apparently deep in her own thoughts and oblivious of his presence.

The door opened without their hearing the sound. Mr. Hilbery looked round the room, and for a moment failed to discover the two figures in the window. He started with displeasure when he saw them, and observed them keenly before he appeared able to make up his mind to say anything. He made a movement finally that warned them of his presence; they turned instantly. Without speaking, he beckoned to Katharine to come to him, and, keeping his eyes from the region of the room where Denham stood, he shepherded her in front of him back to the study. When Katharine was inside the room he shut the study door carefully behind him as if to secure himself from something that he disliked.

"Now, Katharine," he said, taking up his stand in front of the fire, "you will, perhaps, have the kindness to explain——" She remained silent. "What inferences do you expect me to draw?" he said sharply. . . . "You tell me that you are not engaged to Rodney; I see you on what appear to be extremely intimate terms with another—with Ralph Denham. What am I to conclude? Are you," he added, as she still said nothing, "engaged to Ralph Denham?"

"No," she replied.

His sense of relief was great; he had been certain that her answer would have confirmed his suspicions, but that anxiety being set at rest, he was the more conscious of annoyance with her for her behavior.

"Then all I can say is that you've very strange ideas of the proper way to behave. . . . People have drawn certain conclusions, nor am I surprised. . . . The more I think of it the more inexplicable I find it," he went on, his anger rising as he spoke. "Why am I left in ignorance of what is going on in my own house? Why am I left to hear of these events for the first time from my sister? Most disagreeable—most upsetting. How I'm to explain to your Uncle Francis—but I wash my hands of it. Cassandra goes tomorrow. I forbid Rodney the house. As for the other young man, the sooner he makes himself scarce the better. After placing the most implicit trust in you, Katharine——" He broke off, disquieted by the ominous silence with which his words were received, and looked at his daughter with the curious doubt as to her state of mind which he had felt before, for the first time, this evening. He perceived once more that she was not attending to what he said, but was listening, and for a moment he, too, listened for sounds outside the room. His certainty that there was some understanding between Denham and Katharine returned, but with a most unpleasant suspicion that there was something illicit about it, as the whole position between the young people seemed to him gravely illicit.

"I'll speak to Denham," he said, on the impulse of his suspicion, moving as if to go.

"I shall come with you," Katharine said instantly, starting forward.

"You will stay here," said her father.

"What are you going to say to him?" she asked.

"I suppose I may say what I like in my own house?" he returned.

"Then I go, too," she replied.

At these words, which seemed to imply a determination to go—to go for ever, Mr. Hilbery returned to his position in front of the fire, and began swaying slightly from side to side without for the moment making any remark.

"I understood you to say that you were not engaged to him," he said at length, fixing his eyes upon his daughter.

"We are not engaged," she said.

"It should be a matter of indifference to you, then, whether he comes here or not—I will not have you listening to other things when I am speaking to you!" he broke off angrily, perceiving a slight movement on her part to one side. "Answer me frankly, what is your relationship with this young man?"

"Nothing that I can explain to a third person," she said obstinately.

"I will have no more of these equivocations," he replied.

"I refuse to explain," she returned, and as she said it the front door banged to. "There!" she exclaimed. "He is gone!" She flashed such a look of fiery indignation at her father that he lost his self-control for a moment.

"For God's sake, Katharine, control yourself!" he cried.

She looked for a moment like a wild animal caged in a civilized dwelling-place. She glanced over the walls covered with books, as if for a second she had forgotten the position of the door. Then she made as if to go, but her father laid his hand upon her shoulder. He compelled her to sit down.

"These emotions have been very upsetting, naturally," he said. His manner had regained all its suavity, and he spoke with a soothing assumption of paternal authority. "You've been placed in a very difficult position, as I understand from Cassandra. Now let us come to terms; we will leave these agitating questions in peace for the present. Meanwhile, let us try to behave like civilized beings. Let us

read Sir Walter Scott. What d'you say to 'The Antiquary,'
eh? Or 'The Bride of Lammermoor'?"

He made his own choice, and before his daughter could
protest or make her escape, she found herself being turned
by the agency of Sir Walter Scott into a civilized human
being.

Yet Mr. Hilbery had grave doubts, as he read, whether
the process was more than skin-deep. Civilization had been
very profoundly and unpleasantly overthrown that evening;
the extent of the ruin was still undetermined; he had lost
his temper, a physical disaster not to be matched for the
space of ten years or so; and his own condition urgently
required soothing and renovating at the hands of the
classics. His house was in a state of revolution; he had a
vision of unpleasant encounters on the staircase; his meals
would be poisoned for days to come; was literature itself a
specific against such disagreeables? A note of hollowness
was in his voice as he read.

CHAPTER XXXIII

CONSIDERING that Mr. Hilbery lived in a house which was accurately numbered in order with its fellows, and that he filled up forms, paid rent, and had seven more years of tenancy to run, he had an excuse for laying down laws for the conduct of those who lived in his house, and this excuse, though profoundly inadequate, he found useful during the interregnum of civilization with which he now found himself faced. In obedience to those laws, Rodney disappeared; Cassandra was dispatched to catch the eleven-thirty on Monday morning; Denham was seen no more; so that only Katharine, the lawful occupant of the upper rooms, remained, and Mr. Hilbery thought himself competent to see that she did nothing further to compromise herself. As he bade her good morning next day he was aware that he knew nothing of what she was thinking, but, as he reflected with some bitterness, even this was an advance upon the ignorance of the previous mornings. He went to his study, wrote, tore up, and wrote again a letter to his wife, asking her to come back on account of domestic difficulties which he specified at first, but in a later draft more discreetly left unspecified. Even if she started the very moment that she got it, he reflected, she would not be home till Tuesday night, and he counted lugubriously the number of hours that he would have to spend in a position of detestable authority alone with his daughter.

What was she doing now, he wondered, as he addressed the envelope to his wife. He could not control the telephone. He could not play the spy. She might be making any arrangements she chose. Yet the thought did not disturb him so much as the strange, unpleasant, illicit atmosphere of the

478

whole scene with the young people the night before. His sense of discomfort was almost physical.

Had he known it, Katharine was far enough withdrawn, both physically and spiritually, from the telephone. She sat in her room with the dictionaries spreading their wide leaves on the table before her, and all the pages which they had concealed for so many years arranged in a pile. She worked with the steady concentration that is produced by the successful effort to think down some unwelcome thought by means of another thought. Having absorbed the unwelcome thought, her mind went on with additional vigor, derived from the victory; on a sheet of paper lines of figures and symbols frequently and firmly written down marked the different stages of its progress. And yet it was broad daylight; there were sounds of knocking and sweeping, which proved that living people were at work on the other side of the door, and the door, which could be thrown open in a second, was her only protection against the world. But she had somehow risen to be mistress in her own kingdom, assuming her sovereignty unconsciously.

Steps approached her unheard. It is true that they were steps that lingered, divagated, and mounted with the deliberation natural to one past sixty whose arms, moreover, are full of leaves and blossoms; but they came on steadily, and soon a tap of laurel boughs against the door arrested Katharine's pencil as it touched the page. She did not move, however, and sat blank-eyed as if waiting for the interruption to cease. Instead, the door opened. At first, she attached no meaning to the moving mass of green which seemed to enter the room independently of any human agency. Then she recognized parts of her mother's face and person behind the yellow flowers and soft velvet of the palm-buds.

"From Shakespeare's tomb!" exclaimed Mrs. Hilbery, dropping the entire mass upon the floor, with a gesture that seemed to indicate an act of dedication. Then she flung her arms wide and embraced her daughter.

"Thank God, Katharine!" she exclaimed. "Thank God!" she repeated.

"You've come back?" said Katharine, very vaguely, standing up to receive the embrace.

Although she recognized her mother's presence, she was very far from taking part in the scene, and yet felt it to be amazingly appropriate that her mother should be there, thanking God emphatically for unknown blessings, and strewing the floor with flowers and leaves from Shakespeare's tomb.

"Nothing else matters in the world!" Mrs. Hilbery continued. "Names aren't everything; it's what we feel that's everything. I didn't want silly, kind, interfering letters. I didn't want your father to tell me. I knew it from the first. I prayed that it might be so."

"You knew it?" Katharine repeated her mother's words softly and vaguely, looking past her. "How did you know it?" She began, like a child, to finger a tassel hanging from her mother's cloak.

"The first evening you told me, Katharine. Oh, and thousands of times—dinner-parties—talking about books— the way he came into the room—your voice when you spoke of him."

Katharine seemed to consider each of these proofs separately. Then she said gravely:

"I'm not going to marry William. And then there's Cassandra——"

"Yes, there's Cassandra," said Mrs. Hilbery. "I own I was a little grudging at first, but, after all, she plays the piano so beautifully. Do tell me, Katharine," she asked impulsively, "where did you go that evening she played Mozart, and you thought I was asleep?"

Katharine recollected with difficulty.

"To Mary Datchet's," she remembered.

"Ah!" said Mrs. Hilbery, with a slight note of disappointment in her voice. "I had my little romance—my little speculation." She looked at her daughter. Katharine faltered beneath that innocent and penetrating gaze; she flushed, turned away, and then looked up with very bright eyes.

"I'm not in love with Ralph Denham," she said.

"Don't marry unless you're in love!" said Mrs. Hilbery very quickly. "But," she added, glancing momentarily at her daughter, "aren't there different ways, Katharine— different——?"

"We want to meet as often as we like, but to be free," Katharine continued.

"To meet here, to meet in his house, to meet in the street." Mrs. Hilbery ran over these phrases as if she were trying chords that did not quite satisfy her ear. It was plain that she had her sources of information, and, indeed, her bag was stuffed with what she called "kind letters" from the pen of her sister-in-law.

"Yes. Or to stay away in the country," Katharine concluded.

Mrs. Hilbery paused, looked unhappy, and sought inspiration from the window.

"What a comfort he was in that shop—how he took me and found the ruins at once—how *safe* I felt with him——"

"Safe? Oh, no, he's fearfully rash—he's always taking risks. He wants to throw up his profession and live in a little cottage and write books, though he hasn't a penny of his own, and there are any number of sisters and brothers dependent on him."

"Ah, he has a mother?" Mrs. Hilbery inquired.

"Yes. Rather a fine-looking old lady, with white hair." Katharine began to describe her visit, and soon Mrs. Hilbery elicited the facts that not only was the house of excruciating ugliness, which Ralph bore without complaint, but that it was evident that every one depended on him, and he had a room at the top of the house, with a wonderful view over London, and a rook.

"A wretched old bird in a corner, with half its feathers out," she said, with a tenderness in her voice that seemed to commiserate the sufferings of humanity while resting assured in the capacity of Ralph Denham to alleviate them, so that Mrs. Hilbery could not help exclaiming:

"But, Katharine, you *are* in love!" at which Katharine flushed, looked startled, as if she had said something that she ought not to have said, and shook her head.

Hastily Mrs. Hilbery asked for further details of this extraordinary house, and interposed a few speculations about the meeting between Keats and Coleridge in a lane, which tided over the discomfort of the moment, and drew Katharine on to further descriptions and indiscretions. In truth, she found an extraordinary pleasure in being thus free to talk to some one who was equally wise and equally benignant, the mother of her earliest childhood, whose silence seemed to answer questions that were never asked. Mrs. Hilbery listened without making any remark for a considerable time. She seemed to draw her conclusions rather by looking at her daughter than by listening to her, and, if cross-examined, she would probably have given a highly inaccurate version of Ralph Denham's life-history except that he was penniless, fatherless, and lived at Highgate—all of which was much in his favor. But by means of these furtive glances she had assured herself that Katharine was in a state which gave her, alternately, the most exquisite pleasure and the most profound alarm.

She could not help ejaculating at last:

"It's all done in five minutes at a Registry Office nowadays, if you think the Church service a little florid—which it is, though there are noble things in it."

"But we don't want to be married," Katharine replied emphatically, and added, "Why, after all, isn't it perfectly possible to live together without being married?"

Again Mrs. Hilbery looked discomposed, and, in her trouble, took up the sheets which were lying upon the table, and began turning them over this way and that, and muttering to herself as she glanced:

"A plus B minus C equals $x\ y\ z$. It's so dreadfully ugly, Katharine. That's what I feel—so dreadfully ugly."

Katharine took the sheets from her mother's hand and began shuffling them absent-mindedly together, for her fixed gaze seemed to show that her thoughts were intent upon some other matter.

"Well, I don't know about ugliness," she said at length.

"But he doesn't ask it of you?" Mrs. Hilbery exclaimed. "Not that grave young man with the steady brown eyes?"

"He doesn't ask anything—we neither of us ask anything."

"If I could help you, Katharine, by the memory of what I felt——"

"Yes, tell me what you felt."

Mrs. Hilbery, her eyes growing blank, peered down the enormously long corridor of days at the far end of which the little figures of herself and her husband appeared fantastically attired, clasping hands upon a moonlit beach, with roses swinging in the dusk.

"We were in a little boat going out to a ship at night," she began. "The sun had set and the moon was rising over our heads. There were lovely silver lights upon the waves and three green lights upon the steamer in the middle of the bay. Your father's head looked so grand against the mast. It was life, it was death. The great sea was round us. It was the voyage for ever and ever."

The ancient fairy-tale fell roundly and harmoniously upon Katharine's ears. Yes, there was the enormous space of the sea; there were the three green lights upon the steamer; the cloaked figures climbed up on deck. And so, voyaging over the green and purple waters, past the cliffs and the sandy lagoons and through pools crowded with the masts of ships and the steeples of churches—here they were. The river seemed to have brought them and deposited them here at this precise point. She looked admiringly at her mother, that ancient voyager.

"Who knows," exclaimed Mrs. Hilbery, continuing her

reveries, "where we are bound for, or why, or who has sent us, or what we shall find—who knows anything, except that love is our faith—love——" she crooned, and the soft sound beating through the dim words was heard by her daughter as the breaking of waves solemnly in order upon the vast shore that she gazed upon. She would have been content for her mother to repeat that word almost indefinitely—a soothing word when uttered by another, a riveting together of the shattered fragments of the world. But Mrs. Hilbery, instead of repeating the word love, said pleadingly:

"And you won't think those ugly thoughts again, will you, Katharine?" at which words the ship which Katharine had been considering seemed to put into harbor and have done with its seafaring. Yet she was in great need, if not exactly of sympathy, of some form of advice, or, at least, of the opportunity of setting forth her problems before a third person so as to renew them in her own eyes.

"But then," she said, ignoring the difficult problem of ugliness, "you knew you were in love; but we're different. It seems," she continued, frowning a little as she tried to fix the difficult feeling, "as if something came to an end suddenly—gave out—faded—an illusion—as if when we think we're in love we make it up—we imagine what doesn't exist. That's why it's impossible that we should ever marry. Always to be finding the other an illusion, and going off and forgetting about them, never to be certain that you cared, or that he wasn't caring for some one not you at all, the horror of changing from one state to the other, being happy one moment and miserable the next—that's the reason why we can't possibly marry. At the same time," she continued, "we can't live without each other, because——" Mrs. Hilbery waited patiently for the sentence to be completed, but Katharine fell silent and fingered her sheet of figures.

"We have to have faith in our vision," Mrs. Hilbery resumed, glancing at the figures, which distressed her vaguely, and had some connection in her mind with the household accounts, "otherwise, as you say——" She cast a lightning

glance into the depths of disillusionment which were, perhaps, not altogether unknown to her.

"Believe me, Katharine, it's the same for every one—for
me, too—for your father," she said earnestly, and sighed.
They looked together into the abyss and, as the elder of the
two, she recovered herself first and asked:

"But where is Ralph? Why isn't he here to see me?"

Katharine's expression changed instantly.

"Because he's not allowed to come here," she replied
bitterly.

Mrs. Hilbery brushed this aside.

"Would there be time to send for him before luncheon?"
she asked.

Katharine looked at her as if, indeed, she were some
magician. Once more she felt that instead of being a grown
woman, used to advise and command, she was only a foot
or two raised above the long grass and the little flowers and
entirely dependent upon the figure of indefinite size whose
head went up into the sky, whose hand was in hers, for
guidance.

"I'm not happy without him," she said simply.

Mrs. Hilbery nodded her head in a manner which indicated complete understanding, and the immediate conception
of certain plans for the future. She swept up her flowers,
breathed in their sweetness, and, humming a little song
about a miller's daughter, left the room.

The case upon which Ralph Denham was engaged that
afternoon was not apparently receiving his full attention,
and yet the affairs of the late John Leake of Dublin were
sufficiently confused to need all the care that a solicitor
could bestow upon them, if the widow Leake and the five
Leake children of tender age were to receive any pittance
at all. But the appeal to Ralph's humanity had little chance
of being heard to-day; he was no longer a model of concentration. The partition so carefully erected between the different sections of his life had been broken down, with the

result that though his eyes were fixed upon the last Will and Testament, he saw through the page a certain drawing-room in Cheyne Walk.

He tried every device that had proved effective in the past for keeping up the partitions of the mind, until he could decently go home; but a little to his alarm he found himself assailed so persistently, as if from outside, by Katharine, that he launched forth desperately into an imaginary interview with her. She obliterated a bookcase full of law reports, and the corners and lines of the room underwent a curious softening of outline like that which sometimes makes a room unfamiliar at the moment of waking from sleep. By degrees, a pulse or stress began to beat at regular intervals in his mind, heaping his thoughts into waves to which words fitted themselves, and without much consciousness of what he was doing, he began to write on a sheet of draft paper what had the appearance of a poem lacking several words in each line. Not many lines had been set down, however, before he threw away his pen as violently as if that were responsible for his misdeeds, and tore the paper into many separate pieces. This was a sign that Katharine had asserted herself and put to him a remark that could not be met poetically. Her remark was entirely destructive of poetry, since it was to the effect that poetry had nothing whatever to do with her; all her friends spent their lives in making up phrases, she said; all his feeling was an illusion, and next moment, as if to taunt him with his impotence, she had sunk into one of those dreamy states which took no account whatever of his existence. Ralph was roused by his passionate attempts to attract her attention to the fact that he was standing in the middle of his little private room in Lincoln's Inn Fields at a considerable distance from Chelsea. The physical distance increased his desperation. He began pacing in circles until the process sickened him, and then took a sheet of paper for the composition of a letter which, he vowed before he began it, should be sent that same evening.

It was a difficult matter to put into words; poetry would
have done it better justice, but he must abstain from poetry.
In an infinite number of half-obliterated scratches he tried
to convey to her the possibility that although human beings
are woefully ill-adapted for communication, still, such communion is the best we know; moreover, they make it possible
for each to have access to another world independent of
personal affairs, a world of law, of philosophy, or more
strangely a world such as he had had a glimpse of the other
evening when together they seemed to be sharing something,
creating something, an ideal—a vision flung out in advance
of our actual circumstances. If this golden rim were
quenched, if life were no longer circled by an illusion (but
was it an illusion after all?), then it would be too dismal
an affair to carry to an end; so he wrote with a sudden spurt
of conviction which made clear way for a space and left at
least one sentence standing whole. Making every allowance
for other desires, on the whole this conclusion appeared to
him to justify their relationship. But the conclusion was
mystical; it plunged him into thought. The difficulty with
which even this amount was written, the inadequacy of the
words, and the need of writing under them and over them
others which, after all, did no better, led him to leave off
before he was at all satisfied with his production, and unable
to resist the conviction that such rambling would never be
fit for Katharine's eye. He felt himself more cut off from
her than ever. In idleness, and because he could do nothing
further with words, he began to draw little figures in the
blank spaces, heads meant to resemble her head, blots fringed
with flames meant to represent—perhaps the entire universe.
From this occupation he was roused by the message that a
lady wished to speak to him. He had scarcely time to run
his hands through his hair in order to look as much like a
solicitor as possible, and to cram his papers into his pocket,
already overcome with shame that another eye should behold them, when he realized that his preparations were needless. The lady was Mrs. Hilbery.

"I hope you're not disposing of somebody's fortune in a hurry," she remarked, gazing at the documents on his table, "or cutting off an entail at one blow, because I want to ask you to do me a favor. And Anderson won't keep his horse waiting. (Anderson is a perfect tyrant, but he drove my dear father to the Abbey the day they buried him.) I made bold to come to you, Mr. Denham, not exactly in search of legal assistance (though I don't know who I'd rather come to, if I were in trouble), but in order to ask your help in settling some tiresome little domestic affairs that have arisen in my absence. I've been to Stratford-on-Avon (I must tell you all about that one of these days), and there I got a letter from my sister-in-law, a dear kind goose who likes interfering with other people's children because she's got none of her own. (We're dreadfully afraid that she's going to lose the sight of one of her eyes, and I always feel that our physical ailments are so apt to turn into mental ailments. I think Matthew Arnold says something of the same kind about Lord Byron.) But that's neither here nor there."

The effect of these parentheses, whether they were introduced for that purpose or represented a natural instinct on Mrs. Hilbery's part to embellish the bareness of her discourse, gave Ralph time to perceive that she possessed all the facts of their situation and was come, somehow, in the capacity of ambassador.

"I didn't come here to talk about Lord Byron," Mrs. Hilbery continued, with a little laugh, "though I know that both you and Katharine, unlike other young people of your generation, still find him worth reading." She paused. "I'm so glad you've made Katharine read poetry, Mr. Denham!" she exclaimed, "and feel poetry, and look poetry! She can't talk it yet, but she will—oh, she will!"

Ralph, whose hand was grasped and whose tongue almost refused to articulate, somehow contrived to say that there were moments when he felt hopeless, utterly hopeless, though he gave no reason for this statement on his part.

"But you care for her?" Mrs. Hilbery inquired.

"Good God!" he exclaimed, with a vehemence which admitted of no question.

"It's the Church of England service you both object to?" Mrs. Hilbery inquired innocently.

"I don't care a damn what service it is," Ralph replied.

"You would marry her in Westminster Abbey if the worst came to the worst?" Mrs. Hilbery inquired.

"I would marry her in St. Paul's Cathedral," Ralph replied. His doubts upon this point, which were always roused by Katharine's presence, had vanished completely, and his strongest wish in the world was to be with her immediately, since every second he was away from her he imagined her slipping farther and farther from him into one of those states of mind in which he was unrepresented. He wished to dominate her, to possess her.

"Thank God!" exclaimed Mrs. Hilbery. She thanked Him for a variety of blessings: for the conviction with which the young man spoke; and not least for the prospect that on her daughter's wedding-day the noble cadences, the stately periods, the ancient eloquence of the marriage service would resound over the heads of a distinguished congregation gathered together near the very spot where her father lay quiescent with the other poets of England. The tears filled her eyes; but she remembered simultaneously that her carriage was waiting, and with dim eyes she walked to the door. Denham followed her downstairs.

It was a strange drive. For Denham it was without exception the most unpleasant he had ever taken. His only wish was to go as straightly and quickly as possible to Cheyne Walk; but it soon appeared that Mrs. Hilbery either ignored or thought fit to baffle this desire by interposing various errands of her own. She stopped the carriage at post-offices, and coffee-shops, and shops of inscrutable dignity where the aged attendants had to be greeted as old friends; and, catching sight of the dome of St. Paul's above the irregular spires of Ludgate Hill, she pulled the cord impulsively, and gave directions that Anderson should drive them there. But Anderson had reasons of his own for discouraging afternoon worship, and kept his horse's nose obstinately towards the west. After some minutes, Mrs. Hilbery realized the situation, and accepted it good-humoredly, apologizing to Ralph for his disappointment.

"Never mind," she said, "we'll go to St. Paul's another day, and it may turn out, though I can't promise that it *will*, that he'll take us past Westminster Abbey, which would be even better."

Ralph was scarcely aware of what she went on to say. Her mind and body both seemed to have floated into another region of quick-sailing clouds rapidly passing across each other and enveloping everything in a vaporous indistinctness. Meanwhile he remained conscious of his own concentrated desire, his impotence to bring about anything he wished, and his increasing agony of impatience.

Suddenly Mrs. Hilbery pulled the cord with such decision that even Anderson had to listen to the order which she leant out of the window to give him. The carriage pulled up abruptly in the middle of Whitehall before a large building dedicated to one of our Government offices. In a second Mrs. Hilbery was mounting the steps, and Ralph was left in too acute an irritation by this further delay even to speculate what errand took her now to the Board of Education. He was about to jump from the carriage and take a cab, when Mrs. Hilbery reappeared talking genially to a figure who remained hidden behind her.

"There's plenty of room for us all," she was saying. "Plenty of room. We could find space for *four* of you, William," she added, opening the door, and Ralph found that Rodney had now joined their company. The two men glanced at each other. If distress, shame, discomfort in its most acute form were ever visible upon a human face, Ralph could read them all expressed beyond the eloquence of words upon the face of his unfortunate companion. But Mrs. Hilbery was either completely unseeing or determined to appear so. She went on talking; she talked, it seemed to both the

young men, to some one outside, up in the air. She talked
about Shakespeare, she apostrophized the human race, she
proclaimed the virtues of divine poetry, she began to recite
verses which broke down in the middle. The great advantage of her discourse was that it was self-supporting. It
nourished itself until Cheyne Walk was reached upon half a
dozen grunts and murmurs.

"Now," she said, alighting briskly at her door, "here we
are!"

There was something airy and ironical in her voice and
expression as she turned upon the doorstep and looked at
them, which filled both Rodney and Denham with the same
misgivings at having trusted their fortunes to such an ambassador; and Rodney actually hesitated upon the threshold
and murmured to Denham:

"You go in, Denham. I . . ." He was turning tail,
but the door opening and the familiar look of the house
asserting its charm, he bolted in on the wake of the others,
and the door shut upon his escape. Mrs. Hilbery led the
way upstairs. She took them to the drawing-room. The
fire burnt as usual, the little tables were laid with china and
silver. There was nobody there.

"Ah," she said, "Katharine's not here. She must be upstairs in her room. You have something to say to her, I
know, Mr. Denham. You can find your way?" she vaguely
indicated the ceiling with a gesture of her hand. She had
become suddenly serious and composed, mistress in her own
house. The gesture with which she dismissed him had a
dignity that Ralph never forgot. She seemed to make him
free with a wave of her hand to all that she possessed. He
left the room.

The Hilberys' house was tall, possessing many stories and
passages with closed doors, all, once he had passed the
drawing-room floor, unknown to Ralph. He mounted as
high as he could and knocked at the first door he came to.

"May I come in?" he asked.

A voice from within answered "Yes."

He was conscious of a large window, full of light, of a bare table, and of a long looking-glass. Katharine had risen, and was standing with some white papers in her hand, which slowly fluttered to the ground as she saw her visitor. The explanation was a short one. The sounds were inarticulate; no one could have understood the meaning save themselves. As if the forces of the world were all at work to tear them asunder they sat, clasping hands, near enough to be taken even by the malicious eye of Time himself for a united couple, an indivisible unit.

"Don't move, don't go," she begged of him, when he stooped to gather the papers she had let fall. But he took them in his hands and, giving her by a sudden impulse his own unfinished dissertation, with its mystical conclusion, they read each other's compositions in silence.

Katharine read his sheets to an end; Ralph followed her figures as far as his mathematics would let him. They came to the end of their tasks at about the same moment, and sat for a time in silence.

"Those were the papers you left on the seat at Kew," said Ralph at length. "You folded them so quickly that I couldn't see what they were."

She blushed very deeply; but as she did not move or attempt to hide her face she had the appearance of some one disarmed of all defences, or Ralph likened her to a wild bird just settling with wings trembling to fold themselves within reach of his hand. The moment of exposure had been exquisitely painful—the light shed startlingly vivid. She had now to get used to the fact that some one shared her loneliness. The bewilderment was half shame and half the prelude to profound rejoicing. Nor was she unconscious that on the surface the whole thing must appear of the utmost absurdity. She looked to see whether Ralph smiled, but found his gaze fixed on her with such gravity that she turned to the belief that she had committed no sacrilege but enriched herself, perhaps immeasurably, perhaps eternally. She hardly dared steep herself in the infinite bliss. But his glance seemed to ask for some assurance upon another point of vital interest to him. It beseeched her mutely to tell him whether what she had read upon his confused sheet had any meaning or truth to her. She bent her head once more to the papers she held.

"I like your little dot with the flames round it," she said meditatively.

Ralph nearly tore the page from her hand in shame and despair when he saw her actually contemplating the idiotic symbol of his most confused and emotional moments. He was convinced that it could mean nothing to another, although somehow to him it conveyed not only Katharine herself but all those states of mind which had clustered round her since he first saw her pouring out tea on a Sunday afternoon. It represented by its circumference of smudges surrounding a central blot all that encircling glow which for him surrounded, inexplicably, so many of the objects of life, softening their sharp outline, so that he could see certain streets, books, and situations wearing a halo almost perceptible to the physical eye. Did she smile? Did she put the paper down wearily, condemning it not only for its inadequacy but for its falsity? Was she going to protest once more that he only loved the vision of her? But it did not occur to her that this diagram had anything to do with her. She said simply, and in the same tone of reflection:

"Yes, the world looks something like that to me too."

He received her assurance with profound joy. Quietly and steadily there rose up behind the whole aspect of life that soft edge of fire which gave its red tint to the atmosphere and crowded the scene with shadows so deep and dark that one could fancy pushing farther into their density and still farther, exploring indefinitely. Whether there was any correspondence between the two prospects now opening before them they shared the same sense of the impending future, vast, mysterious, infinitely stored with undeveloped shapes which each would unwrap for the other to behold;

but for the present the prospect of the future was enough to fill them with silent adoration. At any rate, their further attempts to communicate articulately were interrupted by a knock on the door, and the entrance of a maid who, with a due sense of mystery, announced that a lady wished to see Miss Hilbery, but refused to allow her name to be given.

When Katharine rose, with a profound sigh, to resume her duties, Ralph went with her, and neither of them formulated any guess, on their way downstairs, as to who this anonymous lady might prove to be. Perhaps the fantastic notion that she was a little black hunchback provided with a steel knife, which she would plunge into Katharine's heart, appeared to Ralph more probable than another, and he pushed first into the dining-room to avert the blow. Then he exclaimed "Cassandra!" with such heartiness at the sight of Cassandra Otway standing by the dining-room table that she put her finger to her lips and begged him to be quiet.

"Nobody must know I'm here," she explained in a sepulchral whisper. "I missed my train. I have been wandering about London all day. I can bear it no longer. Katharine, what am I to do?"

Katharine pushed forward a chair; Ralph hastily found wine and poured it out for her. If not actually fainting, she was very near it.

"William's upstairs," said Ralph, as soon as she appeared to be recovered. "I'll go and ask him to come down to you." His own happiness had given him a confidence that every one else was bound to be happy too. But Cassandra had her uncle's commands and anger too vividly in her mind to dare any such defiance. She became agitated and said that she must leave the house at once. She was not in a condition to go, had they known where to send her. Katharine's common sense, which had been in abeyance for the past week or two, still failed her, and she could only ask, "But where's your luggage?" in the vague belief that to take lodgings depended entirely upon a sufficiency of luggage. Cassandra's reply, "I've lost my luggage," in no way helped her to a conclusion.

"You've lost your luggage," she repeated. Her eyes rested upon Ralph, with an expression which seemed better fitted to accompany a profound thanksgiving for his existence or some vow of eternal devotion than a question about luggage. Cassandra perceived the look, and saw that it was returned; her eyes filled with tears. She faltered in what she was saying. She began bravely again to discuss the question of lodging when Katharine, who seemed to have communicated silently with Ralph, and obtained his permission, took her ruby ring from her finger and giving it to Cassandra, said: "I believe it will fit you without any alteration."

These words would not have been enough to convince Cassandra of what she very much wished to believe had not Ralph taken the bare hand in his and demanded:

"Why don't you tell us you're glad?" Cassandra was so glad that the tears ran down her cheeks. The certainty of Katharine's engagement not only relieved her of a thousand vague fears and self-reproaches, but entirely quenched that spirit of criticism which had lately impaired her belief in Katharine. Her old faith came back to her. She seemed to behold her with that curious intensity which she had lost; as a being who walks just beyond our sphere, so that life in their presence is a heightened process, illuminating not only ourselves but a considerable stretch of the surrounding world. Next moment she contrasted her own lot with theirs and gave back the ring.

"I won't take that unless William gives it me himself," she said. "Keep it for me, Katharine."

"I assure you everything's perfectly all right," said Ralph. "Let me tell William——"

He was about, in spite of Cassandra's protest, to reach the door, when Mrs. Hilbery, either warned by the parlormaid or conscious with her usual prescience of the need for her intervention, opened the door and smilingly surveyed them.

"My dear Cassandra!" she exclaimed. "How delightful to see you back again! What a coincidence!" she observed, in a general way. "William is upstairs. The kettle boils over. Where's Katharine, I say? I go to look, and I find Cassandra!" She seemed to have proved something to her own satisfaction, although nobody felt certain what thing precisely it was.

"I find Cassandra," she repeated.

"She missed her train," Katharine interposed, seeing that Cassandra was unable to speak.

"Life," began Mrs. Hilbery, drawing inspiration from the portraits on the wall apparently, "consists in missing trains and in finding——" But she pulled herself up and remarked that the kettle must have boiled completely over everything.

To Katharine's agitated mind it appeared that this kettle was an enormous kettle, capable of deluging the house in its incessant showers of steam, the enraged representative of all those household duties which she had neglected. She ran hastily up to the drawing-room, and the rest followed her, for Mrs. Hilbery put her arm round Cassandra and drew her upstairs. They found Rodney observing the kettle with uneasiness but with such absence of mind that Katharine's catastrophe was in a fair way to be fulfilled. In putting the matter straight no greetings were exchanged, but Rodney and Cassandra chose seats as far apart as possible, and sat down with an air of people making a very temporary lodgment. Either Mrs. Hilbery was impervious to their discomfort, or chose to ignore it, or thought it high time that the subject was changed, for she did nothing but talk about Shakespeare's tomb.

"So much earth and so much water and that sublime spirit brooding over it all," she mused, and went on to sing her strange, half-earthly song of dawns and sunsets, of great poets, and the unchanged spirit of noble loving which they had taught, so that nothing changes, and one age is linked with another, and no one dies, and we all meet in spirit, until she appeared oblivious of any one in the room. But suddenly her remarks seemed to contract the enormously wide circle in which they were soaring and to alight, airily and temporarily, upon matters of more immediate moment.

"Katharine and Ralph," she said, as if to try the sound. "William and Cassandra."

"I feel myself in an entirely false position," said William desperately, thrusting himself into this breach in her reflections. "I've no right to be sitting here. Mr. Hilbery told me yesterday to leave the house. I'd no intention of coming back again. I shall now——"

"I feel the same too," Cassandra interrupted. "After what Uncle Trevor said to me last night——"

"I have put you into a most odious position," Rodney went on, rising from his seat, in which movement he was imitated simultaneously by Cassandra. "Until I have your father's consent I have no right to speak to you—let alone in this house, where my conduct"—he looked at Katharine, stammered, and fell silent—"where my conduct has been reprehensible and inexcusable in the extreme," he forced himself to continue. "I have explained everything to your mother. She is so generous as to try and make me believe that I have done no harm—you have convinced her that my behavior, selfish and weak as it was—selfish and weak—" he repeated, like a speaker who has lost his notes.

Two emotions seemed to be struggling in Katharine; one the desire to laugh at the ridiculous spectacle of William making her a formal speech across the tea-table, the other a desire to weep at the sight of something childlike and honest in him which touched her inexpressibly. To every one's surprise she rose, stretched out her hand, and said:

"You've nothing to reproach yourself with—you've been always——" but here her voice died away, and the tears forced themselves into her eyes, and ran down her cheeks, while William, equally moved, seized her hand and pressed it to his lips. No one perceived that the drawing-room door had opened itself sufficiently to admit at least half the person of Mr. Hilbery, or saw him gaze at the scene round the tea-table with an expression of the utmost disgust and expostulation. He withdrew unseen. He paused outside on the landing trying to recover his self-control and to decide what course he might with most dignity pursue. It was obvious to him that his wife had entirely confused the meaning of his instructions. She had plunged them all into the most odious confusion. He waited a moment, and then, with much preliminary rattling of the handle, opened the door a second time. They had all regained their places; some incident of an absurd nature had now set them laughing and looking under the table, so that his entrance passed momentarily unperceived. Katharine, with flushed cheeks, raised her head and said:

"Well, that's my last attempt at the dramatic."

"It's astonishing what a distance they roll," said Ralph, stooping to turn up the corner of the hearthrug.

"Don't trouble—don't bother. We shall find it——" Mrs. Hilbery began, and then saw her husband and exclaimed: "Oh, Trevor, we're looking for Cassandra's engagement-ring!"

Mr. Hilbery looked instinctively at the carpet. Remarkably enough, the ring had rolled to the very point where he stood. He saw the rubies touching the tip of his boot. Such is the force of habit that he could not refrain from stooping, with an absurd little thrill of pleasure at being the one to find what others were looking for, and, picking the ring up, he presented it, with a bow that was courtly in the extreme, to Cassandra. Whether the making of a bow released automatically feelings of complaisance and urbanity, Mr. Hilbery found his resentment completely washed away during the second in which he bent and straightened himself. Cassandra dared to offer her cheek and received his embrace. He nodded with some degree of stiffness to Rodney and Denham, who had both risen upon seeing him, and now altogether sat down. Mrs. Hilbery seemed to have been waiting for the entrance of her husband, and for this precise moment in order to put to him a question which, from the ardor with which she announced it, had evidently been pressing for utterance for some time past.

"Oh, Trevor, please tell me, what was the date of the first performance of *Hamlet?*"

In order to answer her Mr. Hilbery had to have recourse to the exact scholarship of William Rodney, and before he had given his excellent authorities for believing as he believed, Rodney felt himself admitted once more to the society of the civilized and sanctioned by the authority of no less a person than Shakespeare himself. The power of literature, which had temporarily deserted Mr. Hilbery, now came back to him, pouring over the raw ugliness of human affairs its soothing balm, and providing a form into which such passions as he had felt so painfully the night before could be molded so that they fell roundly from the tongue in shapely phrases, hurting nobody. He was sufficiently sure of his command of language at length to look at Katharine and again at Denham. All this talk about Shakespeare had acted as a soporific, or rather as an incantation upon Katharine. She leaned back in her chair at the head of the tea-table, perfectly silent, looking vaguely past them all, receiving the most generalized ideas of human heads against pictures, against yellow-tinted walls, against curtains of deep crimson velvet. Denham, to whom he turned next, shared her immobility under his gaze. But beneath his restraint and calm it was possible to detect a resolution, a will, set now with unalterable tenacity, which made such turns of speech as Mr. Hilbery had at command appear oddly irrelevant. At any rate, he said nothing. He respected the young man; he was a very able young man; he was likely to get his own way. He could, he thought, looking at his still and very dignified head, understand Katharine's preference, and, as he thought this, he was surprised by a pang of acute jealousy. She might have married Rodney without causing him a twinge. This man she loved. Or what was the state of affairs between them? An extraordinary confusion of emotion was beginning to get the better of him, when Mrs. Hilbery, who had been conscious of a sudden pause in the conversation, and had looked wistfully at her daughter once or twice, remarked:

"Don't stay if you want to go, Katharine. There's the little room over there. Perhaps you and Ralph——"

"We're engaged," said Katharine, waking with a start, and looking straight at her father. He was taken aback by the directness of the statement; he exclaimed as if an unexpected blow had struck him. Had he loved her to see her swept away by this torrent, to have her taken from him by this uncontrollable force, to stand by helpless, ignored? Oh, how he loved her! How he loved her! He nodded very curtly to Denham.

"I gathered something of the kind last night," he said. "I hope you'll deserve her." But he never looked at his daughter, and strode out of the room, leaving in the minds of the women a sense, half of awe, half of amusement, at the extravagant, inconsiderate, uncivilized male, outraged somehow and gone bellowing to his lair with a roar which still sometimes reverberates in the most polished of drawing-rooms. Then Katharine, looking at the shut door, looked down again, to hide her tears.

CHAPTER XXXIV

THE lamps were lit; their luster reflected itself in the polished wood; good wine was passed round the dinner-table; before the meal was far advanced civilization had triumphed, and Mr. Hilbery presided over a feast which came to wear more and more surely an aspect, cheerful, dignified, promising well for the future. To judge from the expression in Katharine's eyes it promised something —but he checked the approach sentimentality. He poured out wine; he bade Denham help himself.

They went upstairs and he saw Katharine and Denham abstract themselves directly Cassandra had asked whether she might not play him something—some Mozart? some Beethoven? She sat down to the piano; the door closed softly behind them. His eyes rested on the closed door for some seconds unwaveringly, but, by degrees, the look of expectation died out of them, and, with a sigh, he listened to the music.

Katharine and Ralph were agreed with scarcely a word of discussion as to what they wished to do, and in a moment she joined him in the hall dressed for walking. The night was still and moonlit, fit for walking, though any night would have seemed so to them, desiring more than anything movement, freedom from scrutiny, silence, and the open air.

"At last!" she breathed, as the front door shut. She told him how she had waited, fidgeted, thought he was never coming, listened for the sound of doors, half expected to see him again under the lamp-post, looking at the house. They turned and looked at the serene front with its gold-rimmed windows, to him the shrine of so much adoration. In spite of her laugh and the little pressure of mockery on his arm, he would not resign his belief, but with her hand resting there, her voice quickened and mysteriously moving in his ears, he had not time—they had not the same inclination—other objects drew his attention.

How they came to find themselves walking down a street with many lamps, corners radiant with light, and a steady succession of motor-omnibuses plying both ways along it, they could neither of them tell; nor account for the impulse which led them suddenly to select one of these wayfarers and mount to the very front seat. After curving through streets of comparative darkness, so narrow that shadows on the blinds were pressed within a few feet of their faces, they came to one of those great knots of activity where the lights, having drawn close together, thin out again and take their separate ways. They were borne on until they saw the spires of the city churches pale and flat against the sky.

"Are you cold?" he asked, as they stopped by Temple Bar.

"Yes, I am rather," she replied, becoming conscious that the splendid race of lights drawn past her eyes by the superb curving and swerving of the monster on which she sat was at an end. They had followed some such course in their thoughts too; they had been borne on, victors in the forefront of some triumphal car, spectators of a pageant enacted for them, masters of life. But standing on the pavement alone, this exaltation left them; they were glad to be alone together. Ralph stood still for a moment to light his pipe beneath a lamp.

She looked at his face isolated in the little circle of light. "Oh, that cottage," she said. "We must take it and go there."

"And leave all this?" he inquired.

"As you like," she replied. She thought, looking at the sky above Chancery Lane, how the roof was the same everywhere; how she was now secure of all that this lofty blue and its steadfast lights meant to her; reality, was it, figures, love, truth?

"I've something on my mind," said Ralph abruptly. "I mean I've been thinking of Mary Datchet. We're very near her rooms now. Would you mind if we went there?"

She had turned before she answered him. She had no wish to see any one to-night; it seemed to her that the immense riddle was answered; the problem had been solved; she held in her hands for one brief moment the globe which we spend our lives in trying to shape, round, whole, and entire from the confusion of chaos. To see Mary was to risk the destruction of this globe.

"Did you treat her badly?" she asked rather mechanically, walking on.

"I could defend myself," he said, almost defiantly. "But what's the use, if one feels a thing? I won't be with her a minute," he said. "I'll just tell her——"

"Of course, you must tell her," said Katharine, and now felt anxious for him to do what appeared to be necessary if he, too, were to hold his globe for a moment round, whole, and entire.

"I wish—I wish——" she sighed, for melancholy came over her and obscured at least a section of her clear vision. The globe swam before her as if obscured by tears.

"I regret nothing," said Ralph firmly. She leant towards him almost as if she could thus see what he saw. She thought how obscure he still was to her, save only that more and more constantly he appeared to her a fire burning through its smoke, a source of life.

"Go on," she said. "You regret nothing——"

"Nothing—nothing," he repeated.

"What a fire!" she thought to herself. She thought of him blazing splendidly in the night, yet so obscure that to hold his arm, as she held it, was only to touch the opaque substance surrounding the flame that roared upwards.

"Why nothing?" she asked hurriedly, in order that he might say more and so make more splendid, more red, more darkly intertwined with smoke this flame rushing upwards.

"What are you thinking of, Katharine?" he asked suspiciously, noticing her tone of dreaminess and the inapt words.

"I was thinking of you—yes, I swear it. Always of you, but you take such strange shapes in my mind. You've destroyed my loneliness. Am I to tell you how I see you? No, tell me—tell me from the beginning."

Beginning with spasmodic words, he went on to speak more and more fluently, more and more passionately, feeling her leaning towards him, listening with wonder like a child, with gratitude like a woman. She interrupted him gravely now and then.

"But it was foolish to stand outside and look at the windows. Suppose William hadn't seen you. Would you have gone to bed?"

He capped her reproof with wonderment that a woman of her age could have stood in Kingsway looking at the traffic until she forgot.

"But it was then I first knew I loved you!" she exclaimed.

"Tell me from the beginning," he begged her.

"No, I'm a person who can't tell things," she pleaded. "I shall say something ridiculous—something about flames —fires. No, I can't tell you."

But he persuaded her into a broken statement, beautiful to him, charged with extreme excitement as she spoke of the dark red fire, and the smoke twined round it, making him feel that he had stepped over the threshold into the faintly lit vastness of another mind, stirring with shapes, so large, so dim, unveiling themselves only in flashes, and moving away again into the darkness, engulfed by it. They had walked by this time to the street in which Mary lived, and being engrossed by what they said and partly saw, passed her staircase without looking up. At this time of night there was no traffic and scarcely any foot-passengers, so that they could place slowly without interruption, arm-in-arm, raising their hands now and then to draw something upon the vast blue curtain of the sky.

They brought themselves by these means, acting on a mood of profound happiness, to a state of clear-sightedness where the lifting of a finger had effect, and one word spoke more than a sentence. They lapsed gently into silence, traveling the dark paths of thought side by side towards something discerned in the distance which gradually possessed them both. They were victors, masters of life, but at the same time absorbed in the flame, giving their life to increase its brightness, to testify to their faith. Thus they had walked, perhaps, twice or three times up and down Mary Datchet's street before the recurrence of a light burning behind a thin, yellow blind caused them to stop without exactly knowing why they did so. It burned itself into their minds.

"That is the light in Mary's room," said Ralph. "She must be at home." He pointed across the street. Katharine's eyes rested there too.

"Is she alone, working at this time of night? What is she working at?" she wondered. "Why should we interrupt her?" she asked passionately. "What have we got to give her? She's happy too," she added. "She has her work." Her voice shook slightly, and the light swam like an ocean of gold behind her tears.

"You don't want me to go to her?" Ralph asked.

"Go, if you like; tell her what you like," she replied.

He crossed the road immediately, and went up the steps into Mary's house. Katharine stood where he left her, looking at the window and expecting soon to see a shadow move across it; but she saw nothing; the blinds conveyed nothing; the light was not moved. It signaled to her across the dark street; it was a sign of triumph shining there for ever, not to be extinguished this side of the grave. She brandished her happiness as if in salute; she dipped it as if in reverence. "How they burn!" she thought, and all the darkness of London seemed set with fires, roaring upwards; but her eyes came back to Mary's window and rested there satis-

fied.   She had waited some time before a figure detached itself from the doorway and came across the road, slowly and
reluctantly, to where she stood.

"I didn't go in—I couldn't bring myself," he broke off.
He had stood outside Mary's door unable to bring himself
to knock; if she had come out she would have found him
there, the tears running down his cheeks, unable to speak.

They stood for some moments, looking at the illuminated
blinds, an expression to them both of something impersonal
and serene in the spirit af the woman within, working out
her plans far into the night—her plans for the good of a
world that none of them were ever to know.   Then their
minds jumped on and other little figures came by in procession, headed, in Ralph's view, by the figure of Sally Seal.

"Do you remember Sally Seal?" he asked.   Katharine
bent her head.

"Your mother and Mary?" he went on.   "Rodney and
Cassandra?   Old Joan up at Highgate?" He stopped in his
enumeration, not finding it possible to link them together in
any way that should explain the queer combination which
he could perceive in them, as he thought of them.   They
appeared to him to be more than individuals; to be made up
of many different things in cohesion; he had a vision of an
orderly world.

"It's all so easy—it's all so simple," Katherine quoted,
remembering some words of Sally Seal's, and wishing Ralph
to understand that she followed the track of his thought.
She felt him trying to piece together in a laborious and
elementary fashion fragments of belief, unsoldered and
separate, lacking the unity of phrases fashioned by the old
believers.   Together they groped in this difficult region,
where the unfinished, the unfulfilled, the unwritten, the un-
returned, came together in their ghostly way and wore the
semblance of the complete and the satisfactory.   The future
emerged more splendid than ever from this construction of
the present.   Books were to be written, and since books must

be written in rooms, and rooms must have hangings, and outside the windows there must be land, and an horizon to that land, and trees perhaps, and a hill, they sketched a habitation for themselves upon the outline of great offices in the Strand and continued to make an account of the future upon the omnibus which took them towards Chelsea; and still, for both of them, it swam miraculously in the golden light of a large steady lamp.

As the night was far advanced they had the whole of the seats on the top of the omnibus to choose from, and the roads, save for an occasional couple, wearing even at midnight, an air of sheltering their words from the public, were deserted. No longer did the shadow of a man sing to the shadow of a piano. A few lights in bedroom windows burnt but were extinguished one by one as the omnibus passed them.

They dismounted and walked down to the river. She felt his arm stiffen beneath her hand, and knew by this token that they had entered the enchanted region. She might speak to him, but with that strange tremor in his voice, those eyes blindly adoring, whom did he answer? What woman did he see? And where was she walking, and who was her companion? Moments, fragments, a second of vision, and then the flying waters, the winds dissipating and dissolving; then, too, the recollection from chaos, the return of security, the earth firm, superb and brilliant in the sun. From the heart of his darkness he spoke his thanksgiving; from a region as far, as hidden, she answered him. On a June night the nightingales sing, they answer each other across the plain; they are heard under the window among the trees in the garden. Pausing, they looked down into the river which bore its dark tide of waters, endlessly moving, beneath them. They turned and found themselves opposite the house. Quietly they surveyed the friendly place, burning its lamps either in expectation of them or because Rodney was still there talking to Cassandra. Katharine pushed the

NIGHT AND DAY

door half open and stood upon the threshold. The light lay in soft golden grains upon the deep obscurity of the hushed and sleeping household. For a moment they waited, and then loosed their hands. "Good night," he breathed. "Good night," she murmured back to him.

Books by Virginia Woolf
available in paperback editions
from Harcourt Brace Jovanovich, Inc.

THE VOYAGE OUT (HB 151)
NIGHT AND DAY (HB 263)
JACOB'S ROOM *and* THE WAVES (HB 37)
THE COMMON READER: FIRST SERIES (HB 10)
MRS. DALLOWAY (HB 81)
TO THE LIGHTHOUSE (HB 82)
ORLANDO: A BIOGRAPHY (HB 266)
A ROOM OF ONE'S OWN (H 020)
THE SECOND COMMON READER (HB 24)
FLUSH: A BIOGRAPHY (HPL 12)
THE YEARS (HB 166)
THREE GUINEAS (H 021)
BETWEEN THE ACTS (HB 189)
THE DEATH OF THE MOTH AND OTHER ESSAYS (HB 294)
A HAUNTED HOUSE AND OTHER SHORT STORIES (HB 105)
THE MOMENT AND OTHER ESSAYS (HB 295)
THE CAPTAIN'S DEATH BED AND OTHER ESSAYS (HB 253)
A WRITER'S DIARY (HB 264)